Rose's head whipped toward the clerk. "Can you possibly hurry things up a bit? I haven't got all day."

"Nor have I. Your pardon, lady, but the letter could not wait." For a clerk, his voice was oddly cultured.

He stood and stepped from behind the writing table. He was clad entirely in black, but now that she saw him fully, Rose could not call him somber. His flowing shirt was unlaced halfway down his chest and tucked into a pair of sable breeches that clung to the hard muscles of his thighs. His bare feet were silent on the wood floor as he approached.

This is no mere clerk, she thought uneasily. *He must be one of the prince's men.* She swallowed hard and stood, taking a step back as he continued to advance. Another step and her back was to the wall.

"I suppose an introduction is in order," he said, sweeping her a bow that no courtier could have bettered for its grace. There was nothing of the humble clerk about him now. How could she have ever been so blind as to mistake this man for a servant?

The
Prince

ELIZABETH MINOGUE

B
BERKLEY SENSATION, NEW YORK

THE BERKLEY PUBLISHING GROUP
Published by the Penguin Group
Penguin Group (USA) Inc.
375 Hudson Street, New York, New York 10014, USA
Penguin Group (Canada), 10 Alcorn Avenue, Toronto, Ontario, M4V 3B2, Canada
(a division of Pearson Penguin Canada Inc.)
Penguin Books Ltd., 80 Strand, London WC2R 0RL, England
Penguin Group Ireland, 25 St. Stephen's Green, Dublin 2, Ireland (a division of Penguin Books Ltd.)
Penguin Group (Australia), 250 Camberwell Road, Camberwell, Victoria 3124, Australia
(a division of Pearson Australia Group Pty. Ltd.)
Penguin Books India Pvt. Ltd., 11 Community Centre, Panchsheel Park, New Delhi—110 017, India
Penguin Group (NZ), Cnr. Airborne and Rosedale Roads, Albany, Auckland 1310, New Zealand
(a division of Pearson New Zealand Ltd.)
Penguin Books (South Africa) (Pty.) Ltd., 24 Sturdee Avenue, Rosebank, Johannesburg 2196, South Africa

Penguin Books Ltd., Registered Offices: 80 Strand, London WC2R 0RL, England

This is a work of fiction. Names, characters, places, and incidents either are the product of the author's imagination or are used fictitiously, and any resemblance to actual persons, living or dead, business establishments, events, or locales is entirely coincidental.

THE PRINCE

A Berkley Sensation Book / published by arrangement with the author

PRINTING HISTORY
Berkley Sensation edition / November 2004

Copyright © 2004 by Elizabeth Minogue.
Excerpt from *The Sun Witch* copyright © 2004 by Linda Winstead Jones.
Cover art by One By Two.
Cover design by Lesley Worrell.
Interior text design by Kristin del Rosario.

ISBN: 0-425-19920-7

BERKLEY® SENSATION
Berkley Sensation Books are published by The Berkley Publishing Group,
a division of Penguin Group (USA) Inc.,
375 Hudson Street, New York, New York 10014.
BERKLEY SENSATION and the "B" design
are trademarks belonging to Penguin Group (USA) Inc.

PRINTED IN THE UNITED STATES OF AMERICA

10 9 8 7 6 5 4 3 2 1

For Calvin
with love

Prologue

Venya

EWAN fled blindly down the twisting stairway, his burden bumping painfully against his spine with every step. Choking, coughing, he wrested open the door and staggered into the courtyard as the windows of the tower exploded outward, raining glass upon the cobblestones below. Screams cut through the roar of flame, shrill, desperate pleas for help.

Ewan did not look back, nor did he slow until his boot slipped on the blood-slicked cobbles and he went down hard upon one knee. The pain was so intense that he cried out, his voice lost in the confusion of running feet and shouts and curses. Bright sparks drifted through the haze to settle on his head and shoulders.

"Get up!" A hand was on his elbow, tugging him. A voice, shrill with fear, was in his ear. "Get up! Go!"

Ewan heaved himself upright and took one step forward, barely catching his balance when his leg gave out beneath him. He reached down and felt something sharp protruding just below his kneecap. He could not get a purchase; cursing, he tried again, and with a groan ripped a six-inch shard of glass from his leg. Breathing in short gasps, he staggered on, one hand beating at the sparks smoldering in his dark hair as with the other he hefted the sack more securely on his back.

"I'm sorry," he muttered, "I'm sorry. I'm sorry—"

He picked up speed, lurching through the smoke. Just as he reached the edge of the courtyard he was halted.

"Who goes there?"

Ewan squinted, trying to make out the form on the other end

of the sword lodged against his breast. Attacker or defender? Not that there had been any defense, or none to speak of. The attack had been entirely unexpected, the Venyans taken completely unaware. Reason told him that this must be one of Richard's men, ordered to cut down any Venyan trying to escape.

"MacIndron of Valinor," he rasped. "King Richard's envoy."

"Sir Ewan?"

The smoke swirled and parted, and Ewan relaxed his hand upon his dagger. Marva be thanked, he knew this man. Roger FitzWarren, a doltish fop not worthy of the title knight, had once been his partner in a game of bowls against King Richard and his current favorite. Bowls was Roger's game; warfare was clearly not. And there was nothing more dangerous than a frightened man with a weapon in his hand.

"Aye, Roger, 'tis I," Ewan said, trying to speak calmly, even as the sweat ran in a river down his face. "Let me pass."

The sword lowered slightly but did not withdraw. "What is that you're carrying?"

Ewan stretched his lips into something he could only hope resembled a grin. "Plunder. By Marva's bone, I've earned it. Stand aside, man; I must reach my ship before the Venyans take it. King's orders," he added hoarsely.

The sword withdrew. "Very well, then, if—who is that?" Roger cried, panic in his voice, as a man staggered through the smoke to Ewan's side and bent double as a fit of coughing seized him.

"My squire," Ewan answered quickly.

Nigel Bastyon, Lord Chancellor of Venya, straightened, stifling his coughs against his sleeve.

"You can pass," Roger said, waving his sword.

"My compliments to the king," Ewan said, forcing another smile as he stepped out into the night, biting his lip against the pain screaming through his knee. One step, two, and then he was running, slipping down the hillside, not daring to pause long enough to see if Bastyon followed him or not.

The ship was in confusion, sailors hurrying about in all directions. Ewan heaved himself over the side and shouted for the captain.

"What's happening?" the captain asked. A good man, Ewan thought, his voice was steady and his glance was sharp.

"King Richard has attacked. Venya is taken."

The captain rocked back on his heels. "*What?* Taken? But we are not at war—"

"We are now. Or we were. 'Tis all but finished."

With a smooth, almost casual gesture, Ewan drew his dagger and rested the point against the captain's throat. "Here's the position. I'm done with Richard—and Valinor. As of now, this ship is mine. I'm taking her out of here, and we shan't be going home. You can come, or you can join King Richard's soldiers. Which will it be?"

"Where are you going?"

"I canna tell ye that."

The captain's eyes flicked downward to the dagger, up to Ewan's face, then past him to the burning castle.

"I have a family in Valinor. But I won't try to stop you."

"Good enough." Ewan sheathed the dagger. "Take all who are loyal to Richard, and leave the rest. Who can sail this ship?"

The captain's eyes narrowed. "Brandon is the best, but he's a king's man. Ulric might do; a good sailor, but a surly rogue. Hates Valinor like the plague. Pressed," he added by way of explanation, "we took him off a Moravian trader six weeks ago."

"Ulric. Right."

The captain gazed again at the castle and frowned, shaking his head. "Good fortune to you, sir."

"And to you. Now go."

The captain strode across the deck, pointing to this man and that, ordering them to follow. A moment later he was over the side with the best part of the crew.

"Which one is Ulric?" Ewan demanded, and a dark-skinned sailor stepped forward. Broad and solid as a rock, he overtopped Ewan, a tall man himself, by half a head. Copper bands circled his heavily muscled arms, the mark of a free Moravian trader. "I hear ye can handle this ship. Is it true?"

Ulric's muscles leaped as he crossed his arms across his chest and regarded Ewan with hooded eyes. "It might be."

Ewan limped forward, a spasm of pain shooting through his leg. The sack he held seemed weighted with lead, and his body ached and stung from a thousand burns. "I've had a bad night, Ulric," he said softly. "A verra bad night. Ye don't want to make it worse. So why don't ye try again, lad, and this time think before ye answer. For if ye waste another second of my time, I will kill ye where ye stand."

By trade Ewan was Valinor's royal envoy to the court of Venya, a position he had accepted with reluctance but for which he'd discovered an unexpected talent. Yet before he'd ever been a diplomat, he'd been a knight—a *real* knight; not one of Richard's puppies, but a man who had seen battle and known the dark joy of the kill. Despite the danger, despite the need for haste, for one wild moment he half-hoped Ulric *would* defy him so he might have the excuse to cut him down.

Ulric looked down at him. Whatever he read in Ewan's face brought a reluctant nod and a muttered, "Aye, sir. I can handle her."

"Fine, then, Captain Ulric. Get us the hell out of here."

"What course? Sir."

Ewan tried to summon a diplomatic answer, but he was too weary for anything but truth. "It makes no matter. Just get us straight away from Venya—and from Valinor and her whoreson king."

Gold flashed in the lantern light as Ulric grinned. "Aye, *aye*. Weigh anchor and cast off," he added in a roar. "Up the mains'l— damn you, look alive!"

Lord Bastyon appeared silently at Ewan's elbow. Venya's chancellor, that fount of dignity, was disheveled and soot-streaked, graying hair standing out about his livid face and a trickle of blood winding down his cheek. Beside him were three men slightly known to Ewan. Lysagh, the Queen of Venya's chamberlain; Carlysle—something to do with the treasury, Ewan thought; and Eredor, the King's Groom of the Stole. All three wore the slack expressions of men trying to make sense of the unthinkable.

"Does he live?" Bastyon rasped.

Ewan laid the sack gently on the deck and fumbled at the knot. The fabric fell away to reveal the small form of a boy. His nightshirt, touched with lace at neck and wrist, was soaked with blood. Beneath tangled waves of golden hair his face was still.

"Leander's beard," Bastyon swore. "He isn't dead, he can't be—"

Ewan pressed shaking fingers to the boy's neck. "No."

"Get that off him—find the surgeon—"

"That blood isn't his. I found him in the throne room. With"—he swallowed hard—"with them."

Ewan shut his eyes briefly, trying to force back the memory of Venya's merry queen and her beloved lord, lying in a pool of their own blood. "Poor wight," he said at last, drawing the tattered remnants of a once-priceless tapestry around the boy, "'tis better this way. Tomorrow we can—"

He broke off, shocked speechless as a wave of icy water splashed over him and drenched the still form of Venya's heir. "What the devil are ye doing?" he sputtered.

"He lives, but does he have his wits?" Bastyon leaned forward. "We must *know*—"

Ewan seized the chancellor's wrist. "Tomorrow is time enough—"

It was too late. The boy stirred, his eyes opening to gaze dazedly around.

"Your Highness—" five men began at the same moment.

A slight frown of puzzlement drew dark golden brows together. Amber eyes snapped open as memory returned.

"It's all right, Your Highness," Ewan said quickly, "you're safe aboard my ship. We'll get you into bed and—"

But the boy was already on his feet and darting for the side.

Ewan tried to rise and fell back with a rasping groan. "Catch him!" he roared. "There—"

A sailor turned, released his line, and dove after the boy, seizing his legs as he went over.

"Hold him," Ewan shouted, struggling painfully to his feet.

The four Venyans were there before him. Bastyon bent and addressed the boy. "Stop this foolishness. Calm yourself at once."

The boy twisted in his captor's grasp. Prince Florian had always been small for his age, and now he looked much younger than his seven years. But for all his seeming frailty, he was strong, and a moment later he slid from the arms of his captor and was once again heading for the side. He was halfway over when he was caught again and dragged, struggling, to the deck.

"That is *enough*," Bastyon snapped. "We have no time for this."

Stupid man, Ewan thought, *that's no way to talk to a child. Particularly this one. Especially tonight.* The sailor cursed as small, sharp teeth fastened on his hand. Before Ewan had covered half the distance between them, he saw Bastyon's arm rise and heard the sharp crack of a palm striking flesh.

Ewan finally reached the boy, who was sobbing pitifully, hands covering his face. Casting a furious scowl at Bastyon, Ewan reached toward the prince but was halted by Lord Carlysle's hand upon his wrist. "Keep out of this," the Venyan ordered.

"Why, you—" Ewan began, wrenching his arm free, but Bastyon had already seized the prince by the shoulders.

"How dare you so shame your parents' memory?" the chancellor demanded, shaking the boy so sharply that his head snapped on its slender neck. "Have you forgotten who you are? Control yourself at once. At once, do you understand me?"

When Bastyon released him, the prince dragged a shaking wrist across his eyes and stood very straight, though he trembled from head to foot and his breath came in ragged, hitching gasps.

"Now listen to me closely. Venya has fallen. The King and Queen are dead." A keening moan burst from the boy's tight-pressed lips, but was quickly stifled when Bastyon raised his hand. "I can help you, and I will, but you must do exactly as I say. Do you understand me? *Do you?*"

The prince's chin jerked in a nod.

"Listen to me, then, and remember what I say. Your loss is nothing to what your people have suffered tonight. You will think of them, not yourself, and be grateful that you live. Leander spared you for a purpose. From this night, your life belongs to him—to Venya. One day you will avenge your parents and rule in their place. We will make a king of you, Your Highness, but you must do your part. You will begin by comporting yourself with dignity and restraint. Is that clear?"

"Y-yes. M-my lord."

The words seemed to be forced from the boy by will alone, punctuated by painful gasps that wracked his slight frame. Ewan could bear no more. Shoving the Venyans aside, he knelt before the prince and took an icy hand in his.

"I grieve with ye," he said as gently as he could. "But Lord Bastyon speaks the truth. This battle's lost. It's over and there's nothing to be done. We will be back, Your Highness. My word on it. I am your man, and with Leander's help, I will see ye home again or die in the attempt."

Ewan cast a look over his shoulder at the four Venyans. "What are ye waiting for?" he snapped, resting a hand upon his sword. "Are ye the prince's men or no? Then kneel and swear your fealty."

"Quite right, Sir Ewan," Bastyon said calmly, going down upon his knees. "My lords, please join me."

The prince hardly seemed aware of what was happening as the four lords of Venya rendered him their oaths. When they were finished, he turned and walked, stiff-legged, to the stern. He stood, fingers clenched about the rail, staring back at the faint glow that had once been a castle.

"Leave him," Ewan said. "Nay," he added sharply as Bastyon started forward. "Give him a moment, for all love. Who can say when he will see it again?"

The sails filled, and the ship sped out to sea. Clean air swept the deck free of the stench of smoke, and cool moonlight washed the masts. When the stars faded into the first gray light of dawn, the small prince still kept his silent vigil, the bloodied nightshirt fluttering around his legs, eyes straining to catch a last glimpse of his home.

Chapter 1

Eighteen Years Later . . .

ROSE darted into the crowd, sweating in her heavy kirtle as the relentless sun beat down upon her uncovered head. Safe within the press, she dared a quick look over her shoulder. As far as she could tell, she had not been followed.

Yet.

Two weeks on shipboard had left her legs oddly stiff. The wooden planks rose to meet her, jarring her off balance. Clap clap, clap clap. Heel and toe of her wooden pattens hit the planks more quickly as she found her land legs. She hurried on, breathing through her mouth against the oily smell of fish, thick as fog on the unmoving air. She kept to the most crowded places, head down, meeting no man's eye. Yet still the sailors noticed her.

"Slow down, Jenny—sweeting—*chevra,*" they called after her. "What can be the rush? Stay a moment, let me show you—"

Despite the paralyzing heat, she wished desperately for cloak and hood. The past year of silent solitude had stripped her of defenses. Even before that, she had never been the focus of so many eyes. On the few occasions she was permitted to appear in public, her cousins were always present. The two of them rendered her as invisible as any magic cloak could ever do.

But today Melisande and Berengaria were far away. She was alone in a place where no respectable woman would be seen. No woman at all just now, not in this unrelenting heat. Even the dockside whores had retreated to some shady chamber to wait for evening's cool.

But Rose could not afford to wait. She must go now, and swiftly, before her absence had been noticed. Eyes fixed on the wooden dock beneath her feet, she concentrated on her destination.

I must be calm, she told herself. *Or,* she amended, wincing as a sailor trod upon her toe, *I must look calm.* But that should present no problem. She was good at looking calm; so good, in fact, that those who knew her best would swear she was half-witted.

But *he* must not think that. He must believe her story, strange as it might seem. She would be bold. Bold and firm . . . yet not overbearing. After all, she was a supplicant. Or would be, if she ever got there.

Almost running, she crashed into a bearded sailor no taller than her chest with a broad basket balanced on his head.

"Forgive me—please, sir, could you tell me—"

"Piss off," he snarled, shoving her away.

She took a few stumbling steps toward the edge of the dock but was halted on the edge by a hand fastened on her wrist.

The moment she regained her balance, her plump dark rescuer released her and turned away, wiping his palm fastidiously upon his flowing crimson robe.

"Wait!" she cried, hurrying after him. "Pardon, sir, but could you tell me—"

"Channa zayra," he snapped, not slowing his pace.

"Alet amia," she answered sharply.

He stopped instantly and turned, one hand moving to his brow. "A thousand pardons," he said in Jexlan. "How may I serve thee?"

"Canst thou tell me where the Prince of Venya may be found?"

He shut one eye in the Jexlan manner, a courteous gesture denoting careful thought.

"I have not seen him," he said at last. "And had I done so, I would not tell thee."

"But I must find him! Please, *serrin,* it is a matter of life and death."

He sighed. "Daughter, whatever this matter is, thou shouldst take it to thy family. The . . . one you speak of cannot help thee." He clicked his tongue, a *tsk-tsk* of disapproval. "To so much as speak his name is to sully thy honor."

Perhaps in Jexal; if it were so in Valinor, every maiden in the country was already sullied beyond redemption. Despite a dozen edicts, half the troubadours in the country made their living courtesy of the Prince of Venya's adventures.

"But I must speak to him," she insisted. "My family is dead; they cannot help me, and I haven't a moment to waste."

He studied her face for a long moment, then gestured toward the row of stalls. "If the Venyans are here at all, that is where thou shalt find them."

He touched his brow again, this time with one finger only. *Why, the man thinks I am a whore,* she realized with a shock as he turned away without the customary bow. *Jehan help me, will he think the same?*

I must behave with dignity, she thought, turning toward the stalls. *Dignified, bold, calm, yet spirited—*

"Good day, master," she said to the man behind the counter. "Are there any Venyans here?"

"Oh, you do not want those sly sorcerers," the man said with an ingratiating smile. "Whatever they have, 'tis no match for what I can offer. See, here is—"

"I thank you, but only Venyan will do."

His smile vanished. "I cannot help you."

She tried the next stall.

"Venyans!" A burly man spat at her feet. "I have no truck with their kind. Move off. You're blocking the way."

An hour later Rose was soaked with sweat and so thirsty she could barely rasp out another question. But all that was nothing to the anxiety gnawing at the pit of her stomach. She started at each footstep behind her, heart leaping to her parched throat. What if he was not here? What if she had misheard or Captain Jennet had been mistaken?

She had no food, no water, not a single coin with which to buy the most basic necessities, let alone passage on a ship. And soon, if not already, she would be hunted.

She dragged shaking hands across her eyes. *I'm not giving up. Not yet. Not while there is still the slightest hope.*

She reached the end of the row of booths and turned the corner, where a single stall stood on a deserted stretch of dock. She held her breath as she approached it.

The shelf was not crowded, but what was there drew and held her eye. A knife with a plain silver hilt, two rings, a glittering crystal on a stand of twisted strands of gold and silver. A tiny bejeweled windmill whirred and chirped a merry tune without a breath of air to stir it.

The man who stood above these offerings was no less exotic. He had the typical Venyan combination of raven hair and deep-set brown eyes, a strong nose, and prominent cheekbones. Small of stature, he stood only a few inches taller than Rose herself, though he held himself with a fierce dignity that seemed to add inches to his height. He was immensely old, his dark eyes nearly lost within a network of wrinkles that creased his weathered face. Raven hair shot with silver was wound into two braids falling nearly to his waist.

"The blessing of the day upon you," she said cautiously in Venyan. The man's eyes lit, and he smiled.

"And upon you, *acelina*," he answered in the same tongue. "How may I serve you?"

He is a filidh, she thought, giddy with relief. *A Venyan* filidh. *So they* do *exist.*

"A *chrysal* ring, perhaps?" he offered. "One for you and one for your . . ." He used a Venyan word that could mean either husband or lover. "It will burn with Leander's fire should he ever be unfaithful, recalling him to his vows."

"No," she said, "Not that. I—"

"Then perhaps this knife. Have him wear it for a moonspan. When he journeys forth, it will be a comfort to you. So long as it stays bright, you can rest easily, knowing he is well. Should it rust . . ." He ran a finger across the shining edge. "Is it not better to know than sit and wonder?"

She shook her head. "No—though they are very fine. I am searching for your prince."

The *filidh* carefully replaced the knife in its sheath. "*My* prince? Lady, I am but a simple wanderer without home or country."

"But you are Venyan."

"Ah, you seek Prince Rico? Then I fear you have gone far astray. You would do better to look in Valinor, perhaps at Larken Castle."

She shook her head. "Not him. Your *true* prince."

"I am sorry, but I do not know of whom you speak."

"Of course you do! Everyone knows of the Prince of Venya! And he is here somewhere, I'm certain of it. Please, can you not take me to him?"

"I am sorry," he repeated, reaching upward. "I cannot help you."

A wooden shutter rolled down across the opening. Rose caught it before it latched and lifted it an inch. "He who will return upon the flood tide with all who have been lost," she said rapidly in Venyan. "His cause is just, his followers true, and you shall know them when they speak the name of Florian of Venya."

She shoved the shutter up another few inches. "Well? I spoke his name, didn't I?"

"You did."

"And I know the words. By right of custom, you must answer me!"

The shutter began to fall.

"I am Princess Rose of Valinor."

It halted.

"And I demand—no, I entreat you to take me to your prince."

The sorcerer bent to peer through the opening, regarding her with hooded eyes. "Venya *has* no prince."

"Until the true prince is restored," she answered promptly. "When Leander's heir returns, the stones will sing and the land rejoice."

When he did not answer, she tried again, raising her voice a trifle. "I *said,* when Leander's heir—"

"My silence was an indication of surprise, not failing hearing."

"I know a half a dozen more, but I really haven't time. So if you don't mind, I'd like to speak with him now."

"Wait. I will see what I can find."

FLORIAN, Leander's heir, the Prince of Venya, Earl of Marech, and Lord of the Northern Marches, hooked bare feet around the legs of his stool in a vain attempt to stop the fleas biting at his ankles. The tiny windowless chamber was stifling, reeking of stale ale and ancient sweat. A hissing, smoking tallow candle added to the heat as it spread into a greasy pool upon the scratched surface of the writing table. He noted all these things with a small part of his mind as his quill flew across the page.

I will arrange for further supplies as quickly as possible, though I fear it will be at least—

"What is it?" he said without looking up as Lord Bastyon appeared silently at his elbow.

"There is a woman asking to see you."

"And . . . ?"

—a sixmoon before I can get there myself. In the meantime, I am sending you a dowser in whom I place the greatest confidence. He will—

Bastyon cleared his throat. "She claims to be Princess Rose of Valinor."

Florian glanced up, frowning. "Rose? Isn't she the one they put away? The one who is . . ." He tapped a finger against his brow.

"Yes."

"Who would claim to be *her*?" He reached for a mug of ale, then thought better of it. Thirsty as he was, it would take a stronger man than he to brave a second taste. "See what she wants, would you? I haven't time today."

"Of course, Your Highness. I would not have troubled you at all, but she spoke the *shibboleth*."

"Did she?" Florian signed the letter, then set it atop a dozen others and rummaged among the parchments littering the table. "You said there was something from Carlysle?"

Bastyon plucked a parchment from a pile.

"Thank you." Florian slipped a finger beneath the seal. He scanned the writing, then laughed shortly. "Ah, Carlysle, he never disappoints. He sends this bill, saying that there must be some error, for surely I could not be guilty of such extravagance in purchasing provender and new boots for the crew."

"Your Highness—"

Florian seized his quill. "Extravagance? Well, Carlysle might expect men to fight on bare feet and empty bellies, but—"

"Shall I send her away?"

"Who? Oh, the woman." Florian set down his quill and bent to scratch his ankle. "How deep was her knowledge?"

"Second level. Andra said he was . . . impressed."

"Has she been searched?"

"Yes."

Florian scrawled a signature across the page and threw it aside, then picked up the next parchment. "Was she followed?"

"Not that we could tell," Bastyon answered cautiously. "But with so few men, it is impossible to be certain."

"Second level is—" Florian froze, staring at the message in his hands. "Bastyon, have you seen this? Eredor—that bastard, that poxed little shopkeeper—he wants—"

"I know what he wants."

"And you did not *tell* me? He says he has arranged for the *Endeavor* to go to Parma for refitting as a cargo vessel. *Arranged? Him?* Who the devil does he think he is?"

In his long years of service to the Venyan crown, Bastyon had withstood many a royal glare. He drew himself a little straighter, his face perfectly expressionless. "The council voted on it."

"I'm sure they did. I'm sure Eredor called for it as soon as I was gone. A pox on his—" Florian broke off, staring at the former Chancellor of Venya. "Don't tell me, Bastyon, do not *dare* tell me you voted with that *scrub.*"

Lord Bastyon sniffed. "I am surprised you feel the need to ask. But Eredor was most persuasive. Will you not at least consider—"

"No," Florian said flatly. "I won't. Don't worry, I'll write and set him straight. In the meantime, you'd best send the woman in. She must want *something* to come up with such a tale, and second level deserves at least five minutes."

Bastyon bowed his head. "As you will." He hesitated at the doorway. "What will you say to Eredor?"

"I will tell him he can take his vote and shove it up his arse. Damn it all, what do you *expect* me to say? I need that ship—I need all my ships to get to Venya."

"The council has agreed we are not ready to make war."

"No, we're never ready, are we? 'Just a little longer, Your Highness. We need a bit more time—more gold—more arms—' Leander's beard, what are we *waiting* for?"

Florian jumped to his feet and began to pace the chamber. "I've tried to be patient, you know that, but they have tied my hands for the last time. I mean it, Bastyon, and you can tell them so from me."

"I *have* told them." Bastyon straightened the pile of parchments, his eyes lowered as he tapped the edges together. "They believe," he said carefully, "that you . . . lack the necessary support in Venya."

Florian sank down on the stool. Bastyon was being tactful. He was sure the council had put it far more bluntly. No doubt they said their prince had lost the support of the Venyan people through his own reckless stupidity.

And they would be right to say it.

"Delay will only weaken my support," he said evenly. "That is one reason we must move quickly."

"The *filidhi* are drifting, my lord. They have little concern for what happens in Venya now, and they feel it is immoral to be kept on stolen wealth."

"So they wish to ease their consciences by committing sacrilege?"

"They do not see it as sacrilege to sell what they have made."

"*They* have made? It is Leander who has gifted them with the ability to turn craftsmanship to something more. *Venyan magic cannot be bought or sold.*"

"Lord Eredor disagrees."

"This is precisely why we must act, Bastyon. The *filidhi* don't need a trade agreement, they need to get out of Serilla and go home. That is what we've been working for, isn't it? I agree that conditions are not perfect for invasion, but we cannot wait for that. I will not give up my ship—*my* ship—so Eredor can use it to peddle wares to Avrila."

"It is not only Eredor," Bastyon began.

"I don't care who it is. The council is subject to their prince, not Eredor, a detail they seem to have forgotten." Florian picked up his quill and dipped it into the ink. "I am sorry to leave this to you, Bastyon. As soon as I have finished with Ewan, I will address the council myself. You may tell my lord Eredor to expect me."

He stared at the parchment as the ink dried on the quill, trying to frame the message he would send. He needed words. Strong words. Ones that would convince the council of his absolute commitment. The trouble was, he'd used them all before, and the council was still not convinced.

One mistake. That's all it had been, a single mistake that had cost him the trust of his council and his people. A terrible mistake, no one knew that better than Florian himself. But were eighteen years of hard work and careful planning to be cast aside for one ill-judged action that he regretted with every breath he drew?

It did no good to dwell upon it. There was nothing to be gained by wondering how many Venyans had died for his mistake. That would only lead him to despair, and soon he would believe that the council was right, that they should invest all their resources in the colony and admit that Venya was forever lost.

Because of his mistake.

Bastyon laid a hand on his shoulder. "I am sorry."

Bastyon's cold fury had been hard enough to bear, but it was no more than Florian expected. Even at his best, he had never measured up to his chancellor's rigid standards. This sudden sympathy could only mean a failure so complete as to render blame or accusation pointless.

"So am I, Bas, more sorry than I can say. But it's not over yet."

His words hung in the air between them. *Say something,* he pleaded silently. *Tell me* you *haven't given up on me. Just a word, a single word will be enough.*

But Bastyon did not speak. After a moment, he tactfully withdrew his hand.

Florian dipped the quill. "Thank you, Bastyon, that will be all. Now send the damned woman in so I can have done with her and get some sleep."

Chapter 2

NOT another round of questions, Rose thought. *I cannot bear it.* Her last inquisitor, an elderly man with a tired face and piercing eyes, had taken far too long to accept that she would give him nothing but her name. Now she followed him into an alehouse and down a tiny passageway, halfway between fury and despair. She wanted to rage at him, to insist that she be taken to the prince, yet she knew she was utterly dependent on his goodwill.

"Please," she said, "I have told you all I can, and time presses."

"You shall have your audience," he said. He opened a door, stepped back, and with a stiff little bow gestured her to enter. Once she was inside, he shut the door behind her.

The squalid little chamber was stifling, and the stench of it made her empty stomach twist uncomfortably. It took her a moment to realize she was not alone. A clerk sat at a tiny writing table in the corner, quill scratching frantically. He looked up briefly when she entered, then lowered his head over his work. One glance was enough to tell her that unlike the man who had brought her here, he was no Venyan.

She sat down on a stool, folded her hands, stiffened her spine, and lifted her chin. After several minutes her neck began to ache and her stomach grumbled noisily. She cast a quick, embarrassed glance at the clerk, but he was oblivious to everything but his work.

You'd think a prince would have offered me at least a cup of water, she thought with an inward sniff, *let alone a crust of bread.*

Standing, she paced the chamber. It only took a moment to go from end to end. A single glance was enough to show her four walls of rough plank, a bare floor, and a straw mattress on a wooden frame. Her silent companion still wrote on. He was youngish, perhaps a year or two older than her own twenty-four, dressed in sober black, light hair combed neatly back into a braid.

She sidled closer, peering sideways at the page he was writing. A black sleeve moved to block her view.

"Good day," he said, though he did not look up again and the quill did not so much as pause.

"And to you," she answered with a sigh, retreating to her seat and fixing her eyes expectantly on the door.

Any moment now it would open and the Prince of Venya would stand before her in the flesh. Her heart gave a nervous lurch. He was the hero of a hundred songs and stories, the sorcerer pirate whose name struck terror into every captain on the nine seas. Bold and dashing, wily and clever, the Prince of Venya was as deadly to his foes as he was loyal to his followers. It was widely sung that a single smile had the power to melt a woman's bones within her flesh.

Not that Rose wanted her bones melted, if such a thing were even possible. All she wanted was one small favor. Surely that was not too much to ask of the Prince of Venya, the living embodiment of every chivalric ideal!

"Your Highness," she would say firmly, "you must help me."

No, that wouldn't do. She had a feeling that a pirate—let alone a prince—would not take orders well.

"Venya and Valinor were once allies. Now I offer you a new alliance, one that will work to your advantage."

She nibbled at a thumbnail. That sounded well. The only trouble was, it was a lie. The moment he asked *how* it would work to his advantage, all would be lost. Perhaps something a bit more spirited would catch his interest.

"What ho, Your Highness, Rose of Valinor here. Damned if I'm not in a bit of a spot. Long story—uncle hates me—think he wants me dead. What say you play the hero and get me to Sorlain?"

She groaned, starting on another nail. Spirited, yes. But she doubted idiotic would appeal to him.

"I am Rose of Valinor, and I am fleeing for my life. Venya and Valinor were allies for many years, and the breaking of that alliance is something I regret with all my heart. Venyans have ever acted with honor toward my people; for that I dare appeal to you to help me to Sorlain."

Yes. That was it. Calm, dignified, yet spirited—if only she could remember it. She drew a breath and closed her eyes.

"Your Highness," she murmured. "I am Rose of Valinor and—and—oh, bloody hell, where in blazes is he?"

"I'm sorry?"

Her head whipped toward the clerk. "Can you possibly hurry things up a bit? I haven't got all day."

"Nor have I. Your pardon, lady, but the letter could not wait."

For a clerk, his voice was oddly cultured, the words tinged with an accent she could not quite define.

He stood and stepped from behind the writing table. He was clad entirely in black, but now that she saw him fully, she could not call him somber. His flowing shirt was unlaced halfway down his chest and tucked into a pair of sable breeches that clung to the hard muscles of his thighs. His bare feet were silent on the wooden floor as he approached.

This is no mere clerk, she thought uneasily. *He must be one of the prince's men.* She swallowed hard and sat a little straighter. The Prince of Venya might commit acts of piracy, but everyone knew he had been driven to such desperate measures by cruel necessity. At heart, he was no pirate, but a nobleman. What she had not considered was that his crew—even his clerk—would be the real thing.

A thin white scar, very prominent against his sun-bronzed skin, ran down one cheek; another through an eyebrow. A gold ring glittered in his ear. Looking into that hard young face, Rose sensed instinctively that this man knew more about survival than she could ever hope to learn.

Or wanted to.

She swallowed hard and stood, taking a step back as he continued to advance. The stool overturned with a small clatter that she barely noticed. Another step and her back was to the wall.

"I suppose an introduction is in order," he said, sweeping her a bow that no courtier could have bettered for its grace. There was nothing of the humble clerk about him now. How could she have ever been so blind as to mistake this man for a servant?

Stupid, credulous fool, she raged at herself, *they never meant for me to see the prince at all. I have been tricked, trapped . . . and sold? Oh, Jehan, not that, not sold. Not me!* But why not her? It happened every day, women carried off by pirates and never seen again. *At least now I'll know what becomes of them,* she thought. She almost laughed, but the sound tangled in her throat and came out as a gasping sob.

She shot a desperate glance toward the door, praying that even now the prince would walk in and rescue her. But that hope died when the pirate spoke again.

"Florian of Venya at your service."

I don't have time for this, Florian thought, straightening from his bow. Yet courtesy—not to mention prudence—demanded that he hear what she had to say, no matter how outlandish it might be.

There was nothing new about a woman bribing or lying her way into his presence, but none had ever claimed to be royalty. In a way, he approved. If one was going to tell a lie, the bold one was more apt to succeed than some timid shading of the truth. But this lie was so patently ridiculous that he found himself intrigued.

She had made no attempt to look the part. A rough kirtle of some indeterminate color hung in baggy folds from neck to feet encased in the wooden pattens worn by the very poor. Brown hair was bundled into an untidy knot with sweat-soaked strands plastered to her brow. And she was filthy into the bargain.

Perhaps, he thought, she had been driven by some fellow feeling for the mad princess of Valinor. After a quarter hour watching her pace and mutter, he suspected that her wits were not all they should be. Now, looking at her ashen face and wild eyes, his suspicion grew to a near certainty.

I will skin Andra alive, he thought, the beginnings of a headache forming behind his eyes. *And Bastyon, as well.*

"You're not," she said at last. "You can't be. The Prince of Venya is—he is—" She waved a hand at him.

"Six feet tall with a glowing halo? You've been listening to minstrels' tales, I fear. I am indeed the Prince of Venya, and I have but a moment to spare. How may I serve you?"

She bit her lip, her long eyes narrowing as she reassessed the situation. Apparently she decided to believe him, for she nodded slightly and said, "I must get to Sorlain."

And . . . ? he thought, but decided he did not really want to know why she felt compelled to inform him of her plans. "Then you must go down to the docks and ask for Captain Ihlan of the *Osprey*," he said. "I believe he is setting sail tonight."

"No," she said, "no, it must be you. *You* must take me to Sorlain."

Must? Indeed, her wits were very much astray if she thought the *Quest* was a passenger vessel and he some hired captain. But looking into her desperate face, his initial flash of resentment faded. "I am sorry, *shasra*," he said gently, "but I am going nowhere near Sorlain."

"But—please wait a moment, listen to me. I must go now, they are looking for me—"

Likely someone *was* looking for her. From whatever place she had been confined. Apparently the *shibboleth*, which he had always thought a bit ridiculous, was not the secret it was meant to be.

"Then you must go swiftly. Here," he added, dropping a few coins on the table. "This will get you to Sorlain. Good fortune to you."

"It must be you," she insisted, ignoring the coins. "No one else can do it. You cannot refuse me, not now, not after—*Please,* there is no one else I can trust."

"I think you have mistaken me for someone else."

"But I—I call upon your—your mercy—"

He laughed. "Now I *know* you have mistaken me for someone else."

"Your honor, then," she hurried on.

"I am sorry, but—"

She clutched his arm, turning him to face her. "Valinor and Venya were once allies, and I regret the breaking of that alliance with all my heart."

"A great pity, wasn't it?" He removed her hand from his arm and took a few steps toward the door. "And now, if you will excuse me—"

"King Esteban will reward you. Well. Lavishly."

He sighed. "Will he?"

She lifted her chin and looked him in the eye. "You have my word."

"Worth a thousand rimals, I am certain. And you are . . . ?"

"Did they not *tell* you? I am Rose of Valinor."

"I see." He leaned against the door. "And why would Rose of Valinor come to me?"

He expected flattery, entreaty, but instead he got a measured look and a decisive, "Because you are the one man my uncle cannot buy or bribe."

Better, he thought. She sounded almost convincing. "And where did Rose of Valinor learn the words that got her in here?" he asked, more for the sake of hearing what she would come up with next than from any belief she was telling him the truth.

"In Riall. When I was there with my cousin."

"Your cousin? Ah, that would be Prince Rico. He who styles himself Prince of Venya."

"He does *not*. It is my uncle who calls him so. Rico is only a child."

Florian massaged his aching neck. He should be gone, he had far too much to do to linger here talking Venyan politics with a madwoman. But for the first time he suspected that this madwoman might possibly be the one she claimed to be.

"When were you in Venya?" he rapped out suddenly.

"Last spring."

"During the uprising?"

She looked away. "And all that followed."

The brutal executions. The blockading of Riall. The famine that followed, the fever that swept through the weakened population—

The uprising had begun in early spring. By midsummer, the most beautiful city in the world had become a nightmare landscape of terror and despair. Those strong enough had tried to flee, only to be cut down by King Richard's soldiers. Those who remained faced almost certain death from starvation or the fever. In the months that followed, they had turned from men and women into something less than animals. Just hearing the stories was bad enough. To have seen it firsthand . . .

But even if this woman were indeed Rose of Valinor, she wouldn't have seen anything. She would have been locked safely in the Governor's compound with the rest of Prince Rico's royal household, while her uncle sat in Larken Castle and mouthed his lies to a world appalled by the tales of brutalized Riall.

Her uncle? Was it possible she was telling him the truth? Could she really be niece to Richard of Valinor, the man who had made Florian's death a personal crusade? Clever Richard, who had heard, no doubt, that the Prince of Venya had a weakness for women in distress.

"How did you find me, my lady?"

"Captain Jennet said that you were here. He said—"

"Captain Jennet?" he interrupted sharply. "Of what ship?"

"The *Conquest.*"

Florian relaxed slightly. Jennet *was* one of Richard's captains, she'd gotten that much right, but his ship was—

"His ship is in dry dock," she went on quickly, "so Jennet has temporary command of the *Conquest.* And he said to his first mate that you would be here now and it was a pity they couldn't stop to hunt for you."

How had they known that? There was only one way, but Florian had no time to wonder who the traitor was. He moved swiftly to the writing desk and gathered the scattered parchments. "But you decided to do so?"

"You were my last hope. My only hope. I escaped—they must know by now that I am gone."

He pulled on his boots, eyes moving quickly over the chamber. "And how *did* you escape?"

"I forced the lock," she admitted modestly.

"How enterprising." He bent swiftly to retrieve a scrap of parchment from a corner. "And then you used the knowledge you had gained in Venya to find me."

He no longer questioned that she had such information. Indeed, he could imagine all too well how she had come by it. Men and women forced to watch their children starve could not be blamed for saying anything at all.

Had she offered to lead them to him? Or did she truly believe they had allowed her to escape? Either way, it did not matter. He'd learned a hard lesson the year before, but he had learned it well. Not even a princess in distress—be it feigned or genuine— could be allowed to endanger Venya's only hope of freedom. He was sorry, for if she was telling him the truth, she was in for a sad disappointment. But his feelings in the matter were the least important consideration of all.

"Yes. I must get to Sorlain. You see—"

He opened the door. "Wait here."

When he was gone, Rose sank back down on the stool and drew a shaking breath. She wanted to believe it had gone well, and yet she knew it hadn't. She had been neither calm nor dignified. It was no wonder he had not believed her at first. And when he did . . .

He had left her.

Taken everything that might identify him.

And gone.

"No!" She burst out the door and down the tiny passageway into the alehouse. "Where is he?" she demanded of the old woman running an ineffectual broom across the filthy floor.

"Who?"

"The—the man I was talking to back there. The one in black."

The woman shook her head. "What, did he run off without paying you? Stinking sailor, they're all the same." She chuckled. "You must get the coin in hand *before* you lift your skirts."

Rose darted past the woman and out the door, peering frantically in either direction. A few sailors staggered past, but apart from them the docks were empty. With a cry of rage she turned back, seized the old woman by the shoulders, and shook her hard.

"Where is he? You must tell me, you must! Is there some other way out? A secret way?"

"Take your hands off me."

"Tell—"

Rose stiffened at the sound of footsteps. No staggering sailors these, but booted feet moving swiftly toward the alehouse.

She turned and bolted into the narrow passageway. There was no back way out, no window in the chamber where she had so briefly glimpsed salvation. Nowhere to run. Nowhere even to hide.

She started at the sound of voices in the alehouse. *Think,* she ordered herself, *where could he have gone?*

A secret passage. That must be it. Rose tested each plank, then dropped to her knees and ran her hands across the floor. She grimaced as her fingers passed over the accumulated filth of generations, tracked on the boots of the endless parade of men who had

stumbled down this passageway into the arms of the whatever unfortunate woman lay waiting on the flea-infested mattress.

"Get the coin in hand before you lift your skirt."

Wise words. She should have heeded them—at least in spirit.
What a fool she had been to blurt out everything without exacting
a promise in return.

Her nails chipped as she tried to pry up each separate plank.
They all held fast. But there must be a secret passage, there had to
be. Not in the alehouse, what would be the use of it in such a public place? Not in the chamber. It must be here. And she would
find it.

Unless . . . oh, dear Jehan, unless it was sealed by a spell. The
Venyan was a sorcerer, after all.

The voices were louder now; the men shouting, the old
woman shrieking curses. Rose flinched at the sound of crashing
crockery, the clatter of tables overturned. In another moment
they would be upon her. She shrank back into the corner . . . and
felt it shift.

With desperate haste she whirled, running her hands across
the floor and walls. Her fingers touched a knothole, and the wall
shifted so suddenly that she lost her balance.

Not a spell, she thought. *Jehan be praised.*

And then there was no time for thought as she pitched headlong into empty darkness.

Chapter 3

"DO you have the messages?"

Florian spoke quietly, but still his voice echoed faintly off the stone walls of the cave. Moisture dripped from the walls and ceiling, falling with little plinks onto the stony shelf that overhung the sea.

Lord Bastyon touched the breast of his tunic as he stepped into the boat. "Yes, Your Highness."

"Then Leander keep you."

Florian used his foot to push Bastyon's boat from the shelf. He watched it move toward the opening, Bastyon's form hunched over the oars silhouetted against the brilliant patch of sunlight at the entrance.

He hated letting Bastyon take this risk. It wasn't right to send an old man into danger. It was necessary, he understood that, but that did not make it any easier.

The small boat vanished. Another ten minutes and he would do the same. He wished now he had eaten the stew Mother Mattie offered. The last time he'd eaten was . . . yesterday? The day before? It felt like weeks, to judge by the hollow grinding in his stomach. As for sleeping—he muttered a curse, thinking of the ragged mattress up above. A full belly, a few hours of sleep— luxuries now far beyond his reach.

All because of the woman. He cursed himself for not having sensed the danger from the first. He had been so certain it was a trick, the not-so-clever ruse of a woman who thought the Prince of Venya was the answer to her problems. There had been so many, after all. How was he to know this one was different?

He should have questioned her at once. He should have let the letter go. Important as it was, it was not worth his life. He should have—

But there was no point in going through the many things he should have done. There would be time for all that later.

Five minutes gone. No warning horn, no hint of trouble. It should be enough.

He had one foot in the boat when he heard the door above slide open. He whirled toward the stairway, his dagger in his hand.

"What—? Oh! Ow!"

A small form landed in a heap at the bottom of the stairway. He sighed and sheathed the dagger. Dare he hope she was unconscious?

"Wait!" she cried, leaping to her feet. "You cannot go without me!"

Not unconscious. No such luck. She was awake, aware, and, judging from her voice, determined to alert the world to what had been one of his most reliable escape routes.

But no more.

Already he could hear them in the passageway, kicking at the walls with booted feet.

"How many?" he demanded.

"I—I did not see."

Useless. He was already in the boat, pushing away, before she reached the water's edge.

"Stop! Wait—I cannot swim—"

"Then you had better stay on land."

"I appeal to you in Leander's name—on your honor as a prince—you *can't* refuse!"

"Watch me."

He was not really surprised when she jumped. She came up sputtering, hair plastered across her face like ropes of seaweed as she gasped for air.

"Stand up," he ordered, "You're not drowning."

She sloshed after him, the water rising swiftly to her neck. "Please do not leave me. *Please.*"

The door—secret no longer—began to splinter. Florian sighed, looking at the terrified face turned up to his.

"Quick, give me your hand." He pulled her over the side. "Now shut up and lie still."

He rowed swiftly toward the opening. At the last moment he turned the boat, shipped the oars, and slid silently beneath an overhanging rock. Bent almost double, he used his hands to guide them down the passageway.

It narrowed until the edges of the boat scraped bare rock. Inch by inch he moved them through the darkness until the passageway began to widen. Then he slipped down beside the sodden form of his rescued princess and let the boat drift.

Only inches from their heads, glittering bits of malachite and chalcedony caught the light. The trouble was, he should not have been able to see them. Someone was here before him. With torches. He resisted the urge to peer over the side and see how many there were.

The tide was on the ebb, which meant there was a substantial shelf on the far side of the cavern. There was no point in going back and no other way out by water.

The trap had been well planned, he thought. The bait stared at him, eyes enormous in a face as pale as parchment.

"Empty!" a disgusted voice said. "Marva damn him, he's given us the slip. There must be some other passage. Jadre, go fetch that boat."

Florian slid a hand over the princess's mouth. She stiffened, and he put his lips against her ear. "Alienor," he breathed.

He eased his dagger from his belt and rolled over the side into the water.

For a moment Rose was tempted to follow him, but what would be the use? She could not swim; if she did not drown at once, they would catch her instantly.

And then they would catch him. *At least this way there is a chance,* she thought. *He might come back for me.* A slender hope—a fool's hope—but better than no hope at all.

She lay unmoving as the sailor approached, as still as poor Alienor was said to lie in her curragh as she floated endlessly through storm and tide, waiting for the lover's kiss that would bring her back to life.

The boat tipped; red spots danced upon her closed eyelids; she felt the heat of the torch held close to her face.

"Damn me," a rough voice cried. "'Tis—"

The words ended in a garbled cry. A splash; the hiss of the torch as it fell into the water. Then silence.

"Jadre? Jadre! Where the devil did he go?"

The boat rocked slightly, then began to drift slowly back toward the opening.

"Go see what happened."

Rose slitted open one eye. She was beneath the overhang, safe in shadow. Slowly she raised herself on one elbow to peer over the side. Before her stretched another cave, smaller than the first, with a ledge running along one side.

Four men stood on the ledge, big men with knives and cudgels in their hands. They looked vaguely familiar; faces glimpsed during her infrequent walks upon the *Conquest*'s deck.

One waded into the water. "Jadre?" he shouted, his voice echoing eerily off stone.

"Go on, damn you," the leader ordered. "Bring that boat over here."

Heart pounding, Rose watched the sailor approach. *If they catch me, they will take me back,* she reminded herself fiercely, biting back her instinctive cry of warning. But now she knew that wasn't the chief goal at all.

They wanted the Venyan. For that they had used her, sent her off to him so they could follow. Her clever escape had been nothing of the sort. Her uncle Richard had planned it all, and she had played into his hands from first to last. "Don't make it too easy," she could hear him saying, "the bitch thinks she's so clever—let her find her own way out."

Of course Richard couldn't have known *what I would do,* she thought, staring transfixed at the sailor moving closer. He had simply gambled on his knowledge of her. And won. Alone, unarmed, she had single-handedly accomplished what the King of Valinor's entire fleet had spent years attempting. The elusive Prince of Venya was at last within their grasp.

Knowing her uncle as she did, Rose had no doubt that her reward for this service would be death. And Richard—crafty bastard that he was—would surely blame the Venyan for the crime. A tidy plan, coldly planned and ruthlessly executed. Richard at his best.

The men on shore were leaning forward, watching their companion's progress. They did not see the dark shape sliding through the shadows behind them.

But Rose did. So did the approaching sailor. He shouted out a warning, and the men turned with startled cries, torches waving wildly.

There was a flurry of movement on the shore, impossible to follow in the leaping shadows. The ring of blades, a shout, quickly followed by another. The torches guttered and went out.

The sudden darkness was absolute. Rose could hear the harsh breathing of the sailor just beside her.

"Calum?" he cried into the empty blackness of the cavern. "Edward?"

The boat rocked wildly as he threw himself inside. Rose gasped as a knee connected with her stomach.

"What the—?"

"It's all right," she said quickly, "don't fear, I am Princess Rose of—"

She shrank back as a hand brushed her face, then suddenly fastened around her neck. "Where is the Venyan?"

"I d—don't know."

The hand tightened, fingers digging brutally into her throat. "You cannot do this," she gasped, "I am King Osric's daughter, you have sworn—"

"I serve King *Richard*."

He jerked her toward the side and began to force her over. The thought of vanishing into black water lent her strength. Kicking and writhing, she twisted from his grasp and gripped the narrow seat with both hands.

Bright sparks exploded behind her eyes as his fist connected with her jaw. She sprawled across the seat and slipped down to the bottom of the boat.

And felt the oar beneath her.

Now, she thought, fighting back waves of nauseous dizziness. *It must be now. Don't think, just do it.*

She came up fast, swinging the oar. It met something solid with a numbing jar up to her shoulder. There came a soft, garbled moan, a sound she felt rather than heard, like a sickening punch straight to her belly. The boat listed heavily, then abruptly righted. She swung the oar again and again, but it met only empty air.

It fell from her nerveless fingers, and she covered her face with her hands. When the boat tipped again she screamed, groping for her weapon.

"It's all right. It's all *right,* calm down, it's only me."

Rose knew that voice. She knew that accent, the one she could not name. She had heard it long ago, in a little room behind a tavern.

"Where is the other one?" it demanded.

"He . . . I . . ."

She remembered the dull thud of the oar against his head. Nausea rose in her, choking off her words. She leaned over the side and vomited.

"Are you hurt?"

She could only shake her head, knowing he could not see her.

"Listen," the Prince of Venya said with swift urgency. "This isn't over yet. You have to talk to me, I have to know if you are hurt."

"N-no. I am fine."

The boat began to move again. Rose wanted to ask where they were going, but she was afraid that if she spoke, she might begin to cry.

This isn't how it is supposed to be, she thought numbly. She had never planned to end up in the middle of one of the Prince of Venya's adventures. Or, she thought, not *this* kind of adventure. Other women got romance and sweet words from him, that famous smile she had yet to see and a memory to cherish all their lives. But not her.

She had killed a man today. Not an honorable death, oh no; no clean sword thrust on a battlefield. It had been ugly, brutal . . .

"Are they *all* dead?" she said aloud.

"It doesn't matter."

"Of course it matters," she cried, dragging her wrist across her eyes. "How could you say—what *are* you?"

"Alive. And so are you. If they had their way, we would be dead."

"But—"

"There is no 'but.' I did what I must. And if you remember, it was you who insisted upon coming."

"If I had not," she said slowly, "they would all still be alive."

"Perhaps."

"They would," she insisted. "You would have been gone if not for me."

She waited for him to deny it, but he only sighed. "Yes."

Five men, she thought. Five families. Mothers and fathers, wives and children who would never see their men again.

"If not for me," she said, her voice shaking, "none of it would have happened."

"True. But something else would have."

"Something—? What do you mean?" She frowned, trying to puzzle it out. "I would have stayed behind. They would have found me." She shuddered, one hand going to her bruised throat.

"Five against one—and the one a woman. Wouldn't that have made their families proud? Men who go in for murder can expect no better than a quick death. And that they had."

The songs and stories had not prepared her for this brutal truth. And yet it *was* truth; dazed as she was, she recognized that much. But it was not a truth she wanted to know. Her throat ached, each breath drew a protest from her ribs, and her mouth was filled with the bitter taste of bile.

The boat scraped rock and ground to a halt.

"Stay with me and keep quiet."

No, she thought, *not me, I've had enough.* But her hand lifted of its own accord and his was there to meet it, warm and strong as it fastened around hers and pulled her to her feet.

Chapter 4

THE sky was streaked with the first crimson of dawn when Rose was hauled aloft the *Quest*, too exhausted to resent the indignity.

The Prince of Venya was waiting for her on the deck, two steaming mugs in his hands. The sharp enticing scent of kava made her stomach grumble.

"Still on your feet, eh?" he greeted her, handing her a mug. "Well done."

His black shirt was torn at the shoulder, revealing a long slash crusted with dried blood, and the skin beneath his eyes was stained with weariness. Yet he made her another of those sweeping bows and waved a hand, encompassing the ship. "Welcome to the *Quest*."

The kava burned her tongue, but she didn't care. It had been years since she had tasted it, and then its flavor had been softened with generous helpings of cream and honey. This brew was strong and bitter. After the first shock, it was wonderful.

She gazed about, taking in the lateen sails that were filling as the ship sped across the water, throwing up a wake that glittered in the rising sun. Her tired mind tried to fit the shattered pieces of her life into a picture that encompassed her aboard the *Quest*. It seemed impossible. How often had she heard that name, standing in some corner of the market square? The dauntless *Quest*. The gallant *Quest* that could outrun any ship in Richard's fleet.

That last thought brought a smile to her lips. She finished the kava and set down the mug, then spread her torn and filthy skirt and sank gracefully to the deck.

"Thank you, my lord. How kind of you to invite me."

"Did I? Strange, I don't remember that part."

And then he smiled.

Rose was pleased to note that her bones remained quite solid. It was her stomach that seemed to turn to mush. A slow tingling warmth spread through her as she gaped at him, wondering how a simple change of expression could transform his face entirely.

Perhaps it was the sudden flash of teeth against his sun-darkened skin, or the way his strange eyes warmed to molten amber in the growing light, inviting her to share a very private jest.

"Shall you dine, my lady?" he asked. "Or would you retire to your cabin?"

"Oh, definitely retire. With your leave, of course."

"Of course," he said with a gracious nod as she raised herself, wincing a little. "Are you really all right? Perhaps you should see the surgeon first."

"I am fine, just a bit bruised. Nothing rest won't cure. But what of you?" she added, nodding toward his wounded shoulder. "That should be looked at."

"What?" He glanced down, then shrugged. "It's just a scratch. Sleep well, my lady."

ROSE woke to the sound of holystones scraping the deck above, just as she had every morning since she'd left Malin Isle.

It was all a dream, she thought. The escape, the meeting in the tavern . . . a dream. Or a nightmare.

She yawned and began to turn upon her side, but the mattress shifted strangely beneath her weight and her reaching hand met only empty air. She was not in her bunk upon the *Conquest,* but on a hanging cot that swayed gently with the motion of the ship. Her eyes flew open, and she stared at the unfamiliar cabin.

Not a dream. It had all been real. She had done it. Jehan be praised, she was aboard the legendary *Quest*.

She rolled out of the cot and turned slowly about, taking in every detail of her cabin. It was not much different from the one she'd had aboard the *Conquest*. A small table fixed to wall and floor, a bench, a bit of sailcloth hanging in the corner to provide a small measure of privacy. One porthole. But this one was not sealed shut; a tiny breeze flitted through the cabin, carrying the scent of fresh salt air. And the door . . . She ran to it and pulled it open. Not bolted. She was not a prisoner. She was free.

She sank down on the narrow bench. *Free*. For a time that was enough, but soon the nagging thought broke through. Free, aye. But for how long?

The Venyan is a nobleman, she reflected, gazing about her cabin. *He does have a sense of honor, deny it as he will. He will take me to Sorlain. He must. I'll promise him some fabulous amount of gold—and then I'll see he gets it.*

King Esteban would pay. No matter how exorbitant the sum, it would mean naught to him. Sorlain was vast, its wealth beyond all measure. Oh, Esteban would pay, she thought, he would pay dearly. It was the least that he could do for the woman who had been married—however briefly—to his only son and heir.

True, Rose had only the haziest recollection of her wedding and had never laid eyes upon the groom. She had been five at the time, summoned from the nursery in her finest clothing. An old man, his beard tied up with purple ribbons, had stood proxy for Prince Cristobal, himself only a year older than Rose.

The words they had spoken were lost now. Only one memory stood out clear and sharp: the dignified old man easing himself onto a mattress beside the giggling Rose and solemnly touching his slippered toe to her ankle.

A secret marriage, it had been, one performed over the objections of Rose's mother. Rose was the only child of the king, Queen Najet had argued, and her subjects would not be pleased to see Valinor become a mere possession of Sorlain.

But Rose's father had stood firm. The king of Sorlain was his friend, this was a great alliance, and one that Valinor could not afford to lose. There would be more children, King Osric insisted, by this time next year they would surely have a son. But being a prudent man, he had kept the alliance private until that son should be born.

Rose was permitted to write to Cristobal once. She received a blotted answer in return and had been most impressed to learn that her husband owned fourteen hounds and could walk upon his hands.

After that, she was forbidden to speak of him. As no one ever spoke of him to her, the entire incident faded to a memory, vague and very distant, forgotten entirely in the troubles that soon followed. She was fourteen before she thought of him again and had just realized the hopelessness of her position in her uncle's court. Then Cristobal leaped full-blown into her imagination.

He would arrive with all the might and power of Sorlain to quell her wicked uncle with a single flashing glance. "Where is my wife?" he would demand, and oh, how shocked he would be to see how she was treated, how angry on her behalf! She could just imagine the faces of her cousins, Berengaria and Melisande, when she, the object of their open scorn, was championed by the most powerful prince in all the world.

Rose anticipated Cristobal's arrival with growing impatience until she realized he had no way of knowing of what was happening in far-off Valinor. So she sat down and composed a letter in which she told him all.

Six months passed without reply. Fearing her message had gone astray, she wrote again, this time entrusting the letter to a squire. Poor lad, he had been too slow in switching his allegiance to King Richard, and his prospects had suffered in direct proportion to his loyalty to Richard's niece.

The squire undertook the office with a good will, nearly as eager as Rose was herself to see an improvement in her fortunes. Eight months later he returned with a tale of daring and intrigue, culminating in the moment when he had slipped the letter into Prince Cristobal's own hand, with a quick word on where he would await the answer.

Days turned to weeks and no answer came. The squire, reduced to abject poverty, barely managed to escape the bailiff by taking a berth on an outbound trading vessel.

Rumor had traveled more swiftly than the squire. Rose had long been aware of Cristobal's betrothal to the Princess of Mivago. She had not wanted to believe it, had clung to hope until the last. With a graceful little speech and a heart burning with betrayal, she gave the squire her last jewel and sent him off to seek his fortune.

Aye, she thought now, she would go to King Esteban. Not to resurrect a long-forgotten promise, though after a score of broken betrothals Cristobal was still unwed. Never a word, not a single reproach or pleasantry would the Sorlainian prince ever have of her. It was King Esteban who mattered now. After all, he had been her father's closest friend. Surely his vaunted sense of justice would move him to aid King Osric's daughter, the woman he had so deeply wronged.

She would not ask for much. A modest household was the height of her ambitions, somewhere far from any royal court. A small income, nothing he would miss, a mere trifle compared to what Prince Cristobal's cast-off wife was due.

Even Richard would not dare touch a woman under the protection of Sorlain. All she need do was reach King Esteban.

And then, at last, she would be safe.

Chapter 5

"FOURTEEN wax candles?" Florian shook his head at the unaccustomed glory of his table. "Isn't that a bit of an extravagance?"

His tone was mild, but Beylik, his cabin boy, turned sharply, black eyes wide with apprehension. "I'm sorry, my lord, did I do wrong?" The young man hunched defensively, as though readying himself for a blow, something Florian had not seen him do for months.

"No, not at all," Florian said easily. "I was surprised, that's all. You are quite right, Beylik, it isn't every day we have a princess at our table."

Beylik let out a shaking breath. "Thank you, my lord. It does look well, doesn't it?"

The table looked magnificent. The silver gleamed and glowed, no doubt the result of hours of frantic polishing. The fourteen candles reflected dimly in the shining wood of the long table, glinted off the plates marching in a perfect line, coruscated off the crystal goblets. The glow softened the stark lines of his cabin, illuminating only the table with its wealth of plunder and leaving the rest of it in shadow.

"'Tis a pity you cannot keep it," Beylik added, pulling out Florian's chair with a little bow.

Florian's brows raised, but he made no comment as he took the offered seat. "At least we can enjoy it while it's here. Yes, thank you," he added as Beylik held up the wine flagon. He repressed a smile as the young man poured the goblet full and set it carefully before him.

"I'll just see to the meal," Beylik murmured and with another little bow left the cabin.

Two bows in one night. That was something for the logbook. Beylik was always attentive, but he was generally more concerned with putting food upon the table than how exactly it arrived there. If a dish happened to be dirty, he might wipe it with his sleeve, but even that was not to be counted upon. Now here he was, polishing silver, pulling out chairs, and bobbing up and down like a courtier.

And that, Florian reflected, is what comes from having a woman aboard ship.

The door burst open and a man bounded into the cabin. Sigurd Einarsson, the *Quest*'s surgeon, gave him a shamefaced smile. He was nearly a giant by Venyan standards, standing nearly a head above Florian, who was reckoned quite tall among his own people. But the difference was not so marked, as Sigurd tended to slump; round-shouldered, he said, from too many years spent poring over books and parchments.

"Am I late?" he asked, blinking as he gazed nearsightedly around the cabin. Time meant almost nothing to Sigurd, Florian knew, save in situations where it was of the essence. Then the surgeon could move very swiftly indeed, his light blue eyes sharply focused and his large hands very nimble.

"You're early. Take a seat."

Sigurd folded his long legs into a chair and whistled softly. "I see we dine in splendor tonight."

"Do not get used to it."

The surgeon held up a plate and peered at his reflection. "The wise tell us that vanity is a weakness," he said thoughtfully.

"So it is. One that ill befits a man of honor."

"And yet . . . is it not an equal affront to all the gods not to appreciate true beauty?"

Florian plucked the dish from his hands and replaced it on the table. "I wouldn't know. All I see is a damned ill-shaven surgeon."

Sigurd sniffed. "You are one to talk! When is the last time you shaved?"

Florian ran a hand across his jaw. "Blast it, I forgot. Well, perhaps I'll grow a beard."

"I hope that is a jest," Sigurd said severely. "Consider, my lord, that if you did, every man from here to Ilindria would be forced to follow suit. It's bad enough that you've plunged half the world into mourning and sent the dye-makers to their knees, praying you'll be crowned before ruin overtakes them. Would you really have the barbers join their number?"

Florian laughed. "A few more prayers could hardly hurt. I know, Sigurd, let's hire a minstrel to make songs about you. Then *you* can set the fashion for a change."

The surgeon shot him a grin, a gleam lighting his ice blue eyes. "There's a thought! The Prince of Venya's surgeon—lancet in one hand and trusty basin in the other! They could do a verse about the time I held your head while you puked your guts out on Mivago. And another about the time on Lanamarr when you—"

Florian held up a hand. "Let's not get into Lanamarr, if you please. I was thinking more along the lines of wounds sustained in glorious battle. But now that I reflect a moment, the whole idea was misguided."

"Perhaps." Sigurd sighed. "But then," he added, brightening, "she might just have a weakness for redheaded surgeons."

"She? Oh, Leander's balls, not you, too, Sigurd! You'd think we've never had a woman on this ship."

"Indeed." Sigurd glanced about. "I don't recall seeing your table ablaze with silver before tonight."

"Beylik's idea," Florian answered shortly.

"And a very proper one it was. I never knew you even possessed such a service!"

"I didn't. And I won't for long. It will be going off with Ewan with the rest of the swag."

"A pity."

Florian glared down at his dish. "Sheldrick didn't give a leg so I could eat my meat off silver."

"But you are," Sigurd said, "so should you not at least enjoy it?"

"Certainly. Why not? Tonight our table dazzles and a princess will share our repast. The silver might be stolen and our would-be princess a liar or a madwoman, but why should such trifles spoil our good time?"

"Oh, she is certainly not mad, and I don't think she is lying," Sigurd said decisively. "I spent ten years in the desert, you know, and the lady definitely has Jexlan blood. The coloring is wrong, but you can see it in the bones and the shape of her eyes. And there's the way she uses her hands. Not pure Jexlan, but then it wouldn't be, would it? No one could manufacture such a performance."

"So she's part Jexlan." Florian shrugged. "And that proves . . . ?"

"Don't be difficult, my lord. I'm certain she is exactly who she claims to be."

"And I'm just as certain that you are smitten. Again. Which renders your opinion suspect, to say the least."

Sigurd rested his chin in his palm. "She *is* rather sweet."

"They always are." Florian wagged a finger at the surgeon. "You want to steer clear of the sweet victims of the world, my lad. That sort will only slow you down, and drag you under, too, if you're not careful."

"You are very hard," Sigurd said reproachfully.

"The world is a hard place."

"Particularly so for women," Sigurd said pointedly.

"Such poor little creatures, aren't they?" Florian retorted blandly. "So charmingly bewildered by the cold, cruel world . . . right up until the moment they sink their hooks into a man they think can help them. Then just try to break their grip!" He laughed, raising his goblet to his lips.

"All women have the right to claim protection from a man," Sigurd argued. "All gentlemen are bound in honor to comply."

Florian choked on his wine. "Bound in honor! She only has to ask, and it is done? Leander's balls, that is a fine arrangement. Oh, I won't deny that it's a heady thing to have some lovely swooning in your arms and declaring you her savior, like finding a magical suit of armor made precisely to your measure. But is it magic? Or is it only a lie that we want to accept as truth?"

Sigurd stared at him with an intensity very much at odds with his usual expression of detached good humor.

"You see, Sigurd, the thing you—and any man—must remember is that it's always *her* story. Oh, we have our place, and we're quite useful, bound by our so-called honor to provide whatever she might ask, no matter at what cost. It is indeed a fine arrangement, is it not? One no man could have possibly devised. I'm afraid the truth is that women are far cleverer than we are, and very seldom helpless. At least so long as there is some poor fool of a man they can beguile into doing precisely what they want."

Florian straightened the gleaming silver dish before him, his fingers lightly tracing its scalloped edge. When the silence had lasted half a minute, Sigurd said, "They say in Jexal that a man is judged by deeds, not words. And unless I am mistaken, it was you who brought the princess aboard."

"Do they not also say that misfortune is but opportunity's disguise?"

Sigurd's gaze sharpened. "What do you mean to do? Do you—can you mean to barter her to King Richard?"

"I'm not sure yet what I mean to do with her. But whatever it is, it will be my decision, not hers, and it will be taken for the good of Venya."

"I see," Sigurd said thoughtfully. "I suppose that Richard might be prepared to bargain if—"

He broke off as the door opened and Beylik, with yet another bow, motioned the princess into the cabin. Before she was seated, the first mate, Gordon, arrived as well, with half a dozen men behind him.

THE captain's table was usually a merry company. It had been months since Florian had presided over such a stiff and formal gathering of men in such a raw-skinned state of cleanliness. Cheeks were scraped bare, pigtails newly braided, and the scent of oil was enough to make him dizzy. No one fell upon his meal, every dish was offered to the woman half a dozen times, and not one swear word marred the conversation.

It was she, Florian noticed, who kept the conversation going. Every time it threatened to lapse into silence, she would come up with a question for one of the men or a compliment upon the fare. It was smoothly done, he thought, the sort of thing a dutiful noblewoman must be taught from the cradle.

Dutiful. That was a good word for her. *Sincere* was another. Simple as brown bread and transparent as fresh water. Sigurd might call that quality sweet, but the word that sprang to Florian's mind was *dull.* Seen in a good light, she was also disappointingly plain. Oh, her features were nice enough, he supposed, and her long almond eyes were rather unusual, but she completely lacked the spark that could transform even an ugly woman to a beauty.

"And what happened then?" she prompted.

Gordon, the first mate, as taciturn a man as Florian had ever known, beamed at her, his face flushed with wine and the tale that he was telling. "Well, my lady, we double reefed the topsails and turned into the wind. What else could we do?"

"What else, indeed?" she murmured.

"Now, the tide had turned when we rounded the headland— like this," he said, pushing the saltcellar to the center of the table and laying his knife at an angle. "So of course there was no help for it."

"There wasn't?"

Florian hid a smile. Lady Rose hadn't the first idea what Gordon was talking about, but she was gamely stumbling along in the wake of his tale.

"None at all," Gordon cried. The saltcellar jumped as he crashed his fist upon the table. "In that tide—did I mention that the moon was full?—there was no other way but forward. And once we rounded the headland, there was the fog so thick you could barely find your pr—ah, that is, you could barely see your hand before your face."

Barely find your prick with your two hands. That's what Gordon had started out to say. A pity, Florian thought, that he had checked himself. It would have been interesting to see how far her courtesy extended.

"Oh, dear," she breathed. "How terrible! What did you do?"

"Set a storm staysail to the mainbrace!"

"I never would have thought of *that!*"

"Really?" Florian raised a brow. "What would you have done, my lady?"

She smiled across the table. "Fallen down into a faint, no doubt. But then," she added to Gordon, "I cannot claim to be a sailor."

"Of course not!" he cried. "What woman is?"

"Anika Brennan?" Florian suggested smoothly.

Gordon frowned. "Well, yes, my lord, but she is the exception. Now, as I was—"

"And Ramika of the *Diarmuid*," Florian put in, lifting his goblet and admiring the candle's flame through the crystal. He smiled a little as he remembered his first meeting with the Moravian corsair. *She* was not plain. Not pretty, either, with her weathered skin and craggy features, but a damned exciting woman just the same.

"A heathen," Gordon growled.

"And of course we mustn't forget Lady Hesperia." Florian met the woman's eyes across the table. "Of Valinor, if I am not mistaken."

She frowned slightly, then turned back to Gordon with a smile. "I met Lady Hesperia once," she said confidingly. "I was very young, but I remember her right well. It was just after Lord Varnet returned from his expedition. The two of them made quite a sensation at court."

"You met Lord Varnet?" Ashkii, the third mate, spoke for the first time, bringing out the words with such charged intensity that they sounded more like a challenge than a question.

But that was Ashkii's way. Lean and focused as the osprey that was the symbol of his house, the Ilindrian had made few friends aboard the *Quest*. Florian wished he could do something to ease the young man's lot, but he knew from long experience that any interference from the captain was like to do more harm than good. With an inward sigh he noted Gordon's frown and suspected there were many midnight watches in Ashkii's future.

Then there was Sigurd, fair skin flushed with wine, glaring at the third mate as though he'd like to throttle him on the spot.

And that, Florian thought, is a woman for you. Even the plainest was naught but trouble from first to last, stirring up resentment in the crew, making enemies of otherwise amiable shipmates.

Some women reveled in the chaos. Others deplored it. But the princess seemed oblivious to the dark currents all around her. "Oh, yes, I met him many times," she said to Ashkii. "My father was his sponsor, you see, and Varnet—of course, he was just plain Aidan Culpepper in those days—was often at our table. He was always going on about the passage he was certain he could find."

"He *did* find it," Ashkii said with a lift of his chin that was just short of insulting.

"Yes, of course he did!" The princess smiled, spreading her hands in a graceful gesture of apology.

"Varnet discovered the passage to the Andrien Sea," Florian put in quickly. "He opened up a whole new world to us. He was the first to reach Ilindria," he said with a nod to Ashkii, "then went farther still, all the way to Chalindar."

"Where he found his Hesperia! Who was indeed a wonderfully accomplished sailor by all accounts," the princess added to Gordon, who was scowling with drunken ferocity at his third mate. "Which, alas, is a talent I completely lack."

She laughed, and Florian wondered if she had done that apurpose, snipped off the loose ends of a conversation that was threatening to unravel. But it seemed more likely she hadn't noticed it at all. Perfectly polite, she continued with every show of interest, "Now do tell me, Mr. Gordon, what happened after you set the storm staysail. Was it successful?"

Chapter 6

AT last it was over. The pudding was eaten, the glasses emptied, and Rose began to count the moments until she could escape.

"My lady," the Prince of Venya said, "would you stay? I'd like to speak to you about your plans."

The men all rose and bade her good night. The first mate, Gordon, beamed at her with approval as he made his bow, staggering a little in the process. The surgeon held her hand a bit too long, smiling with a somewhat befuddled charm. The third mate did not deign to smile. He merely bowed in what she assumed was the Ilindrian manner, very stiff and formal, hands clasped behind his back. The prince stood and walked with them to the door.

Alone for a moment, Rose sank back in her seat and closed her eyes, every muscle vibrating with tension. She had expected a private interview tonight, not a gathering. And such a formal one! She hadn't thought such luxury existed aboard the *Quest*. All the tales agreed that the prince lived as meanly as his own people and used every scrap of plundered wealth to support his Venyan cause. But apparently the tales were exaggerated. His table was as fine as King Richard's—indeed, it was identical, for the silver was marked with the same curling leaves and vines she had often seen in Richard's hall.

It was a small thing, yet oddly disconcerting. The Prince of Venya was not meant to dine off silver—he was the champion of the downtrodden, the hope of the oppressed, the proof that somewhere in the world there lived a prince who always placed the welfare of his subjects above his own comfort.

*And if you think that any man alive could measure up to that
ideal, you are as credulous a fool as Richard named you.*

Fool that she might be, Rose wished she hadn't seen it. She
had admired the prince too fervently for far too long to take even
such a small disappointment lightly. If only he had thought to
warn her what was planned tonight, she would have made some
excuse to keep to her cabin. She felt as though she had walked the
gauntlet, surviving more by luck than by design. All those men
watching her like starving hounds with a bit of meat, ready to
turn and rend each other at the slightest provocation, had been an
unexpected—and unwelcome—honor.

Not that it was any compliment to her. As she'd said, her father had taken an avid interest in his fleet, often inviting his captains to his table. Their stories had made little sense to a child, but
Rose had listened and remembered. And she knew that after
months at sea, a woman suddenly introduced into an exclusively
male company was a danger to herself and to the crew.

The prince knew it, too. She suspected that when it came to
his ship, very little passed him by. Had it been some sort of test,
then? Or merely a diversion? She rubbed the rigid muscles of her
shoulder, then straightened, opening her eyes as the door closed
behind the last guest.

"I hope I didn't say the wrong thing," she said as the prince resumed his seat. "That pale young man was so angry."

"Oh, that was nothing you said. Ashkii's always like that. He
has no conversation, it's all challenges and insults. Not his fault,
poor lad, he had a rather . . . unusual upbringing."

"He is Ilindrian, I gather?" She had never met one before,
though she had heard the tales of the sorcerer-beasts who inhab-
ited Ilindria. Kohkahycumest Ashkii, with his dead white skin
and the feather trailing from his silvery hair, resembled no man
she had ever seen before. But despite his sharp-edged features, he
was unmistakably a man.

"Yes, but we try not to hold it against him."

"I had thought an Ilindrian would be less . . ." She waved a
hand at the prince.

"Like us? On the contrary, they are generally *more* like us—
until the transformation. But Ashkii is only half Ilindrian."

"However did he end up here?"

The prince shrugged. "I've spent quite a bit of time in Ilindria over the years. The *Qaletaqa* flirts with the idea of lending me support, but he can never quite make up his mind to do it."

Rose considered this. "It would not be a popular alliance."

"No, they have rather a rather bad odor in these parts, don't they? Though on the whole, I think it's undeserved. Ilindrian magic is strange to us, but that doesn't make it evil—or it wouldn't if we used it as they do. The trouble is that we don't have their customs to guide us. In the wrong hands, their elixir is a danger, though mostly to the poor fools who think it would be fun to have a taste of magery. I've seen plenty of them—or what's left of them—on the docks, begging or stealing or worse for the price of one more Ilindrian draught."

"Have you tried it?" Rose asked.

The prince smiled at her and slumped in his seat, looking charmingly disheveled with the candlelight gleaming on the golden stubble on his cheeks and chin. "I have plenty of vices already. Speaking of which," he said, picking up the flagon at his elbow, "will you join me? Unless you don't drink spirits—I noticed you refused wine before."

Rose held out her empty goblet. "I didn't dare," she confided. "I'm afraid I'm not much used to company."

He filled it and set the flagon down, taking up his own goblet and raising it to her before he drank. She raised hers as well, feeling as though she had stepped into a pageant. Was she really sitting upon the *Quest* (*the gallant* Quest, a voice sang in her mind), sipping wine with the Prince of Venya?

Perhaps he did indulge himself with stolen silver, but was that really such a crime? Really, it was a bit endearing. The small flaw made him somehow more approachable, a man instead of just a legend.

His eyes (piercing, merry, or a flashing with a righteous anger, depending on the song) turned to the graceful sweep of the stern window. Their expression was . . . tired, she thought, a little sad, as though his thoughts were not happy ones. Somehow she had never imagined that *he* could be sad or weary, which was a bit ridiculous when she came to think of it.

Then he turned back to her, and she jumped a little as his eyes fixed on her face.

"Not used to company? And why is that?" He relaxed further

in his seat, hooking a leg over the arm of his chair as though settling in for a comfortable chat.

"Since my parents died, I have lived a very . . . sheltered life. My uncle does not allow me out in public very often."

"Is that why you wish to go to Sorlain?"

"Not entirely," Rose answered slowly. "Though it is certainly a part of it."

"And what is the rest?"

He looked at her expectantly, as though he were genuinely interested in her answer.

"My uncle is an ambitious man."

"I have noticed," he said dryly.

"Yes, of course you would have. Well, when my father died, my position was a bit uncertain. He had always expected to have a son, you see, and so he never acknowledged me as his heir. Right up to the last, he was still hoping. He died very suddenly, you know."

"And yet King Osric was not a young man. Surely he must have known there was a chance you would be his only child."

"I suppose he must have," Rose said, "though if he did, he never spoke of it. Not to me, at any rate. Nor to my mother either, from all that I could tell. But then, I don't think he ever talked to her much at all."

"Your mother was of Jexal, was she not? It is unusual for a woman of the tribes to wed an outlander."

"Yes, it was unusual. But my father wanted the trade agreement, and he was desperate for an heir. You know perhaps that his first wife and their sons died in the red fever?"

The prince nodded. "Yes, I've heard that. Three sons, wasn't it? Gods, it must have been terrible for him, losing them all in one blow, and his queen as well."

"I don't think he ever recovered from the shock. Of course he married again at once; it was his duty. My father was a great one for doing his duty." Rose turned the goblet in her hands, surprised to find it empty. "What a pity that all he got for his trouble was a daughter."

The prince held out the flagon with a questioning lift of his brow and she nodded.

"Of course he never said that," she went on. "But I always knew . . . It wasn't his fault, he'd lost his entire family and never had the chance to mourn them. And my mother was so much younger, just sixteen when I was born. It was only . . ."

"Only what?"

Rose managed a laugh. "Well, he never seemed quite certain who we were. Oh, not that he was mad, it wasn't that at all. But if he came upon us suddenly, he would look so surprised, as though he had no idea where we'd come from. And he was always so . . . *polite*. It wasn't so bad for me. I had my mother. But I think it was rather terrible for her, all alone in a strange place with such very different customs."

She stopped, a little alarmed at the things she had just said, private things that she had never imagined confiding to anyone.

"She must have been very lonely," the prince said, his voice so warmly sympathetic that Rose forgot her reservations in the relief of speaking the truth to someone so disinterested and kind.

"Perhaps if she had borne a son, he would have . . . but she did not. Then he died and my uncle came back. Once my mother was dead . . . and my cousin Rico was born . . ." Rose shrugged. "The barons swore their fealty to Richard and his heir."

"Then why did your uncle not marry you off to one of his trusted men? It seems the obvious solution."

"There is no one Richard trusts so much as that! My father *was* the king, and I his only child. There has never been a woman ruler of Valinor, but it seems there is no actual law forbidding it. No, he wouldn't risk it. He wanted me where he could keep an eye on me, so I became part of Rico's household. And after Venya . . ."

The prince leaned forward, suddenly alert. "Venya? What has Venya to do with this?"

"I was there, I told you that. Through the uprising, the famine . . ." Shuddering at the memory, she tossed off the rest of her wine. The prince refilled her goblet instantly.

"I have heard," he said, replacing the stopper in the flagon, "that there was some ill-feeling against me for that."

"Well," she said carefully, "there was a rumor that you were invading the country and a bit of grumbling when it was proved false."

"Yes, but—" he began, then checked himself. "I have heard rumors, as well, as to what happened in Riall. How bad was it really?"

"Terrible. Worse than I could say."

Her stomach clenched as Riall came back to her in a rush of jumbled memories. The dead piled in the streets, the living wandering like ghosts, skeletal faces etched with blank despair. The grinding helplessness. The rage. And the fear. Oh, yes, the fear.

"I did what I could. It was very little, I'm afraid, but they were grateful. Too grateful," she added ruefully. "There were some—not many, but Jehan's garter, they were loud—who took up what they were pleased to call my cause."

The prince's eyes sharpened. "I never heard of this."

"You wouldn't have. There was nothing to it, really, just a few desperate people who would have seen me in my uncle's place. Of course Richard heard of it. He hears of everything," she added with a shiver.

"Why would Richard care what a few Venyan peasants had to say?"

"It wasn't only them. He was aware of me already. For years, even before Venya, he had me watched every moment of the day. It was"—she swallowed hard—"unpleasant."

Unpleasant. Weighing every word she spoke, taking only from the dishes her cousins ate from, suspecting every show of kindness. Sitting alone in her chamber day after weary day as her life slipped irrevocably past.

"I was allowed no private conversations that Richard did not arrange. For the most part, I was kept confined—for my health, or so he said. But every so often he would send someone with a new plot to put me on the throne."

"What did you say to them?"

To her own surprise, Rose laughed at what had never seemed amusing before. "I would stare at them, like so"—she widened her eyes and tipped her head to one side—"and say, 'But I do not understand. My uncle is the king. You must speak to him about these matters.' And I would go on repeating that until they went away."

The prince laughed as well. "Oh, very good! You look quite half-witted when you do that."

"Thank you. I practiced hard to get it right. But after Riall, I made a terrible mistake. When I returned, I challenged my uncle on his Venyan policy. Worse, I did it publicly."

"I did not know we have a champion at Richard's court," the prince said, lifting his glass to her. "I thank you, lady."

"*Had*," she corrected wryly, returning his salute. "And not a very good one, I'm afraid. Richard had me locked up at once and told everyone I had suffered a collapse after my ordeal. And then . . ." She gestured toward the stern window.

"You were sent to Malin Isle"—he leaned slightly forward—"to the Handmaidens. I've heard something of them. But no one seems to know just what they do on Malin Isle or even who they serve."

"What no man can know or woman tell," Rose murmured.

The Prince of Venya smiled winningly. "Just so. But *you* know, don't you? And you could tell me."

"Yes." Rose moved restlessly in her seat. "I *could* tell you," she said, trying hard to smile. "But if I did, I am afraid you would be cursed for life—or what remained of it, which by all accounts would not be long. Or pleasant."

He began to laugh, then stopped and eyed her thoughtfully. "Do you believe that?"

"I'm not sure. When I was there, I saw—" She caught herself up sharply. "In your place, I would not take the chance."

He frowned, then shrugged. "Come to think of it, I don't suppose I'm quite so curious as that. So Richard packed you off to the Handmaidens. Why did he not leave you there?"

"I don't know. I expected that he would. When he sent for me, I thought—I was certain that he meant to do away with me for good. So when I saw a chance to get away, I took it. I did not know it was a trap. I am sorry—"

He waved her apology aside. "But why did you come to me?"

"I knew that I could trust you."

"Did you?" he said softly. "And how did you know that?"

"Well, I told you one reason, that I was sure Richard could not buy you off."

He nodded. "Sound enough. But you said that was *one* reason. Were there more?"

"Well, yes," she said, "one more. Everyone knows the Prince of Venya would never refuse a lady in distress."

"Oh, *everyone* knows that, do they?" He shook his head, smiling. "Then of course it must be true."

"My lord, I do beg you to take me to Sorlain. King Esteban was more than my father's ally; they were true friends. I know he will assist me."

"Ah, so now we come to it. In what way will Esteban assist you? What do you want from him?"

The ship had stopped, she noticed. The cabin was silent, the air filled with the pungent scent of swamplands.

"A home," she said at last, the words catching in her throat. "Just a place to . . . be. Nothing much, I don't ask for a grand manor or riches."

"But what of Valinor?"

"Valinor belongs to Richard now. There is nothing there to hold me. Save for Rico," her voice wavered when she spoke his name. "I'm very fond of him. And my cousin Jeannie, she is different from the others, though I never had the chance to know her well. I was always kept apart, you see, and I could never be quite sure of anyone. I am so weary of it," she whispered, "always watching, trying to fathom Richard's mind and keep one step ahead. I only want to be free of it and be . . . myself. Whoever *that* is. After all this time, I honestly don't know."

Florian poured himself another glass of wine. He didn't really want it, but he needed some excuse to look away, lest she see how well he understood her. Some things were too private to be shared, even in a glance.

"I don't expect it sounds like much to you," she said with an embarrassed laugh. "It isn't very interesting compared to"—she waved a hand—"well, to this. But it is what I want."

"Then you should have it."

"Do you mean—will you help me?"

Florian smiled and inclined his head. Why not? She was fairly useless as a hostage. If even half of what she'd said was true, Richard was probably hoping she was dead. Florian didn't think she had lied to him, though she had probably exaggerated her Venyan sympathies a bit, which could play to his advantage once she reached Sorlain. Perhaps she would put in a good word for him with King Esteban. Leander knew he could use *someone* at Esteban's court to plead his cause.

"Venya's champion deserves something from her prince!" he said lightly. "I am afraid I cannot take you to Sorlain myself, but we will soon reach Hufre, and I know a man there who can be trusted."

"Thank you. But . . ."

As Sigurd had said, her speech was that of Valinor, but the

way she used her hands was Jexlan. The desert tribe observed three days of silence out of every seven, and through the years had developed a second language made entirely of signs. Every Jexlan spoke as much with gestures as with words, and given that her mother had been a desert woman, it was no surprise that Princess Rose would do the same. Now she lifted one hand, palm upward, and with a graceful flutter of fingers turned it over.

Florian had never been quick with languages, but he understood her instantly. "Do not trouble yourself about that. He owes me several favors."

"I will repay you—"

"It is nothing, lady, truly. Do not even think of it."

"How long to Hufre?"

"Three or four days. We cannot go directly there, I have . . . business that cannot wait. Until then, you are my guest. If there is anything you need, just ask."

"I have everything I need." Suddenly she wasn't plain at all; her long, dark eyes glowed in a face transformed with joy as she smiled brilliantly into his eyes.

Chapter 7

ALONE, Florian sat down at his writing table, but he could not rouse himself to tackle the work before him. He stared at the same page for a quarter of an hour, then reached into the cabinet above his head for another book, with the name of Aidan Culpepper etched in gold across the spine. It fell open to a chart, the place marked by a scrap of parchment that he unfolded and spread out upon the page.

He wasn't sure why he bothered. It wasn't as though he had forgotten the words scrawled in haste upon its crumpled surface. But he read them over for what must be the hundredth time since he had written them the year before.

> *"The sword to conquer Venya's foes,*
> *The shield protects us from our woes,*
> *When sacrifice of uncrowned king,*
> *Is offered in the sacred ring,*
> *Then two are one by oath forsworn*
> *And hope unites the land reborn."*

No new wisdom was revealed to him, no fresh interpretation burst upon his mind. Frowning, he traced a finger over the third and fourth lines of the prophecy, then slapped the book shut and strode up the steps leading to the forecastle deck.

Huge moths fluttered about the hanging lantern that cast a warm yellow glow on the men below. The crew was at ease tonight, lying about half dressed, dicing or winding hair into complicated pigtails, swatting insects, and drinking steadily. The click of the tiles, low curses, and laughter were comforting, familiar sounds, for Florian's childhood and youth had been passed in just such company as this.

But now things were very different. A captain had no business on the forecastle deck. Gordon had the watch; if Florian went round the ship, the first mate would be insulted. He could go to bed, but sleep was far away. He leaned his elbows on the railing and gazed at the swirling tendrils of fog rising from the brackish water as though he could find the answers he needed in the mist.

Filidhi and *fheara.* Mages and tribesmen, the two peoples of Venya. Since Lord Leander's time, they had lived as one, bound to each other and the land. Now the *fheara* were crushed beneath Richard's heel and the *filidhi* had fled to Serilla, where they practiced their magical arts until such time as their prince should lead them home.

> *Then two are one by oath forsworn*
> *And hope unites the land reborn.*

Florian needed no prophecy to remind him of his duty. It was the task he had prepared for since the age of seven. Now some on his council would have him accept that it had all been a mistake. Venya is lost, they said. Just let it go. You are no prince, but just a man, free to make your own destiny.

Free. A seductive word, one he dared not think too often. What had the princess said? *"I only want to be free of it and be . . . myself. Whoever that is. After all this time, I honestly don't know."*

He pushed the memory away. He *did* know who he was. What he had been born to be. The Prince of Venya, who would return upon the flood tide with all who had been lost. There was no freedom for him. None at all. To even think the word was folly.

All at once the air was too thick to breathe, the twisted vines and creepers the bars of a prison he could not escape. He wanted wine—no, the burn of *usqua*—as much as he could stomach. He wanted a game of *cheran* in some stinking tavern where no one knew his name. A fight—a whore—either would ease the pressure threatening to choke him.

"Jashera Venya," he muttered, fingers splayed in his hair and the heels of his hands pressed against his eyes. "Meara jasra." *My soul for Venya. I accept my destiny.*

But the words did not bring their usual comfort. Not tonight. Tonight he wanted off this prison ship.

He wanted *out.*

The pressure gathered itself into a fist that clenched around his heart, and icy sweat broke out over his entire body. *Not now,* he thought, *not yet, it is too soon—*

A swim will ease you.

The thought slid full-formed into his mind. He could almost feel cool water caressing his skin, dark water rippling his hair. Yes, of course. A swim. That was exactly what he needed.

He stripped quickly and started down the ladder. Only when the water lapped around his thighs did he stop, wondering what the devil he was doing. He must be mad to even think of going alone into a swamp in the middle of the night. The brackish water was filled with snakes and eels and scaly beasts with long, sharp teeth. He could sense them out there, hungry, hunting . . .

But he could sense something else, as well, like a half-remembered song tugging at the edges of his mind. Sweetly it sang, and softly, promising ease and joy and the freedom of the sea. He shivered, his fingers clenched on the ladder as a wave of sick dizziness passed over him. Then it was gone and he was sharply alert, every sense heightened to the breaking point. Frogs croaked, insects hummed, and the eerie call of a waterfowl pierced the still night air. A small splash in the darkness sent him leaping half out of his skin.

"So, Prince of Venya."

The heavily accented words rippled sweetly as cool water over stone.

Florian leaned down, fingers tightening about the ladder. He could just make out a dim shape before him, all sinuous arms and flowing hair. The tail was invisible beneath the water, but he knew it was there. His heartbeat quickened, and the hair stirred on his neck.

"Merrow," he said, the word not quite a question. Instinctively, he touched his brow in a gesture of respect.

"The spawn of Valinor is with you?"

"The Princess? Yes. How did you know?"

"We see. We watch. We watch *you*."

"I am honored," Florian said. "Or am I? They say men only see you in the moments before death. If that is so, merrow, it is an honor I can do without."

The liquid sound of laughter came softly in the darkness. The clouds parted, and moonlight glinted off sleek blue-tinted flesh. Hair flat and shining as a seal's pelt cupped the merrow's lovely skull. Florian stared fascinated at the ripe, lush mouth, the eyes, too large for any human, but somehow perfect on that delicately molded face. Eyes that glowed with a dark beauty, drawing him, beckoning him . . . He wrested his gaze from hers.

"Oh, I have held the sailors in my arms and kissed the last breath from their lips. It is sweet," the merrow crooned, "sweet to take and sweeter still to give. They beg me with their eyes for more . . ."

Florian imagined that her kiss would be sweet indeed, dark and cold and endless.

"But for you, that time is not tonight."

"Then what do you want of me?" he asked, his voice harsh in his own ears.

"No more than you want for yourself. *Venya*."

"Why?"

"For reasons of our own, of course, and they are no concern of yours. But we wonder . . . How strong is your resolve? How far are you prepared to go?"

"As far as necessary," Florian answered steadily. This time, he held the merrow's gaze without flinching. "Will your people help me?"

Again that laughter, faintly mocking, piercing sweet. "We do not *help*. We only watch. But this much I can tell you: The *Lord Marva* has set sail from Valinor."

Florian swore. "The *Lord Marva*? Are you certain?"

"I have seen it. They will be here in two days."

"But I will not."

"Go, then. Our hopes go with you." Her voice changed to a warning hiss. "Do not fail us."

"Or what?"

A faint splash, a flip of a phosphorescent tail, and Florian stood alone, watching moonlight glittering on empty water.

Chapter 8

"GOOD evening, Gordon."

"Your Highness." Gordon nodded from his place at the helm. "All's quiet."

"Good. There has been a change of plan. We're leaving now."

"Now? You mean tonight? But I thought—"

Florian raised his brows.

"That is, I understood—"

"I believe you have the course."

"Aye, my lord, I have it here. We'll get under way at once."

"Thank you."

Florian went back to his cabin. His logbook still sat open on the table, the blank page a mute reproach. He sat down and dipped the quill, but before the first word was written, ink spattered in a fine spray across the page. He waited a moment, staring at his hand until the tremor ceased. Then he forced himself to begin again, focusing on each letter until Gordon arrived to make his report.

"If the wind holds, we'll reach the rendezvous by tomorrow sunset," the first mate said.

"That is well." Florian set down his quill and rubbed the space between his eyes. "I have learned tonight that the *Lord Marva* is in pursuit."

"But how could you—?" Gordon stared, the high color fading from his face. "Oh. I see."

Florian knew quite well what Gordon saw. Sorcery. During his first weeks aboard the *Quest,* the first mate had watched Florian with nervous, sidelong glances, braced against some sudden display of magic. For of course everyone knew that the prince was the most powerful of all the Venyan *filidhi*.

"Mmm," Florian murmured. "The point is, we must keep well ahead of them. So let's find Sir Ewan as soon as possible and then head for . . . for . . ." The cabin swung in a sickening arc before his eyes. He blinked hard, and it steadied once again.

"My lord, are you well?" Gordon asked, peering at him with concern.

"Yes, quite. We'll make for Serilla by the northern route. If the *Lord Marva* picks up our trail, we can lose her in the islands."

"Aye. Will there be anything else?"

"Not tonight." Florian reached for the quill, then withdrew his hand and clenched his fingers tightly. "Or—yes. Send Sigurd to me, if you would."

Gordon nodded, backing toward the door. "I will see to it at once."

Chapter 9

ROSE counted four bells as she lay on her hanging cot, arms folded beneath her head, and watched a tiny splash of sunlight dance upon the ceiling.

She had slept far into the morning and woken only long enough to eat before drifting off into a doze. Her mind roamed lazily among hazy images and half-formed thoughts; every limb was deliciously relaxed. Three days to Hufre. Four if she was lucky. A small space in which to rest before taking up the next task. She did not intend to waste a single moment.

She was just remembering the Prince of Venya naming her his champion, her memory sliding into a dream in which he took her hand and raised her to her feet. "Venya's champion deserves something from her Prince," he murmured, and bent to her . . . and then a pounding on her door jerked her awake.

"Come in," she called, and the dark young man who had served at table the night before opened the door. *A Jexlan lad,* Rose thought, *one of my mother's people*. A rather beautiful young man, with the same high-arched brows and long eyes that Queen Najet had gifted to her daughter.

"My lord says you are to come below," he said. "He says you are to take what you need from the hold."

"Give him my thanks, but I need nothing."

"He says you are to come," the boy repeated stolidly.

"Oh, then I suppose I must." The boy did not return her smile, but merely stood back and bowed his head, waiting for her to pass.

"Art of Jexal, little brother?" she asked as they stepped into the passageway.

He shook his head. "I am of the *Quest*."

"Yes, but before . . . I can see it in thy face and hear it on thy lips, even if thou wilt not speak our tongue."

"I am of the *Quest*. Please wait a moment." He disappeared through a door, emerging a moment later with a candle in his hand.

"And what is thy name, child of the *Quest*?" Rose asked as they walked down a short flight of steps.

"They call me Beylik."

Rose looked at him closely, wondering if she had misheard, for *beylik* was the Jexlan word for slave. "That is not a name."

"It is what they call me." He opened a door. "In here, if you please."

Her breath caught as she stepped into a small, windowless chamber and Beylik held the candle high. Gold and silver glittered in the flickering light, and rich velvets and shimmering silk were heaped in careless piles on the tables. She smiled as she inhaled the spicy-sweet aroma of Jexlan spice.

"A treasure!" she exclaimed. "Is it all for me?"

This time Beylik did smile. "My lord says you should choose stuff for a gown."

"Very kind of him, but I'm no hand at sewing, and I seem to have forgotten my seamstress."

"The men will see to it."

Rose stepped into the chamber and spent a happy few minutes imagining herself in crimson velvet or sapphire silk. But at last she chose a bolt of fine green wool. "This, then," she said. "With my thanks."

As she lifted it, a faint gleam of gold caught her eye. She pushed rolls of fabric aside and found a tapestry beneath. A man sat upon a throne, holding a garland of golden blossoms above the head of the woman kneeling at his feet.

Beylik moved to stand beside her. "I have seen them before," he said. "On tapestries and coins. Who are they?"

"This is Marva, the first King of Valinor. He was humbly born and lived by the sea, a fisherman by trade. Leander was his friend and kinsman, a maker of nets. He was clever with a knife and carved such things as people needed, bowls and spoons and such.

"One day," she went on, "they went out into the boat together. They cast the nets and brought in a fish that spoke to them and claimed to be the sea king's daughter. She pleaded with them to release her and offered in return whatever they most wanted. Marva asked for wealth, and it was granted him. Leander took longer to decide, but in the end he said he would take whatever the sea king's daughter thought he had earned.

"Well, Marva became the leader of his tribe. He called the land Valinor and declared himself its king. Leander's gift was slower to show itself, but when it did, he was delighted. For what he crafted with his own hands was just as he imagined it. His nets would never break or tangle; his chairs were not only beautiful, but brought ease of mind and body to those who sat in them. It was said that no matter what was served in Leander's bowls or cups, it tasted of the very thing you liked the best.

"He also had a special feeling for wind and tide and storm, so that in time all the fishermen consulted him before setting out and farmers waited for his word before planting or harvesting their crops. And though Marva ruled without dispute from his castle, the hearts of his subjects belonged to the gentle Leander in his tiny cottage by the sea."

"But who is the woman?" Beylik asked when she paused.

"We'll come to her. Now, as Leander's power revealed itself, Marva's seemed to diminish, if only in his own eyes. He claimed that as the boat was his, so was the catch, and all the gifts of the sea king's daughter belonged to him. He would have kept his kinsman as a vassal, harnessing Leander's wisdom for the good of Valinor. They debated this, first in a friendly fashion, and then in one that was not so friendly. And when Leander refused outright, Marva bade him reconsider the matter from a prison cell.

"But Jehan"—Rose touched the woman's bent head—"who was Lord Marva's promised bride, took Leander's part. She unlocked his prison and helped him escape across the mountains. For this deed, Jehan was banished, but Lord Marva, in his mercy, took her back. He crowned her with *carna* blossoms and made her his queen."

"And Lord Leander settled in his new land, and in time became the first King of Venya," a voice said behind her. She jumped a little and turned to see the surgeon, Sigurd, in the doorway. "I have heard the tale before, though I do not think they tell it thus in Valinor."

"No, they say it differently there," she agreed, "with Leander as the evil sorcerer who turned traitor to his king. But I have read the old books, and I think they do not lie."

"And now King Richard has taken back Venya. All he need do is catch our lord and make him High Mage of Valinor to be Lord Marva come again."

Rose laughed and flicked the tapestry over. "I don't think even Richard would try that!"

"What have you chosen?" Sigurd asked, stepping inside and looking at the bolt of wool. "Bah, so plain! No, you must have"— he picked up a roll of dusk-pink silk shot through with golden thread—"a good color for you." He thrust the fabric at the cabin boy. "See that the work begins at once, *beylik.*"

Sigurd pronounced the word in the Jexlan manner, with a curl to his lip that made it the insult that it was. The boy looked up at the surgeon, dark eyes smoldering beneath his silky fringe of hair.

"Art truly a *beylik,* little brother?" Rose asked gently. "I see no collar."

Beylik shook his head. "I wear none . . . now. My lord struck it off when he took me from the galleys."

"Then why—"

"Thy kindness does thee credit, lady, misplaced as it may be," Sigurd said to her in Jexlan. "The boy knows exactly what he is. Don't you, Beylik?"

Beylik stood very straight, his eyes fixed on a point over Rose's shoulder. "Yes," he said. "I do. Would you like me to take you back to your cabin, lady?"

"No," Sigurd answered for her. "You may go." He turned to Rose and held out his arm. "If you are finished here, I have arranged a meal on deck."

Rose was thoughtful as they left the hold and Beylik locked the door behind them. She was not happy with the way Sigurd had spoken to the cabin boy, for whom she felt an immediate and instinctive sympathy of blood. Nor was she happy with herself for standing by and saying nothing. But what else could she have done? She was but a guest here, after all, and courtesy forbade her from interfering in what was none of her concern.

They went up the narrow stairway and passed from the dimness of the passage to light so dazzling that Rose was momentarily blinded. She closed her eyes, and when she opened them again, it was to find herself in a world composed of superlatives.

The sun did not merely shine, it blazed with a power that would have been unbearable had it not been for the wind, scented with salt and tar and the faintest touch of Jexlan spice. It filled the sails to bursting, driving the ship onward through a sapphire sea. The rise and fall of the prow was at once soothing and exhilarating; each dip flung up an arc of spray on either side, and where sunlight caught the water, rainbows danced.

Rose's heart filled as she tried to take it in. She wanted to swallow it whole and keep it always, the scents and sights and the lovely crisp smack of wood on water, of canvas against wind, the music of sailors talking in a dozen languages at once. They were everywhere, it seemed, swarming deck and shrouds and sails in a confusion of color. She saw skin of every shade from alabaster to onyx, scarves of periwinkle and crimson and vermillion, ornaments of gold and silver and copper flashing as they moved, each to his own purpose but every one directed toward a single goal.

"Welcome to the *Quest,*" Sigurd said, echoing the prince's greeting of the day before.

Rose glanced quickly at the quarterdeck, where Gordon stood at the wheel. The first mate smiled and sketched her a little bow, and she waved at him.

"This way," Sigurd said, gesturing her toward a small table tucked into the prow beneath a canvas awning. It was set for two, she saw, and once she had taken her seat, Sigurd sat down across from her and lifted the cover of a dish.

"Will you try some of these prawns?" he said, spooning them onto her dish, and she realized she was ravenous.

The prawns had been simmered with hot peppers and garlic and unfamiliar spices. The first bite set her mouth afire and flooded her eyes with tears. Sigurd laughed at her expression and poured a pale liquid into their cups.

"You must sip immediately after each bite," he said, and when she had emptied half the cup, the fire subsided to a glow. She tried another bite, and when she followed it directly with a mouthful of sweet, cool liquid, the flavors combined into a taste so varied and delicious that she barely stopped herself from moaning aloud with pleasure.

"What is this?" she said, only managing to force herself to pause for conversation when her dish was nearly empty.

" 'Tis a Sorlainian dish. And this"—he held up the flagon—"is *osran,* a liquor brewed from berries. It is rather strong," he warned as she held out her cup. "Sip it slowly, or we shall have to scrape you off the deck."

Rose laughed at the idea, and Sigurd laughed as well as he poured her cup half full.

A shout from up above drew her attention, and she looked up, her breath catching when she saw several of the younger members of the crew high above the deck, racing with all speed through the rigging.

"Skylarking," Sigurd said, following her gaze. "Foolhardy, but there is no stopping them."

A dark-haired boy was in the lead. It was Beylik, Rose realized, flinging himself from one hold to the next with an abandon that left the rest struggling in his wake.

"Thou wert full harsh with the little brother earlier," she remarked, slipping without thought into Jexlan.

"Speak thee as a daughter who has never felt the sand beneath thy slipper?" Sigurd chided gently. "The ways of Jexal are strange to thee, I deem. Yet I have dwelt in the tents for many a season, and I say to thee that this *beylik* is no brother of thine. His name was lost to him when he was sold, 'tis no kindness to ask that he recall it."

Rose looked at him, uncomprehending. "But he is free now! Why should he not remember his own name?"

"No, lady. He cannot be free unless his master—his true master, the one who paid for him in gold—releases him. So long as that debt remains, he has no right to his birth name."

"Do you believe that?" she demanded.

Sigurd set down his cup and relaxed back in his seat. Even in the shade of the canopy, his red hair flamed, curling in ringlets about his strong neck and high brow. His wide mouth quirked in the half-smile that was his usual expression.

"The question is not whether I believe it, but whether Beylik does, and the answer is absolutely. The naming ritual in Jexal is at the heart of their beliefs. Each Jexlan name is rooted in an ancient story; each story is but part of a tale that has been, and is, and will continue until the tale is told in full. When the task of one lifetime is completed, the soul departs to another realm in which the next task is revealed. The duty of the tribes is to greet each soul as it returns with the proper name, for only then can the story continue as it is written in the stars. Did Queen Najet tell you nothing of this, lady?"

"No," Rose said, "my mother did not often speak of her life in Jexal."

"Hardly surprising," Sigurd said thoughtfully. "Her brother broke with all tradition when he sent her away. They were still talking of it when I was there. I gather there were some who thought that her name should be taken when she was sent to Valinor, but in the end they decided she might keep it."

"How kind of them."

Sigurd smiled faintly at the sarcasm in her voice. "Kinder than you know. The loss of one's name is worse than death to any Jexlan. Without it, one cannot perform the sacred task that is the purpose of this life, and the name that is lost to death is lost forever. There is no rebirth for such unfortunates; never again will that name be bestowed upon a living child. Their part in the tale can never be completed, only ended, their destiny left forever unfulfilled. 'For what is done cannot be undone,' " he quoted softly, " 'and shall endure forevermore.' "

"Is that what they say in Jexal? Then you are right in one thing, Master Sigurd: I am no daughter of the desert, no more than you are a true son of the tents."

"Right you are, lady," he answered with a smile. "I was born among the ice floes of the north, as far from the desert as one can possibly imagine. Yet our ways are not so very different, either. Any man who has worn the collar is dead to us, and should his shade return, the tribes would drive it out."

"Wicked superstition," Rose snapped.

"Perhaps. But tell me, lady, if you had been carried off by pirates and lived among them for a time, what sort of welcome could you expect in Valinor?" When she did not answer, he laughed. "Wicked superstition, indeed!"

He was right, Rose thought, any woman who had lived among thieves or pirates would be regarded as forever damaged, even if she had been carried off against her will. People believed all manner of strange things, and there was no point in being angry with Sigurd for saying what her own mother had likely thought to be the truth. *They are wrong,* Rose thought, then sighed, knowing she could argue herself hoarse and never overset so firmly planted a belief—just as no Jexlan would ever change her mind, no matter how persuasively he spoke.

She wondered suddenly what the Prince of Venya made of all this. Did he, too, believe that poor Beylik was doomed to eternal death because he had been taken as a slave?

"Where is the prince today?" she asked casually.

"Abed. Asleep, if he has taken the draught I left him, though more likely he is fretting over charts. I will go and scold him after we have eaten. Will you have a biscuit?" He offered her a plate.

"Thank you. He is ill?"

"A touch of marsh fever," Sigurd said dismissively, helping himself to a biscuit. "He took it in Venya years ago. No doubt you know of the occasion?"

"Of course." Everyone knew of the prince's adventure in the Venyan marshes when he was but sixteen; his daring escape from Richard's soldiers was the foundation on which his reputation had been built.

"The songs never mention tedious little details such as fever," Sigurd said. "Odd, really, since I'll wager that he was in far more danger from that than all King Richard's men and arms. Not that he is in any danger now," he added. "It comes on him from time to time as these fevers tend to do, inconvenient but hardly life-threatening. If he follows my orders, he will be up and about tomorrow."

"And if he doesn't?"

Sigurd grinned. "He will still be well tomorrow. But that, lady, is only for your ears. The prince drives himself too hard, you see, in his zeal to win back Venya."

"All the world knows that!" She laughed.

"Indeed," Sigurd agreed dryly, "he makes quite sure they do."

Rose frowned a little at his tone. "It is only natural the minstrels sing of him. There is no greater hero in our time."

"So I thought once," he murmured, so low that she wasn't sure if she had heard him properly. "I joined the prince's crew last year," he went on in his normal tone, "but alas, I find I am no hero, only a poor surgeon, more concerned with the saving of lives than the taking of them. The death of any man is an ugly thing to me, no matter how just the cause he dies for."

Rose shuddered, remembering the cavern. *Ugly* was a good word for what she had seen—and done—there. "But the prince kills only by necessity."

"Necessity is a hard master," the surgeon agreed. "It is always worse, of course, when the innocent die, particularly when they are his own subjects. But I don't have to tell you that! You were in Riall."

Rose nibbled at her biscuit. "That was no fault of the prince's."

"Of course it wasn't! The whole business was a tragedy, and I'm sure the prince deeply regrets having been the cause of it."

Rose set down the biscuit. "What do you mean, the cause of it?"

"Well, after Kendrick's—" Sigurd began, then broke off, casting an uneasy glance over his shoulder.

"Kendrick's Mine? But that was just a rumor started by my uncle's men."

Not that Rose had believed it for a moment. They said the prince had begun the riots in Riall to divert the Valinorian forces while he raided Kendrick's Mine, killing a hundred of the workers—his own subjects—in the process. They said he sailed away from Venya with a hold full of gems, leaving the people of Riall to pay the price. Wicked, she had thought it then, to try to lay the blame on *him* for what her uncle had done.

"The prince wasn't really at Kendrick's Mine," she insisted. "He couldn't have been."

"I'm sorry, lady, I thought you—I see I've spoken out of turn."

"But if this is true—"

"I never said it was," Sigurd interrupted hastily. "I know nothing at all about it. I wasn't even with him at the time. I should never have spoken of such a thing, let alone to you. I beg you to forget I mentioned it." He unclenched his fingers and brushed crumbled biscuit from his palm. "Lady," he whispered, "please—*please* do not say anything of this to him."

Sigurd was wrong. He *must* be. He said himself that he wasn't even with the prince at the time. His tale she could have discounted, and yet his manner troubled her. It was so strange, completely at odds with all that Rose had heard about the Prince of Venya. He was reputed to be as just and kind a lord as had ever lived, and it was widely sung that his followers served him out of love and loyalty. Not fear. Never that. Yet Sigurd was unmistakably afraid.

"I will say nothing," she promised.

The surgeon released a long breath of relief that he hid beneath a laugh. "Thank you. I wouldn't want him to be troubled by such ridiculous rumors," he said, an explanation that rang as false as his laughter. "Now, lady," he continued heartily, "the sailors will sing and dance for you. They have been practicing all morning at the prince's order. You wouldn't want to disappoint them, would you?"

"No." Rose forced herself to smile, trying to recapture her pleasure in the day. "Of course not."

Chapter 10

DURING the past year, Florian had often considered dismantling the great bed in his cabin. He had never used it for sleeping in the first place, or at least not alone. For that, he much preferred the comfort of a hanging cot, and now that it was no longer serving its intended purpose, the very sight of the bed irritated him. It was a relic of another life, a flagrant waste of space where every inch was precious.

Somehow he had never found the time, and over the months, it had become a sort of storeroom, piled high with clothing, weapons, broken instruments, and other odds and ends, the curtains drawn to hide the mess. But lately he had found another use for it.

A hanging cot was all well and good for sleeping, but it did not lend itself to any other occupation. And if Florian had to spend a day alone upon his back, at least he could be doing something useful. Or trying to, he amended, squinting at the chart resting against his drawn-up knees. In truth, he was accomplishing very little except to give himself a headache. It was impossible to concentrate when his skin pricked hot and cold until he could hardly bear the pressure of the thin coverlet drawn up to his waist.

He gave up and rested his head against the bolster, staring at the canopy with aching eyes. Closing them was even worse, for without an anchor he was soon tossed by waves of dizziness. He tried to study the chart again, gave up, and began to count the tiny tridents embroidered on the canopy. He had just reached eighty-two when Sigurd walked in without knocking.

"Well?" the surgeon demanded, standing just beside him. Florian winced as his voice lanced through his temples. "How are you feeling?"

"Well enough."

Sigurd knuckled his brow with an exasperated sigh. "Really, my lord, if you would just take—" He broke off, staring at the cup he had lifted from the table. "Oh. You have. How long ago?"

Florian closed his eyes, fighting back the waves of nausea as he considered his response. An hour was more than enough time for the draught to work. But it hadn't. He did not want to admit this to Sigurd—he didn't like admitting it even to himself. The implications were too disturbing to face in his present state.

Don't think about that, he told himself, *just concentrate on getting through tonight.* But concentration was beyond him. He could only wonder with a dull hopelessness how much longer he could go on before the truth could not be hidden. *But from whom do you want to hide it?* he thought dizzily. *Sigurd? Or yourself?*

"How long ago, my lord?" Sigurd insisted.

"At six bells," he rasped.

"Hmm." Sigurd touched his brow again. "It doesn't seem to have had any effect at all. You must be growing accustomed to the dose. Wait here, and I'll bring you something stronger."

Where would I go? Florian almost laughed, but it came out as a groan.

"I won't be long," Sigurd promised. It seemed an age until he returned, but at last he held a cup to Florian's lips. "Drink it all," he ordered, "and you will sleep."

The bitter draught lay uneasily in Florian's empty stomach, and for a terrible moment he feared he would vomit it up again, which would surely burst his skull. The moment passed, but the nausea subsided only slightly, and the spike driving through his temples did not withdraw.

"I will be back in a quarter of an hour," Sigurd said.

Good man, Florian thought. *He knows I can't bear to be fussed over.* And yet . . . he didn't want to be alone. Not now. Tomorrow would be different, but just for one night he wished there was someone who would sit with him and drive away the thoughts he dared not think. Someone with a sweet voice and gentle hands.

He remembered the princess's hands sketching patterns in the

air. Such pretty hands, so graceful . . . He thought of her voice
with its pretty accent, Valinorian tinged with the faintest trace of
Jexlan . . . So low and soothing . . . He imagined light fingers
brushing his brow until at last he slept.

He dreamed he walked through ravaged fields. Florian was no
farmer, but even he could see that the waist-high crops would
never reach maturity; they were all dead, bleached to a skeletal
whiteness by the sun burning in a cloudless sky, pale blue tinged
with yellow.

The drought had not lifted, then. He gazed over the barren
fields that stretched as far as he could see, burning with helpless
anger and despair. Had Venya not suffered enough without this
new trouble added to the burden? Huddled shapes lay by the side
of the path he walked, the bodies of swine and cattle. Flies
buzzed around the carcasses, and he passed by quickly, his stomach twisting at the sickly sweet stench of rotting flesh.

Without any warning, he found himself in the remains of a
great forest. Desiccated earth crumbled beneath his boots, and
the grotesque forms of blasted trees rose starkly against a leaden
sky. The only sound was the whisper of the wind among the dry
and twisted branches. *What is the time?* he wondered suddenly, *I
must go, get back to the* Quest. He turned about, searching for the
path, but it was gone.

There must be a way back, he told himself, trying to control
his ragged breathing. *Be calm, and you will find it.* He tried first
one way and then another, only to find himself moving deeper
into the forest with every step. When something brushed his
cheek, he panicked, running blindly back the way he had come,
tripping over roots and forcing his way through the tangle of dead
branches. Twigs fastened in his hair and cloak, binding him until
he could not move a step, forcing him to be still.

To listen.

Over the pounding of his own heart, he heard it, the song of
the wind in the trees. A chant, a death rattle, it repeated until the
words were burned into his mind.

The tide is ebbing.

He did not understand—and yet he did, and rejected the understanding instantly.

"No!" he shouted, twisting furiously, "No! Let me go, I have to get back to the *Quest*—"

The tide is ebbing.

His struggles weakened. *I am too late,* he thought, the flood tide has passed. Despair drained the strength from his limbs. He sagged against the branches, and they released him so suddenly that he fell to the earth, sinking down into dust and ashes that clogged his nostrils and choked the breath from his body until he could not struggle anymore.

Is this death? he wondered, surprised that he did not feel frightened anymore.

"No."

Florian turned his head and found a man standing beside him, a common fisherman, neither old nor young, with a weathered face and mild eyes, clad in a rough tunic with a net over his shoulder. How long had he been standing there, watching the Prince of Venya fight against a tree?

Florian found that he could sit up easily, and he raised himself on one elbow, wiping sweat and ashes from his face with his sleeve. He sought for some light words to cover his embarrassment, but one look from the fisherman stilled them on his lips. Instead he heard himself say, "The tide is ebbing."

The man nodded, his teeth flashing in a grin. "Then you must make haste to catch it." He took the net from his shoulder and threw it with a practiced turn of his wrists. It flew over the forest, stretching to encompass the whole of it, and where it settled, color flowed over the blackened branches, turning them to living brown and green.

"The time comes when a man must cast his net," he said, looking down at Florian, "and take what fortune sends."

"How?" Florian demanded. "I have no net."

The fisherman laughed at that, bracing his hands on his thighs. "Oh, but you do, one of your own fashioning. 'Tis none of mine, but I think that it will serve." His laughter stopped abruptly. "It will have to. There is no time to weave another. The tide is ebbing."

"But—"

"My lord. My lord."

"What have you given him?"

Florian looked around, startled, at the sound of these new voices. When he looked back, the fisherman was gone.

"Wait," he cried. "Wait, come back—"

"My lord." A light blow stung Florian's cheek, and the forest faded into swirling blackness. "It is time to wake."

Florian opened his eyes to see Sigurd bending over him, Beylik hovering anxiously at his shoulder.

"That's better," the surgeon said, straightening. "Are you with us?"

"Yes." Florian's pulse began to slow and he blinked, still caught up in the dream. "What is the time?"

"Two bells," Beylik answered, his voice trembling. His swarthy skin looked gray in the sunlight streaming through the stern window. "And the *Endeavor* has been sighted. You wouldn't wake," he added in an uncertain whisper. "I—I was—"

"I'm fine, Beylik," Florian said. "More or less. Gods," he muttered, dragging a hand through his hair. "What *did* you give me, Sigurd?"

"That's right, blame the surgeon! Had you not driven yourself to the brink of exhaustion, you would have woken long ago. And if your dreams disturb you," he added primly, "you must examine your own conscience for the cause."

"Thank you, Grandmother." Florian swung his feet to the floor. "Beylik, have Gordon load the skiff. Tell him to put in a cask of *usqua,* as well."

He moved into the sunlight and stretched like a cat, groaning with contentment as he worked the kinks out of his spine, and was rewarded with a glorious surge of energy.

"You are well," Sigurd observed, sitting down on the bed.

"Never better."

"Good. I was a bit concerned last night . . ." Sigurd frowned down at his feet. "Your fever was quite high."

"Was it?" Florian asked vaguely. "Well, whatever you gave me did the trick."

"You should really spend the day resting—"

"I'm fine."

"At least put on some clothes before you take a chill."

This far south, heat stroke was more likely, but Florian made no argument as he pulled on a pair of light trousers. He was still Venyan enough to be most comfortable in nothing but his skin, but Sigurd came from the northern reaches, where layers of wool and fur were the norm and customs were very different.

"Gods, I need to shave," Florian said, swiping a hand across his jaw, "and to eat before I go. I think I'll take the princess with me."

"Why?"

"Why not?" Florian began the pattern of movements Ewan had taught him long ago to increase flexibility and balance. "The sun is shining, the sea is calm—and I daresay she's had enough of *your* company." He grinned at the surgeon. "Did you spend the entire day with her?"

"Yes," Sigurd answered smugly. "We had a lovely time choosing the stuff for her new gown and then we dined together on the deck, where I dazzled her with my wit and learning. How do you do that?" he added, frowning. "It looks impossible."

"Practice, Sigurd. Discipline." He did not say that nothing seemed impossible today, though that was how he felt. He balanced easily on one foot and stretched, feeling every muscle hum with energy. He broke the pose when the door opened and Beylik returned, a pot in one hand and a dish in the other. "Kava," he breathed, "and food. Bless you, Beylik."

Beylik smiled and poured the pungent kava. He looked better now, the ashen tinge faded from his cheeks, though his hand still trembled slightly. He must have been frantic to fetch Sigurd, given that the two could hardly speak a civil word to one another. It seemed a foolish custom that made Beylik something less than human through no fault of his own, and Florian had always been a bit surprised that an educated man like Sigurd could believe such nonsense. Yet there was nothing he could do to stop him. Only a fool or tyrant sought mastery over anyone's conscience but his own.

"Thank you, Beylik," he said, sitting down at the table and accepting the cup. "Send someone for the princess, would you? I'll see her in a quarter of an hour. Would you like a cup and plate, as well?" he added as Sigurd pulled out a chair. "There is enough for two."

"No, I have eaten. I remain for the princess's sake. It is not fitting for you to receive her alone, half dressed in your cabin. And I must say, my lord, that it do will her reputation no good should the two of you go off without an escort."

"I can assure you that I have no intention—"

"Intention has nothing to do with it. A reputation once lost can never be regained. Would you have hers fall into such disrepute as the four score ladies who have preceded her?"

"Four *score?*" Florian choked on his kava. "Is that what they say? Gods, do they think I am part goat?"

"I have sometimes wondered," Sigurd murmured, then ducked the biscuit Florian threw at his head.

"I never claimed to be a Hurian priest, but this—! It is nonsense."

Sigurd shrugged. "At least your legend will live on."

Florian set down his kava, his amusement vanishing abruptly. His *legend?* Is this how he would be remembered, as Venya's rutting prince? The man who couldn't keep his trousers buttoned for five minutes at a stretch?

Richard always made a point of referring to Florian's mother as the Great Whore of Venya, an epithet completely undeserved. *I am the one who has earned that title,* Florian thought. Shame coiled in his belly as he imagined the conversations that must be heard daily in every tavern on the nine seas, for no one loved gossip like a sailor.

Well, what else can you expect from a Venyan? Everyone knows what they are like. Got up to things that would make a drover blush, leastways until King Richard put a stop to all that nonsense. Like mother, like son, some drunken old sailor would pronounce, nodding wisely into his ale, *it's in the blood.* And then someone would drag up the whole scandal of Queen Ailís's marriage as though this somehow proved the point.

Unfair. Unjust. They were ignorant fools who knew almost nothing about Venya, and what little they knew they did not understand. Like all Venyan monarchs, Queen Ailís had married in her own time, to her own purposes, and was answerable to no one for her choice. It was only Richard who had been affronted by the union for reasons that had nothing to do with propriety. And it was Richard who, not content with their deaths, had twisted their marriage into a filthy jest.

At least Florian had the comfort of knowing that Richard lied about his parents. He only wished he could claim such innocence himself. Oh, the stories were wildly exaggerated, but many of them contained an uncomfortable grain of truth: a gift given or received, a detail of a tryst, even a joke he had thought private until he heard it on some stranger's lips months later and a hundred leagues away.

The first time his face had burned with shock and mortification as his own words were bellowed out in a Moravian tavern, with a sly twist that made the sailors laugh and clap him on the back. He did not recognize the smooth stranger in the song—not then. Later he had become far too familiar, and Florian learned to choose his words with care, lest some awkward phrase or hint of weakness should mar the legend. It was not a game he would have invented, but he played it with what skill he had, and for some years had taken a perverse pleasure in exceeding every expectation of debauchery.

In any other man, such behavior could be dismissed as youthful folly. In any other prince, it would rank as a minor indiscretion. But he was not just any man or even any prince. He was the Prince of Venya, who had sacrificed his people's pride to serve his own and made a public mockery of their beliefs by confirming every rumor of their practices.

Gods, it was no wonder they were ashamed to own him. If only he had shown the least discretion . . . But he hadn't. Not until last year, when everything had changed.

And by then, it was too late.

No, he told himself, *it isn't too late. There is still time to prove myself. But I must make haste, the tide is ebbing . . .*

"You're shivering," Beylik said with swift concern. "Is it the fever?"

"What?" Florian looked up. "No. No, I am fine. Is that hot water? Good, then you can shave me. Sigurd, you are quite right about the princess. Please join us."

"With pleasure," Sigurd said, smiling. "Atherson promised me some timnonweed when last I saw him. And I shall do you the honor of shaving you myself. Give that over, *beylik,*" he ordered, taking the razor from his hand. "Make yourself useful and fetch my bag. You'll find it hooked over the door. Mind that you don't drop it."

Beylik stiffened, his gaze moving to Florian. "If you would be so kind," Florian said, repressing a sigh as Beylik turned without a word and vanished out the door.

Chapter 11

AS Sigurd had predicted, the prince showed no ill effects from his fever; he looked fit and rested, freshly shaved and glowing with health and energy. He smiled at Rose as she came on deck, and all at once she was a little breathless. "Good morning, lady. I trust Sigurd looked after you yesterday?"

It was then she noticed the surgeon standing by the taffrail. She fancied she saw a trace of anxiety in his eyes. "He did indeed," she answered, casting him a reassuring smile.

"Good," the prince said, buckling a sword about his hips. "We have sighted another Venyan ship, and we are off to inspect the cargo. Will you join us?"

During the past night, Rose had thought much of what Sigurd had told her about the prince, turning the matter over and over in her mind. It seemed impossible that the world could be so mistaken in his character. Only a monster could do the things of which he was accused; a man so obsessed with wealth and power that he would coldly plan the murder of his own subjects to advance his interests. A man like Richard. *It can't be true,* she thought, looking at him now. *I don't believe it. I won't.*

"With pleasure," she answered a bit defiantly.

Sigurd's lips curved in a wry smile and he nodded slightly, for all the world as if he was privy to her thoughts. Unaccountably embarrassed, she followed them down the ladder.

A few minutes later she was wedged into a small boat amid casks and crates, with Sigurd far astern. The prince raised the single sail, and the laden boat moved slowly through the water. He did not speak much on the journey, keeping himself busy with the sail and lines, though from time to time he would draw her attention to a bird or school of fish with absentminded courtesy.

"And there," he said, pointing, "is the *Endeavor*, recently returned from Venya."

They tied up beside the ship and a man leaned over the side, his face in shadow.

"Who goes there?"

"'Tis I, Renauld," Florian called up. "May I board?"

"Your Highness! We did not expect you yet." He flung a ladder over the side. "Is that Sigurd Einarsson as well? Athelson will be glad to see you."

"You first, Sigurd." Florian turned to Rose. "Can you manage it?"

She eyed the flimsy rope ladder. "Certainly."

"Just follow me and do what I do."

Rose soon realized that what had looked so simple was not easy at all. The thick rope scored her palms and slipped beneath her feet. Looking down, she froze, suspended halfway between safety and the sea.

"Don't stop"—the prince's voice came from far above—"and don't look down."

Good advice. Too bad he hadn't given it sooner. She stared transfixed at the brilliant blue water far below.

"Stay put, then. I'll have them lower the chair."

The chair, a narrow plank, was the way she'd first boarded the *Quest*. Undignified and terrifying, she had thought it then, and now she rebelled at sitting helpless once again as she was drawn aloft. The first rule of a sailor, she had once read, was to never let go of one line until you had hold of another. She had smiled at the time, thinking it a joke, but she now understood the wisdom of the words.

She tipped her head up and opened her eyes to see the prince's boots vanishing up the ladder. The soles were Shansian leather, sturdy yet supple as kidskin. Her own footgear had been supplied to her on Malin Isle; wooden soled, secured with baked leather that bit painfully into her skin. With an effort, she unclenched the fingers of her right hand long enough to slip the straps from her ankles. The shoes fell, one after another, making tiny white puffs as the water closed around them.

That was better. Her toes curled around the rope, rough and

comfortingly solid beneath her skin. Her grip secure, she released her left hand and grasped the rope above her head. Now the right hand, then the feet . . .

"Don't bother, here she is," the prince remarked over his shoulder as she pulled herself up the last bit, spurning his offer of assistance.

"Aye, so she is, but who . . . ?"

Rose straightened with a snap and found herself facing a man clad in a scarlet shirt and bright blue waistcoat with a golden sash wound about his waist. Black hair fell loose about his shoulders, held back from his face by a silken scarf of blue and scarlet that he had bound, caplike, about his brow, the ends fluttering in the breeze.

He was staring at her with fierce intensity. She lifted her head, met his eyes, and felt the deck shift beneath her feet. She remembered her mother saying that just looking into those eyes made her feel quite homesick, for such a brilliant blue was only to be found in the Jexlan sky.

He had been pale then, compared to the swarthy stranger who faced her now. Gone was the elegant young knight with his love of lace and velvet, and yet, she thought, feeling a flutter of laughter in her throat, he had not outgrown his penchant for the peacock-bright colors of his house.

"S-Sir Ewan?"

"Ye gave me quite a start, lass." Ewan laughed a little shakily. "For a moment . . . ye are the image of your mother."

Rose felt herself blush. "I'm not. I'm nothing like her."

"Not the coloring, no, 'tis in your bones, the way ye hold your head . . . why, just look at ye!" he said, taking her hands and holding them out to the sides. "Wee Rosamund, all grown up."

He brought her hands to his lips and kissed them formally, then laughed and pulled her into a hard embrace.

"They said you had died," she said, the words muffled against the silken fabric of his waistcoat. "In Venya. They said—my uncle said—"

"The filthy catiff, I'm sure he wishes it were so. I'm sorry if ye were . . . troubled by his lies."

She drew back and looked into his face. Troubled? It had been bad enough when Richard sent Ewan off to Venya. When news came of his death, she had been sick with grief. Sir Ewan had been her childhood hero, a flash of bright color and laughter to lighten the dark days after her father died. The courtiers who had once been so attentive had drawn back a step, waiting. When her uncle came, they slunk away like the curs they were, abandoning King Osric's relics for their new liege.

But not Sir Ewan, that braw and bonnie knight, as her mother had once called him. How Ewan had laughed! Queen Najet's Jexlan accent was so pronounced that the attempt to mimic Ewan's speech had sounded passing strange. But for all his laughter, Rose had known the knight was pleased, as much by the words as by the thought. Losing him so soon after her mother's death had seemed the final blow.

"I see introductions will not be necessary," the prince observed from his perch atop the rail.

"Nay, Princess Rosamund and I are old friends." Ewan tucked her hand into the crook of his elbow.

"Rosamund? Rose of the World?"

"My true name," Rose said, laughing. "Though no one has called me that for years." She turned to Ewan. "What happened to you?"

Ewan shook his head, a grim set to his mouth. "The whoreson Richard packed me off to Venya with his gifts and assurances of friendship. The lies had barely left my lips when he attacked. I'm sure he meant for me to die as well. He never did much care for me."

He smiled, though his bright eyes were clouded as he looked at Rose. "He knew full well where my loyalty lay."

"You hardly made a secret of it," Rose said.

"Nay, nor am I sorry for it. Better to be dead in truth than serve that animal. What he did in Venya was"—he glanced sideways at the prince—"weel, it wasna what ye might call honorable warfare, attacking in the dead of night."

"Ewan got me out," the prince said. "And has been ordering me about ever since. Shocking, it is, the way he goes on, but you know how it is with these ancient retainers. You just can't get rid of them."

Rose studied the dark-haired knight. He had been barely twenty the last time she had seen him, and the ensuing years had passed over him lightly. He was a bit broader in the chest and shoulder, but the added weight suited him and the golden sash encircled a waist as slender as the young knight's had ever been. His raven hair was yet untouched by silver, and only a few rather attractive lines radiated outward from blazingly blue eyes, the kind of lines that came from days staring into the sun.

"Ancient?" he growled. "Why, ye insolent young pup! Ye would be lost without me, laddie, and don't forget it."

"How could I, when you remind me constantly?"

The words were spoken lightly, though there was an edge to the exchange that Rose did not understand. But when the two men grinned at one another, she forgot her questions in a sharp stab of jealousy.

Ewan had been her mother's champion, utterly devoted to his queen. The times the three of them had spent together were the happiest Rose had ever known. She used to pretend that the dashing, merry knight was her real father, not the gloomy old king who never seemed to know her name. Her favorite dream had been that one day Ewan would take them far away from Larken Castle and they could all live together always.

She had mourned him as she never mourned King Osric. And all that time he had been alive, his service given to the Prince of Venya.

Something of her thoughts must have shown on her face, for Ewan gave her hand a squeeze. "Lady, never think I have forgotten ye. I wanted to write—many a time I sat down and did just that. But I never dared to send it. Had Richard intercepted a message from me—"

Rose shuddered at the thought. "You were right not to. Though I am glad you thought of it."

He smiled, relief showing in his eyes. "Now tell me what brings ye here."

"He does," she said, nodding toward the prince. "My uncle and I had a . . . falling out . . ."

"Aye," Ewan said, "I heard as much. Ye were sent to Malin Isle?"

"Yes, and I have decided not to return to Valinor. The prince has kindly agreed to help me to Sorlain."

"For the coronation?"

The prince looked up sharply. "What coronation?"

"King Cristobal's."

Rose leaned weakly against the rail. "King Cristobal? But—but King Esteban . . . ?"

"Is dead."

"When?" the prince demanded.

"Not long. The news reached Venya when I did myself."

Rose stared down at the deck, her mind working furiously. Cristobal was to be king? Cristobal, the faithless churl, the man who had callously ignored her pleas, who had not even bothered to answer her messages, was to sit on Esteban's throne?

"My lady," the prince said, "this way, please."

Feeling numb, she followed the two men across the deck, bits and pieces of their conversation drifting back to her.

"Not as many as we had hoped," Ewan was saying, ". . . guards have doubled . . . twelve lost . . ."

I cannot go to Cristobal for help, Rose thought. *How can I trust him? But where else can I go?*

". . . the last one, Ewan, so we'll have be careful where we sell . . . not Hew, Palander is giving better prices . . . my lady. Lady Rose?"

She started from her thoughts to find that Ewan was gone, though she heard his voice at the far end of the ship, directing the unloading of the skiff.

A hatch opened nearly at Rose's feet, and from the depths of the ship rose a fetid stench of illness and unwashed bodies, mingled with the scent of boiled porridge. She recoiled with a gasping cry, feeling as though she had plunged into a nightmare. She'd had the same one often since Riall, standing in the mason's hall beside an empty cauldron while an endless line of gaunt and starving Venyans stared at her in mute appeal.

Sigurd's red head emerged from below, and a moment later he was standing on the deck, wiping his hands on a rag. "It is not the red fever," he said, "but still, I would not advise that you go down."

"Thank you, Sigurd, but I must." The prince turned to Rose. "Please wait here, my lady. I won't be long."

He vanished down into the hold. Rose withdrew another step, one hand covering her mouth. "What—" she began, but broke off as a voice shrilled in Venyan from below.

"Fools . . . a fewkin' lie . . . they mean to sell us all—"

A door slammed shut, cutting off the cry.

"Those aren't *slaves* down there?" Rose demanded.

"No. Of course not."

"Then who—"

"I don't know," Sigurd said, not looking at her.

"You do. Tell me." She seized his sleeve, but he shook her off.

"You'd do better to ask the prince. Or Sir Ewan."

He turned on his heel and walked away without looking back.

FLORIAN drew a deep breath before descending, dreading what he would find below. But he had to go. He had to see it for himself. As his eyes adjusted, he could make out a row of pallets stretching down the hold. Half were empty; the rest held what looked like bundles of rags. Most of the children were lying very still, but a few were sitting up, eyes bright in skeletal faces as they regarded him.

"It's him, it's really him," the whispers went down along the rows. "It's the Prince of Venya!"

"Fools! 'Tis but a trick, a fewkin' lie! He doesn't give a rat's ass for the likes of us! 'Tis only gems *he's* after, him and his fine *filidhi*. They mean to sell us all as slaves!"

Florian closed the door behind him, then bent to the tiny ragged figure. "What is your name?" he asked.

"Shana. What is *yours?* Certes, you are *not* the Prince of Venya!"

Like all the others, her head was shorn to a stubble, accentuating the pointed bones of cheek and chin. Unlike the others, she was on her feet. Hands fisted on her hips, she glared up at Florian defiantly.

"But I am."

She sniffed. "Oh, certainly you are. You wouldn't catch *him* in a place like this. He wouldn't lift a finger for the *fheara!* He cares naught for Venya now, not since the *filidhi* left. He's too busy plundering and murdering to pay us any mind."

"Who told you that?"

"My father!" she cried. "*He* told me that. But everyone knows it's true. Everyone but these fools." She cast a contemptuous glance about the hold. "They don't know anything."

"Well, Shana, your father was mistaken. I am indeed the Prince of Venya, and I care very much what happens to you and all my people."

She continued to stare up at him, completely unimpressed. "Prove it."

"Well, this is my seal ring. And here is my sword."

She leaned forward, staring suspiciously at the blade hanging at his hip.

"Carbonec. Perhaps you have heard of it? It once belonged to my father, King Rafael, and before him, to my grandfather, King Sean, and before him to King Caleigh. And so on and on, back to Lord Leander himself. Draw it, Shana, and see it for yourself."

She put one hand on the jeweled hilt, the other on the sheath, and tugged. "It's stuck."

"No, it is Carbonec. Would you like to try again?"

He obligingly held the sheath so she could use both hands to draw the sword. She spat on her palms, rubbed them together, and braced her feet, tugging until her face was red with effort.

"Shall I try?" Florian set thumb and forefinger on the hilt and half a foot of gleaming steel slid from the sheath. "Carbonec. It can be drawn only by Leander's heir—as King Richard learned, to his sorrow. You have heard, perhaps, how it was taken on the night that Venya fell . . . and how regained?"

"The Prince of Venya crept into Larken Castle all alone," a boy cried eagerly from his pallet, "and stole it back again!"

"So I did," Florian agreed, smiling at the boy, "and a fine time I had doing it! What is your name?"

"Alain of Revnar. Your Highness."

Florian took the boy's outstretched hand. "I am pleased to meet you, Alain of Revnar. How do you fare?"

"Better than most," Alain answered stoutly, though his hand was as fleshless and fragile as a bird's claw. "I'll be up and about in no time."

"Good lad." Florian smiled at him, then turned to the girl at his side. "Now, Shana, if you are satisfied as to my credentials— you are satisfied, are you not?"

Shana's teeth worried her lower lip. "I suppose so."

"Then would you do me the honor of presenting me to the rest of your friends?"

The girl hesitated a moment, then took his hand. By the time they reached the end of the row of pallets, she was chattering away as though she had known him all her life. *See?* he thought, ridiculously relieved, *it isn't hopeless. Once my people come to know me, they will trust me once again.* His smile faded when he reached the last pallet, where a serving woman was attempting to feed a pitifully wasted boy of five or six.

"Come on, now, let's try again," the woman urged. "Be a good lad and open up. You can do that for me, can't you?"

She pushed the spoon against his lips. Broth dribbled down his chin to the coverlet, which was splotched with moisture. She sighed and raised herself stiffly to her feet.

"Is he wounded?" Florian asked. "Fevered?"

"Nay, my lord." She shook her head, the weary lines deepening around her eyes. "He is just . . . slipping away. It happens like that sometimes."

Florian touched her shoulder. "You've done wonders with the others. Thank you."

She smiled, and he realized she was far younger than he'd thought. "They'll be better when we reach land."

"Better still if they had been left at home," Florian said grimly. He forced a smile as he turned back to the boy. "And what's your name?"

There was no answer. The child didn't even seem to hear him. Florian had seen children equally as thin today, but they all had some vestige of liveliness, a determined grasp on whatever life was left to them. There was none of that in this child. He had an air of hopelessness that had been lacking in the others.

"That's Corin." Shana caught Florian's hand in hers. "They brought him but a week or so before Sir Ewan came. He comes from up in the Kirian hills; they're horse breeders up there, you know. His father died before he was born, so it's just him and his mother. He used to cry for her at night, but now he doesn't talk at all. He won't eat, either."

Florian squeezed her fingers in thanks. "Welcome, Corin," he said. "I'm so glad to see you. I've been waiting for you and all your friends to get here."

Still the boy did not answer, nor did he turn his head as Florian sat cross-legged on the floor beside him. "I know you're very tired, but you must eat and get your strength back. We have a lot of work to do, you know."

Corin's lips moved almost imperceptibly. Not a sound did he

make, not even a whisper, yet Florian knew what he had said, the word that spoke of childhood as no other could have done, weighted with a pain and loss that no child should ever have to bear.

"I know, lad. I expect your mum is missing you, too," he answered softly. "Just now she has no idea where you are, but just think how she'll feel when she sees you well and strong! Why, it will be the finest surprise she's ever had!"

He took the boy's limp hand in his. "You wouldn't want to miss that, would you? Seeing her face light up when she learns that somehow, against all hope, you managed to survive? You can tell her all about it, what it was like in the mine and how Sir Ewan came and carried you away on his great ship. Why, she'll be clean amazed when she hears of your adventures! And you can tell her that even though you were very sad and very frightened, whenever you imagined her there waiting, you knew you couldn't give up, no matter how you wanted to. Oh, Corin, she'll be so proud and happy when she hears that. Can't you just imagine it?"

Corin's gaze flicked to him, then back to the wall. A tiny gesture, so swift that had Florian blinked, he would have missed it.

"It won't be easy," he went on, "and it will take some time, but one day we'll all go home together. I'll need a lot of help, though, Corin. Every man I can get. Can I count on you?"

He realized he had forgotten to draw breath when at last the boy's head jerked in a nod.

"That's fine, then. Why don't you sit up and have something to eat?" He snapped his fingers, and Shana put a wooden bowl into his hand. "Just a bite or two for now, no need to rush."

Corin struggled up as far as his elbows, then fell back, panting. Florian put the bowl on the floor and scooped the boy into his lap. "There you are. That's better, isn't it?"

Corin looked up at him with shadowed eyes, a single tear winding slowly down his filthy cheek. Shana wiped it away, saying with rough kindness, "There's nothing to cry about, silly. No one's going to hurt you."

"That's right, Corin," the serving woman said gently, "you must show the prince what a brave little man you are."

Florian bent and set his lips on the boy's brow, holding the wasted body hard against his chest. "Don't you mind them, Corin," he whispered, "they mean well, but they don't understand. There is no shame in tears."

He did not speak again while the child sobbed against his chest. If the words existed that could heal such grief, he didn't know them. All he could do was sit in silence until the worst of it was past and Corin's breath was coming evenly again.

"That's better, then," he said. "Do you think you can eat something for me now?"

Corin nodded, his fingers relaxing their hold on Florian's tunic.

"Good lad. Just a bit, then a bit more later . . ."

Florian fumbled for the bowl, trying to grasp it one-handed, but before he could manage it Shana was kneeling beside him, holding the roughly carved spoon to Corin's cracked lips.

Chapter 12

ONCE Sigurd was gone, Rose went in search of Ewan. She found him leaning far over the rail, guiding the crates from the skiff as they were drawn aboard.

"Careful, now," he was shouting to the men in the skiff below, "watch that line—"

"Ewan?"

He did not turn. "One moment, lady. Not like that," he bellowed to the sailors, "secure it twice around. *Twice,* d'ye hear me?"

"Ewan, who is in the hold?"

"What? Oh, those poor wee souls." He shook his head, his mouth set in a grim line. "They're bound for the *filidhi* colony on Serilla."

"Where did they come from?"

"I picked them up in Venya. 'Tis a sorry business, but the prince—Marva's bones, Toma, what are ye about?" he shouted, glaring over the side. "Ah, never mind, leave it—no, I said leave it. I'll see to it myself."

Suiting word to action, he swung himself nimbly over the side.

"Pardon," a young sailor said, shooting her a winning smile, "if you'd just take a few steps over there."

"Out of the way," another sailor snarled when he backed into her, his arms filled with lines and grapples. "Go on, shift yourself, you've no business here. Get below with the others."

"Oh, Willy, have a heart. She's been cooped up all this time with those misbegotten brats, and a sad and sorry job it is." The first sailor grinned at her again. "She just wants some company, that's all. Ain't that right, Jenny?" he added with a wink. "Two shakes and I'm your man."

"I doubt that very much," the prince said from behind her.

The sailor fell back a pace, one hand flying to his brow. "M'lord," he mumbled, "I didn't mean—"

"Oh, I think you did. But no harm done—or is there? Lady?"

"No," Rose said, "none at all." She was rewarded with another smile from the sailor, albeit a very quick one before he bowed clumsily and hurried to the side.

"I am sorry to have kept you waiting," the prince said, "but if Sir Ewan is finished, we can return to the *Quest.*"

His words were courteous enough, but his expression was so grim that she could not blame the young sailor for his fear. She was a little afraid of him herself.

"You," he said, gesturing to a passing sailor, "find my surgeon and tell him we are leaving."

"That's the last of it," Ewan said, leaping lightly over the rail. "You've been busy, my lord. It looks to be a damn fine haul."

"I need to speak with you, Ewan. Lady." The prince gestured toward the ladder. "I will join you presently."

Rose looked from the prince to Ewan. She had just found him, and now she was to lose him all over again. But he was a stranger to her now. Indeed, he always had been. She had been a mere child when she saw him last, only half-comprehending all that was happening around her. The one certainty she'd had was that the knight was her mother's loyal servant. If Queen Najet had lived, Ewan would never have allowed himself to be packed off to Venya.

But he did not stay for me, she thought. *He went away and never came back.* She understood how it had happened, and reason told her it had been no fault of his. Yet for a moment she felt as lonely and abandoned as a child.

"A moment, my lord, to say farewell." Ewan took her arm and drew her aside. "Lady—Rosamund—tell me this: Are ye still bound for Sorlain?"

"Yes—or, I am not certain—"

"Have ye had word from Cristobal?"

Rose stiffened. "Why would I?"

"I thought—as ye were promised to him as a child—"

"You knew of that?" Rose asked, astonished. The alliance with

Sorlain had been a closely guarded secret. The King and Queen had been the only witnesses, and Cristobal's proxy had departed for home within the hour, carrying with him all record of the vows.

"Oh, aye, the Queen told me. But when I heard no more about it, I assumed that King Esteban had changed his mind."

"You assumed correctly. And 'tis for the best." Rose gave a scornful flick of her fingers. "I wouldn't have Cristobal on a platter."

"Then what are ye to do?"

Rose had a sudden longing to fling herself at Ewan and sob against his scarlet waistcoat as she used to do when some childish tragedy befell her, certain he could make everything come right. But childhood was far behind her, and Ewan was the Prince of Venya's man.

"I'll have to give it careful thought. Don't worry, Ewan, I'm quite capable of looking after myself. I've been doing it for years now."

Ewan looked away. "Aye. Of course ye have. But Rosamund, ye musn't go to Sorlain. Cristobal isn't to be trusted. He and Richard are thick as thieves these days."

"Thank you," Rose said. She would not weep, not here before them all. "Jehan keep you until we meet again."

Chapter 13

WHEN Rose was safe aboard the skiff, Ewan leaned back against the railing, crossing his arms over his chest.

"Why did ye bring her here?"

"I thought she might see the children for herself," the prince replied, then sighed. "I hoped she would put in a good word for us with Est—with Cristobal, I should say." He shook his head. "King Cristobal. Gods. I still see him as eight years old."

"He's a year older than ye are," Ewan pointed out. "And by all accounts, he's been managing Sorlain for the past sixmoon on his own. Esteban didna want anyone to know how ill he really was, but now the truth of it is coming out."

"Well, I'm sorry to hear that Esteban is gone. I liked him well." He shot Ewan a halfhearted grin. "I would have liked him better if he'd given me an army, but he did me many a good turn in his day. I suppose Cristobal will go on as his father did."

"I wouldna be too quick to suppose that."

"Why not?"

"Two months ago, Cristobal traveled to Larken Castle and stayed near a fortnight."

"What was his business there?"

Ewan shrugged. "Richard has three daughters."

"What, another betrothal?" Florian laughed. "How many does this make for Cristobal? Ten? An even dozen? It won't come to anything, Ewan; it never does with him."

"But he is King now," Ewan pointed out. "And Sorlain must have a Queen. I'm sure Richard is quite determined to put one of his daughters on the throne. The youngest is still a child, but the other two . . ." He sighed heavily. "Ye have heard of them, o' course. Berengaria and Melisande."

"The two loveliest princesses in the world," the prince finished thoughtfully. "Or so they say. Is it true?"

"They were snot-nosed bairns the last I saw of them," Ewan answered with a shrug, "but their mother was reckoned a famous beauty in her day. Aye, there may be some truth to the rumors."

"But still," the prince protested, "even if Cristobal is wifehunting in Valinor, he is still my kinsman. Surely he'd not betray his own blood for a woman!"

Ewan laughed. "Oh, lad, I wouldna be too sure of that. Mayhap *ye* have never looked twice at any lass but she was leaping into your bed, but there is a whole world of women ye know naught about, the kind who keeps her legs shut tight until every one of her conditions has been met."

"So I have heard. But even so—"

"Men have been driven to madness for wanting a woman— another thing ye may have trouble believing, but which I promise ye is true. Things such as honor and kinship have a tendency to fly straight out of a man's head when he is looking at the woman he wants and canna have."

"*All* men? Or is it yourself you speak of?"

Ewan smiled wryly. "Verra shrewd, my lord. But my experience is far more in the common way of things. I wouldna count too heavily upon Cristobal the now."

"I bow to your greater experience." The prince's smile vanished. "Ewan, you don't think—"

"Nay, the colony on Serilla is safe enough for now. Just after he returned from Valinor, Cristobal waived the tithe again. In that respect, he seems determined to carry on as Esteban did before him. 'Tis *you* I fear for."

"Noted. I will take care until I know which way the wind blows from Sorlain."

Florian spoke lightly, but Ewan noted the subtle straightening of his shoulders, as though he braced himself against an extra bit of weight added to the burden he already carried. Ewan felt his own shoulders tense as he sought the words to speak the rest of his tidings.

"And what of Venya, Ewan? What news from there?"

"None good," the knight answered directly. "The drought

continues, and lately a murrain has struck both swine and cattle. They say there have been fearsome windstorms, as well, with great bolts of lightning blasting field and forest. With everything so dry, the fires canna be contained. The people are afraid. They say Leander has turned his face from Venya since—because . . ."

"Because of me," the prince finished. Though his voice was calm, Ewan saw that his lips had gone dead white.

"Some say that, aye. Richard's men have been hard at work to make sure they say it loudly."

"How much support do I have left?"

Ewan scowled at the turquoise water below. He would have done anything to spare his prince this knowledge—anything but lie about it.

"None."

He was careful not to look at his prince as he spoke, yet even so he sensed the younger man's start.

"None at all? But what of Marlin? He wrote to me not long ago about the drought. I sent a dowser—"

"His holding burned to the ground; no one survived."

The prince dragged a shaking hand through his hair. "Gods. He was a good man, I'm sorry. But even so—surely there are some—"

"None," Ewan repeated harshly. "If ye moved today, half the Venyans would fight for Valinor against ye."

"And the other half?"

"Would keep out of it. A call to arms would yield perhaps two hundred men—and only if ye first showed them the gold."

"Leander's balls," the prince said softly. "Once the council hears—"

"They'll say we must abandon Venya and save the colony," Ewan finished glumly.

"The colony," the prince spat. "That's all they care about, the *filidhi* and the colony and their thrice-damned trade agreements."

"'Tis what they say of *ye* in Venya," Ewan pointed out. "The prince won't bother with the dregs who were left behind when the *filidhi* fled. Let Richard have them."

The prince slammed a fist against the rail. "How can I fight a shadow? A whisper?"

"Are ye sure ye want to?" Ewan asked quietly. "The *filidhi* are your people, too. I ken ye do not care for Lord Eredor—I don't care for him myself—but there's no denying he's done wonders on Serilla. Ye do him a disservice not to hear him out, at least, before rejecting his proposals."

"I don't need to hear him out. I know already what he wants. But I cannot give it to him, Ewan, I will not divide our people further. Venya—"

"Has waited eighteen years for your return," Ewan interrupted. "If a few more are needed, then so be it. Ye must think, my lord, before ye act, not rush into a battle ye canna win. I ken the waiting is not easy for ye," he said soothingly, putting a hand on Florian's black-clad shoulder, "not when your people suffer. But ye must use all your skills to build support, both on Serilla and in Venya. Ye need to take your time here, and—"

"I don't *have* time. It must be *now!*"

The prince jerked away and glared at Ewan. *As if I were the enemy,* the knight thought, feeling his own spine stiffen as he faced his liege lord.

"Why? Because of Riall?"

There, he had said it, the word that none dared utter in the Prince of Venya's presence. He half expected the younger man to turn and walk away, but the prince held his place.

"In part," he answered evenly, "but there are other reasons."

"What are they?" Ewan demanded.

The prince looked away for a moment, as though gathering his thoughts. "For one thing," he said, "the younger *filidhi* have no memory of Venya; all they know is Serilla. Already they look to Eredor as their leader."

Ewan nodded reluctantly. That much was true, though he hadn't realized the prince was aware of it.

"Should I give in to Eredor now, he will use the opportunity to bolster his position. And once the trade routes are established, he and his Serillan *filidhi* will have that much more to risk in open warfare for a land they can't remember and people they don't know. Every day drives the wedge a little deeper, and I need the *filidhi,* Ewan, they are the heart of Venya. I will *not* surrender them to Eredor."

"He has support on the council," Ewan warned.

"I know. Carlysle certainly, and perhaps Lysagh. That leaves you and me . . . and then there is Bastyon."

"Bastyon will support ye," Ewan said.

"I wish I could be so certain." The prince rested his elbows on the railing and frowned down at the water. "There is another thing," he said. "Someone is passing information to Valinor. They knew where to look for me."

"So ye have a traitor to contend with, and the council, and the situation in Venya could not be worse. I ken that things look black, but given time—"

"I don't have time," the prince said again, though this time he sounded more weary than angry. "It must be now."

"What folly! Ye are still young, my lord, and I ken that youth is impatient, but I beg ye to consider that diplomacy will do more for your cause than—"

"If I only had the Venyans with me, I could convince the council," the prince went on in a low voice, as though Ewan hadn't spoken. "But if it's truly as bad as you say . . . Gods, what am I to do?"

Ewan fought back the impulse to seize Florian by the shoulders and shake him hard. He'd just *told* him what to do. Diplomacy was the only prudent course, anyone could see that—anyone save the prince. Since Riall, he had seemed oblivious to reason, bent on Venya to the exclusion of all else, closing himself off from the very people who wanted most to help him.

Couldn't he see that he was driving away his dwindling supporters and turning potential friends to enemies? They were saying he was arrogant and reckless, too hungry for power to ever wield it wisely. Ewan had defended his young liege lord against these charges and would continue to defend him to the last. But by all the gods, he didn't make it easy.

The prince turned suddenly, his eyes blazing with some fierce emotion. "I know you think I haven't heard you, but I have. I've listened to everything you've said, and I am grateful for your advice, but now you must listen to me. I cannot afford to waste years running Eredor's errands and attempting to win supporters to my side. The time is now. If I hesitate, Venya will be lost. I know you don't understand, and if I tried to explain, you'd likely think me mad. All I can say is that I *know* this and ask you to accept it."

The prince was right, Ewan didn't understand. Frowning, he said, "My lord, are ye saying ye have had a . . . vision?"

The prince hesitated, then asked quietly, "Would you believe me if I did?"

Ewan shrugged helplessly. "I ken naught of Venyan magic. 'Tis the *filidhi* ye should be talking to, not me."

"The *filidhi* only listen to Eredor now. But you—" He laughed without amusement. "Aye, Ewan, I know. Why should you believe me, when— This past year hasn't been easy for you, either, I'm well aware of that. After all you've borne from me, I have no right to ask for more. Yet I need you to go on trusting me, I-I need—"

He turned away abruptly. "Never mind. You've done more than enough already." He began to walk toward the ladder, speaking over his shoulder, "When you get to Serilla, would you see that the boy Corin goes to to Rab's stable? I think he will do well there. And remember, don't take the silver to Hew's; Palinder is giving better prices." He rested a hand on the ladder and glanced back with a smile that did not reach his eyes. "I think that's all, then. Safe journey, and I will see you in—"

"My lord, wait. There is something ye should know."

"Yes?"

"The Venyans will not fight for ye, 'tis true. But there *is* one they would follow. One name that even Richard canna silence, try though he might. Only one who can oppose him now."

"What name?" The prince whirled to face him. "Who but I dares contest Richard's right to rule my people?"

Ewan drew a ragged breath. For a long moment he did not answer, nor would he meet the prince's eyes; instead he stared down at the skiff below.

"Well? Whose name would rouse my people to arms when mine cannot?"

"Hers." Ewan sighed, nodding toward the skiff. "Rose of Valinor."

Chapter 14

ROSE lifted her face to the sun and let the wind blow through her hair. The skiff, relieved of the heavy crates they had carried to the *Endeavor,* glided swiftly across the sparkling sea. Sigurd had rejoined them at the last and now sat far astern, gazing at the water rushing past.

"It was wonderful to see Sir Ewan again," she said, speaking almost randomly. Ewan's news had been disturbing; the question of those poor Venyans shut up in the hold even more so. Slaves? No, not the Prince of Venya, the very idea was unthinkable. Yet she could not get the shrill, desperate voice out of her mind, and even now the stench of sickness seemed to cling to her.

The prince made no answer. He had seemed distracted since he joined her, hardly speaking at all, though once or twice she'd turned to find him watching her closely. Now she glanced at him and found his eyes fixed upon her face with an intensity that made her shiver.

"My lord," she said, "tell me of your errand on the *Endeavor.* Who was down below in the hold?"

"Children, lady, bound for the *filidhi* colony on Serilla."

"Where did they come from?"

"Venya. They came from Kendrick's Mine."

Sigurd looked up sharply at the name.

"What were children doing at the mine?" Rose asked.

"Mining," the prince answered shortly. "Your uncle opened Kendrick's Mine," he went on evenly, "on what was our most holy shrine. The whole thing is unstable as all hell. Not that Richard lets that stop him. One vein collapses, they dig a new one—and they dig small, so small that no miner can fit through. So they use children. Venyan children. And when they die—as they do quite soon, for no vein has ever lasted long—it's off to the countryside to find some more. It matters not how small the yield of gems might be; Richard still profits. Venyan children cost him nothing."

Appalled as she was, Rose was conscious of a sharp relief. Perhaps the prince had been at Kendrick's Mine the year before, but it was not gems that had taken him there. He had gone to the rescue of those poor Venyan children. She threw Sigurd a glance—*I told you so!* The surgeon acknowledged it with a nod.

"But they had no idea of this in Riall!" she said. "At least not when I was there."

"The mine was very new then," the prince said. "They had not yet hit upon the brilliant scheme of sending children down to perish in the darkness. Mayhap by now the truth has leaked out, though Richard does his best to keep prying eyes away. And Riall had plenty of its own troubles at the time. Lady, when you were there—"

"Let us not speak of Riall," she interrupted, not trusting herself to discuss the matter calmly. "I would just as soon forget it altogether."

"Why?" he persisted. "Were you not locked safely in the Governor's castle?"

"Rico—Prince Richard—and I were in no danger," she answered evasively.

"So . . . ?" He raised his brows, inviting her to explain herself.

"People died," she said abruptly. "All around us. Men, women, children. I could not escape the knowledge of what was happening outside the walls."

"You did tell me," the prince began carefully, "that you had helped them. I assumed it was no more than a few baskets of scraps. But Ewan said—" he broke off, making an adjustment to the sails. When he turned back, he continued, "I gather there was more to it than that."

"A bit more. Are you certain you want to hear it?"

"No." He laughed without humor. "But I think I should."

"It all started with a girl—a Venyan girl, Lira, my chamber-maid, coming to my chamber late one night," Rose began haltingly, and then the memories rushed back. "She told me that the storerooms were stocked to the rafters, but they were sealed by the

Governor's order before he fled. She learned this from her lover, one of the castle guards. They took a terrible risk to come to me."

"What did they expect you to do?"

"Help them empty the storerooms. It took time; longer than it should have. But we managed in the end. Lira and her Kevan did most of the actual work, of course. I was just responsible for the arrangements."

The prince drew up one knee and rested his chin upon it. "What sort of arrangements?"

"Setting up the times, finding ways to distract the guards, making sure there were carts outside driven by people who wouldn't run off and sell the food. And that there was someone on the other end to make sure it got where it was meant to go."

"Ah. Was there anything else you . . . arranged?"

"I did manage to get some families out of Riall. There were so many," she said sadly, "and I could help so few . . ."

"How many would you say you helped to get out?"

"Not more than five hundred."

He lifted his head. "Five *hundred*?"

"Families, that is. If only I had more time, I think—I really believe I could have done better. It took so long to find the proper people—the ones who could really *do* something—and then convincing them to do it."

"Yes, I imagine it did. I'm sure it wasn't easy to convince Richard's soldiers to commit treason. Or to get Venyans in positions of authority to risk their lives. How did you manage it?"

Rose shrugged. "Most people want to do the right thing. It only takes someone to show them how to do it."

"You mean," the prince said slowly, "someone to *lead* them."

"Yes. Then they're usually quite willing to go along."

"And if they were not?"

"Well," she answered carefully, "I've found that almost everyone has a price."

"Yes, I've found that, as well," the prince agreed. "How did you pay it?"

Rose extended her free hand palm downward, fingers spread. A tiny hesitation, then she closed her fingers tight and drew it back again.

"You *stole* it?"

"Rico had so much—jewels that he had never had the chance

to wear, an entire service of gold that the Governor presented to him when we arrived. Very pretty, but quite unsuitable for a child."

"I had no idea your talents extended to theft and smuggling."

She did not return his smile. "Needs must, my lord."

And it was what you would have done, she thought, just as she had thought back then. Many and many a time when her courage or ingenuity faltered, she had asked herself, *What would the Prince of Venya do?* imagining entire conversations in which he encouraged and advised her. It was childish—she'd known that even then—but very comforting to think that there was one person in all the world who would understand and approve of what she'd done. In that, at least, she had been right.

"Yes, of course," he said at once, "I did not mean to make light of it. You acted with great courage." Despite everything, Rose felt a warm glow of pleasure at his praise.

"Though I imagine your uncle might see it differently," he went on. "Did you never stop to think what he would do if he found out about all this?"

Once again, she was disarmed. He really was the Prince of Venya—perhaps not quite as she'd imagined, but still a good, kind lord who cared for all his people. He was nothing like Richard, who she could easily believe would use children in his mine. She had good reason to know just how far Richard would go to satisfy his pride and his ambition—as did the prince, of course, who looked genuinely concerned as he waited for her answer.

"Once or twice," she said, "or, well, perhaps a *bit* more often. In the event, I told him myself. He was starting to ask too many awkward questions. Of course I didn't tell him the truth," she added quickly. "I named no names. I only said that I had given orders to distribute the food and taken—borrowed—some of Rico's things."

"He could have charged you with treason."

"Like his third wife, Queen Analise?" Rose shook her head. "He forced the council to condemn her, but there was a lot of ill feeling about it. The eastern barons nearly rebelled. And I *am* Osric's daughter. He was much loved in his time. I did not think Richard would risk an execution."

"You did not *think.* You could not have been certain."

"I was more worried about an accident. Richard's very good at accidents, you know, a quick push down the stairway or a bit of nightshade in the stew. But instead he just declared me mad and packed me off to Malin Isle."

She was pleased that she could say that name so calmly, as though it were just another place she'd been. If she must carry the scars forever, so be it. At least they could be hidden.

"Would you do it again?" the prince asked unexpectedly. "You obviously have no great affection for your uncle. If you were offered the chance to . . . help the Venyan people, would you take it?"

Reluctantly, Rose shook her head. "I wish I could say yes, but the truth is, I don't think I could. I seem to have lost my taste for intrigue. And the courage for it," she added in a lower voice.

A slight frown drew his dark gold brows together, and she sensed that her answer had disappointed him. Then his face softened with something that looked terribly like pity. "Yes," he said, "I understand. I'm sorry."

Rose felt the heat rise to her face, though this time she blushed from shame. Bad enough that he had forced her to admit her own cowardice, did he really have to stare at her as though she was some poor dumb beast about to be taken to the slaughter?

"When I was in Riall," she began, "they said . . ."

"Yes?"

If his tone had not alerted her, one look at his face was enough to warn her that she was venturing onto dangerous ground. Yet it was he who had raised the subject over her objections, and she felt entitled to a question of her own.

"At first they said you had returned with an army at your back. Then later, when it was clear there was no army, they said—*some* said—"

"I assure you that I did not sail by stealth to Venya so I might plunder Kendrick's Mine."

"But you—"

"Nor did I murder any Venyans who happened to stand between me and the gems."

"Then why—"

"Riall was a tragedy for which I take full responsibility, but I did not intend for it to happen. I certainly did not plan it."

Rose wanted to believe him, wanted it so much that she was tempted to just take him at his word. But she could not allow herself to do it. She had to know.

"If not for invasion or plunder," she asked, "what *did* take you to Kendrick's Mine?"

A muscle jumped in his clenched jaw; he would not hold her gaze. "It is a tedious story, lady," he said, "and it makes no matter now."

He stood and jerked a line, causing the skiff to heel so sharply that Rose had to catch herself with both hands to keep from falling. Sigurd was not so lucky. She heard a muffled thump as the surgeon was spilled unceremoniously to the deck. With a muttered curse, the prince yanked another line and they righted. He kept his back to Rose, making several adjustments—unnecessary ones, she would have wagered—to the sail.

Well, she had her answer—or enough of one to convince her that whatever had taken the Prince of Venya to Kendrick's Mine had been no honest errand. Not plunder—she would not believe that of him—but something he was ashamed to own.

It might be nothing of importance. A wager, mayhap, or a tryst, or some reckless bit of daring had brought thousands of his subjects to a cruel and bitter end. Had it been something else, he would have said so plainly, not only to her, but to the world, if only to stop the rumors that had reached even Sigurd on the *Quest*.

She had no reason to feel betrayed that the man she had admired so much for so many years was not the spotless hero she'd thought him. It was better to know the truth. Of course it was. She was far too old to go on believing in fairy tales.

She leaned her head against her hand, wondering wearily where she would go from here. King Esteban, a dubious ally at best, was dead. Cristobal was on the throne of Sorlain. There was no safe haven for her now. *I will go to Jexal,* she decided, *to my mother's kin.* Not to the *Melakh,* Najet's brother who had exiled her for the Valinorian alliance, but to Chandra, Najet's sister, who lived . . . Rose realized she had no idea where her aunt lived, save that she had stayed in Jexal.

Eight weeks by sea to Jexal's nearest port, another four weeks through the desert—and that was assuming she could find a guide who could be trusted. If she did manage to survive the journey that no respectable woman would consider making unescorted, she had no idea where to begin searching for her family.

They passed the rest of the journey in silence. Only when they had climbed aboard the *Quest* did the prince speak to her again, turning to offer her his hand as she made the long step onto the deck.

"Thank you for your company, lady. Will you do me the honor of dining with me tonight?"

His smile looked forced—or was it only that she could see through the illusion now? He was not the Prince of Venya, but a stranger she did not really wish to know. She certainly didn't want to dine with him. It was on the tip of her tongue to refuse, when she realized that she could not possibly get to Jexal without his help.

"Yes," she said, "I would like that."

"Good—and here is Ashkii," he added, gesturing the third mate over. The Ilindrian approached, the long feather trailing over his shoulder, a swathe of dusk-pink silk spilling from his arms. "He has been hard at work upon your gown."

Ashkii was so stiff and solemn as he offered it to Rose that she was careful to show none of the amusement she felt at the idea of this proud young man hunched over his needle. "I am sure it is—" She drew a sharp breath as she held it up and the sun glistened off the golden threads. "Beautiful. Thank you."

A curt nod was her only answer. "Well done, Ashkii," the prince added, and the young Ilindrian's face lit up in a smile that transformed his sharp features into a wild beauty.

"At your service," he said, and though it was to Rose he bowed, she knew it was not to her he spoke.

Here was one, at least, who did not serve the prince from fear. But Ashkii was an Ilindrian, and too new to the Venyan's service to know his liege lord well.

He isn't who you think he is, she wanted to caution the young man, *you mustn't believe all you have heard.* But to attempt to disillusion him would be both futile and unkind. *There is little enough of honor in this world,* she thought with a sigh; *even the dream of it is better than nothing.* She only wished that she still had her dream, as well, but reality would have to do for her.

The reality was that she needed the Prince of Venya's help. How she would gain it, she wasn't certain, but looking down at the thin silk in her arms, the dim outline of a plan began to form. If he could play a part, surely she could do so, too. The only question was what role would suit her needs.

Chapter 15

"WILL you try some wine?"

Florian smiled and tipped the flagon over the princess's goblet without waiting for an answer.

"It is Tiernaviel," he went on, "best when it is chilled."

She obediently lifted her goblet and drank. "Mmm. Yes, it is very nice. Thank you."

Tonight they sat alone at his table with an extravagant sunset blazing through the stern windows. Gone was the silver candelabra, off with Ewan to the nearest merchant with the other swag. Their crockery bowls had been removed by Beylik, and now a chipped plate of biscuits sat between them as they sipped their wine.

The princess wore her new gown tonight. The dusky rose brought color to her cheeks, and the simple Ilindrian style suited her. Ashkii had made a neat job of it, considering he had never held a needle before joining the *Quest*.

Princess Rose—or no, Rosamund, Florian thought—had accepted it with dignity and poise, and the result was more attractive than he'd thought possible. All in all, things could have been much worse.

She could have been a giggling fool, hideous or cruel. But even if she had been all those things, he would still be sitting here with her in the sunset, urging her to drink the sweet Tiernaviel wine that was far stronger than it tasted.

There was no question in his mind of what must happen. His plan had been made by the time he had left the *Endeavor*. Ewan wasn't altogether pleased about it; Florian wasn't happy, either, although he'd known for some time that he must marry and provide Venya with an heir. Each day that passed made the need a bit more urgent, and although he accepted the necessity, he had dreaded the inevitable complications. The very last thing he needed was one more person questioning his decisions and prying into matters that were his concern alone.

He had intended to find a woman who would suit him, one who was either so dazzled by the Prince of Venya that she would not dare question or so slow that the idea would not occur to her. Princess Rosamund was proving to be alarmingly intelligent and damnably persistent; like a terrier with a rat, she had worried him with her questions until he had no recourse but a flat refusal to answer.

A bad beginning, he thought now. Not only was she no longer dazzled, he suspected that she held him in contempt. It would not be easy to win her over, but he would. He must.

Her body he could have for the taking; she was completely in his power, and many a bride had come gagged and kicking to her vows. But if he wanted her to speak for him in Venya, she must come to him willingly.

"It grows late," she said, setting down her wine. "I should—"

"Please stay. I grow weary of sitting all alone," he added wistfully. "Unless, of course, there is something you would rather do."

"No. No, there is nothing."

She picked up her goblet and drank so quickly that she choked a little. So she could still be flustered! Perhaps things were not quite so black as he had thought.

"A game of *cheran?*" he suggested. "Do you know it?"

"A little. But I have nothing to wager."

He smiled slowly and was rewarded by a deepening of color in her cheeks before he twisted in his seat to reach into a drawer behind him and pull out the *cheran* tiles and a small bag. A shower of coins spilled on the table as he emptied it between them. He divided it into two roughly even piles and pushed one across the table.

"A loan."

"What I win, I keep," she said, surprising him.

"And if you lose?"

She was already far out of her depth, obviously a stranger to even the mildest flirtation. He wanted her intrigued, not terrified, so he looked down as he spread the tiles facedown upon the table.

"You'll have my marker," she said at last.

"As the lady wishes."

There was a small silence as they each selected their tiles and examined them.

"How many?" he asked. Three tiles clicked as she laid them on the table. He slid three more across the polished wood and made a show of frowning over his own.

"I'll take one."

He exchanged a tile, allowed himself a smile, and placed three coins between them. After the briefest hesitation, she matched his wager. There was a longer pause while she decided whether to increase it.

So cautious, he thought, *so very serious. Where do I begin with her? When she looks at the Prince of Venya, who does she see?*

It was a game he had played many times before, guessing a woman's secret fantasy. Usually he had a good idea before the first course was off the table. Tonight, he found himself at a loss.

The trouble was that this game must last beyond a single night. And when it came to women, Florian had never considered the concept of tomorrow. Today—tonight—had always been enough for him. The type of woman who interested him looked for nothing more. They saw a night with the Prince of Venya as an adventure, perhaps the only one they'd ever have. Wed to men they did not choose, their lives bounded by duty and obedience—was it any wonder they would seize a chance to cast dull care aside and step into a fantasy?

But what was Princess Rosamund's fantasy?

Surely not the bold pirate—always a favorite—who would accept nothing less than complete surrender from his captive. He was glad of that, for it made his head ache to imagine another night of feigned shrieks and faux struggles. Not that the struggles were all so very faux; he'd had his eye blacked and back scratched raw by some of his more enthusiastic "captives." And for what? The pleasure of watching the lady achieve a climax? There *was* pleasure in that; of course, it was always nice to know one had succeeded, but he couldn't help but think the whole thing a bit ridiculous. Not to mention one-sided.

Then there was the world-weary rake disarmed by the sweet innocence of the woman in his bed. Many women liked that one.

Too many, really; he was bored with it. All right, perhaps he *was* a little jaded, but he was far from weary of the world or all the women in it. And of course the women involved were seldom sweet and never innocent. He supposed they wished they were, but why? He liked them as they were—clever, experienced, spirited enough to go after what they wanted. Why spoil it all by pretending to be less?

The callow youth, all wet kisses and eager, fumbling hands? No, at twenty-five, he suspected he'd at last outgrown that role, though he nearly smiled at the thought of Rosamund playing teacher to his student.

Yet this was no joking matter. He had no time to waste upon deciding his approach. The thing must be done, and quickly, before she realized what he was about.

His focus sharpened, narrowed on the woman across from him. She gazed down at the table, expression pensive, and absently tugged a lock of hair.

He set down a tile with a little click and adjusted it so the scored marks lined up with one beside it, joining three tiles in a pattern known as the Plough. Her eyes widened as the shape took on a faint aqua glow.

"How . . . ?" she breathed.

"They are Venyan tiles. You've never seen a set before? I thought King Osric had purchased one, though perhaps Richard does not use it."

She shook her head, eyes fixed upon the glowing Plough. "No, I've never seen one. But I thought Venyan magic could not be bought or sold?"

"This is not Venyan magic. These, the chrysal rings, the daggers—they are baubles that apprentices produce while studying the *filidhi* art. The truly enchanted talismans are never bought or sold, but given to those for whom they are intended. Now, let me see. A Plough should be worth . . ."

Florian pushed a substantial pile of coins into the center. She bit her lip, eyes moving from the gold to the formation on the table then back to her unused tiles.

Judging from her expression, she saw nothing to reassure her. Would she give up now, he wondered, with the game barely begun? Did she really have so little interest in the outcome? He was relieved when she matched his wager. His brows rose when, after the briefest hesitation, she added half her remaining coins. For the first time, he gave his complete attention to the game.

"What do you have?" he murmured, studying the blank backs of her tiles. Nothing much upon the board, while he was showing not only the Plough, but most of the Chalice, lacking only two tiles to complete the pattern. One of which he did not possess, but she had no way of knowing that. Was she actually attempting to bluff him? He suppressed a smile and pushed an equal pile of coins beside hers.

Her hand hovered over her tiles, selected one, and set it out. A Scepter? he thought, studying the new arrangement. Is that what she was after? It would best the Plough he had showing, but not the Chalice he seemed so close to making. Ignoring her feint, he chose not to block her Scepter. Instead, he placed the next sequence to the Chalice and added a few more coins to the pot. She looked up at him, eyes searching his face. He smiled and leaned back in his seat, reaching for his wine.

Two tiles remained before her, both of which she needed for the Scepter he was now certain she had. Yet in making it, she would leave him free to use his final tile to complete the Chalice. She hesitated, teeth worrying her lower lip. Would she forfeit now, keeping her remaining coins for a second game? He thought she might, rather than risk all. To his surprise, she matched his wager, and in two moves the game would be hers.

But having come so close, she faltered. She went for the block, the safe route. The moment the tile was laid, she realized her mistake. She frowned, then with an angry, almost defiant gesture, pushed all her remaining coins into the center.

Worse and worse, he thought. Indecision was bad enough, and the mistake had been a stupid one. All that he could excuse, as she was obviously a novice to the game. But to throw good gold after bad revealed a reckless petulance that troubled him.

"Too bad," he said, sliding his final tile almost randomly into place. It did not matter now. The game was over, and she could see he'd never had the Chalice at all. His faintly glowing Plough was the only completed pattern on the table.

He half-expected an outburst, but she only sighed. "Yes," she said, "it is."

And she made her final move.

Crimson lit the markings, then streaked across the board, joining every one of her tiles. It took him a moment to comprehend what she had done. The Tribute was so rare that he had seen it only twice before.

"Well," he said at last, then shook his head and laughed. "Well done, indeed, my lady. I never saw it coming."

"You weren't looking for it."

"No."

Her lips curved in a secret smile as she swept the pot to her side of the table.

"Underestimating an opponent is always fatal," he remarked. "A mistake I do not intend to make again."

"Good. Then shall we play? I'll wager you all this," she flicked a finger toward her coins, "against your Venyan tiles."

Chapter 16

ROSE won the tiles on the second game. This round had been decided by sheer luck; it happened like that sometimes, a draw so blatantly unequal that even the dullest player would be hard put to lose. She was pleased with her winnings, but even with the Venyan *cheral* pieces, it wasn't nearly what she needed.

Jexal. Not a pleasant thought, but there was no other choice. Her winnings would have easily paid her passage to Sorlain, but they would not come close to getting her to Jexal's nearest port. That was a far longer journey, and more dangerous, for it led through waters often traveled by Richard's ships. The prince sometimes hunted in those waters, but he was not hunting now; he had said earlier that he was heading for the Venyan colony on Serilla by a northern route, while Jexal lay directly south.

She had considered explaining her predicament and once again casting herself upon his mercy, but she suspected she had already strained his mercy to the limit. He would have to call in a very large favor indeed to find anyone to take her near to Jexal.

Then, too, the thought of explaining Cristobal's rejection did not appeal. Oh, there was nothing personal in it; the new King of Sorlain had never even laid eyes upon her, but still, it rankled, and she chafed at the idea of telling such a humiliating little story to the Prince of Venya. And why should she? It was no business of his, where she went or why . . . save that she needed his help to get there.

She studied him through downcast lashes as she ran the tiles through her fingers. How to go about this? She had always considered herself a good judge of character, but the man before her remained a mystery.

He had started out the evening very formally, clad in a high-necked tunic of black silk over loose trousers, belted about his hips with joined links of obsidian. Sometime during their game he had kicked off his low boots and loosened the jet clasp at his neck, baring the strong line of his throat. Now he was half-turned in the great chair, one knee hooked over the arm and a bare foot dangling above the floor. One hand cupped his clay goblet, the other rested casually on the table, his heavy seal ring glinting in the candlelight.

Tonight he had been flirtatious and grim, engaging and withdrawn, first entreating her for her company and then lapsing into a silence so deep it seemed he had forgotten her entirely. At least until she had beaten him the first time. Then he had thrown off his bad mood and played with both skill and pleasure, as though the fall of the tiles was the weightiest matter on his mind.

That, she thought, had not been feigned. Whatever else the Prince of Venya might be, he was a gambler.

But, perhaps, not quite as good a one as she.

" 'Tis late," she said with an unconvincing yawn. "I expect you must be tired. Thank you for—"

"Oh, no. Not yet." Leaning across the table, he caught her wrist. "Give me one more chance. I'll wager . . ." He released her wrist slowly, fingertips lingering against her skin, then drew the dagger from his belt and tossed it on the table between them.

Rose did her best to ignore the sudden pounding of her heart and the slow warmth spreading up her arm. She frowned and leaned over the dagger, pretending to examine it closely. "Are these real?" she said, poking at the hilt. "They look like glass to me."

"Very funny. I had that dagger straight from the hand of Shideezhi Liluye of Ilindria."

"Ooh." She widened her eyes in mock awe, though in truth she was a little impressed. "Did you? How unchivalrous to wager a love token!"

A small smile played across his lips. "Shideezhi Liluye is old enough to be my mother. It was a gift, Princess. One I value highly."

"Like the tiles?"

His smile widened. "You have no mercy, do you? Good. Then I won't be sorry to win them back again."

Two games later he had regained dagger, tiles, and the best part of his gold.

"It grows late," he said, stretching. "Perhaps we should—"

"Either give me the tiles," Rose said crisply, "or lay them out yourself."

By the time they came to the final tiles, Rose had wagered all, though her victory was very much in doubt. The prince held his last tile in his hand, shaking it lightly as he bent over the board between them. A Scepter and a Star glowed in emerald and amber. Her Star. His Scepter. She held the second Star in her hand. Game to her, unless he really held the Crown. Of course he could be bluffing, though she wished she could be sure . . .

Smiling, he pushed his last two coins to the center. "Oh." He made a show of looking carefully at her side of the table. "I see you cannot match my wager. What a pity. I believe that is a forfeit."

"Wait. I'll wager"—she rested her chin in her palm—"my jewels."

"What jewels?"

"The ones I left in Valinor."

"Oh, *those* jewels. I am sure they are very fine, though collection may present a problem."

"What problem? Just nip round to Larken Castle and slip in through a window." She grinned and waved a hand. "Child's play."

"True. *If* I were bound for Valinor, which, alas, I am not. No, I'm afraid your jewels will not serve. But I'll tell you what I will accept." His amber gaze drifted over her face and lingered on her lips. "A kiss."

Rose didn't answer. She could not, for her heart seemed to have lodged somewhere in the back of her throat. But her luck was in; by the time she found her voice, she'd found her wits, as well.

"For such a prize, you must hazard more than this," she said, flicking her hand toward the table.

"What would you ask, then?" he asked, smiling indulgently.

"Let me think. Perhaps"—she slanted him a smile—"your ship?"

Now it was his turn to be silent. Only the tiniest widening of his eyes betrayed his surprise before he laughed. "You set a high price on your kisses, lady."

Rose lifted her chin. "Think you so, my lord? *I* would call it a bargain."

Had she overdone it? Hard to tell, when she could not for the life of her imagine why he had suggested such a wager in the first place. Habit, she thought, that must be it; no doubt he had made a hundred such wagers before, and been answered in the same terms. *At least,* she thought with satisfaction, *I have managed to surprise him.*

"Of course," he murmured, eyeing her intently, "a bargain indeed. And what would you do with the *Quest*?"

"Oh, I don't know. Perhaps sail it to . . . Jexal."

"Jexal? I thought you were bound for Sorlain."

Rose pushed her last tile in a little circle upon the table. "Well, yes . . . eventually. But I have always wanted to meet my mother's kin, and who knows when such a . . . unique . . . opportunity will come again? I'll tell you what: If I win, I will keep you on as captain as far as Jexal, and once we arrive, I will give you back the *Quest* as payment."

"Let me be sure I understand you," the Prince of Venya said in measured tones. "Should I lose, I turn my ship around and sail eight weeks to Jexal. If I win, I get a kiss."

Yes, she had definitely overdone it. The whole thing was absurd. A traitorous blush was rising to her cheeks, but she only shrugged and said, "Precisely."

"Then it is done. Your move, I believe."

Rose's hand trembled slightly as she slid her tile into place.

"A double Star!" the prince said admiringly. "You don't see that very often. Though I did see a treble once, on the isle of Raval. You know of Raval, don't you? The dwarves don't take kindly to strangers as a rule, but they're mad for *cheran*. Well, on that night—"

"Play," Rose interrupted.

"Play? Oh, I see, I've forgotten the last one." He laughed, flipping the tile in the air and catching it again. "What was it I meant to do with this? Wait, now, give me a moment, I'm sure I had something in mind . . ."

"Would you please—"

"*Now* I remember." He held her gaze as he slipped it into place and the board flared emerald between them. "I believe the game is mine."

* * *

BY the time they walked onto the deck, the sky had lightened to a pearly gray and a freshening breeze tautened the sails. Rose could just make out the prince's smile as he paced silently beside her.

"Good night, my lady," he said formally when they reached the hatch. "Or should I say good morning? In any case, I thank you for a most entertaining evening."

"You only say that because you won." Rose folded her arms across her chest. "Go on, then."

She tipped her face up and squeezed her eyes shut. It seemed an eternity until he responded, long enough for her to become painfully aware of how she must look to him, lips pursed, eyes shut, practically begging for his kiss. *Just get it over with,* she thought, so focused upon the impending kiss that she was taken completely unaware by the touch of his hand upon her cheek, just below her ear. She tensed as his hand moved in a slow caress across her jaw, down her neck and up again. He stroked the base of her skull; his fingers were in her hair, freeing it from its knot. The weight of it fell upon her shoulders, and she heard the pins drop to the deck beside her feet.

Whatever she had expected, it wasn't this. Not this touch, so gentle and unhurried, demanding nothing as he soothed the tension from her neck. It had been so long, so terribly long since anyone had laid a hand on her except to punish that she was defenseless against the feeling that welled up in her, an ache that held both joy and sorrow and yet was not fully either, but some new emotion for which she had no name. She only knew that she never wanted it to end. She dared not move or speak; even breathing seemed beyond her as he lightly traced the outline of her mouth. She was dimly aware of her tight-pressed lips relaxing as she swayed forward, resting her hands on his shoulders to support herself.

Her entire body felt the shock of this new contact, soft cool silk, warm flesh, and solid muscle. Instinct demanded that she run her hands across his shoulders to clasp his neck. She did not even think to argue. The next step was as inevitable as the pattern of a dance, and he took it neatly, closing the space between them.

His palms were rough and warm against her skin as he cupped her face, tipping it to his. His breath was soft against her lips, and then he spoke, saying words that seemed to make no sense.

"No. Perhaps not . . . *yet.*" She opened her eyes and saw that he was smiling, his eyes alight with mischief and amusement. "It is late. You are weary."

His hands brushed her cheeks, then fell slowly to his side. "I think we should await a better moment."

The meaning of his words was slow to penetrate the fog that had crept into her mind, but at last she understood. He didn't want her. Not as she had wanted him. No, of course he didn't, it was just a wager, after all. A game. One the Prince of Venya had played a hundred times before.

Her hands still rested on his shoulder. She snatched them back and stepped away. But no matter how firmly she ordered herself to meet his eyes, she could not bring herself to do it.

WHAT was wrong with her? Florian thought impatiently. Surely she must know that he meant only to prolong the game, not end it. But she didn't seem to understand. Well, she wouldn't, would she; she was a novice. He had *known* that. How could he have made such a stupid mistake? How was he to recover from it?

As he hesitated, she began to walk away. His paralysis broke; acting on pure instinct, he went after her and caught her by the arm.

"Wait," he said. "On second thought . . ."

"I think not, my lord."

Her voice was cold, but she lacked the artifice to hide her feelings. All she could do was turn away, hoping that he would not see—or would not understand—what he had done.

But he did see. And he understood. Not only did she not know the rules, she had been playing a different game entirely. One that was no game at all. He knew a moment of complete confusion, during which she attempted to wrest her arm from his grasp and he could do no more than hold on, like some dockside ruffian who would force from her what a moment ago she would have given willingly. Not just a wagered kiss; her trembling and sighs had not been feigned, but a genuine emotion that he had been too blind to see. Stupid girl, to hand him such a weapon. Did she not know better than to trust a man like him?

"You were right," she said, "I *am* weary. Let me *go.*"

Well, she knew better now. There was no softness in the look she turned on him, only anger. He knew only one answer to such a look, and he gave it, wrapping her in his arms and bending to set his mouth on hers.

Now he was on surer ground. He was good at this; he'd been told so often and had no reason to doubt it was the truth. Leander knew he'd had enough practice to melt the anger from any maiden's heart. Taking great care, he kissed her softly, and then not so softly, urging her lips apart with his, inviting her response. Yet she did not accept the invitation. She stood, arms at her sides, not struggling, but not responding, either.

He drew back to look into her eyes. As soon as he broke contact, she stepped away and raised her hand. For a moment he thought she meant to slap him, which would have been unpleasant, but encouraging. He'd been slapped too many times before to mistake such a clear signal of incipient surrender.

It served as a direction, too, though not a reliable one; slow down, one woman might be pleading, while another was urging him to hurry up and seize the moment. The devil of it was that either would expect him to understand precisely what she wanted and supply it without hesitation. A clumsy means of communication, he'd often thought, and it hardly helped matters that this lightning-quick moment of decision would invetiably follow a sharp smack to the face.

The princess did not tread this well-worn path. Instead she wiped the back of her hand across her mouth, and she did it slowly, so he could not mistake the insult.

"I trust you are satisfied, my lord."

The gesture he could have forgiven. It was new to him, though he'd seen its like before and ranked it little more important than the token slap. The cold contempt in her voice was a different matter. *That* was real. His chest tightened painfully—with anger, he thought, which was only natural—and a sort of hollow surprise, as though he had missed the last step on a stairway.

"No," he replied evenly, "I am not. Let us try again."

"That was not part of our wager."

She was right. It hadn't been. He knew that, but he no longer cared what they had wagered for. Without another word, he pulled her into his arms. This time his mouth came down on hers blindly, not inviting but demanding. After one heart-stopping moment, she wound her arms around his neck and pulled him close. She held nothing back; for all her inexperience she flared with a passion that ignited a hunger he had denied for far too long. He parted her lips roughly and plundered the sweetness of her mouth until both of them were breathless.

When at last it ended, she clung to him, trembling. He came slowly back to awareness of himself, and her, and that he was holding her too tightly, possessed by a mad urge to keep her here forever, an elemental need to shelter and protect the woman in his arms.

But she was in no danger. Except, of course, from him. From that, he could not save her even if he wanted to.

Where had *that* thought come from? Gods, he must be losing his touch if one kiss could undo him so completely. Either that, or he was losing his mind, which should come as no surprise after a year of celibacy. Yes, of course, that's all it was; his self-imposed penance was having unexpected consequences, unfortunate but hardly fatal.

He rested his cheek on her soft hair, allowing himself a small sigh of relief. He had been lucky this time. Playing blindly, he had played well. But he would not trust to luck again. From now on, he would be more careful.

Deep within a haze of absolute contentment, Rose sensed his withdrawal. He held her just as tightly, but the subtle tensing of his muscles was like the raising of a shield beween them. Even as they stood clasped, she began to wonder if they had really shared that perfect moment or if she had imagined it.

"*Now* I am satisfied," he murmured against her hair. "I hope you are, as well."

He loosed his grasp to look down at her, one brow raised in question. His anger was gone—if it had ever really been there. She wasn't sure now whether she had imagined that, as well, or if it had been some elaborate game he was playing to add spice to his victory.

"Yes, quite." She moved away, not sure whether she was relieved or disappointed when he released her.

"Lady," he said, "I have one question more: How soon can we have another game?"

She smiled uncertainly, trying to match this new mood. "No more. I know when I am outmatched."

"You give yourself too little credit. A bit of practice and you will have the best of me." He bent, his voice dropping to a velvet purr. "Just name the time and place. I am completely at your disposal."

He was teasing her again, his eyes warm as they carressd her face. Rose shook her head in mock reproof. "I think you are something of a rogue, my lord."

Something flickered in his eyes, then was gone. "I am the Prince of Venya." He shrugged, shooting her a smile of such wicked charm that she was momentarily struck speechless. "What else did you expect?"

Laughing, he walked off. Who *was* the Prince of Venya? A few weeks ago, she could have answered that question easily, but now she did not know. How *could* she know when he changed from one moment to the next? Yet when he kissed her—not the first time, that had been part of whatever game he played—but the second, when he held her so closely that she could feel his heartbeat racing as madly as her own—he had seemed like someone else completely. Someone . . . real. Or had that, too, been an illusion?

She was suddenly aware of a sound that had been going on for some time, just below the edge of consciousness. Holystones. It was dawn. The night was past, the game ended, and a new day had begun.

This new day was weighted with too many questions for her to take pleasure in its arrival. They crowded into her mind, demanding answers. And she would answer them. But no matter where she went or what might befall her, she knew she would carry the past night with her. Strange as it had been, she had enjoyed it. Matching wits with such an opponent had been a pleasure, and even if she'd lost, she hadn't come out of it too badly. It wasn't every woman who could say she'd had her first kiss from the Prince of Venya.

Shivering in her thin gown, Rose watched him walk away, the salt breeze whipping her hair into her eyes and a strange emptiness around her heart.

Chapter 17

"SAIL ho!"

Florian stopped halfway down the hatch and looked up to the rigging.

"Where away?" he called.

"Two points off the starboard bow."

Florian was up the rigging in a moment. Bracing himself against the mast, he drew a crystal and a square of leather from the pouch at his waist. A quick glance around ensured he was alone, invisible to the lookout and no more than a speck to the crew below. He set the crystal in the leather, twisted the whole thing into a cylinder, and raised it to his eye.

Immediately the hazy shape of sails sprang into sharp relief against the dawn-splashed sky. He cursed, jerked the crystal from the leather, and bundled the whole thing into his bag. Ten seconds later he was catching his balance on the deck.

"Reef the mains'l," he shouted. "Hard about, three points to larboard."

"What is it m'lord?"

Gordon blinked in the growing light, hair kicked up on one side of his head, and nightshirt fluttering about his shins.

"The *Lord Marva*. She's after us. Don't just stand there gaping, man, there isn't a moment to be lost."

"What is the course, my lord?"

Florian frowned. "We'll make for Andrien Straits with all speed. All speed, Mr. Gordon, do you understand me?"

"Aye, aye, my lord. The Andrien Straits it is."

Chapter 18

IT was midday when Rose ventured onto the deck again and was blown half off her feet.

The prince stood at the wheel, legs spread against the rolling of the ship and face lifted to the rushing wind. He was every inch the captain today, taut and focused on his ship. "Good morning, my lady. The kava is still hot. Beylik, light along and fetch the lady a mug."

Rose accepted the steaming mug with a nod and welcomed the hot bitter brew that cleared the last sleep from her mind. There was very little talk on deck. The men went about their work with barely suppressed tension that showed in the sharpness of the orders and curses when they were not obeyed upon the instant.

"What is it?" she asked. "What is wrong?"

The prince nodded toward the stern. "That."

Rose peered across the water, one hand shading her eyes against the sun. "That ship? Why? What is it?"

"The *Lord Marva*."

"Are you certain?"

"Quite. The only question is which one of us it's after."

She groped blindly behind her for the rail. "Will you set me ashore?"

"Would you? If you were in my place?"

He sounded honestly curious, as though they were discussing some hypothetical question instead of what remained of her future.

Her fingers gripped the wood. "I might."

"Why?"

"You have more lives than mine to consider."

He scanned the horizon, eyes narrowed against the sun, and made a minute adjustment to the wheel. "True. Loyalty isn't worth much if it doesn't run both ways. I owe it to my crew to protect them."

"Would it help," she said carefully, "if I were to beg?"

"You could try it and find out."

She forced herself to return his smile. "On second thought, I think I'd rather not."

She turned away to gaze out over the stern, past the creamy wake of the *Quest*. The sea was a vast coverlet of blue, stretching to the horizon where the *Lord Marva*'s sails glinted in the sunlight. It looked tiny at this distance, a toy ship on a painted sea. *How far is it?* she wondered. *How long will I have?*

With an effort, she released the rail and straightened.

"Send for me when we make land."

She had gone two steps when a hand on her shoulder halted her. "Hold on, now, don't rush off. I never said I was going to put you ashore. That was your idea. As I recall, I said you were my guest until I could assist you to . . . where was it? Sorlain? Jexal? Or have you come up with something new today? If you like, I can show you the Andrien Straits while you decide."

She was afraid to turn and look at him, fearing this was some new jest. "You—do you mean that?"

He sighed. "That's the trouble with this whole pirate business. You board a few ships, carry off a bit of plunder, and suddenly everyone is doubting your word. If I were any other prince you would believe me."

"Not if you were"—*Cristobal,* she thought—"Richard," she finished with barely a pause. "And he's a king."

His fingers tightened on her shoulder. "I suppose I deserved that. Forgive me," he added, turning her to face him. "I shouldn't have joked about it. Though I was rather hoping—not that you would beg, exactly, but that you might come up with an . . . interesting offer."

Relief made her giddy. "If I had, surely your honor would never have allowed you to accept it!"

"We'll never know now, will we?" He smoothed the wind-blown wisps of hair back from her face. "Unless you'd like to make it now. You know, a token of gratitude . . . ?"

She caught his hand in hers. "I *am* grateful. Truly."

"And I am truly honored to assist you."

He raised her hand and brushed his lips slowly across her skin, the laughter fading from his eyes.

"I make it twelve knots," a boy cried from the side.

"Twelve knots!" an older sailor called.

"Twelve it is, at . . ." The prince paused, then nodded as the bell struck. "At eight bells. Beylik, make a note."

The boy bent, tongue caught between his teeth as he clamped an elbow across one edge of the wildly fluttering log and dipped a quill into the weighted inkwell.

The prince swung Rose's hand lightly as he gazed up at the sails. "I believe," he said, "that we can make it thirteen. Raise the sprits'l."

A moment of dead silence greeted his words. To a man, the sailors looked upward where the sails strained against the wind. Then the moment passed and they swarmed aloft.

It was a mere scrap of canvas compared with the other sails, hardly to be noticed. Yet Rose imagined she could feel the crew holding a collective breath as it filled. The mast creaked and groaned, and Beylik glanced up uneasily from the logbook.

"That will do nicely," the prince declared. "Lady, I am famished. Will you join me? Call me if there is any change," he added to Gordon.

Gordon's face worked as he eyed the new sail, but he only said, "Yes, m'lord."

It was not until Rose was inside, away from the wind, that she realized every muscle had been braced against its force. She relaxed into her seat with a little sigh and stretched her legs before her.

"You are really going to the Andrien Straits?" she asked, nodding her thanks as a sailor presented her with a platter of fresh fish.

"With all speed," the prince answered around a mouthful of biscuit. "Lord Varnet's discovery, if you recall."

"Yes, I remember," Rose said, breaking off a slice of biscuit and dipping it in oil. "Ashkii has impressed it on my mind forever. He's a great admirer of Varnet's, isn't he?"

"As is every sailor. The Andrien Straits opened up a new world. I used to pretend I had been with him . . ." He laughed, a little shamefaced. "Me and every other boy who ever punted on a millpond. The pass is damned tricky if you don't know it well."

"But I suppose you do?"

The prince merely smiled. "We'll lose them there."

Rose had been taught that a lapse of conversation at mealtimes was a crime to be laid at the door of the eldest lady present. But it seemed that the rules were a bit different on a ship. Meals were not mere social occasions attended by the overfed, and food was not something to be picked at while awaiting the next witticism or piece of gossip. Here, hunger was the issue, and she had learned it was perfectly permissible to relax in silence until the plates were emptied.

"So," the prince said conversationally, setting down his knife, "what do you have against Cristobal of Sorlain?"

Rose stilled, a bite halfway to her lips. "I? Nothing at all. I've never even met him."

"Then why have you changed course? A journey to Jexal is not without danger, the very thing you claimed you wanted to avoid."

This was a conversation Rose had meant to start herself, when she had decided on the best way to approach the matter. But now that he had brought it up, she was relieved.

"King Esteban was my father's friend, but Cristobal is unknown to me. Jexal seemed the safer route, though difficult to manage. I feared it was too much to ask of you."

"So you decided to wager for it instead?"

The prince did not sound angry, merely curious. Rose forced herself to hold his gaze. "It was a shoddy trick after all the kindness you have shown me. I cannot abide duplicity in others and am ashamed I stooped to it myself. There is no excuse for such behavior. I hope you will accept my apology."

"There is no need to apologize. It was a fair wager, lady, and I accepted it freely. I enjoyed the game right well." His lips curved in a wicked smile. "Nearly as much as the prize."

Had he really enjoyed it? She thought he had, but now she wasn't sure. The memory was too confused by her emotions for any measure of detachment. Not that she hadn't tried to remember exactly what had happened. Jehan knew she had thought of little else since they had parted.

One moment she was certain it had been an extraordinary experience that altered everything between them; in the next, she was equally sure that it changed nothing. She had hoped he would give her some sign of what it meant—and yet he had, earlier, when he laughed and walked away.

Likely every maiden wants to believe her first kiss a matter of cosmic import, Rose reminded herself sternly. At fourteen such delusions are excusable. At twenty-four, they are pathetic.

She tried for a sophisticated smile. "You are too kind."

"Not at all. Indeed, if you would like to play again, I am completely at your service."

What did *that* mean? *You are being pathetic again,* she thought, willing herself not to blush. *Feeble. Absolutely useless.*

"But I agree with you about Cristobal," the prince added, surprising her. "You *should* be wary of him. Particularly as he has lately gone a-wooing at Larken Castle."

"What?" Every muscle in Rose's body tensed with outrage. "Which one? Berengaria or Melisande?"

"I cannot say. There has been no announcement . . . yet.

Knowing Cristobal, Rose thought, *there may never be one.* By all accounts, he had been promised a dozen times at least, yet always managed to slip free before he reached the altar. But she also knew her cousins, who would not easily let such a prize escape.

"I see," she said evenly. "Well, I wish him joy."

Not that Cristobal would get that from either of her cousins. Really, it was the best vengeance she could wish on him, to be chained to one of them forever. But, oh, it wasn't fair. Between the two of them, her cousins had taken her title, her jewels, her chamber—even her place at table. Now one of them would leave Larken Castle to live in unimaginable splendor with *her* husband, without a single care more pressing than which gown would set off her slender figure to advantage or what jewel would best adorn her milk-white hands.

Rose stared down at her own hands, clasped before her on the table. Her skin lacked the exotic Jexlan luster of her mother's—or the cabin boy Beylik's—but was several shades darker than the cream so prized in Valinor. Her hair was not a jet-black waterfall or a froth of golden curls, but only a stubbornly waving brown. Even the crown of Sorlain could never disguise the fact that she was short and plain, though once she had imagined that it would, and that Cristobal would learn to love her in spite of her deficiencies.

"I'm sure he will have that," the prince said, "I think Cristobal was born for joy." Rose stared at him, surprised at the bitterness in his voice. "But that leaves us with the question of your future," he added quickly. "Do you really think Jexal is the answer?"

"I have family there."

"But they do not know you ... or you them. Jexlans do not take kindly to strangers, and I fear a woman of your ... spirit ... would have a difficult time fitting in among the tribes. Have you ever thought that you might do better to marry?"

The question was so unexpected that Rose laughed. "No, I have not. Why, do you have someone in mind?"

He did not smile. "I might."

He couldn't mean—no, of course not, she was being feeble again. It was someone else he was thinking of. Everyone knew the Prince of Venya was seeking an heiress, pereferably a royal one, with a family so powerful they could give him the support he so desperately needed. He might flirt—and more—with other women, but he had never offered marriage to even the wealthiest among them. He was surely not about to offer it to a penniless fugitive without so much as a leaky dinghy or a brass coin to bring to his cause.

Not that she wanted him to offer, of course she didn't, though she wouldn't mind another kiss ... She caught herself up sharply. It was her life at stake here, and she could not afford to lose her head over such a trifle as a kiss, even one that muddled her thoughts and set her blood afire. *Especially* a kiss like that. Particularly when given by a man she barely knew and did not trust, a man so completely unimpressed by the experience that he could talk of marrying her off to someone else without the slightest pretense of regret.

"It is a thought," she said neutrally.

"So you are not averse to marriage?"

"Not in principle, no, though I am particular."

"In what way?"

He was doing it again, watching her with those sharply slanted eyes, as though he hung upon her words. Beneath that penetrating gaze, Rose hardly knew where to look, let alone what to answer. The idea of marriage had been so far from her thoughts for so many years that it had not occurred to her as a solution to her problems. Yet now that it had been presented to her, she could not deny it had advantages.

"It's difficult to say ..."

"Try," the prince said, leaning his chin on his fist.

"He couldn't be a sailor," she began tentatively, "gone for months at a time. Or a soldier, either. Age is not important, though given my choice, I'd rather older than younger. The most important thing," she went on, warming to her subject, "is that he is . . . steady. Dependable."

The prince made a wry face. "What of wit? Charm?"

"Vastly overrated," Rose answered crisply. "My uncle's court is full of charming gallants. They practice their smiles in the glass and sharpen their wit on anyone they think is weak. I—"

"Did they think you weak?" the prince interrupted.

"Yes," Rose admitted with some reluctance, then lifted her chin and added, "but only because I wanted them to think it."

"I see. So wit and youth and charm are expendable, dependability is not. Is there anything else that you require?"

"The most important thing of all is honesty. Too many people lie as easily as breathing—I should know, I was one of them for years. I am not proud of it, but I could see no other way to live. 'Tis what I fear most about Jexal," she confided, "that I will end up as a pawn between my uncles, mired in some web of intrigue and deception and jostling for power."

"It is not a groundless fear. Your uncles are both strong rulers with a profitable alliance, but it is no secret that they detest each other. Hand either one a weapon, and he will wield it. Not openly—both of them need the alliance too much for that—but the *Melakh* is renowned for subtlety and Richard is a master of intrigue. If I were you, lady, I would avoid Jexal at all costs."

"I take your point." Rose sighed. "Still, I do have cousins somewhere . . . All I ask is a quiet life," she burst out. "Is that really so impossible? I don't need a castle or riches—"

"Just a steady, honest fellow, not too young and completely lacking charm. That shouldn't be too difficult," the prince said encouragingly. "Come to think of it, I know a goatherd on Serilla who might suit. I've often marked him of a morning with his flock, an oldish sort who never fails to greet me with a grunt as he goes by. If it's dependable you want, you'll have it. He creaks up the mountain every morning and down again at night, steady as the tide. Now, I've never heard him speak—I don't think anyone has—so I cannot guarantee that he isn't a very witty fellow. But in any venture, you must accept some risk."

Rose tried to frown, but spoiled it by laughing. "I thank you, but no."

"No? Don't tell me you mean to be difficult about this! I suppose you want a nobleman? Perhaps . . . a prince?"

"I do not look so high." Rose forced a laugh, willing herself not to blush as she stared down at her dish. She picked up a biscuit and turned it between her fingers. "A knight would do—even a yeoman, if his family is respectable. He really must be educated, I do insist on that. Kind, well mannered, honest—"

"You mentioned that before."

"Did I? Oh, yes, that's right—" Flustered, she broke her biscuit into tiny pieces. "A country knight, perhaps, one who is content to be no more. Certainly not a courtier. Oh, and he must be brave, of course, and kind and generous and honorable—"

"In short, a paragon of manhood." The prince sighed, for what reason she could not begin to guess, then grinned and reached to tug at a lock of her hair. "What you need right now is a tie-mate."

"A what?" Rose asked, wondering if this was some Venyan marriage custom.

"Someone to plait your hair for you." He stood and moved behind Rose's chair. "The men do it for each other, turn and turn about. I used to be rather good at it, though it's been years . . ."

"Really, there is no need—" she began, though not with much conviction, for his fingers had begun to wind through her hair, sending a delicious shiver down her spine.

"These are no good," he said, ignoring her feeble protest as he tossed her woolen net and pins before her on the table. "Wait. Don't move."

He turned, reached into a drawer, and produced a comb. "You're all knotted."

"Thank you, but—"

"Just sit."

She braced herself but barely felt a tug as he teased out the tangles with more patience than any of her serving women had ever shown. He seemed to have forgotten that the *Lord Marva* was in swift pursuit. Or else, she thought, he was so accustomed to pursuit that it had lost the power to alarm.

"What a lot of hair you have," he remarked, "'tis a shame to keep it hidden in that thing. Turn a little, would you, and tip your head back."

"I can do it myself—"

"But I want to. I think I'll give you the four-plait—my specialty, guaranteed to hold in a typhoon."

She gave up and rested her head against the chair back. Why not? It wasn't as though she had anything else to do. She was headed for the Andrien Straits, which gave her at least a fortnight to consider her next move. Tomorrow—or the next day—she would begin to worry. Today she was safe aboard the gallant *Quest,* protected by her trusty crew. And the Prince of Venya was combing out her hair in long, luxurious strokes, until she wanted to curl up in his lap and purr.

Chapter 19

FLORIAN was thoughtful as he passed the comb through the princess's hair. His thoughts were busy with a hundred things at once: calculating the course, measuring the provisions, weighing the well-being of the crew against the need for haste. But the *Quest* had outrun Richard's ships before, so these considerations occupied only a small portion of his mind. Another part imagined what he would say to the council when they met, which depended on the woman sitting before him now.

And how quickly he could convince her to marry him.

Well, now he knew her fantasy. *Steady,* she had said. *Dependable.* Neither word had ever been applied to the Prince of Venya—for good reason. He felt more comfortable with *educated.* Thanks to his council, he was certain he could measure up in that respect. What were the other qualities she'd named? Kind—well, he hoped so—honorable, certainly, brave enough for most things and as generous as the next man. But there was one more thing, wasn't there? What she had called the most important thing of all.

Honesty.

That was a bit of a problem. Actually, more than a bit. Given her distaste for intrigue and her fear of being used as a political pawn, it was a huge concern. Florian did mean to use her—from the purest of motives, of course . . . but wasn't that what anyone would say in his position?

Damn all this, he thought impatiently, *I will just explain the situation and ask her straight out. If she says yes, the matter is settled. If she says no . . .*

Well, she couldn't say no. Or she could say it, but it would make no difference. Which meant there wasn't really any question to be asked, but only a matter of persuasion.

"Rosamund is a Jexlan name, isn't it?" he said.

"Yes, my mother's choice," she answered dreamily. "I like to think it was a courtesy my father gave to her, though I suspect he just couldn't be bothered to come up with one himself."

"Either way, it is a lovely name."

Her lips curved in a smile. "It doesn't feel like mine now."

No true Jexlan would say the same. But then, no Jexlan would allow their name to be altered in any manner. Sigurd, a master of all desert lore, had once explained the Jexlan naming customs to Florian.

Queen Najet had apparently had high hopes to honor—or burden—a mere scrap of an infant with the name of Rosamund. Florian was only passingly familiar with Jexlan legend, yet even he had heard something of this tale. It involved a flower—the Rose of the World—that bloomed in an enchanted garden at the very heart of the world (which, of course, was Jexal), and the sorcerer's curse that had turned paradise to barren desert.

The rose still bloomed, the Jexlans said, though no mortal eye could look upon it now, and one day it would heal their blighted land. Should it die, the desert tribes would perish. They had all manner of rituals to ensure the continued existence of the rose, most of which no outlander could ever know.

Rose of the World indeed, Florian thought, smothering a grin. He wondered what the elders of the tribe would make of Queen Najet's presumption. Najet's daughter was only half-Jexlan, after all, and had been engendered in far-off Valinor.

And it was in Valinor, at Richard's court, that she had learned to fear—and recognize—deception.

His misstep last night had put her on her guard, and the kiss they had shared, sweet though it had been, had obviously not robbed her of her wits. He doubted she would lose her head over the bold pirate's blandishments or the world-weary rake. If he wanted to disarm her, he would have to give her something real.

He cast about for some piece of himself that he could bear to part with. It was unexpectedly difficult to find one. He had played so many roles for so many years that he hardly knew himself where they left off and he began. So go back to the beginning, he thought. The beginning . . . when had that been?

"Years ago," he began haltingly, "when I was sixteen, I went to Venya. It was all a great secret, of course, no one was meant to know I was in the country and everyone was terribly careful. Not careful enough, as it turned out . . ."

No, he thought, *not that tale, I cannot.* Not the treachery that had alerted Richard's men to his whereabouts, or his flight into the marshes, or the devastating price his supporters had paid. He scowled, drawing the comb through thick brown hair cascading down the chair back, waving almost to the floor. A half-formed memory shimmered in his mind of the time in Venya before Richard's men had found him. He pursued it, speaking almost without thought.

"One day I was sent into the forest to meet my next escort, and he was delayed, so I had to wait an hour by a forest pool."

It sprang into his mind, then, very sharp and clear, the faces of the people who had bidden him farewell, glowing with hope and happiness.

"I thought I remembered everything about Venya," he said, "but once I got there, I found there was much I had forgotten. I was not used to forests, or anything on land, really, not beyond the docks. It was very quiet. Too quiet. The silence seemed to bear down on me, and it felt very odd to be cut off from the horizon. The light was different, too; it didn't seem to come from anywhere, but it was all around me, very soft and green. It made me . . . uncomfortable, not knowing where I was or how to get my bearings."

Uncomfortable. He almost laughed at the understatement. After ten minutes he had been a mass of jangling nerves, trapped and helpless in an alien landscape. The worst part about it was that Venya had not changed; it was exactly as he had dreamed of it. It was he who did not belong there anymore.

"After a time, though," he continued, "I began to notice things: the tall oak trees around me, the scents of earth and plant, all the little noises I hadn't heard at first. Small animals hurried through the undergrowth . . . and the birds! There were so many birds, so busy up above. I couldn't see them, but I could hear them, and it seemed that once I'd known their names, but I couldn't quite remember. It was like a dream . . . or the memory of a dream I'd once had long ago . . ."

His voice trailed off, his hands stilled. The princess seemed to have fallen asleep; her breath came evenly, her face was peaceful and relaxed, dark lashes fanned against the soft skin of her cheeks.

"I sat beside a little pool," he went on quietly, speaking almost to himself, "and a shaft of sunlight, very small, found its way through the leaves above and fell just on the water. It was so clear, so still that I could see right down to the bottom, carpeted with last year's leaves. The colors were"—he lifted her hair and let it slide through his fingers—"so . . . rich. So various. Always when I think of Venya, it is that forest I see, that hour by the pool that I remember."

"It sounds very beautiful."

He started a little at the sound of the princess's voice, and looked down to find her watching him. For the first time he noticed that her eyes were not plain brown as he had thought, but flecked with tiny bits of green and gold, like sunlight upon leaf and bough and earth.

"A subtle beauty," he said slowly, "one must take the time to look for it. But no less beautiful for that."

She smiled and closed her eyes. "I hope you will see it again soon."

"So do I."

He gathered the thick sheaf of her hair and divided it, his hands faltering at first, then moving more swiftly as they remembered their old skill.

"Who was your tie-mate?" she asked after a moment.

Florian clenched his jaw hard. Damn her perception—once again she'd managed to ask the one question he wanted least to answer. But he was the one who had opened the door and invited her inside. Now that she had taken a step forward, he could not afford to slam it in her face.

"His name was Rhysiel," he said, biting off the words.

"Was?" Of course she'd caught the past tense, had he expected any less? "I'm sorry—was he a good friend?"

"He was my only friend." Florian laughed shortly. "That was a joke between us," he added in answer to her questioning look. "After Venya fell, I was kept . . . apart. With the council. After nearly five years of that, Ewan decided I needed a companion closer to my own age. Rhysiel was the son of a Venyan noble who had died defending his king and queen, a fitting companion for a prince—or so the council thought at first. Once they came to know him . . ." He laughed again, this time more naturally. "Rhys was not quite what they'd envisioned."

"What was wrong with him?"

"That would depend on who you asked. The council thought him a terrible influence. They had me so well trained by then that I never dreamt of questioning an order. But Rhys was dead lazy and didn't care who knew it, and if he could find no mischief to get into, he made his own. Any day not spent in the pursuit of comfort or amusement was a wasted day to him. I was horrified—at first. But he made me laugh, and . . . well, once I got over my shock, I grew to like him well. So, yes, he was a good friend—and my only friend."

"I'm sorry," Rosamund said again, and now her eyes were warm with sympathy. "What happened to him?"

"He was with me on that first journey into Venya, the one that ended in the marshes. The council did not want him to go, but I insisted on bringing him along." This was hard, even worse than Florian had thought it would be. He was careful not to look away as he continued. "Rhys was never meant for the hardships of a soldier's life. He said so himself—daily—but I didn't listen. My mistake. No sooner did we arrive in Venya than he sought out Richard's men and struck his bargain."

"He *sold* you? To my uncle?"

"Indeed. I thought you might have seen him at Richard's court."

"No." She shook her head. "No, never, I would remember."

"I will find him one day," Florian said, finishing the plait. "He knows me well enough to be sure of that. I doubt he's slept a night since he heard that I survived."

"How did you?"

"That is a story for another day"—he flipped the braid over her shoulder—"and duty calls. Will you join me later for supper?"

"Yes," she answered without a moment's hesitation.

Florian could barely force himself to smile as he left her with a bow. It had been ten years since he'd spoken Rhysiel's name. He had thought that surely so much time and a host of small betrayals would have diminished the impact of that first one, yet it had not. Perhaps, he told himself, he should take it as a timely reminder of the danger of letting anyone get that close to him again.

Not that Rosamund would ever pose him such a threat. She was cleverer than she let on, and her courage in Riall could not be doubted. For that alone he would have liked her, and there was no denying that she stirred his blood. But he was in no danger of losing his head over her or any woman.

Over the next few hours, as the *Lord Marva* gained upon them steadily, he was snappish with the crew, earning many a startled glance before he took himself in hand. His bad temper wasn't their fault. It was hers. Or no, he amended, it was his for being too squeamish—or too proud—to simply take what he needed. He wanted her willing, but surely there was some other way to win her than to tear open old wounds for her amusement.

How the devil did one go about wooing a woman? Florian had never attempted it—he'd never had to. They pursued him—or rather, they pursued the Prince of Venya, which was a different thing entirely. The Prince of Venya wasn't real, he was a chimera. He was every woman's secret fantasy, the blank page on which they wrote the tale they wanted most to hear. Since his birth soon after Florian's escape from Richard's soldiers in the marshes, the Prince of Venya had been both bane and blessing, though in the beginning Florian had been as dazzled by him as the rest.

No one could have been more surprised than Florian himself when ladies who had never glanced twice at the awkward, penniless young scion of a fallen house were not only looking at him, but talking to him, too, and making little excuses to touch his hand or cheek, their words and touches underscored by languishing looks that were by turns fascinating, bewildering, and terrifying. When the touches became more intimate, the words more explicit, he could not help but understand their meaning, though he could not fathom why so many ladies had developed such a sudden and inexplicable desire to instruct him in the arts of love.

At sixteen, still devastated by his disastrous journey into Venya, he had not stopped to question such incredible good fortune. His only fear was that his performance would not live up to expectations. But he was eager—desperate, he thought now—to please, and they were determined he should please them. They all but handed him a script; he only had play the part to be rewarded with a night of dizzying delight and a closeness he had naively mistaken for affection.

As the years went by, he *did* question his good fortune, and the answer was not hard to find. It wasn't he who made those ladies scream with pleasure. Oh, he always did his best—and he'd had some very imaginative tutors—but when all was said and done, there were only so many things two people could do in bed and he doubted he did them that much differently than other men. But the Prince of Venya was something else again.

Brilliant. Dashing. Amazingly perceptive, he had the magical ability to discover a woman's deepest desires and satisfy them all. At least the ladies believed he did . . . because they wanted to believe it, and there was nothing as erotic to a woman as her own imagination.

Once Florian realized that he was the living equivalent of the pleasure-sticks so favored by the ladies of Moravia, he could never summon quite the same enthusiasm for the games. Which hadn't entirely stopped him from playing them, or not all at once—until the night a year ago when he had fled Kendrick's Mine and known the time for play was over.

But Rosamund was not a game. She was his future princess. If he had to woo her, then he would, though he was no more the paragon she'd described than he was the Prince of Venya. But first he had to lose the *Lord Marva,* which, he noted with annoyance, had gained another half league while he was lost in thought.

Chapter 20

ROSE drifted upward from the depths of sleep, her pleasant dream dissolving into the familiar sound of holystones upon the deck. It was a far nicer sound to wake to than the birds that used to chatter outside her window at Larken Castle.

She stretched, yawned, and closed her eyes again. In the past weeks she had discovered a new passion for sleep. For years, it had been something she did because she must, and she had submitted to it grudgingly, usually far into the night, starting up at the least sound and waking before dawn. But then, she had never slept in a hanging cot before, surely the most wonderful invention of all time. Now she no sooner put her head down than she was gone, and nothing at all could wake her before she had slept her fill.

She dozed a while longer, swaying gently with the motion of the ship. There was no point in getting up, for she would be much in the way if she ventured on deck before the ritual was completed. Every morning was the same. No matter how hot the chase—and in the past week it had been very hot indeed—the decks must still be cleaned, the brass polished to a burnished glow, the sailors fed, the glass turned, and the bell rung.

It was a very ordered little world, complete unto itself. And it was ruled, absolutely and completely, by the man who was even now at his place on the quarterdeck, a mug in his hand and his eyes everywhere at once.

Rose didn't need to see him to know exactly how he looked, amber eyes narrowed against the rising sun and his old black shirt fluttering in the wind. It would be no good speaking to him, for his mind was far away. They said in Valinor that the *Quest* was speeded on by Venyan magic—which surely must be so. How else could they continue to evade the *Lord Marva,* the pride of Valinor, sleek and new and rigged with an intricate arrangement of sail that even Beylik had admitted was the last word in ingenuity?

Rose had watched closely, hoping to see how it was done, but so far whatever magical rites the prince performed had been carried out beyond her sight. But certainly there was an uncanny bond between the Prince of Venya and his ship. He was aware of every movement and could sense a crossed line or a sloppily sheeted sail even when his back was turned.

The slap of cloths against the deck slowed, then stopped. As happened every morning, the last trace of sleepiness vanished and Rose leapt from her cot, eager to begin the day.

FLORIAN, perched high among the rigging, saw with satisfaction that they had gained at least two leagues during the night. It wasn't enough, but it was something. The past sen'night had been a nightmare of murderous shoals negotiated at a speed just short of suicidal, but the Andrien Straits were behind them now.

At one point he had considered going straight through and taking refuge in Ilindria, but even Ashkii could not guarantee their welcome with Richard's ship so hard upon their heels. The *Qaletaqa*—damn his eyes—played a cautious game. Venya was a question; Valinor an acknowledged force in the Western Sea, and Richard, clever bastard that he was, had already made overtures of friendship to Ilindria. To force the *Qaletaqa* to a decision now was a risk that Florian dared not take.

So it was round the straights and back again, and where they would go next was a decision Florian must make very soon. But at least he had a breathing space. For the first time in seven days, he was not flying from one peril to the next, fully expecting disaster to overtake them at any moment.

He glanced down at the deck and was reminded of the problem he had shelved in the face of more pressing concerns. There she stood, his future princess, talking to Beylik down below. She had taken a great liking to the lad, it seemed, for in the past days he had often noticed her speaking to him in Jexlan. She was doing so now; he could see her hands forming graceful patterns as she chatted on. Beylik listened attentively, dark head bent, his own hands clasped firmly behind his back.

Florian slid lightly down the backstays and landed just beside them, startling a soft cry from Rosamund. "Good morning, my lady," he said with a flourishing bow.

"Do you always do that?" she said crossly. "Appear out of nowhere?"

"I try." He grinned at Beylik, and the boy smiled before leaving them.

Rosamund watched him go, a small frown creasing her brow. "He won't talk to me."

"Has he been discourteous?" Florian asked, surprised.

"No, it isn't that. He won't talk to me in Jexlan. Oh, he listens, and he understands everything I say, but he won't speak a word of it."

"What shall it be for him, my lady? Thumbscrews? The rack?"

"Very amusing. But I don't see why—"

"Beylik's reasons are his own and, short of torture, I doubt he'll give them up. It matters not to me what language he speaks. He writes a fine, clear hand and makes a damned fine pot of kava."

Rosamund glared at him. "You don't care *why* he won't speak his own language? No, I don't suppose you do, so long as you are well served by your *beylik*."

Florian held up his hands. "Don't look at me like that, lady, I only call him as he calls himself."

"Because he believes that his name was taken from him."

"It *was* taken from him, part and parcel of the sale. Or so Jexlan custom has it. By his law, Beylik can buy it back—if his master is inclined to sell—or win it in a duel against whatever champion his master cares to name. As I do not own Beylik, but merely freed him from the galleys, I am of no use to him."

"Unless you were to buy him and restore his name to him," Rosamund retorted sharply.

"Why do you care, lady, what becomes of a Jexlan *beylik*?"

"Beylik!" she exclaimed, disgusted. "If it had been me—if I had been bought and sold in some market, at least I would still be who I am, no matter what they called me. But he—he is nothing, at least in his own eyes. I do not know the *Venyan* custom, but in

Valinor, any man, no matter what his station, is entitled to the protection of his liege lord."

She was enchanting this morning with her hands fisted on her hips, the wind whipping fresh color into her cheeks, and the light of battle in her gold-flecked eyes. He wondered how he'd ever been so blind as to think her plain. Or dull. There had been no time to woo her properly, but when he had the chance to dine with her, he had found her good company.

She had a trick of being silent when he needed most to think and distracting him from care when he had a moment to relax. Her lively curiosity about the ship was something new to Florian, and he often found himself answering as directly as he would any member of his crew. Had she really been one of them, he would have given her full marks for close attention and a faultless memory for what she'd learned. But of course she wasn't. No member of his crew would dare challenge his decisions as she was doing now for the sake of a boy she thought ill-used.

"It is the same in Venya," he answered mildly. "But I took Beylik from the *Golden Net*—your uncle's ship—and I doubt Richard would treat with me for the legal ownership of a galley slave he believes I stole from him. I pay Beylik a fair wage and train him as I do the other lads, and I have told him more than once that Jexlan custom holds no sway with me. What he chooses to believe is his concern."

"I worry for him," Rosamund said. "He is . . . lost. I can see it in his eyes. You must watch over him carefully, my lord."

"Beylik will be fine. He's on the *Quest* now, isn't he? Everyone knows there is no finer berth for a sailor!"

"Oh, everyone knows that, do they?"

"I heard it in a song," Florian answered gravely, "so of course it must be true." He turned and rested his elbows on the rail, squinting out to sea. "Lady, do you know who has command of the *Lord Marva* now?"

"Alamont."

He shook his head. "I know Alamont. He is an able seaman, but no more. This man"—he nodded toward the stern— "is very much more. He seems to know what I will do before I've thought of it myself. No Valinorian captain I have encountered knows the Andrien Straits as well as this one."

"I'm sorry." She made that pretty, helpless gesture he had come to know so well. "I wish I could say. Richard never had the captains up to the castle as my father did. He was so proud of his fleet," she added with a sigh.

"With good reason. In your father's day, the fleet of Valinor could not be matched, not even by Sorlain. When I think of the care he put into his ships, the brilliant men—"

Florian stopped mid-sentence, struck by a sudden thought.

"I know," Rosamund said. "So many have been lost since my uncle took the throne. They've gone to Sorlain or Moravia—"

"Or into retirement," Florian said quietly.

"Like Lord Varnet?" Once again, she had followed his thoughts with unerring accuracy. "Richard treated him disgracefully; I cannot blame Varnet in the least. After all his courage—and all the time he spent on his memoirs! Such knowledge belongs to the world, not Valinor alone. Richard behaved like a barbarian, suppressing his work and ordering every copy burned. Such a waste—I never even got to read it."

"You can borrow mine," Florian said, "if you promise to treat it gently. It took me years to find and cost a king's ransom, though the chart of the Andrien Straits alone was worth the price. Varnet is still alive, isn't he?"

"Oh, yes. Or he was last time I heard, living deep in the country with Hesperia—Lady Varnet, that is, though she prefers to be called Hesperia. At least she did," Rosamund added wistfully, "when she was at court. I can just remember her—and him—and, oh, it was so thrilling when he came back after everyone had given him up for lost. We had a whole week of feasting, speeches in the square, dancing every night. He was so distinguished and she was so lovely—so exotic—and both of them so *nice,* not proud at all. They had five children last I heard, though by now there may be more."

"But he must be very old!"

"Not very, no. Why, he was hardly five-and-twenty when he made his voyage."

"So young as that? I did not know."

A shout drew Florian's attention upward, where some of the younger members of the crew were skylarking among the rigging. His gaze rested on his third mate, Ashkii, who was struggling along far behind the rest. He was scowling, his pale skin flushed with exertion, and when he came to a seemingly impassible space, he stopped dead, obviously having no idea where to go from there.

At least he was trying. When Ashkii had first come aboard, he'd been terrified of heights. His progress had been good—but then, he had a strong motive to succeed.

Before Varnet had opened the Andrien Sea to trade, the Ilindrians lived in complete isolation. Varnet had stayed only a short time before sailing off in search of new adventure, but he had clearly made a good impression on at least one member of the royal family. In due course, Ashkii arrived, the first halfling born to them. If not for his mother's impeccable lineage, he would have been exposed at birth.

Times had changed; halflings were no longer considered freakish oddities, but that tacit acceptance had come too late for the first. Ilindrians didn't set much store by fathers as a rule, but in that, as well, Ashkii was the exception, though he never claimed any connection to Lord Varnet. Florian alone knew why Ashkii had left his home and what he hoped to find.

The Ilindrian was trying very hard to adjust to his new life. When one of the boys called back to him—an insult, judging by the tone—he did not fly into a fury as he would have done before. His scowl deepened, but he called back something that made the others burst into laughter.

The one who had first spoken—it was Beylik, Florian saw, looking merry as a grig, so much for the princess's fears—laughed as heartily as the rest as he made a swift descent to stop just beside the third mate. A short argument ensued, and after a good deal of hand waving, Ashkii kicked off his low boots. Beylik stared, which was only natural, as Ashkii had but four toes upon each foot. The fifth and smallest was a curving talon that the Ilindrian had been at great pains to conceal.

Florian could hardly blame him; Ashkii had taken more than his share of insults about the feather growing from his temple. Beylik raised his head, his lips moved . . . and Ashkii's laughter floated down to the deck. Then they were off again, Beylik moving slowly—at least for him—with the Ilindrian trailing in his wake.

It would be a sorry thing if Ashkii's first meeting with his father came at the wrong end of a sword. It would be more than sorry for the rest of them. It was likely to be deadly. Florian glanced back at the *Lord Marva,* and his guess at whose hand was on the helm sharpened to a certainty, like an icy finger laid upon his neck.

"Lady, I must leave you now," he said. "But if you'll come on deck before sunset, I can give you a glimpse of Venya."

"Venya? Do you mean to go ashore?"

"Abandon ship? Not while I have breath. Varnet may have charted half the nine seas," he added grimly, "but when it comes to Venyan waters, I believe he's met his match."

Chapter 21

ROSE was on deck long before sunset, hoping for a glimpse of the azure cliffs of Venya. They were famed in song and story, and she had always longed to see them for herself. But it was Venya's prince she watched, and for once she had no trouble knowing what he felt: joy and sorrow, longing and regret, they were all there on his face, plain for anyone to see. Then he was gone, leaning over the rail as the log was drawn aboard.

"Six by the helm, seven by the deep . . ."

Two voices called out the depth in a rhythmic chant. Rose glanced up and caught her breath as the cliffs rose to her right. The westering sun was caught in peridot and adamite, topaz and sapphire, the facets reflecting back the light in a thousand shimmering shades of blue. She leaned over the rail, gazing at a dark spot on the cliffs, the only flaw in its perfection. Looking more closely, she noticed a thin trail winding down the cliff into the sheltered cove below, as though the very stones bled into the sea.

"Kendrick's Mine," a voice said beside her.

She turned to Sigurd, who was staring moodily at the cliffs with his elbows resting on the rail.

"That?" Rose pointed at the gaping wound. "That is Kendrick's Mine? Oh, how *could* he?"

She was filled with helpless anger at the sight of such beauty marred forever, anger that sharpened into rage as they passed by the cove. It must have been beautiful once, before the water had been sullied by the steady stream of filth flowing downward from the mine.

"You tell me, lady," Sigurd said. "You know your uncle."

"I do not know him," Rose said. "I cannot say why he would do such a thing. Perhaps he cannot endure such beauty to exist only for itself, but must somehow turn it to his own profit."

Sigurd glanced at her sideways. "It is . . . magnificent. Yet people starve beneath its shadow." His eyes moved to the prince. "What ruler would not be tempted by such abundance, just waiting to be tapped?"

"Him." Rose nodded toward the prince. "He never went after the gems, Sigurd. Did you not hear him say so?"

"Yes, and I was right glad to hear it. After we spoke, I realized how heavily it had been weighing on my mind. I inquired among the crew, but none of them could tell me anything—well, nothing save that he did indeed travel to Venya."

"But for some other purpose," she said. Now that she had come to know the prince a little better, she thought he must have had a good reason for his presence at Kendrick's Mine. He simply did not speak of it because . . . well, no doubt he had a good reason for that, too.

"Of course," Sigurd agreed. "Not that I ever wanted to believe the rumors—but they were so persistent—which just goes to show how easy it is to confuse truth with legend! Especially where the prince is concerned."

"Yet I think many of the legends concerning him contain at least a grain of truth."

"The good ones, certainly," Sigurd said, smiling, "though in this, at least, it seems they were entirely mistaken. Perhaps," he added casually, "it was for the lady's sake that he risked the journey to Venya."

"What lady is that?" Rose asked.

"The one he brought with him from the colony on Serilla. A young *filidh,* the daughter—or is it the granddaughter?—of the High Magaea of Venya. The crew was quite taken with her; apparently she is wondrous fair, though something of a mystery. She spent most of her time closeted with the prince. The crew barely saw hide nor hair of either one of them during the entire voyage! No doubt they were conferring over Venyan matters, though there were many who thought— But we both know that rumor is not to be relied upon. After all, there has been no formal announcement . . . yet."

So there had been a woman with him. She should have known.

There was always some woman or other tangled up in the Prince of Venya's stories. Oddly enough, they were never old or plain or bent upon some ordinary errand. But if it was a matter of state that had taken him to Venya, why had he not said so?

She remembered the way he had averted his eyes from hers when she asked him why he had gone to Kendrick's Mine. It would have been easy enough to tell her the truth, even if that truth had been that he could not in honor tell her. But there had been no mention of honor. Or of Venya. Certainly none of a young and beautiful *filidh*. *A tedious story,* was what he had said, *I will not bore you with it.*

This is none of my concern, she told herself fiercely, trying hard not to remember the feeling of his hands in her hair, his lips parting hers, his arms tightening around her as the strength drained from her limbs . . . Or later, the longing in his voice as he spoke of the Venyan forests, the pain as he told her of his betrayal by his only friend, things she had been so sure he had never confided to another . . .

"Lady," Sigurd said, breaking into her thoughts, "please do not think me impertinent, but . . . I understand that you have left your uncle's keeping, and I am certain you must have had good reason for it and for your decision to seek the prince's aid. But he is consumed with his own cares—as well he should be—and I cannot help but wonder what will become of you. Do you have a plan?"

"Yes," she answered, "I do. I mean to seek out my Jexlan kin."

"A wise decision," Sigurd said. "You know I spent many years in Jexal. It is my home in every way that matters. I have been thinking—hoping—to go back. I should never have left. I thought—when I had the chance to serve the prince—" He smiled wryly. "But I find the life of a ship's surgeon is not quite what I imagined. If I can be of any assistance—if you need a guide through the desert—you can rely on me entirely. I know my way about quite well and am familiar with the customs . . ."

He trailed to a stop, his fair cheeks flushed, then added in a fervent burst, "You needn't fear that I would take advantage of the honor. Your uncle—the *Melakh*—was my patron. I know what is due to him and his."

"My uncle does not know me," Rose said, "and he is Richard's ally. I had hoped to find my cousins—the children of my mother's sister."

"Sammar and Rihana? They would be overjoyed to have you, though I would suggest that you go first to your uncle. Richard's ally he might be, but kinship is far more important to him than the Valinorian connection. I attended him during an illness, lady, and he spoke often of his lost sister. He bitterly regrets sending her to Valinor."

"Still," Rose said slowly, "the Jexlans rely upon the Valinorian trade. Regret is one thing, but he has a duty to his people."

"Yes, that is so. But your uncle grows old and sees things very differently than he once did. Kinship ties are at the very heart of Jexal, and now, with death approaching, the *Melakh* looks beyond this world to the next. His conscience is uneasy. Given the chance to atone, I can assure you he would take it. It would give him such joy to do you honor! And if you are . . . temporarily out of funds, do not worry. I have saved more than enough to make the journey."

"You are too kind—" she began, but he cut her off.

"No, lady, not at all. It would give me great pleasure to restore you to your family—and in all truth, you could do me a great service if you would. Much as I have longed to return, I did not see how it could be done. I gave up a good place at the university, and they were not altogether pleased with me for leaving as I did. One word from your uncle would make all the difference."

Rose studied him thoughtfully. As pleasant and attentive as Sigurd had always been to her, she could never quite bring herself to like him. In part, it was for Beylik's sake, though she knew it was unfair to condemn Sigurd for believing what he had been taught. Now she wondered if her coolness sprang from another cause, as well, that he told her the very truths about the Prince of Venya that she did not want to hear. Still, he seemed sincere in this, even to admitting his own motives . . .

"I thank you for your honesty," she said.

Sigurd beamed at her. "Then we are agreed?"

This was what she had wanted, wasn't it, the chance to find a place where she belonged? She should be leaping at this opportunity. "I will ask the prince where he can put us ashore," she said slowly, "then we can—"

"Lady, it would not be wise to announce our plan too openly. The prince is committed to Venya's good, and you are King Richard's niece. I doubt he will surrender a potentially valuable hostage—"

"Hostage?" Rose interrupted sharply. "No, Sigurd, I am nothing of the sort. The prince has sheltered me in need, and it is I who was reluctant to leave the safety of the *Quest* until my plans were formed."

"I—well—" He bit his lip, staring up at the cliffs. Then he squared his shoulders and turned to her. "Lady, it grieves me to say this, but that is not what the prince has said to me. He told me plainly that he was not certain what use he would make of you, but the decision would be his, made for Venya's benefit, with no regard for your wishes in the matter."

"He *said* that?"

"Upon my honor. I beg you not to reveal our plans to him, but wait until such time as we can slip away."

She searched his face, and he met her gaze without flinching. "I will think about it."

"Think quickly, lady. It cannot be long before we make land; our provisions are perilously low. In the meantime, I beg you to be careful. If the prince suspects that you want to leave the ship, he will take measures to ensure that you do not."

"You think he would imprison me?" she asked incredulously.

"Only as a last resort. The Prince of Venya has no need of shackles to keep a lady at his beck. His reputation must be known to you. Take care, my lady, and remember what he himself has said, that he means to use you as he will for Venya's good."

Before Rose could answer, the ship heeled sharply and the cup she had been holding flew from her hand. She took the opportunity to step away from Sigurd and chase it across the deck. Just before it rolled into the sea, the prince leaned down and picked it up. He handed it to her without taking his eyes off the water.

"Five by the helm," the boy chanted, and the prince lifted one hand. The ship heeled again and Rose caught the rail. The water here was as brilliant as the cliffs above, so clear she could see right down to the bottom. It was alive with fish, flashing by like living rainbows. She caught her breath and leaned closer to the water.

A long, dark shape undulated through the shadow of the *Quest,* scattering the fish in all directions. A shark? Or no, not a fish at all, for surely those were arms. She froze, her startled cry dying on her lips when the creature turned, looked straight into her face . . . and smiled.

She leaned far over the rail, but the merrow was gone. If indeed it had ever been there. Rose stared until she was dizzy, but she saw no sign of it again.

But there were many other things to see, a whole world before her eyes. She stayed at the rail, her eyes moving between the water and the prince, thinking of all that Sigurd had said. They drifted along, barely moving, as the sun sank into the sea, the silence broken only by the voice of the boy calling out the depth. At last the sun vanished completely, and the world below faded into shadows against shadows. Rose straightened with a little sigh and was instantly aware of the tension on deck. Every eye was fixed on the prince, who stood by the railing with the boy.

"Five by the deep," he called, and the men went completely still. The prince lifted his hand again, and silence was absolute as they waited for his signal.

"Six by the helm."

Another flick of the hand, and the ship moved almost imperceptibly. "Eight by the deep," the boy cried, and the men released a collective breath.

Rose leaned far out and stared back at the *Lord Marva,* sitting motionless at the mouth of the cove.

"HE'LL never get through. He can't."

King Richard's sorcerer gripped the rail of the *Lord Marva,* straining forward as the *Quest* vanished into the shadow of the cliff.

"A shallow draught, a good pilot . . ." Lord Varnet shrugged. "It has been done before."

"By him?"

Varnet nodded.

"I *told* you to stop him before he got here," the sorcerer snarled. "I told you—"

"If I could have caught him, I would have done so. And now . . ." He shrugged, doing his best to look regretful.

"And now *what?*"

"If he goes to ground, there is no more I can do."

"Then you'd better pray he doesn't go to ground. Not if you expect to see your lady and children again."

Varnet stiffened. "King Richard commanded my skill, and that I have given. What more do you require?"

"The Venyan. That's what the king requires. Until he has him, the terms still hold."

When the sorcerer was gone, Varnet stood unmoving for a time, eyes fixed on the cliffs. Then he turned and strode to his cabin. A few minutes later, a light tap sounded on the door.

"Come."

The first mate entered. "Are we going back?"

"No. Here is the new course."

"But they're saying the Venyan's gone to ground."

Varnet shook his head. "He's going through."

The first mate frowned. "You sound so sure. Not that I'm arguing, sir," he added quickly, "I'm just wondering what makes you think that."

A humorless smile touched Varnet's lips. "It is what I'd do in his place."

"But it's mad! The wreckers make a good living from those waters."

"For most people, it would be mad," Varnet agreed. "But not for everyone. He'll make it through all right. And when he gets to the other side, we will be waiting."

Chapter 22

ROSE stared into the darkness of her cabin, wondering what had woken her. The night was very still, the ship moving steadily through the water.

Then she realized what it was. The silence. By now the holystones should be scraping the deck, and yet they weren't. She dressed quickly and hurried up as the last stars were fading from the sky.

Venya was behind them, a huddled shadow off the stern. Ahead stretched the open sea. The prince was on the quarterdeck, a place she did not dare approach without an invitation.

"Come up, lady."

How did he know? He hadn't turned, and she would have sworn she hadn't made a sound. Beylik appeared silently to hand her a mug, then vanished without a word. She sipped the hot brew gratefully and waited for the prince to speak.

"What do you see?" he called softly.

"Nothing," came the answer from above, echoed by two other voices.

"What should they see?" Rose asked.

"The *Lord Marva*. She's about somewhere."

"But I thought we lost her!"

The prince shook his head. "Varnet will be here. The only question is whether he's here yet."

"And if he is?"

"Then we'll go back—if we can. If not"—he smiled faintly—"you'll be home in time for Midsummer feast."

Rose shuddered. She'd never cared for Midsummer feast. The entertainments, lavish though they were, did not disguise the fact that Midsummer was the time for sacrifice. The bellowing of the bulls and rams in their pens and the thought of the prisoners awaiting execution always spoiled her enjoyment of the holiday.

"I'd just as soon miss it," she said.

"So would I. The idea of providing the midday entertainment does not appeal."

Rose laughed nervously. "Surely there's no chance of that!"

"We'll see in a few minutes."

The wisps of cloud turned pink as dawn spread across the sky. Rose found herself scanning the horizon until her eyes ached.

"Here goes," Florian muttered, then turned his head and gave a series of soft orders.

At once the riggings sprang to life as clouds of sail unfurled. The *Quest* leaped forward, throwing up a spray of water that caught Rose full in the face.

"Anything?" Florian called.

"Not yet."

"Aye, there—sails! A point to larboard."

Florian was up the rigging in a flash, his heart in his throat. There she was, the *Lord Marva,* setting every sail as quick as she could manage. They caught the morning sun in a blinding flash of white, plainly visible even at this distance.

Florian let out a long breath and closed his eyes as he sagged against the mast. He still had a chance. It wasn't over yet. As for how it would end, he could not imagine. In other days, he would have headed for Sorlainian waters and Richard would not have dared to follow. King Esteban had always made it very clear that Sorlain was neutral in the conflict between Valinor and Venya, and it was a decision Richard had no choice but to accept.

But not now. Cristobal was an unknown; the risk was far too great. *I'll think of something,* Florian told himself. *Later.*

He went down very carefully, grasping each line with hands that shook. When he reached the deck, he called for Gordon.

"You have the helm. Keep to the course, and wake me if there's any change."

He managed to smile at Rosamund as he passed. "It's all right, they're miles off. I'm going to get some sleep."

He dragged himself to his cabin, only to find it full.

"We're down to salt meat and biscuit, my lord, and that last lot we opened didn't look too promising."

"Halve the rations," Florian said through a yawn. "We'll provision as soon as possible."

"The men are showing signs of scurvy," Sigurd put in. "We must have fresh food."

Florian tossed him a key. "Have Beylik show you to my private storeroom. There's a cask of baska juice there somewhere. Yes, Aubright? I hope *you* have good news for me."

"Not bad, m'lord," the carpenter said, hooking his thumbs into his belt. "A few nicks and cuts is all, nothing we can't handle."

"Good work. Beylik, just pile everything on the table. I'll look at them when I've rested. And now, if you'll excuse me . . ."

Alone, Florian stretched and shed his clothes, standing for a moment by the window, watching the foaming wake spread out and letting the sun sink into his skin. When he was warm at last, he headed for his cot. But once there, he stopped and turned back to gaze out the window once again.

A perfect day, blue sky and a sweet wind blowing from the south. Surely there was no need . . .

But he knew he would not sleep well without first checking. Yawning hugely, he opened a cabinet and extracted a finely carved box inlaid with silver tracery. Carefully he took out the contents and set it on the table before him.

A lovely thing it was, made from Yarlmay glass, shaped rather like a flagon with a long spout curving to the top. He'd found it in a tiny market on an island so small it did not appear on any map. A curious thing, he'd thought, not believing the stallkeeper's claim but liking the look of it.

Yet the stallkeeper had not lied. Time and time again, Florian had found the thing to be accurate, though how it worked he could not begin to say. Now he stared at it for a long moment, gently tapped the glass with a nail, and watched the liquid settle.

"Leander's balls," he muttered. Leaning over, he picked up his shirt from the floor, every muscle groaning in protest. He stared at it, blinking stupidly, then rested his brow on the cool wood of the table. Five minutes later he jerked upright to stare wildly about the cabin until his gaze fell on the Yarmlay glass.

He replaced it with careful hands, pulled his clothes back on, and went up on deck.

"Gordon," he called, gesturing the first mate over. "We have some weather coming."

Gordon looked from the cloudless sky into Florian's face. "My lord, you need to sleep. The day is—"

Florian raised his brows.

Gordon swallowed hard. "Oh. I see. Are you . . . ?"

"Quite sure."

"How bad?"

Florian thought of the liquid's level. "Bad enough. Suggestions?"

Gordon stared into the distance, eyes narrowed. "Ospir is not too far; they have a solid harbor. But there's only the one narrow pass."

"Can the *Lord Marva* make it in?"

"Tricky, but with a sure hand at the helm . . ."

"She'll make it. Other options?"

"Wattle Island, but it isn't much good in a real blow."

Florian nodded. He'd thought of these already, but in his present state he didn't trust himself to consider every angle. He rubbed his eyes hard, forcing himself to think.

"Ship the deadlights, secure the decks, and make for Ospir with all speed. Put as much distance as you can between us and the *Lord Marva*. Flat out, Gordon, do you understand me? Wake me the moment land is sighted."

"Aye, my lord."

VARNET lifted his head and tapped a finger against his lips, squinting in the sunlight pouring through the stern window of the *Lord Marva*.

"Ospir?" he murmured. "One passage, no way out . . . he can't be thinking to engage us." He ran a finger along the chart, thinking hard, measuring distances. At last he shook his head. "It must be Ospir. But why? Why there?"

By mid-afternoon he had his answer.

"Storm staysails—and rig a lifeline here," he roared into the wind, reaching out an arm to catch a sailor as the sea swept over the bow. He turned to his first mate. "He knew. Damn his eyes, he saw it coming. Or else he called it up himself. We'll make Ospir in another two hours. And by Marva's bones," he added fiercely, "this time we'll have him."

"LAND!"

The cry was ripped from the sailor's mouth and flew across the deck below.

"Wake His Highness," Gordon ordered.

"It's all right, I'm here." Florian braced himself against the pitching of the ship. "It's Ospir?"

"Aye, my lord."

"The *Lord Marva*?"

"We haven't seen her this last hour."

"Well done, Gordon. Now make it four points to larboard and get us out of here."

"BUT you *said* he would be at Ospir. He must be hiding—a cove—"

Varnet dragged a hand through his dripping hair and accepted the goblet his steward offered. Beyond the barrier the sea still raged, but here the rain fell in a steady sheet and the ship rode easily.

"No. He never came in at all. He's riding out the storm."

Clever bastard, he thought, draining the goblet in two swallows and holding it out for more. *He led us here and went on.*

"Then go after him!"

"We could," Varnet said neutrally. "But going through that passage once was a risky business. I won't answer for getting out again in this. And even if we do, this storm is no joke. What we've seen so far is only the beginning."

"What kind of fucking cowardly answer is that? If he can ride it out in that little pissant ship of his, I don't see what the trouble is. You get us out and find him. The king gave me full responsibility—"

"Very well," Varnet said, his face perfectly expressionless. "I have acquainted you with the dangers, as is my duty. Now we shall, of course, do as you command."

Chapter 23

THE full force of the wind in Rose's face sent her staggering. The prince, standing at the wheel, caught her wrist.

"You shouldn't be out in this!" he shouted, his lips against her ear.

"I wanted to see it."

"Get below!"

"No!"

He muttered something she didn't catch, then raised his voice and shouted, "Clap on to the man-line and keep out of the way."

After several hours huddled below in darkness, feet tucked up above the water sloshing through her cabin, Rose had been sure that whatever was happening above could not be nearly so terrifying as her imagination made it.

Now she saw that she'd been wrong.

She was surrounded by solid walls of water that reached beyond the tallest mast. If one—just one—should crash down upon the deck, they must surely sink like a stone. She gazed from side to side as the ship rose, bowsprit pointed to the sky. Their speed increased as they climbed, the small sails filled and then they'd done it, they'd reached the crest, only to hurtle down again with a speed that brought a startled cry bursting from her lips.

Now the water was around them once again, gray walls marbled with yellowed foam. The ship slowed, then seemed to stop completely as the stern swiveled slowly round.

Now she understood what Beylik had tried to tell her. So long as they kept the bow into the wave, all would be well. The danger came in the troughs, where no wind could reach the sails. Should the ship turn broadside to the wave, they would be broached and sunk between one heartbeat and the next.

The shrieking of the wind slackened, and she could hear Florian beside her, his voice strong but very rough as he shouted a stream of orders up above. The ship turned; they faced the wave and began their painful ascent, reached the crest, and flew down the other side, only to begin again.

And again. And again. Each time Rose's heart was in her mouth, every muscle clamped tight against the pounding of the wind, the pitching of the deck, the cold shock of the smaller waves breaking over the deck at either hand. After an hour—and that just watching—she was exhausted. Yet she did not go below. She did not even think of it. So long as this mad race went on, she wanted to be part of it.

As they tipped the next crest she glanced over at the prince. He had stood at the wheel through two watches and showed no sign of relinquishing it. He was wrapped in a long oiled cloak, his head bared to the storm. Water streamed down his face, and when he turned to her, Rose saw with a shock that he was smiling.

With a greater shock, she found herself answering with a grin as fierce and reckless as his own.

It was hours later that she followed him to his cabin. He said the wind was slackening, though to Rose it seemed just the same as ever. But she was more than willing to take his word for it. Half a dozen of his men were already seated at the table, faces drawn with weariness in the lantern light. With a sigh, Rose eased her trembling legs into a chair.

The pitching was not quite so fierce now, and Beylik came nimbly across the floor with a covered dish of soup, setting it down without a splash. It was amazing, Rose reflected as he ladled it out, what they could do with ship's biscuit and dried meat. Soups, roasts, stews, and fricasees, all highly spiced in a brave attempt to disguise the flavor of the meat.

What kind of meat it was, she never asked. She was afraid to hear the answer.

Though the prince's table was usually a congenial place, today there was no conversation, just the sound of spoons scraping against crockery, Rose's scraping as quickly as the rest. When she had finished two bowls she remembered her duty. Shipboard etiquette forbade the men from opening a conversation; that right belonged to the captain and, as his guest, to her. Raising her head, she began, "Do you think—"

But she never finished the question. Instead she stood and filed out silently with the others, leaving the Prince of Venya fast asleep, one cheek resting on his folded arm and the spoon still in his hand.

IT seemed only moments after Rose had fallen into her cot that she was woken by hammering that seemed to come from inches from her ear. With a muttered oath she turned over, opened her eyes, and saw sunlight streaming through the porthole.

She jumped up from the cot and splashed through ankle-deep water over to the table, where Beylik had laid out a dry set of trousers, a shirt, and the small knife she used at meals. She pulled on the clothes, and went on deck to a scene of furious activity. The hammering was louder here, and sailors ran in all directions, calling orders to their mates who were splicing and mending far above. The pumps sent high jets of water to either side in glittering sprays.

There was none of the laughter Rose had expected, no sense of triumph at having made it through the storm. When the prince waved that she might approach the quarterdeck, she greeted him with a smile.

"Are they not to rest at all?" she asked. "They must be exhausted."

"There is no time for that."

Rose turned to peer over the stern. It was difficult to see much, for though the day had brightened, the sea still ran high. "Has the *Lord Marva* been sighted?"

"Not yet."

"Then . . . ?"

"Lady, you have heard of a typhoon?"

"Yes, of course. But it is past now, isn't it?"

Florian sketched a swirl in the air. "This is a typhoon. It moves like this, round and round, do you see?" He circled thumb and forefinger and said, "One of its peculiarities is that it has this little clearing in its center, which we call the eye. And this"—he pointed to a spot in the middle—"is us."

Rose felt a sudden hollowness in her stomach. "Then—you mean we have it all to do again?"

"I'm afraid so. Which is why we need to make all the repairs we can before it starts again."

"When will that be?"

"An hour if we are lucky. Half that if we are not. I suggest you enjoy the sunlight while you can."

BACK in her cabin in the dark, Rose lay strapped into her wildly swinging cot and tried to sleep. She knew now what was happening above; there was no need for her to see it. She could only trust that the prince would bring them through as he had done before.

"We've seen worse."

That's what all the men had told her as they filed from the prince's cabin. "It was a good one, all right, but we've seen worse."

The words had been echoed by Beylik when he had come by to lash her into her cot. When had that been? Hours ago? Days? It seemed a lifetime. She wished desperately that he would come back and tell her again that this was nothing compared to other storms the *Quest* had weathered. She longed to hear his voice with its comforting Jexlian accent saying, "It's bad enough, all right, but we've seen worse."

She could have sworn that it *was* worse now, far worse than it had been before. She tried to dismiss it as imagination, but as the moments passed, she was certain it was so. After one terrible twisting crash her flailing hand touched water and she panicked, fumbled for her knife, cut the ropes, and spilled to the floor with a splash. She lurched to her feet, staggering as the ship bucked, and grabbed the table for support. She couldn't stay here. Better to face whatever happened up on deck, in the company of the crew, than to drown all alone in darkness.

The water was knee deep in her cabin now, higher in the passage. She half ran, half stumbled to the stairs and made her way to the deck, wincing as her blistered palms fastened on the manline. At first she could see nothing but water—blinding sheets of rain, foam-flecked seas rushing over the deck—and coherent thought was impossible in the deafening shrieking of the wind.

She had been right. It *was* worse.

Inch by inch she pulled herself to the wheel, where Florian stood alone. He was not smiling now. His face was set as he stared ahead with narrowed eyes. He acknowledged her with a flicking glance and a nod.

No protest. No order to get below. He knew just why she was here and agreed with her decision.

Which meant . . . it meant . . .

Rose had no time to finish the thought. With a groan that seemed to come from the depths of the ship, the mast cracked and fell across the bow, trailing clouds of sail.

The ship halted with a jerk and began to slew around. Florian leaped from the quarterdeck and raced across the heaving deck to pull himself far out on the bowsprit, where he vanished in a crash of foam.

The wave pulled back and he was still there, steel glinting as his arm rose and fell, cutting the sails away, the sails that were trailing like dead weights through the water. Another sailor joined him, but when the next wave broke and receded, the prince was once again alone.

Someone pushed past Rose and she staggered, nearly falling. It was Gordon, eyes starting from his livid face as he fought to control the wheel.

Rose went down, clinging desperately to the man-line as the sea washed over her. Choking, she struggled to her knees and peered across the streaming deck. The prince was still there. She couldn't imagine how, but he had held his place and his arm still rose and fell as he tried desperately to free his ship from the dragging sails.

"One more like that," Gordon was saying, a meaningless litany that went on and on. "One more like that—one more—"

Rose dragged herself forward, toward the bow, with no clear idea what she would do if she managed to reach it. A shout—a cheer—the sails were going, sweeping away into the sea.

"She answers! She answers!"

Gordon's hoarse cry came from behind her, and they were moving again, turning to meet the next wave head-on. They rose toward the crest with only a tangle of line streaming from the bowsprit, still caught fast on the ship.

Or no, Rose realized. Not on the ship. The prince was clinging one-handed to the bowsprit as he slashed at the line tangled around his boot.

"Help him!" she screamed, looking wildly about, almost weeping with relief when she saw it was all right, that others had seen and help was already on the way. They were running, calling out to him to hold on, not to lose heart, they were coming.

Yet it was not all right. In the space of a heartbeat, Rose measured their distance—and hers—and the speed of the gathering wave. In the next, she was scrambling over the lines, down on her hands and knees as she fumbled for her knife.

She reached him as the ship was rising, rising on the wave. Without daring to look up, she sawed through the line, dropped the knife, and caught his wrist in both hands, bracing herself on her knees as she strained to pull him up. He rolled aboard and covered her body with his own as a fury of foaming water crashed over them. *I am drowning,* Rose thought, *so this is what it's like.* And then the rushing darkness pulled her under.

"Breathe, *breathe*—"

The words were punctuated by a pounding on her back, driving her against the deck. "Don't," she wanted to say, "you're hurting me," but when she opened her mouth, water gushed out in a burning stream. She coughed and choked, trying to force air into lungs that were too busy expelling the sea to obey her.

"That's out. Good. Now clap on, lady, clap on hard."

From a great distance she was aware of a pain in her palms as her hands scraped against a rough surface, then fell away. A sharp crack, a different pain, stinging on her cheek, and she forced her eyes open to see the prince's face dancing crazily above her, blood streaming down his brow.

"Wake up and take the line," he ordered fiercely, pressing her numb fingers around the line. "Now. Take it. Damn you, *clap on to the line.*"

She tightened her fingers and felt his hands close briefly around her own.

"Hold hard," he was saying, "hold fast—"

And the deck beneath her vanished.

She hung suspended for an endless time, staring at the bowsprit pointing to the sky. *We're going over,* she thought dizzily, *there's a name for that. What do they call it when a ship goes over backward?*

Screams rent the air. Rose clutched the line and sent a wordless prayer into the wind. Slowly, slowly the bowsprit began to dip toward the water; they had done it, somehow they had crested the wave and were hurtling down the other side. Before Rose could be grateful, she hit the deck with a shock that tore her bleeding palms from the man-line.

Hard hands grabbed her beneath the arms, pulled her to her feet, forced her toward the hatch and down into the darkness.

"You stay below," the prince shouted. "*Below*. Do you hear me? Do you understand?"

"Y-yes, yes—"

He took her by the shoulders and shook her. "What were you thinking?" he demanded, and then he pulled her hard against him. She felt his body shaking and the wild pounding of his heart beneath her cheek.

"Of you," she answered in a sobbing gasp, winding her arms around his neck. "Of you."

His beard scraped her cheek and for one searing, heart-stopping moment his mouth closed over hers.

"You stay below," he said again in a shaking voice.

And he was gone.

Chapter 24

SHE had been walking down the corridor forever, sloshing through the endless darkness, bracing herself against the wall as the floor shifted and the water swirled to her waist, then receded in a rush that sucked the strength out of her legs.

Don't fall, she told herself, *don't go down, you won't get up again.* Lurching, stumbling, sobbing with exhaustion, she tripped on a stairway and went up, away from the water, and found herself in another corridor, fully as dark as the one she had just left. But at least this one was dry.

Her reaching hand fastened on a latch, twisted, and pulled open the door. A sudden lurch sent her sprawling to the floor. When she looked up, she saw by the wildly swinging lantern that she had reached the prince's cabin.

The long table was empty, the chairs gone. The hanging basket seat swung in a wild arc. Still on hands and knees, she made her way to the cot and tried to straighten it. It was hopelessly twisted, tangled upon itself in a knot that even the ablest of sailors could not possibly sort out. She crawled toward the bed, pulled herself up, and fell facedown upon soft feathers.

She lay there for a long moment, clinging to the edge with both hands, her body rolling back and forth with the movement of the ship. At last she found the strength to pull off her sodden trousers, cursing in a sobbing whisper as her bruised and shaking fingers fumbled over the unfamiliar buttons. At last they were gone, the shirt as well, and she pulled back the heavy coverlet and crawled beneath it. *At least I will die warm,* she thought as she pitched headlong into sleep.

* * *

DAWN broke. It seemed impossible, but there it was, pink clouds edged with gold against a pale blue sky. Florian had seen many sunrises before, though never one quite so beautiful as this. The difference being, he supposed, that he had not expected to see another one.

With a jerk, he forced his gaze from the rising sun and surveyed his ship. Not good, one part of his mind said, while the other cried that it was wonderful, a miracle unparalleled since the beginning of all time. For battered and beaten as she was, the *Quest* still floated.

"Aubright," he said, turning to the carpenter standing anxiously at his elbow, "what news?"

"Four feet in the well and drawing fast."

"Is she holed?"

The carpenter shook his head. "Pump and caulk job, m'lord."

"Pumps, then, at once. Gordon, we'll go in watches, turn and turn. You are with the first watch. Beylik," he added, raising his voice, "in what condition is the galley?"

"Wrecked entirely, m'lord," Beylik answered cheerfully, "but we can get a fire going somehow."

"Do so. The men need hot food at once. As soon as you've anything to offer we'll pipe the first watch to breakfast. Let us get started on the pumps."

"Aye, m'lord."

Bend and pull. Bend and pull again, aching muscles loosening until they found an easy rhythm, spurred on by the sight of water pluming far into the sea. The watches changed, and the carpenter's face was red with exertion and pleasure when he made his next report and hurried off.

Bend and pull. Each stroke lightening the ship, bringing her to life. Florian started, his rhythm breaking as a hand touched his elbow.

"My lord," Gordon said, "you must rest. Sigurd has been crying out for you this hour past."

Florian straightened, staggering a little. "What?"

"Sigurd, m'lord, he is waiting. You must go to him."

Then Sigurd was there, weary but smiling, his hand warm on Florian's shoulder. "It is enough. There is no danger. Come, my lord, come below."

"Not now."

"Yes, now. It is all well, you are not needed here."

"But . . ." Florian blinked hard and tried to focus on the faces around him.

The carpenter, saying, "Down two foot and dropping." Gordon saying, "Go, my lord, it's all right, I have the watch." Sigurd's fingers parting his hair. "Once again, you have Leander's luck. A stitch or two will set you right."

Florian nodded, relinquishing his place. "Very well, Sigurd. Just as you wish. Thank you, Aubright. Mr. Gordon, the watch is yours."

A stitch or two had turned to eight by the time Sigurd cut the thread and straightened. "It is not wise for a man to reach perfection, but once again I have come dangerously close. A bandage to protect my handiwork . . . thus. Now you may sleep."

"Thank you, Sigurd. How many in the sick bay? How many lost?"

"Have I not said 'sleep'? We will speak later."

"I saw two go over," Florian said. "Tamlin and . . . Rusk, I think it was."

"Yes, it was Rusk. Cilben was lost, too."

"Cilben? Gods, he was to be married." Florian rested his brow on his clenched fist. "I suppose it could have been worse. It nearly was."

"Drink this," Sigurd said, setting a cup before him. "It is only wine, but it should help you sleep."

Sigurd was right, Florian thought, forcing himself to swallow the wine, he should get to sleep. He knew it, but he could barely lift the cup to his lips and swallow, let alone stand and walk to his cot. His eyes were gritty with exhaustion, and every muscle ached, but his mind would not be still. It buzzed and hummed, flitting from one thought to the next.

Florian did not believe in discussing his decisions with the crew. Right or wrong, the responsibility was his alone. But everything seemed a bit unreal that morning. "I don't see what else we could have done save ride it out," he said, hardly aware that he was speaking aloud. "Gordon suggested Wattle Island, but it would not have served. I suppose I could have tried—no, we never would have made it. It was the only way—at least the only way that I could find. If I could just be sure . . ."

"Who can ever be sure they have done the right thing?" Sigurd's voice was soothing, and he tipped the jug over Florian's cup again, filling it to the brim.

"I used to be."

Once—gods, was it only last year?—Florian *had* been sure, effortlessly confident in all he did. Faced with the loss of three crew members, he would have mourned them and gone on, secure in the knowledge that he had done his utmost. Last year . . . it seemed an age ago. Another life entirely.

"Thank you, Sigurd," he said wearily. "That will be all."

He stood, catching the edge of the table for support, then walked carefully to his writing table and squinted at the empty shelf. Where had Beylik put the books? He pulled out a drawer, then another, and finally found the one he sought, with Varnet's name across the spine. It fell open to a chart, the place marked with a scrap of parchment.

> *"The sword to conquer Venya's foes,*
> *The shield protects us from our woes,*
> *When sacrifice of uncrowned king,*
> *Is offered in the sacred ring,*
> *Then two are one by oath forsworn*
> *And hope unites the land reborn."*

The sacrifice of uncrowned king . . . Not on the sea, but in the sacred ring. Were all his choices an illusion? Was he no more than destiny's minion, walking blindly through the world, his steps leading inexorably down a path foretold by prophecy? His weary mind tried to grasp exactly what that meant, but after a moment he gave up and flipped the book closed.

Yawning, he dragged off his clothes and stared stupidly at the twisted knot that used to be his cot. With a groan, he stumbled across his cabin and fell upon the bed. He pulled the curtains shut and burrowed under the coverlet, turning on his side and flinging out an arm.

His hand met flesh. Living flesh, very warm, and, he found after a brief exploration, curved in unmistakable lines.

There is a naked woman in my bed, was his last thought as he hooked an arm around her, pulled her close, and fell asleep.

Chapter 25

FOUR hours later, Florian woke from a dream in which he walked through endless passageways dim with smoke and echoing with screams. His mind surfaced briefly, enough to assure him that the ship had lightened, the sails were rigged, and they were under way, making perhaps three knots and heading north.

He was just relaxing back into the mattress when a soft sigh brought him up sharply. He turned his head and met a wide hazel stare shining in the dimness.

"Good morning," he said a little hoarsely. "Or is it afternoon?"

Rosamund blinked. "Are we alive?"

"Apparently we are, strange as it might seem."

"You're hurt—"

"This?" He touched the bandage around his brow. "It's nothing. But how are you today?"

She shifted, doing interesting things to the coverlet gaping over her breasts. Very nice breasts they were too, as far as he remembered. She had a nice belly, as well, sweetly rounded, flowing into full hips and a lush bottom. He had apparently managed to notice quite a bit in the seconds before he slept. The memory was vivid in mind and body as he peered down into the shadow, catching a tantalizing glimpse of pale flesh before she moved again and quite destroyed the view.

She groaned. "One solid bruise from head to foot, I would imagine."

"Shall I have a look?"

She slapped his hand away. "No, sir, you shall not."

"As you wish," he said, sighing a little, then shifted so his face was inches from her own. "Now that I begin to wake, I recall what I meant to tell you yesterday. Has anyone ever mentioned that you are quite mad?"

Her lips curved in a smile. "Oh, well spoken, very nicely said indeed. First shouting, now abuse. And this from the Prince of Venya, famed for his gentle courtesy."

"Did I neglect to thank you? How remiss." He took her hand and raised it, but when his lips brushed the torn skin of her palm, the events of the day before came back to him in a rush. She had nearly died. He had almost lost the *Quest* and everyone aboard. They were safe today, but what of tomorrow?

And tomorrow and tomorrow and all the days after that, each one bringing more decisions to be made, decisions that would affect not only the crew of the *Quest* but all of Venya. Each day leading him closer to the final confrontation with Richard of Valinor.

Florian knew what he must do, though Leander only knew how he would do it. Somehow he must begin the battle that would be the saving of Venya, though he would not see its end. There could be no victory without sacrifice. The prophecy left no doubt what that sacrifice would be.

Florian had gone into many a battle knowing that he might not live to see it finished. Every fighting man must make his own peace with that possibility. But it was one thing to say, "My life for Venya"—and mean it with his whole heart—while still believing that through skill or luck or some combination of the two that he might just make it through. It was quite another thing to walk into a battle knowing beyond doubt that survival was impossible.

That took a different sort of courage. In the year since Florian had learned his fate, every day had been a new battle to find that cold resolve within himself. So far, he had succeeded. But this morning, weary and aching and grieving for the men who'd died under his command, he could not summon his defenses. Too many things had happened to him lately, too many more were still waiting to happen, and he had lost sight of whatever part he was supposed to play.

"I am sorry" was all he could manage. "Rosamund, I am so sorry—"

"For what?" she asked softly.

The storm. That my misjudgment nearly killed you. That I have lied to you and will go on lying. That you have no more choice in this than I.

Instead he brushed a lock of hair out of her eyes. "It didn't hold. The plait. I said it would hold in a typhoon . . ."

He wrapped his arms around her and pulled her close. There were no words left to him, no tricks or ploys or clever strategies. He only wanted her to hold him until the world was right again. Her warm, soft body pressed close to his, and she stroked his head, a touch completely chaste and yet more intimate than any he could remember. With a ragged sigh, he rested his head against her breast and lost himself in her embrace.

ROSE hardly knew how she had come to this place, but here she was in the Prince of Venya's bed, his body clasped within her arms. The strangest thing of all was how natural it felt. He made no demands, but seemed content to simply rest. She stroked his head, wondering at herself, and him, and the tale that this would make, the two of them naked in a bed . . . sleeping. If such a story got about, his reputation would be ruined.

Sigurd had said something about the prince's reputation—a warning, she thought drowsily, that she was his hostage and he would not hesitate to use seduction to keep her on his ship. But Sigurd was wrong. This was no wild libertine in her arms, but a man barely older than herself, worn with worry and exhaustion. Surely she had nothing to fear.

Or perhaps she did. He stirred and raised his head to look into her face. Staring into his eyes, she remembered how it had felt when she began to drown; her body dissolving, the thoughts flying from her mind. She drew a sharp breath as his lips touched her neck.

His palm was on her cheek, his thumb lightly tracing the outline of her ear. She gasped as he took her earlobe between his lips, his soft breath sending a thousand bright shivers racing through her body.

And then his mouth found hers. She had thought of his kiss a thousand times, but her memory had fallen far short of this. Nothing could compare to the reality of his lips parting hers, the teasing exploration of his tongue. His fingers moved in small circles across her shoulder, and he caught her soft cry of pleasure in his mouth when his palm feathered the taut peak of her breast.

He bent his head, lips following his hands—and oh, Jehan, she'd never imagined such sensations. Her thoughts began to scatter like clouds before the wind.

One tiny part of her mind was still clear and sharp. *You should not be doing this,* it said, straining to be heard above the tumult of her senses. *This is dangerous and foolish.*

Just another moment, she promised, yielding herself to his mouth, tugging with gentle insistence at her breast; his hand, trailing up the tender skin of her inner thigh as gently, slowly, he explored her until she arched against him and set her teeth into his shoulder to still her cry.

Small shivers, the aftermath of some great upheaval, rippled through her body, leaving her limp and langorous in his arms. Wanton, she thought, trying to summon a wisp of shame. Who would have imagined that of her? But then, who would have imagined that she would ever find herself here?

It passed all understanding. But then, so did everything these days. She, who had been so very careful for so many years was now hurtling along from one moment to the next with no idea where she was going, let alone what would happen when she got there. Worse, she didn't care. Worst of all, her very unconcern, which should have been a cause for grave alarm, didn't bother her at all.

His hands were on her breasts, and he claimed her mouth again. Like a dance, she thought dizzily as he teased her lips apart; advance, retreat . . . She had always longed to dance, but of course no one would dare to partner her . . . until now . . . and, oh, if this was her reward for missing all those dull pavannes, it had been well worth the wait.

She ran her hands across his back, his arms, his warm skin, and his coiled muscles, breathing in his scent until she lost all sense of time or place. Advance, retreat; she grew bolder, her fingertips brushed his manhood, drew back again over his taut belly, then dipped again. He angled his mouth over hers, deepening the kiss, and caught her hand, guiding it between his legs.

"Yes," he whispered, "ah, gods—please—"

His breathing was as ragged as her own, his voice low and urgent as he strained against her palm. His hand slid up her leg and—oh, Jehan, she couldn't—not again—but she could, she felt a quiver of anticipation deep in her belly, a slow heat gathering as it crept through her sweat-slicked limbs—and she wanted, needed—

He shifted, and she moved instinctively beneath him. His knee glided between her legs. He poised above her, she arched to meet him, and then, in one swift movement, he was inside her. She froze, the sharp pain between her legs bringing her abruptly to her senses.

SO right. So perfect. Deep in the dizzying waves of pleasure, Florian heard her gasp and felt her go rigid beneath him. He stilled, every muscle shaking with the effort, then groaned when she shifted beneath him. He moved slowly, his teeth gritted as he held his own need at bay, and gradually the tension eased from her body. "That's it," he murmured at her first tentative response, "like that, ah, Rosamund, yes—"

She made a sound, half sigh, half moan, and when she arched against him, he lost every semblance of control. He thrust deeply, and soon—too soon, he knew—was lost in the shattering pleasure of release.

When he could think again, he realized that there was more to this than what they had just shared. She was his now, just as he had wanted. Only . . . he had not expected it to be like this. He had not planned it, nor, he knew, had she. It had just happened. So simply. So naturally. No games, no roles, just himself and Rosamund, an experience unlike any other he had known and far sweeter than he had imagined possible.

Under any other circumstances, asking for her hand in marriage would have been as pure and right as all that had just passed between them. But if he was honest, Florian would have to admit that her life with him would be one wary step after another through a landscape fraught with danger, a twisted path leading to an end he knew too well. After that, he did not know what would befall her, only that she must face it on her own.

He could have loved her. That, too, would have been a simple thing, as natural as drawing breath. Yet if he truly loved her, he would send her away to find the peaceful life she craved. Love was like a sickness, he thought, something that would weaken him when he needed to be strong. But the taste of salty tears on her cheeks was almost more than he could bear.

"Shh," he murmured, "do not weep. It will be all right, Rosamund. I will marry you."

She drew back and stared at him, her eyes wide between lashes spiked with tears. "*Marry* me?"

"Yes, you mustn't worry, all will be well."

"Marry *me?*" she repeated.

"Of course. Did you think I would dishonor you? Surely you can see that you must—that is, *we* must marry now."

She pulled herself free and sat up, wrapping her arms around her knees. "*Must?*"

Too late, he realized his mistake. He had assumed that she would welcome his offer, or at least greet it with relief. But she was staring at him through narrowed eyes, every line of her body taut with suspicion.

He should have talked of love, not need, no matter how the lie might stick in his throat. "Rosamund," he began, groping for the words that had always come so easily before, "surely you know what I feel for you! You are my heart, my joy, my—"

"Stop," she whispered, "just stop. Please don't pretend to feel things you don't."

A mistake. Another one. It seemed everything he did these days was wrong. But having set this course, it was far too late to alter it. "Can you doubt my love?" he protested, though even to his own ears his words sounded unconvincing.

Her eyes were shadowed, impossible to read. "You are very kind. But I have told you, I am bound for Jexal."

"Well, yes, before, but everything is different now!"

"Is it? Or am I still a hostage?"

"A *hostage?*" He sat up and reached for her hand, but she pulled it from his grasp. "Don't be ridiculous, you are nothing of the sort."

"Then if I wanted to leave the *Quest* and make my way to Jexal, you would let me go?"

"Leave the ship?" he repeated sharply. "When we have no idea where the *Lord Marva* is? They will be searching every port—and offering good gold for information. You wouldn't have a chance of reaching Jexal."

"That would be my care," she said evenly, "and you have not answered my question."

He looked down at her hand, clutching the coverlet across her breasts like a shield. *So much for winning her affection. I should have played the prince for her,* he thought. *No, I should have wed her that first night and saved myself all this. Yet all might not be lost. There is always the chance that she has conceived. Then, from sheer desperation, she might be forced to have me. If not, she will be forced by other means.*

All at once he was aware that his head was pounding fiercely; it must be that, and the bone-deep weariness that a few hours sleep had done little to assuage, that made him feel so low. What difference did it make if she detested him? Their marriage would be a short one by necessity. Next time, she could wed to please herself.

"Lady," he said, "I would not have you rush off into danger on my account. We had agreed to speak of this when we reach Serilla, and we shall hold to that agreement. You are quite safe, I assure you," he added with a laugh that rang bitter in his ears. "You need not fear that I will press my attentions when they are so obviously unwelcome."

"It isn't that you—that I—" she stammered. "It has nothing to do with this—" She waved a hand to encompass the rumpled coverlet, the scent of their lovemaking still clinging to the sheets.

"Of course not," he said politely. "I'm sure you have many good reasons for wishing to go ashore in a strange place and undertake such a difficult and dangerous journey unprotected."

Even in the dimness, he saw the blush rise to her cheeks. "My lord—" she began, but her words were lost in the rattle of chain as the curtain was pulled back and bright light flooded the bed.

"Good day," Beylik said, "Mr. Gordon's compliments and would you like to come on deck? We've sighted—sighted . . ."

The word trailed into silence, broken by a murmur of voices outside the open door.

"Good day to you as well, Beylik," the prince said over his shoulder. "My compliments to Mr. Gordon, and I shall join him directly to see what he has sighted. Not the *Lord Marva,* I trust?"

"No." Beylik spoke stiffly, his face turned studiously away. "Land. Mr. Endriss and the others are without, waiting to make their reports."

"Tell them I will be with them in a quarter of an hour."

"Of course." Beylik drew the curtain closed.

"Please excuse me, my lady," the prince said with a cool smile, "I will send someone with dry clothing for you."

Rose's heart was pounding, though now it was fear that quickened her pulse. What had she just done? And, sweet Jehan, what was she going to do now?

"Thank you," she choked out.

"Beylik," he called, putting his head out the curtain. "My clothing, if you please."

"He's awake now!" a voice cried impatiently, and all at once the cabin was filled with men.

"If you will wait here," the prince said to her, "I will be rid of them as quickly as possible. Good morning, gentlemen," he called, "I am sorry to have kept you waiting. Another moment and I am yours."

He vanished through the curtain on the far side of the bed, away from the waiting men. *The Prince of Venya made me an offer of marriage,* Rose thought, putting her fist against her mouth to stifle a half-hysterical burst of laughter. *All I had to do was say yes and the most burning question of the age would have been settled for all time.*

Why *hadn't* she said yes? What had she been thinking? It was her every dream come true, more wonderful than any dream could ever be. He had asked her—*her,* Rose of Valinor—to marry him . . . and she had refused. It had not been by design—her answer had come without any thought at all, with a certainty too urgent to deny. She did not understand it even now or why every instinct had screamed that there was something very wrong about his offer.

She didn't trust him. No matter how sweetly he made love to her, there were shadows in his eyes. He claimed to love her, but his words had been so stiff and stilted that only a fool could be deceived. Yet his actions had been real enough when he held her, and later, when he shook with passion, every semblance of his control destroyed by something so simple as a touch—her touch—that had been real. Or had it? Why else would he have asked her to marry him?

In the eyes of the world, such an alliance could only be ranked as a disaster. He needed gold and ships and men, a strong ally with a stake in his success, not a penniless fugitive with no connections. Even if she could believe that she had won his heart, he was no greensick lad to cast aside his duty for the sake of pleasure.

She closed her eyes and imagined herself accepting his offer. Princess of Venya. Oh, to spend every night in his arms . . . but she wouldn't. Once wed, she would barely see him. Jehan only knew where he would leave her while he sailed off on his next adventure. Probably on Serilla, the tiny, barren village on the edge of Sorlain where King Esteban had graciously allowed the Venyan *filidhi* to settle when they fled their stricken homeland.

He would make the occasional visit, if only to beget the heir he needed. But once the royal duty was performed and the first flush of passion faded, there would be nothing to bring him back to her. Even if he succeeded in his goal and they returned to Venya, what kind of life would they have together?

Rose knew how little joy was found in royal marriages. Her own father had barely spoken to her mother; Richard had murdered at least two of his wives and treated the others with scant respect, openly flaunting his mistresses before their faces. All kings had mistresses. Their management was a thing that every princess was taught, along the proper way to speak to servants and visiting nobility.

One must never bow to a visiting king, but always to his queen. Servants must be treated firmly. And when faced with one's lord's current mistress, one must never show by word or sign that one is aware of the relationship.

Given the Prince of Venya's history, his lady would have much to overlook.

And yet . . . she would be safe. Whatever his reasons for marrying her, once he had done so, he would protect her. Wasn't that what she wanted? A place in the world that was secure, one that belonged to her alone? She didn't know anymore what she wanted, or what she feared, or whether she had just made the most terrible mistake of her life.

She rolled over and peeked through the curtain. He was already half-dressed, his back to her as he reached for the black shirt hanging on a peg. His muscles moved smoothly beneath his sleek brown skin, nicked with lighter knots of scar tissue. So many scars. She had not noticed them before. There was a weary droop to his shoulders that made her want to reach out and draw him back to bed, make him smile, hold him in her arms until he slept. But for good or ill, such an impulse could hardly be carried out with half a dozen men in the cabin. She lay back, sighing, and let the curtain fall together.

A moment later, voices burst out, hurrying over one another.

"Good morning, my lord, I have your breakfast. 'Tis—"

"My lord, we have Iona in sight, but you know—"

"We must take on provisions, the—"

"That is looking well, if you'll just turn your head—"

"—only biscuit, but the kava is still not, and—"

"—the master is a grasping devil—"

"—water is down to—"

The prince's voice cut through the confusion, rough with weariness and tinged with his own indefinable accent.

"Gentlemen, good day. Iona, is it? Thank you, Sigurd, that will do for now. Beylik, lad, you look half dead, have you not slept at all? Drink this and get below until I send for you. Mr. Endritch, you are quite right about the Ionian master, but we really have no choice. Mr. Aleman, take charge of the provisioning and water; Ashkii, please be so kind as to assist him. We must be ready to leave by tomorrow sunset."

A moment of silence greeted this pronouncement.

"Tomorrow? But—perhaps you did not see the damage—"

"I have not yet seen a full report, but I have an idea what we need and I shall see to it that the Ionians work through the night. Whatever they have completed by tomorrow afternoon will have to do. The *Lord Marva* must not find us in the dockyard."

"But we've seen nothing of the *Lord Marva*! Surely they took refuge in Ospir."

"I wish I could share your certainty, Mr. Endritch. As I cannot, we shall begone tomorrow sunset, and may Leander send us a fair wind."

Chapter 26

OF the three men in the sick bay, Sigurd chose the youngest. He was a Moravian of perhaps two-and-twenty years, with several kinsmen among the crew and a host of friends. Sigurd had removed the splinter from his belly and stitched up the wound, and though the gash had looked alarming, it was healing cleanly and there had been no perforation of the intestine.

Sigurd put a hand on his brow, cool now. The ferbifuge had been successful; he would have to make a note of it. He was mentally reviewing the ingredients when he sliced into the sailor's jugular. He held an ewer to catch the stream of blood, his gaze focused sharply on the young man's face, watching for any change to mark the passage from unconsciousness to death.

There was none. Sigurd noted that, as well. He was thoughtful as he laid out candle, herbs, and ewer. Had the Moravian known that his soul had been set free of his body? If he had been dreaming, did the dream simply stop, or did it go on for all eternity? Thinking of his own dreams, Sigurd fervently hoped that was not the case. Was the man's spirit awake, perhaps watching even now? Or did he merely go on sleeping?

That was the worst thought of all, that death was but a dreamless sleep from which there was no waking. That when life ended, one would simply . . . cease.

It was intolerable. He would not think of it. Not tonight, when he had so much else to do. For if once he let that idea take hold of him, he would tip the blood into the sea and be damned to King Richard, the Prince of Venya . . . and himself, into the bargain.

But then, he was already damned. Several times over. Or so he had been told by people who claimed to be in a position to know. Fools, every one of them, if they believed that Sigurd Einarsson could be held to the same standards that bound other men. They had no idea of his power, no concept of what true power was. Only a man free of the petty tyranny of rules could begin to grasp it for himself.

He took the key from round his neck and unlocked his cabinet. Reaching inside, his fingers fastened on a small chest, which he set upon the table and fitted a second key into its iron padlock. He withdrew a small crystal vial from inside, which he placed carefully upon the table, then locked both chest and cabinet again and tucked the keys back into the neck of his tunic.

He had just laid out the herbs he needed, along with a larger vial of sweet oil, when there came a knock upon the door. With a muttered curse, he thrust ewer, herbs, and vial back into the cupboard and bent to the sailor. He wiped all traces of blood from his neck, then turned his head to hide the mark. Casting one quick glance around the cabin, he strode to the door and pulled it open with a jerk to reveal a group of Moravian sailors outside, all but invisible in the darkness save for the gleam of their eyes and the glitter of copper upon their arms.

He had known they would come, though he had not expected them until morning. But no matter, he was ready for them now.

"What do you mean by making such a racket?" he demanded sharply. "Are we attacked?"

"No," one answered, "we only wanted to see how Rashad fares."

"He is dead," Sigurd said, stepping back and allowing them to enter. "He died just now. I am sorry."

Seven men filed into the cabin, touched fingertips to lips, and bowed to the body of their messmate.

"Was he—was it easy?" one asked.

Sigurd looked away, biting his lip, giving them ample time to imagine a long and painful ending for their friend. "Yes, quite easy," he said at last, his voice quick and overhearty, "he did not suffer."

He turned to his former patient and regarded him with a sorrowful gaze. "I know how deeply you will feel his loss. He was such a cheerful lad. And so young. He should have had many years before him. Had we but taken shelter from the storm, he would be with us now. If only the prince had listened to Gordon . . ." He sighed and drew the sheet over the young Moravian's face. "I fear he will not be the last before this madness is over. P-poor lad—"

His voice broke, and he sank down on his stool, shading his eyes with one hand. "Forgive me. I-I did try to save him—"

"Of course you did," the men said, "we all know you're the best. Don't think we're blaming you."

Sigurd drew a few ragged breaths. "It comes hard to lose a lad of such promise, especially when—"

"When what?" a young man prompted, so like the dead lad lying on the cot that Sigurd knew this must be his brother.

"When his death could have been prevented," Sigurd answered, his voice pitched low so they all strained forward to catch his words. "But the prince will have his way at any price. He would not alter course, though they begged him—for the crew's sake—May the gods have mercy on us," he added in a choked whisper, his head falling forward in despair, "we are all helpless in his hands."

He sat thus for a time while the wind sang through the rigging and the ship groaned and creaked and each stroke of the hammers up on deck drove home the fragility of this little world, a tiny speck upon the endless sea.

At last he raised his head and stood. "Rashad was your brother, was he not?" he said gently, resting a hand on the man's trembling shoulder. "I mourn with you, my friend. Let us pray that this is the last needless loss we suffer. Now say your farewells so I might prepare him for his final journey."

Alone again, Sigurd retrieved his instruments from the cupboard. That had gone rather well. The Moravians had not dispersed when they left the cabin, but gone off in a group, muttering among themselves.

He smiled as he crumbled the herbs into a bowl and added a pinch of Jexlan spice. The sweet aroma stole through the stuffy cabin; two of his patients stirred slightly and drew in deep breaths. Rashad, of course, lay motionless. He would not move again, nor was Sigurd haunted by any ghostly apparition as he poured oil over the herbs and spice and set the bowl aflame. He dripped the blood in slowly, counting each drop, breathing deeply of the smoke. Finally, he unstopped the crystal vial and swallowed the Ilindrian draught.

It ran through his blood like rain upon parched earth, quenching a need he had denied for far too long. Oh, bless that greasy clerk for a true man, for this was real, it was right, it was everything that mattered—

It was *power*. Sheer, shattering power that filled him to the soul. He was himself at last, soaring high above the dead flesh of his body, the prison of his mind. He reveled in it, but only for a moment. With an almost physical wrench he forced himself to focus on his errand.

The *Lord Marva*. No sooner had his mind formed the words than he saw it, a tiny lighted speck upon the churning waves. He swept down and down, through the clouds, across the waves, and past the men on deck. He found the cabin he sought and imagined himself inside. A moment later he was watching the King of Valinor's sorcerer bent over a table, gazing deeply into a pan of clear water.

I could kill him now, Sigurd thought. *All I need do is stretch out my hand, close my fist, and stop his heart.*

"You could," said the sorcerer, "but my death would serve no purpose, or none that would help *you*. Say what you have come to say."

"Write it down," Sigurd ordered coldly. "I didn't come all this way to have my message garbled. He's not going to Serilla yet; he doesn't want to pass through Solainian waters."

"Why not?"

"He knows King Cristobal was in Valinor, but not why. He won't risk it until he has more information."

The pen scratched. "Go on."

"We're headed for the Straits of Janus, and he will take an eastern route to Serilla, through the Oslan Islands."

The pen halted. "You could save us so much trouble . . ."

"Do *not*," Sigurd said in a low and deadly voice, "so much as ask it. The king himself has said he will be satisfied with the return of his niece."

"Lucky Sigurd"—the sorcerer laughed unpleasantly—"you never did have the stomach to see it through. The Prince of Venya will die in the end."

"No one looks forward to that day as much as I. But it will not by my hand. My oath—"

The sorcerer waved the quill. "Yes, yes, we all know about your *oath*. Gods, a man like you—it wouldn't be anything you haven't done before! Or is it that you only take pleasure in killing sweet young maidens?"

Sigurd could not repress a start. Damn him, how had he found that out? The sorcerer laughed. "I know all about you, Sigurd Einarsson. You have been my study. How old was she? Fifteen?"

So he didn't know everything. Only the first—the one who had cost Sigurd his home and family and sent him into exile. He had been barely older than the girl himself, too stupid to conceal the body properly. He had learned much since then.

"We were speaking of the prince," he said coolly.

"And your ridiculous pretensions to honor. What difference does it make if you do it or if you give him to us so we can?"

Only my life, Sigurd thought, then cursed himself as the sorcerer laughed softly. "Ah, so it isn't honor at all. I should have known. What is it then, a *geas?*" He leaned back in his seat, eyes gleaming in the shadow of his hood.

"A curse. When I took the healer's oath to the prince, my life was bound to its performance."

"Does he require this of all his men?" The sorcerer laughed. "He has grown wise. There was a time he trusted all too easily. You should have told me, Sigurd. The prince's magic is no match for mine. Say the words he used, leaving nothing out, and I will break it."

"It was not the prince."

"Then who?"

"Shandra Yal," Sigurd spat, his face conorting as he named the Master Physician of the Jexlan university at Yalmet.

"Ah." The sorcerer leaned his chin upon his steepled fingers. "Well, that is a different matter. Why did the old man do it? The prince is no friend to Jexal."

Sigurd laughed harshly. "Ask the gods. They're the ones who told him to, or so he claimed when he babbled some gibberish about broken oaths and retribution. He said no word about the prince; I only understood what he had done when it was too late. Yal is mad—they all are, those *hajomati*—their brains are baked to a pudding by the desert sun while they seek a vision from their Rose of the World."

"Yet clever enough to toss you out on your ear! Yes, Sigurd, I know that, too, though I did not discover why. So you broke your healer's oath, did you? And now you are bound by it on pain of death. I suppose that is Yalmet justice. Well, mad or no, Shandra Yal is not a man I care to meddle with. The prince is ours to deal with."

"He will not stop again until Serilla. Should we reach there, have someone waiting at the wine shop by the olive grove and I will bring the princess."

"How do you plan to get her off the ship?"

"She will come willingly. And I expect full payment for my services upon delivery."

"Yes, yes. Just control yourself, all right? She's no use to us dead. Has the Venyan attempted to take her to his bed?" When Sigurd hesitated, the sorcerer drew a hissing breath. "What are you not telling me? He has not succeeded?"

"I am not certain."

Pale eyes flashed. "You were supposed to watch over her."

"The storm made that impossible."

"Damn you!" the sorcerer cried, his voice thin with fear. "If there is a child—"

"There will be no child," Sigurd promised. "I will see to it."

The sorcerer's long fingers tapped the tabletop. "Do not fail me."

"I will not. What does the king intend to do with her?"

"That is none of your affair. Just deliver her to me, and you will return home with enough gold to buy and sell the one who drove you into exile."

"And the title that was promised me," Sigurd added sharply, "or all the king's gold will be worthless."

"The title shall be yours, as well, the man's lands and kin and kine—all yours to do with as you will. The king does not forget his servants. But you will forget what you did in his service, will you not?"

"Gladly."

"Good. Then go."

The man flicked a finger, sending Sigurd spiraling back into the night. With a searing pain, he descended back into the prison of his flesh, slumped over the table, the scent of blood and smoke acrid in his nostrils.

Moving stiffly, he went out onto the deck and poured the blood into the sea, followed by the charred herbs and the empty crystal vial.

Chapter 27

"FIRE!"

A boulder arced through the morning air and crashed into the raft, sending a plume of water into the air.

"Arm!" the prince shouted.

Rose held her breath, counting the seconds as the arm of the ballista was drawn back and secured, a new boulder fitted in the basket, and the call of "Ready!" was shouted out.

"Fire!"

This time the shot fell wide, and the sailors let out a collective groan.

"Better," the prince called down. "You've cut near a minute off the time."

He descended in his usual heart-stopping fashion, landing silently on deck. During the past week, Rose had barely seen him, as he was completely absorbed in the never-ending work to repair the ship and train the crew in the use of this new weapon.

She had thought him busy before, but it was nothing to the way he drove himself now in his haste to reach Serilla. "The men are exhausted; we must make Serilla before the *Lord Marva* finds us," he had said to her when they shared a hasty meal on the quarterdeck. "I dare not risk another flight like the last. We've lost too many men already."

She knew he was thinking of the four men the storm had taken. Three had been lost to the sea; the fourth, a young sailor named Rashad, had died of a splinter wound. Rose had been moved by the simple burial service, and more so by the expression on the prince's face when he thought himself alone. Only she had lingered long enough to watch him add a private prayer.

She had gone to him, standing silently at his side and watching the sunlight on the waves. He did not look at her or speak, but when she reached out, he took her hand and held it for a time before turning away abruptly.

He greeted her now with a quick smile, then bent to the ballista. True to his word, he gave no sign that she was more than his guest, or that anything of importance had ever taken place between them. It was as though he had not kissed her until her senses spun, or held her so close she could feel the beating of his heart, or rasped a plea against her cheek. He had spoken words of love to her—had they really been as false as she had feared?

But I am the one who sent him away, she thought, though she could not remember now why it had seemed so important. She only knew that she longed for him—not only to lie in his arms again, but to sit together in the twilight over a game of tiles, or share a hasty meal as he bent over his charts, pointing out the route they were taking and telling her stories of the places they would pass. She missed the sound of his voice, and most of all she missed his laughter. She had not heard him laugh since the storm. Even the crew seemed affected by his mood; they had lost their cheerful easiness, and once or twice she had turned quickly with the feeling of being watched by hostile eyes.

"Aubright, what do you think?" he asked the carpenter. "Is it the sight?"

"Nay. 'Tis as true as man can make it."

"Then we must practice harder. But not today. Good work, lads," he called, raising his voice. "Seven out of ten is better, but tomorrow I expect to see nine."

He squatted down and tugged at a rope, his expression rapt.

"You look," Rose said, "like a boy with a new hoop."

"I never had a hoop."

"What did you get for Midsummer, then?"

He squinted through the sight, one hand resting on the wood. "A sword, a dagger, a set of throwing knives . . . Once, Ewan brought me a garrotte. But I think that was a joke."

"Very funny," Rose muttered. She stared moodily at the ballista. "It's hideous."

"It's not here as an ornament, lady." He ran a hand along the wood, caressing it in a way that deepened Rose's annoyance.

"Perhaps you were not aware that Venya is at war. Anything that will give us an advantage is important."

"Then why don't you use sorcery?"

The prince went very still. "Venyan magic does not lend itself to warfare."

"But the Prince of Venya has powers beyond all other *filidhi*. Or so I have heard."

"The royal gift is sacred to Leander. He was no warrior, you know, but when forced to battle, he defeated King Marva only with such earthly weapons as he had to hand."

"What exactly *is* the royal gift?" Rose asked bluntly. "None of the tales agree. Some say it is weather-working, others that the Venyan monarchs can transform into animal shape, or read the hearts of men, or turn invisible."

He glanced up at her. The bandage was gone, but where it had been, his clipped hair curled onto his brow, making him look younger than his years. "Invisible? I've never heard that one. The gift varies according to Leander's will, but it is forbidden to use it in any form to harm another. My father had no gift—he was not of Venya—but my mother could speak the tongues of certain animals."

"And you? What is your gift?"

"Nothing that would help me against Richard. For that, I am grateful . . . in my better moments."

"I wonder," Rose said, "what Leander would have thought of this." She kicked the ballista lightly.

"I think he would have used it in great need."

"And yet did he not say that every life was precious? This"—she kicked it a little harder, then winced—"is different than a sword or dagger. You will never even see the faces of your enemies."

"I do not see the faces of the men my soldiers kill, but I am still responsible for their deaths. That is what it means to command."

"A good leader will avoid bloodshed."

"True, though not at any cost. I did not start this war; Richard did. But now that it is begun, I *will* defeat him."

"No matter what the cost?"

The sunlight turned his eyes to molten amber. "I would sell my soul for Venya. Indeed," he added with a short laugh, "there are some who would say I already have."

Rose regarded him seriously. "And what do you say?"

She never heard the answer to her question, for a cry came from above.

"Sail ho! Three points to starboard and closing fast!"

The prince straightened with a snap, his jaw clenched as he turned to look over his shoulder. "Excuse me, lady," he said, "My soul will have to wait. It seems the *Lord Marva* has found us once again."

"THE *Lord Marva* is a strong ship, commanded by a deadly captain," the Prince of Venya said, his voice raised to carry across the deck, where the sailors stood shoulder to shoulder in the waist, sweating in the pitiless sunlight. Their faces were taut; most grim, a few of the younger ones looked starkly terrified.

"Richard of Valinor has sent his best against us," the prince continued. "They've run us ragged through storm and sea until we have almost nothing left. I won't lie to you, lads, our backs are to the wall. We'll have two clean shots, a third if we are quick. Each one of them must count. Everything depends on speed. You all know what I expect of you, and I know you will perform with honor. Leander guide our hands and hearts. To your stations!"

It was midday when the *Quest* limped into the cove. Her sails were flapping, and the deck was strewn with the clear evidence of hasty carpentry under way. There was a great deal of hammering and shouting and sailors scurrying about in confusion.

To Rose's eye, the scene was not confused at all, but staged as carefully as any masque. The sails were rigged precisely to the prince's order, and for all the swarming up and down and shouted orders, the ship could not move more quickly, for it was slowed by a sunken barge they towed behind. The *Lord Marva* had been gaining steadily all morning, exactly at the rate the prince decreed, and when the *Quest* rounded the headland into the bay, it was hard upon their heels.

"Now, lads," the prince cried, and the sailors moved as one to clear the decks, make fast the sail, and cut the barge. Others lined the rail, nocking arrow to bowstring and fitting spears into their holders. The wind caught the sails and sped them to the center of the cove just as the tips of the *Lord Marva*'s sails appeared over the headland.

The *Quest* turned with a speed that nearly pitched Rose from her seat. Beylik pumped the bellows, and the brazier burst to life.

"Load," the prince called, and the stone, wrapped tight with oiled rags, was set into the iron basket.

The *Lord Marva* rounded the headland.

"Sight. Now, Beylik," he said, and the boy set the rags aflame. "Fire!"

The flaming missile shattered the deck of the *Lord Marva*. "Load," the prince shouted, "sight and . . . fire!"

The second shot hit the sails. Flame licked across them as the *Quest* approached. "One more, lads," the prince shouted over the cheering of the crew. "Archers—spears—" The third shot caught the top of the highest mast as arrows and spears rained down upon the *Lord Marva*'s deck.

There was no time for more, for the *Quest* was bearing down on the *Lord Marva*—they were passing the ship, close enough that Rose could hear the shouting of the sailors as flaming sails crashed down around them.

She recognized Lord Varnet, standing on the quarterdeck. Beside her, Ashkii leaned so far over the rail that she feared he might fall over, straining to catch a glimpse of his hero. Varnet's face was wooden, though one finger touched his brow in an almost imperceptible salute as the Prince of Venya swept by with a bow.

The crew was cheering, dancing on the deck as the *Quest* flew through the passage and into the open sea.

The cheering faltered as a ship appeared from behind a small island. Silence fell as a second ship joined the first.

"Battle stations," the prince called. "Lady Rosamund, you are with me."

He raced down the hatch to his cabin, where he pulled open a cupboard and began shoving documents into a sack, followed by a heavy stone. "Lady, this time you *will* stay below. Go to Sigurd, give him my compliments, and bid him ready the surgery."

He pulled the drawstring closed and shoved a dagger into his belt. "Keep to the surgery; you will be safe there."

"Good fortune to you!" Rose called helplessly as he strode out the door.

He turned his head and smiled. "And to you, sweet Rosamund."

* * *

SIGURD was not in the surgery when she arrived. She found him up on the foredeck, standing among a group of Moravians, his red head bent in earnest conversation. He caught sight of her and broke off, hurrying to join her.

"We'll go below directly," he said when she told him of the prince's order. "But there is no danger yet."

She had thought—unfairly, she saw now—that Sigurd might be something of a coward. But for a man who professed to abhor violence, he seemed in no hurry to escape the approaching battle. His ice-blue eyes were gleaming as they moved avidly across the deck.

FLORIAN could see that it would be a hard-fought battle. Each of the Valinorian ships was larger than the *Quest*; together, they were formidable. And the *Lord Marva* would be joining them soon enough; she was only delayed, not seriously damaged. He did not need Gordon tugging at his sleeve and mumbling something about surrender to tell him that the odds were not in his favor.

Surrender. Where had that word come from? It seemed to be everywhere at once, blowing across the deck like a whisper of wind upon dry leaves, no one quite daring to speak it aloud. It was unthinkable. Had his crew been Venyan, there would be no question of surrender—but most of them were not. They were worn out and frightened, and the Moravians in particular had been sullen since the death of poor Rashad. He realized now that it was with them the word had started, and it was they who hurried from group to group, spreading the contagion.

Florian stood quite still, a hundred small incidents and remarks he had heard over the past week snapping together to form a single image: *mutiny.*

Before he could respond to this new threat, Beylik took matters into his own hands. The cabin boy leapt to the rail of the quarterdeck and shouted with all the power of his lungs, "Who *dares* speak of surrender? Are we not the Prince of Venya's men in life or death?"

The men on the forecastle deck stilled, eyes stretched wide as they gazed at the boy above. Beylik stood straight, face burning like a flame, his voice ringing like clear silver through the heavy air. "Wouldst live as dogs, thy families shamed forevermore? When this day is sung—and they will sing of it, so long as memory remains—what wouldst thou have them say? That the men of the *Quest* abandoned their prince in his last hour, slunk away, and bent their necks to the collar? Or will they sing that we were true men to the last and sold our lives at such a cost as beggared the whoreson King of Valinor?"

"Death!" The cry came from but half the men, but their voices drowned out the sullen mutters of the rest. "Death before surrender!" The chant was taken up, and soon it was only the Moravians who stood silent while the rest drew off a little, leaving them alone.

Beylik jumped lightly from the rail and fell to one knee before the prince. "Go, my lord," he urged, "now, while they are with you."

Ashkii stood watching, his green eyes solemn as he met the prince's gaze.

"You did well, Beylik." Florian touched the boy's brow. "Thank you. Now get to your post. Ashkii, to me."

He looked hard into the young Ilindrian's eyes. "You saw the captain of the *Lord Marva*?"

Ashkii nodded. "I saw him."

"I want you to go below. Ilindria has no part in this. I promised your mother—"

Florian broke off, remembering his parting from Shideezhi Liluye of Ilindria and what she had given him then. What had he done with it?

"You promised her that I should be a full member of your crew," Ashkii argued hotly. "It is not right that I should hide while a child"—he jerked his chin toward Beylik—"should stay and fight."

"I will not force you. But I will think no less of you if you go below."

"I stay."

Florian nodded absently, his mind searching back, trying to remember where he had put Shideezhi Liluye's gift. He had accepted it from courtesy alone, for no matter what his need, he was no trader in Ilindrian elixir. But she had meant the gesture kindly, and in the same spirit he had taken it and thanked her, fully intending to throw it overboard at the first opportunity.

But had that opportunity ever come? No, he had locked the rosewood case away and forgotten it.

He thrust the weighted sack into Ashkii's arms. "Our logbook and records. If we are boarded, throw it over. Do not let them take it."

"If . . . ?" Ashkii breathed, but Florian did not stay to answer. He bolted down to his cabin and twisted the key in the cabinet door, groaning with relief when he saw the casket was still there. Seizing a small crystal vial, he thrust it into his purse and ran back to the deck, sprinting past the bewildered sailors and heading for the rigging.

Once he had gained the topmast, he turned his gaze to the approaching ships. He drew the vial from his purse and held it tightly, remembering the warning of the High Magea of Venya.

"The elixir of Ilindria is not without value, though to the unitiated, it is slow poison," Magea Gwythian had said, "all the more more deadly for its sweetness. It might wake your gift . . . for a time. But it will be no true waking, and the shock could do irreparable harm."

Not as irreparable as the harm Richard will do, Florian thought, unstoppering the vial. "Lord Leander," he said aloud, "I am in your hands."

He tossed the bitter contents back, then flung it from him, far out into the sea.

He watched it fall slowly, arcing in a glitter that seemed to last a lifetime. Sparkling, turning . . . and then the sparks grew into a dazzling light that encompassed the entire scene below, stretching before him like a tapestry of blue and gold and silver.

He saw the *Quest* and the two Valinorian ships, tiny specks among the twelve islands that made up the chain. Oh, how simple it all was, how ridiculously easy! He laughed, one hand laid lightly on the mast of his ship, feeling the hum of power in his palm.

They had only to move—just so—to slip the trap. The opening was tiny, but it was enough. His fingers tightened as he saw it in his mind's eye, and the *Quest,* Leander bless her, answered as sweetly as she ever had. *Faster, it must be faster*—the thought was no sooner formed than the ship below him quickened, sped through the gap and beyond.

Florian laughed aloud as the wind whipped through his hair. He had always known his ship, but only now was he truly one with her. He needed no wind, no helm, nothing but the power of his thoughts. Faster and faster still . . . He held out a hand, laughing, half-expecting to see lightning shooting from his fingertips. The *Lord Marva,* still trailing clouds of inky smoke, joined the two Valinorian ships. But they were far behind the *Quest* now, for she had already reached the last two islands in the chain.

He staggered as the wild magic began to drain away, leaving a deathly chill in its wake. It flared, but now the surge of energy was more akin to pain than pleasure.

So quickly? he thought. *I must get down before I fall . . .*

Slowly, carefully, he began his painful descent.

WHEN the men began to cheer, Rose pushed through the crowd to see what was happening. No one noticed her; they were staring at the topmast, where the Prince of Venya stood, one hand laid on the mast and his face turned to the wind, laughing as his ship sped toward the narrow gap between the Valinorian vessels. They passed so close that Rose could have reached out and touched the ships on either side, but not a single shot was fired. She glimpsed the bowmen of Valinor, arrows nocked, frozen to their places as they gazed upward, too, mouths fallen open in astonishment.

Then they were gone. The *Quest* was through the opening and into the channel, not tacking to the wind but flying straight into its teeth. Gordon stood at the wheel, hands hanging at his sides.

The prince staggered, caught himself, and stood a moment longer, the wind whipping his flowing black shirt against his chest. He began to descend, but slowly, jerking from one hold to the next. His hand, always so sure upon the rigging, missed a line, and he fell but caught himself at the last moment to land clumsily upon his knees.

"Gordon," he shouted hoarsely, "the helm is yours. Make for Serilla with all—"

He went rigid, his head flung back, and he cried out, a terrible cry that hung in the air as he crumpled to the deck.

"Sigurd! Where's the surgeon—someone fetch him—stand back, you fools, give him air—"

"What is all this?" Sigurd demanded, his red head rising

above the crowd. "Get to your stations, what can you mean by standing about like this in the middle of a battle?"

The men fell back and Sigurd dropped to his knees. He put a hand to the prince's brow, lifted an eyelid, and sank back on his heels, frowning. Then he leaned forward, his face inches from the prince's, pried open his mouth and peered within.

"What is it?" Rose asked.

"Quiet. Let me think." Sigurd closed his eyes for a few seconds, then they snapped open and he called, "Someone lend a hand here—where the devil are they?"

"You sent them away," Rose said, peering anxiously over his shoulder. "Is he—?"

"Not yet. But he will be if one of those fools doesn't—you!" he roared, pointing at a passing sailor. "Get over here. Take up his feet—gently, man, this isn't a sack. We'll take him to the surgery."

Rose hovered in the doorway as they laid the prince on two sea trunks pushed together to form a makeshift table. "Get out," Sigurd snapped, and the sailor went.

"He look bad, lady," he muttered to Rose as he passed. "Look *dead. Feel* dead." He made an unfamiliar sign, thumbs crossed, and hurried toward the hatch.

"Fool," Sigurd muttered beneath his breath, though whether it was the sailor or the prince he meant, Rose could not tell.

"Sigurd—"

"Step in. Sit. If there is one thing I cannot abide, it is someone hovering over me when I am working."

Rose took the seat he indicated. This was a very different Sigurd than she had ever seen before. She did not dare point out that he didn't seem to be working, or doing anything at all but staring into the prince's face and muttering. Disconnected phrases reached her, though they made no sense.

"He wouldn't—why *would* he? But even if he did, it wouldn't . . . or would it? Still, 'twas by his own hand—" His eyes squeezed shut, and his features contorted into a rictus of pain. "Damn you, Yal," he whispered fiercely. He drew a shuddering breath and passed a hand across his eyes. "Venyans," he said, "Venyans . . . I wonder—"

He leapt to his feet, narrowly avoiding the beam above his head, and whirled to his cabinet. "I had it—I know I did, it was in the blue—ah! You, hold his head. *Now,* if you please." Rose hurried forward and laid her hands on the prince's temples. His skin was icy to the touch, and his lips had a bluish tinge that frightened her. "That's it, don't let him move."

Sigurd forced a bottle into the prince's mouth and pinched his nose shut. Florian choked once, then his throat worked as he swallowed.

"Now we shall see."

It could hardly have been more than a few minutes, though it seemed much longer to Rose before the prince gasped and his eyes opened. "Where am I?"

"In the surgery." Sigurd stood and began to straighten the shelf he had disarranged. "That was a very foolish thing you did, my lord."

"No. It was Leander's will."

"Then Leander very nearly got you killed." Sigurd turned and laid a hand on his brow. "And now you are fevered. You will take to your bed and remain there for two days. *Two*. And no complaints, if you please." He glared down at his patient.

"Stop *fussing*, Sigurd. You know I can't abide it." The prince smiled. "Oh, and thank you."

Sigurd's face worked, but at last he said, his voice choked, "Your servant, my lord."

The prince reached for Rose's hand. "Thank you, as well, lady. I'm glad you are here."

His cheeks were flushed, his eyes bright with fever, but still, a triumphant smile curved his lips.

"What did you do that was so foolish?" Rose asked.

"Magic. It always has its price." He turned on his side, tucked her hand beneath his burning cheek, and closed his eyes, still smiling.

Chapter 28

THE prince was up in one day, not two, though Rose thought he should have listened to Sigurd. The fever was gone, but he still looked unwell as they docked at the harbor of Serilla, a small fishing village on the very tip of Sorlain. It was dusk when Rose and the prince arrived at the inn. No one showed the least surprise to see the Prince of Venya appear in the last stages of exhaustion. No questions were asked, no gold demanded, and he was taken at once to a chamber where a dark-robed woman seemed to be awaiting his arrival.

Rose left him there and was shown to a smaller chamber. A few minutes later, a serving man appeared with wood, a pitcher of ale, and a large bowl of stew that she fell upon at once. By the time he had built up the fire, she had finished her meal. Before the door closed behind him, she was asleep.

The next day she received word that the prince would keep to his bed. She followed his example, waking only long enough to consume the meals that appeared with wonderful regularity, and after a long sleep, woke anxious to explore the village.

She ate and dressed in her kirtle, which had been brushed and mended while she slept, then ventured down the stairway. The taproom was deserted at this hour, and sunlight poured through the open shutters. She sat down and had barely begun to wonder what she would do next when she heard footsteps on the stairway. Turning, she saw a young man walk into the taproom. Her breath caught in her throat when she recognized the prince.

This was not the man she'd last seen, weary, ill, and careworn. She had forgotten that he could look like this. His hair was a ripple of pale gold, and for the first time in many days, he was clean-shaven, revealing the strong lines of cheek and jaw. His eyes were clear and shining, his lips and cheeks ruddy with health. In deference to the heat, was clad in a thin black tunic that left his arms and legs bare, with thin sandals laced to the knee.

"I did not expect to see you today! And you look so well!" She jumped to her feet, laughing as she took step forward, her hands outstretched. "I was so worried—"

"It was nothing," he said brusquely.

She stopped, her hands falling to her sides, feeling both ridiculous and impertinent.

"And how are you?" he added after a moment, breaking a very awkward silence. "Have you rested?"

"Yes. Thank you."

He walked to the window and looked out. "It is a fine day, isn't it?"

"Lovely."

Having exhausted the topic of the weather, silence fell between them. Rose searched for some way to break it, though she could not imagine what to say. There were things that *must* be said, the conversation they had delayed until they reached Serilla. Now they were here. There was no excuse to put it off. Yet she dreaded what he might say to her—almost as much as she feared what she might say to him.

Jehan, grant me dignity, she prayed. *Don't let me humiliate myself.*

"The council meets this afternoon," he said abruptly, "but first I must visit the *filidhi* hall. Would you like to see it?"

"Yes, very much."

His smile was as brilliant as he offered her his arm, and suddenly everything was well between them as they stepped out the door into the sunlight.

The *filidhi* hall of Serilla was not a hall at all, but a network of buildings that ambled haphazardly along a rise in the rolling, barren landscape. Most of the buildings were constructed of wood, though there was one squat tower of stone as well.

The prince stopped and stared at it, his eyes hooded. "That is new," he said. "I have not seen it before."

His lips were drawn into a tight line as he led the way to the door and lifted the knocker. It was a beautiful thing, fashioned in the image of a fish, a thick brass ring clasped in its jaws. "This is new, as well," he remarked, then rapped it forcefully upon the brass plate.

Instead of the sharp clang Rose expected, a clear voice sang, "Hark, the Prince of Venya seeks entrance to the hall. Make haste to answer."

"Well, that's handy, isn't it?" Rose said. "I wonder what would it would say if I knocked." She lifted the ring, but before she could let it fall, the door opened.

A young woman in a midnight blue robe greeted them with a smile. "Your Highness," she said, dropping into a deep reverence, the fine wool of her skirt pooling gracefully around her on the flagged floor.

"Caelan!" The prince stepped inside and took her hands, raising her. "Since when do you run about answering doors?"

"Since the Prince of Venya has decided to grace us with his presence," she answered, laughing. "We all heard that you were back, and Magea Avenic has been expecting you."

"Magea Avenic? But—"

Rose lifted a hand to catch the door before it swung shut on her. "May I?" she said, stepping inside.

"My lady," the prince said, "this is Caelan, fourth-year apprentice *filidh*. Caelan, this is Lady Rosamund of Valinor."

Caelan made her a reverence, too, though it was somewhat brief and sketchy. "My lady," she murmured. "You are welcome to our hall."

Nowhere near so welcome as the prince, Rose thought, managing a smile and a nod as she followed them across the flagstones. Caelan, fourth-year apprentice, appeared to be about twenty years. Her steps were firm, as was her voice, and her black hair was drawn severely back to fall in a thick braid to her waist.

"I wanted to see Magea Gwythian," the prince was saying.

"She is no longer mistress of the hall," Caelan said, opening a door and standing aside for them to enter. "Not for nearly a year now. Magea Avenic has taken over her duties."

They exchanged a glance that was obviously significant, though of what, Rose could not say.

"Please wait here," Caelan said. "She will be with you shortly."

"Thank you."

A touch of color rose to Caelan's cheeks when the prince

smiled. She was younger than Rose had thought, and rather attractive in a dark, Venyan way.

"Can I bring you anything, my lord?" she asked. "Some wine, perhaps? Or if you are hungry—"

"No, thank you," Rose said crisply, walking between them into the chamber. "We broke our fast at the inn."

"If you think of anything, just send."

"We will, Caelan. Thank you."

The chamber was warmed by a small fire, and a brazier in one corner sent a pleasantly spicy aroma into the air. Rose kicked off her ill-fitting slippers and sighed with pleasure as her feet sank into the thick, soft carpet. A long table held piles of parchments and several bright objects that glittered against the dark wood.

"Oh, look," she said, picking up several squares of onyx and ivory inlaid with traceries of gold and silver, "more tiles! Aren't these fine ones? And these, are they chrysal rings? How beautiful!"

"Beautiful indeed," a voice said behind her, "but not chrysal rings, I fear. Not yet, at any rate. I have great hopes that young Edmund will do better on his next attempt."

The speaker was a Venyan woman of middle years, with a lean face and mild eyes. "My lady," she said, bowing courteously, "I am Magea Avenic. Welcome to Serilla. And my lord," she turned slightly to include Florian in the bow, "it is a pleasure to see you again. Please sit down and let me serve you."

When they were seated at the table, she took three goblets from the shelf and filled them from a small pot warming by the fire. Rose noticed that the prince's lips compressed again as he took the goblet and turned it in his hands.

"And what brings you here, Your Highness?"

"I had thought to see Magea Gwythian."

Magea Avenic shook her head. "She has relinquished her post. Age, my lord, has caught up with her at last."

"I see." Florian sighed and sipped his wine, his brows rising a little. "Jexlan, is it?"

"You have a discriminating palate."

"As do you, Magea. How nice that you can accommodate it."

"Isn't it?" She smiled. "We have been doing rather well this past year, you know."

"No, I didn't." He smiled, as well. "I wonder why I was not informed of your newfound prosperity."

"Perhaps it was that you have never shown much interest in the *filidhi* hall," she replied pleasantly. "It has been . . . what, a full year since you last graced us with a visit?"

"Has it really been so long as that?" He leaned back in his seat. "Let me see, it was just after my last visit that I took the *Spindrift* off the Jexlan coast. This carpet came from her hold, I believe. And the tapestries—Moravian, are they not? Yes, from the *Mako,* as I recall. I have reason to remember that encounter particularly, for three men lost their lives. Then there were the months I spent in Ilindria, trying to convince the *Qaletaqa* that any men and arms he might give me would be put to good use. From there back to Jexal, another two months at sea—"

He held up the goblet. "But I see you are already familiar with *that* voyage. Yes, Magea, I believe you have the right of it. It *has* been a full year since I sat at my ease in the *filidhi* hall."

Rose glanced from the prince to the Magea, but the woman only smiled serenely. "Well, you are here now," she said, rising smoothly from her seat, "and very welcome. Perhaps you would like to visit the apprentices?"

The prince stood as well. "I'm afraid I haven't time today. The council meets this afternoon."

"What a pity. They would be so pleased so see you, I am sure. Indeed, my lord, if I might make a suggestion . . . ?"

"Please do."

"Make the time for us. We are all aware of your many sacrifices on our behalf. Let us show you what all your hard work has wrought. I think you will be pleased with our progress."

"I'm sure I will be."

"The apprentices should meet you for themselves," Magea Avenic continued. "You are nothing but a name to them. And if you were to perhaps give some small demonstration of your own abilities, they would feel that you are indeed one of them."

"In that, I fear I cannot oblige you," he answered with a slight shrug. "As you know, I have received no formal training."

"But the royal gift—"

"Is not one that can be used for show. But as to the rest, I would be very pleased to spend an afternoon with the apprentices. After

Chapter 29

THE prince was silent as they went back down the hill and toward the small village nestled at its foot. They passed along the busy dock, and Rose stared openly about, for as she had an escort the sailors did not trouble her.

The docks were a confusion of noise and color, filled with people hurrying about their business. Men and women, pale and dark, dressed in a bewildering variety of colors thronged the narrow planks. Sailors came and went up the gangplanks of the ships, carrying rolls of fabric, nets and fish, and baskets piled high with bread and fruit. Women with children hanging on their skirts waited patiently by the gangplanks, and other women, dressed in scanty gowns of gaudy hues, called boldly to the men on board.

As Rose stared about, wide-eyed, the prince walked easily through the crowd, calling back friendly greetings as dozens of voices cried his name aloud. It seemed he knew everyone and would often stop to inquire whether the journey had been successful or how a sailor's ailing father was or whether one of the women had found the man she sought. Rose noticed how the people brightened when he spoke to them.

Even with no mark of rank and clad as plainly as he was, there was something about him that drew and held the eye. Certainly it was drawing the eyes of the women. They turned to watch him pass, young and old, maid and mistress, and for a moment they all wore the same expression—soft, almost wistful, as though they had been reminded of some half-forgotten dream.

They passed into the village itself, a small collection of buildings roofed with red tiles. A lemon tree stood in the center of the square, and the path was lined with flowering shrubs. Bright blossoms spilled from window boxes and trailed down the white-washed walls.

Florian drew a long breath. "Serilla," he said. "I'm glad to be back." He paused beside a livery stable. "I'd like to stop here for a moment, if you're not too tired."

"Not a bit," Rose said.

They stepped inside and were assaulted with the pungent scents of hay and horses. "Mmm," Rose murmured. "Lovely." She laughed at Florian's expression and reached past him to stroke the gray nose of a horse that thrust its head out of what had seemed to be an empty stall. It submitted to her attentions with typical equine arrogance.

"You do ride, don't you?" she asked.

"When I must. *Only* when I must." The blunt nose butted him, and he edged away.

"Don't you like horses?"

"Not much." The horse stretched its neck over the stall and nipped at Florian's wrist. "It is a mutual aversion."

"He's only being friendly."

"I do not consider biting friendly. Well, generally speaking. There are exceptions, of course, but none of them involve horses."

Rose rolled her eyes and bent to kiss the horse's velvet nose. "Don't listen to him. He doesn't mean a word of it."

"On the contrary, I—" Florian sneezed three times in rapid succession. "Hay," he said succinctly in answer to Rose's questioning look. Raising his voice, he called, "Master Rab!"

A young Venyan hurried from a far stall, shaking a shock of jet-black hair from his eyes and wiping his hands on a rag.

"My lord!" he said, smiling as he bobbed his head. "I heard you had arrived. How are you?"

"As you see me. Let me present you to Lady Rosamund of Valinor."

"Lady—Lady *Rose?*" The young man's eyes widened and he made her a much deeper bow. "I—this is a great honor—will you sit down? Can I bring you some ale—or—"

Florian shot Rosamund a sideways grin. "Thank you, but we broke our fast at the inn. You're looking rather prosperous these days, master ostler. Trade is brisk?"

"Quite. We added on ten stalls this spring, and all of them are full."

"And how does young Corin come along?"

"Much better. You did well to send him to me—and not only for his sake. He's been a great help; he's got a real feeling for the horses. But then, all those hill folk are born to it, aren't they? Here, let me call—"

Rab broke off as a young man strode into the stable. A very lordly young man, Florian noticed, lean and high-nosed, wearing the long robes of a *filidh*. A green mantle was flung over his shoulders, and a green gem glittered in his ear.

"Boy," he said to Rab, "where is my horse? You did get my message, didn't you?"

"Aye, sir. We're just getting to her now." Rab turned his head and called, "Corin, saddle Damson. Master Daigh is here."

The young *filidh* let out a sharp breath of annoyance. "I have an appointment. Now I shall be late."

"Your pardon, young sir," Florian said mildly. "It was I who distracted Master Rab."

"Next time keep your gossip for the tavern," Daigh snapped, "and leave the servants to their work."

"Servants?" Florian repeated softly. "Is that what they are? I did not know."

"Well, now you do. Oh, come along," he added impatiently as a very small boy led an enormous black beast forward. "I'm late already."

Florian could hardly recognize the wasted child he had last seen aboard the *Endeavor*. Though still thin, Corin had filled out wonderfully and his hair had grown into a tight cap of dark curls. He did not look up at them, but kept his eyes fixed on the horse's saddle as he fiddled with the girth.

"It's twisted," he said. "I can't get it—"

"Let me," Rab said, moving to the horse.

"Stand away, both of you. I'll do it myself." Daigh pushed past Rab and knocked into Corin, throwing the boy off-balance. Corin tried to right himself, reaching out to grasp a hanging bridle for support, but it pulled from the nail and he fell to the floor.

Rab rounded on the *filidh*, his mild eyes kindling. "That was ill done. *Sir*."

Daigh, bent over the girth with his back to both Rab and Corin, straightened with a snap. He turned, his gaze moving quickly from Corin, sprawled awkwardly in a pile of stable sweeping, to Rab. The young ostler took a step forward, hands fisted at his sides, and Daigh rose instantly to the challenge, his eyes flashing as brightly as the gem in his ear as he drew back his hand.

Florian stepped between them and grasped Daigh's wrist.

"Get your hands off me!" Daigh snarled. "Who the devil do you think you are?"

"I am the Prince of Venya."

Daigh threw back his head, the better to look down his nose at Florian. "Yes, and I am the King of Sorlain. You insolent—"

"He is," Rab and Rosamund said together.

Daigh stared at the fingers imprisoning his wrist, his eyes widening as he noticed the seal ring on the prince's hand. "My lord," he whispered, "I did not know."

Florian released him. "Is it the custom here to speak so rudely to a stranger? And to abuse a boy who is doing his work as best he can?"

"He made me late," Daigh said defensively. "And you saw for yourself that this one was insolent."

"No, Daigh, I saw nothing of the sort. What I saw was a young apprentice who does not seem to know his place. This is Rab's stable, not yours."

"My lord, I am a *filidh*."

"And Rab is an ostler. I cannot speak for you, but I know that *he* is damned good at what he does. For that he deserves to be treated with respect, if courtesy is beyond you. Unless you would like to stable your own horse, arrange for its feed, shoe it, and dose it when it is sick? No? Then I suggest you either apologize or learn to do without a horse. Because I tell you, Daigh, Rab is not bound to serve you or any man. He is a *fheara* of Venya under my protection."

Daigh's cheeks flushed. "As you say, my lord." He turned to Rab. "Boy—"

"Rab," Florian corrected. "*Master* Rab to you. For he has completed his apprenticeship, which you have not."

Rab was now as red as the young *filidh* before him. "My lord, that isn't—" he protested, but Florian held up a hand.

"Go on, Daigh."

"Master Rab," the young *filidh* said, the words hissing through clenched teeth, "I apologize for my discourtesy."

"And I for mine," Rab said at once.

Daigh nodded, looking somewhat mollified. "Now may I have my horse?"

"Of course, sir," Rab said. He bent and twisted the girth. "She is ready."

Daigh turned quickly away, his cloak swirling about his boots as he strode to the horse without another word. Florian watched gloomily as the *filidh* mounted and turned his horse's head toward the door. Just before passing through, he halted and looked over at Corin.

"Boy," Daigh said, then bit his lip. "I do not know your name."

"Go on," Rab urged, giving Corin's shoulder a little shake.

"Corin. Sir."

"Corin, Damson is looking splendid. I can see you've taken good care of her. Thank you."

Corin glanced up shyly. "She's a wonderful horse."

Daigh smiled. "She is, isn't she? Good day."

He passed through the doorway without looking back.

"Hello, Corin," Florian said, dropping to one knee. "Do you remember me?"

"Yes."

"Then give your prince a proper greeting and tell me how you have been getting on here."

Corin hesitated but a moment, then flung himself into the prince's arms, his voice rising as he gabbled out a long and complicated story without pausing to draw breath.

Rose could not quite grasp the tale, but the words "Sir Ewan" and *"Endeavor"* were repeated more than once, along with a mine that figured largely in young Corin's nightmares, though Master Rab—a man who really understood horses, Corin added in what was clearly the highest praise he could bestow—had come up with the cure for that by allowing Corin to bed down in the stable.

As the high, excited voice went on, Rab leaned against the wall beside Rose.

"I've seen them up at the hall," he said quietly, "weaving their spells and making their illusions. Very pretty. Very impressive." He glanced at the door through which the young *filidh* had passed, then shook his head and grinned. "But *that*," he said, "was magic."

Chapter 30

TWO hours later the prince stood at bay in the center of the tap-room of the Gilded Dragon, facing the five men seated at a long table opposite the hearth.

"Are you implying," he asked in a dangerously low voice, "that I have been irresponsible?"

Ewan had hoped this meeting might reconcile their differ-ence, but there was no denying that it had started badly and promised to get worse. Even the weather had turned against them. The sky that had promised so fair at midday had turned to a mass of roiling clouds. Rain drummed upon the roof, and waves broke in thundering crashes upon the Serillan cliffs be-yond the windows.

The shutters behind the council table were shut tight, and the only illumination came from the hearth across the room. Backlit by the fire, the prince was a faceless shadow. The stark black he wore heightened the impression of darkness, relieved only by the ring glinting in his ear.

Ewan glanced uneasily at the grim faces of his fellow coun-cilors, ruddy in the firelight, then stood and took three candles from the mantel and set them on the table. No one spoke as he touched a waxed spill to the fire and lit them one by one. Only when he had resumed his seat did the discussion continue as though there had never been a pause.

"It is all well and good to say that you could not abandon the princess to King Richard's mercy," Lord Carlysle said, "but once the *Lord Marva* appeared on the scene, you must have seen that she posed a danger to yourself and to your ship."

"What would you have had me do, my lord? Toss her to the sharks?"

"There must have been some opportunity to set her ashore," Carlysle answered irritably.

"As it happens, there was not. At least not in a place where she would have had the slightest chance of survival."

"Then—"

"Leave it, Carlysle," Lord Bastyon said wearily. He wasn't looking well, Ewan thought. It seemed he had aged ten years in the months since they had met. "The prince did what he felt was right, and it makes no matter now. Princess or no princess, the *Lord Marva* will not dare attack Serilla."

"True," the prince replied, "but that still leaves us with the question of how the *Lord Marva* found me in the first place. *Someone* has been keeping Richard very well informed about my plans."

"Now, Your Highness," Ewan said, catching the prince's eye and frowning, "I'm certain ye dinna mean to imply that it was one of *us*."

The prince's amber eyes moved over the members of the council, holding each one's gaze in turn.

"Tempers are running a bit high today," Ewan said, shooting the council members a warning look. "We're already looking into the matter of where Richard got his information, but it will be the devil's own luck if we turn anything up."

"I'd say that the most likely candidates are among your crew," Carlysle said. "That Ilindrian—"

"His name is Ashkii—Lord Kohkahycumest Ashkii to you— and I would stake my life on his loyalty."

"Well, you did, didn't you?" a cool voice drawled. "And look where it got you."

It was Lord Eredor, the youngest of the council members, who spoke. He was a slender man with the typical Venyan combination of black hair and pale brown eyes. Ewan had never cared much for Eredor personally, but even he must admit that the young lord had done an able job of stepping into his father's place the year before.

"As Sir Ewan said, we're looking into it, Your Highness," Bastyon said impatiently. "And I suggest you do the same."

Eredor leaned forward in his seat. "But in the meantime, Your

Highness, perhaps you would be so good as to explain why you countermanded the council's decision regarding the *Endeavor*."

The prince rounded on him. *"What?"*

"Not now, Eredor," Ewan snapped. "He's barely on his feet."

"And by the time he is firmly on his feet, they will no doubt have carried him away again," Eredor said, his light brown eyes fixed on the prince with a predatory gleam. "Leaving us to deal with the problem of Serilla on our own."

"On your own? I would hardly say so, my lord," the prince retorted sharply. "You seem to have made quite free with the gold that I have sent, gold that was intended to raise an army. Where are the weapons I ordered the council to purchase? The men who should be training even now?"

Eredor sat a little straighter in his seat. "I have sent you a full accounting of every copper spent. Would you have the *filidhi* starve?"

"Of course not. But I do not recall signing any order for a new tower for the hall, and I am quite sure I never approved disbursing Jexlan wine or golden goblets for the personal use of the Magea! Serilla is a temporary measure, Eredor. Your father understood that."

"But I am not my father," Eredor answered smoothly. "And times have changed. We must trim our sails to the prevailing wind."

"No, you are clearly not your father, nor are you a sailor," the prince replied, obviously keeping tight hold of his temper. "Or you would know that once a course is set, the variation of the wind is no excuse to alter it."

"Unless," Eredor countered, "the course was set for an impossible destination. Then, I believe, even the most doughty sailor would agree that to persist in it is folly."

"Venya is not an impossible destination," the prince snapped. "I fully intend to reach it, no matter how much hot air I endure from the most junior member of my council. Hear me, Eredor: I have sworn a sacred oath to my people—to *all* my people, not only the *filidhi*—and I will fulfill that oath or die in the attempt."

The silence that followed was as charged as the air before a storm. Ewan tried to think of some way to break it, but this storm had been brewing for so long that it was far beyond his ability to control. All he could do was wait it out and hope the destruction was not irreversible.

"And how," Eredor said, each word clipped short, "do you intend to do that? Had you troubled to read the latest report I sent you—"

"I read it."

"Then you must know that our goals have changed. We are doing our utmost to become self-sufficient."

"What I know," the prince replied, "is that you and Magea Avenic seem to think that Venyan magic is a commodity to be bought and sold. Leander knows how she ever became Magea when she clearly had no concept of what it means to be a Venyan *filidh*. As for you—"

"You need not remind me that I am no *filidh*," Eredor said. "We are all well aware that I am but a *fheara*."

"It is you who make that distinction, Eredor, not I. *Fheara, filidh*, what difference does it make? We are all *Venyan*."

"Most of the *filidhi* have no memory of Venya. They are Serillan, my lord, and take pride in that—too much pride to continue living off the spoils of your conquests."

"Then they should be pleased that I have made my last conquest. Now we can all turn our attention to Venya and get the *filidhi* home, where they need not concern themselves with anything beyond their art."

Eredor's eyes narrowed. "A fine dream. But tell me, Your Highness, have you never wondered why in eighteen years you have not managed to win a single outside supporter to such a lofty and admirable cause?"

"You forget the Ilindrians," the prince answered. "I have received a message from the *Qaletaqa* arranging a meeting with his ambassadors."

"The *Ilindrians?*" Carlysle cried. "I thought that was all finished. Do not tell us you are once again considering allying us with that—that filth?"

"The Ilindrians are not filth, but even if they were, it makes no matter. I would ally us with Rakshasa himself if he offered men and arms."

"Which the Ilindrians have not," Bastyon put in, sounding more exhausted than ever. "Nor do they intend to. They will make no commitment until they are certain of success."

"Lord Bastyon is right," Eredor said. "Surely even you have fathomed that the *Qaletaqa* is playing you and Richard against each other to his own advantage. You have no solid support at all, Your Highness, nor any prospects of gaining any. In the eighteen years since Venya fell, has it never once occurred to you that maybe, just possibly, you are wrong to persist in this misguided course?"

"Yes," the prince answered, flicking Eredor a scornful look. "It has occurred to me. But I dismissed it as a base and cowardly notion."

"That is your prerogative. But some of us must take a more practical approach. Perhaps you have not noticed, but while you have been off on your adventures, we have built something fine here on Serilla." Eredor struck his palm upon the table. "How dare you ask us to throw it all away to feed your pride?"

The prince drew an audible breath. "Do you think I do this for my own pleasure? The Venyan people—"

"Have rejected you. The *fheara* do not want you back, and the *filidhi* will not fight for you. The time has come to face the fact that Venya is lost to us."

"Richard of Valinor has destroyed the trust the *fheara* once had in me. But I will win it back."

Eredor laughed. "Oh, will you? Really? I'd like to see even the Prince of Venya produce such a miracle as that!"

"Then you shall see it, Eredor. Tonight. For at dusk I will wed Rose of Valinor, who holds the hearts and trust of the Venyan *fheara* in her hands. With her at my side, they will rally to me once again."

Ewan barely restrained his exclamation of surprise. He had been prepared for this announcement when the two of them arrived on Serilla, but when it did not come, he had assumed the prince had either changed his mind or been rejected. He had not expected it to be flung at Eredor as a challenge. Nor was he the only one taken unawares. A shocked silence filled the taproom as every member of the council assessed this unexpected development.

"The wedding will take place here, at sunset," the prince continued coolly, "and I expect every one of you to attend. In fact, you can consider it a royal command. I would advise you not to disappoint me."

With that, he turned on his heel and strode out of the taproom. When the door closed behind him, the council sat in stunned silence for a moment. Bastyon dropped his head into his hands.

"What the devil was that?" Lysagh asked.

"That, lads, was your prince," Ewan said, leaning back in his seat and hiding his smile in his beard.

"That—that—" Carlysle sputtered. "How dare he address us in such wise? Why, if not for us, he would be dead!"

"We put him where he is," Eredor said, "and we can take him down."

"Lad," Ewan said, "watch yourself. One more word and ye will be talking treason."

"Treason?" Carlysle demanded. "Why, it is he who has betrayed us! Bastyon, surely you don't intend to let him go through with this."

Bastyon raised his head. "The decision has been made. I will support the prince, as will you."

"Surely you do not expect me to attend that—that farce!" Eredor began.

"Indeed I do," Bastyon said coldly. "Your prince has commanded it."

"*My* prince?" Eredor's eyes narrowed as he stared at the door. "Is he really?"

Ewan brought his palm down sharply on the table. "You go too far! I'm willing to believe that ye spoke without thinking, Eredor. Now I suggest ye shut your mouth before I am forced to shut it for ye."

Eredor began to speak, then he took another look at Ewan's face and reconsidered.

"Fine, then," Ewan said. "Now get your arse up and put on your finery. You're going to a wedding."

Eredor walked out of the room, his back stiff, Carlysle trailing in his wake. Lysagh followed more slowly. He opened the door, then hesitated and looked back.

"I cannot like Eredor," Lysagh said, "but I fear that he is right."

Bastyon raised his head. "Eredor is a fool. He understands nothing that cannot be tallied up and entered in a ledger. I will see you at dusk, Lysagh."

When Lysagh was gone, Ewan rounded on Bastyon.

"If that is how ye feel," he cried, "why do ye not say so to the prince? Your silence hurts him, Bastyon, can ye no see that for yourself?"

"If I am silent, it is for good reason."

"He needs you. Leander knows why, but your opinion matters to him. What reason could be so damnably important as to—"

"He knows why I stay silent. Were I to speak, it would be in support of Eredor."

Ewan's jaw dropped. "But ye just said—"

"I said Eredor lacks imagination, and that is true. But he has other qualities equally important. And Ewan, much as it pains me to admit this, I believe Eredor has the right of it. The prince has done his best, I will not deny him that, but his best was just not good enough. In his heart, he knows this. He won't admit it, not even to himself, but were I to say it, he would listen. And it would destroy him. So I remain silent.

"Though"—his voice trembled and he compressed his lips, then went on firmly—"I do not know how much longer I dare continue. This marriage is a disaster. He is using the princess to shield himself from a truth he cannot face. It will do nothing but delay the inevitable, at Leander knows what cost. This union should be stopped. *I* should stop it. I know my duty, Ewan, but I-I—" He rested his brow on his clenched fist. "I cannot bring myself to do it. I am too weak—"

Ewan rested a hand on Bastyon's shoulder. "That is not weakness, Nigel, it is faith. Ye are as bad as Eredor in your way, wanting everything all neat and tidily in place, but I say to ye that the prince isna finished yet. And ye discount Lady Rosamund too quickly. This marriage could be the making of them both."

Bastyon's frail shoulders trembled. "I wish I could believe that," he whispered. "I would give anything to have your faith. But I do not."

"DAMN him," Eredor swore, pacing up and down before the hearth in his chamber. "What does it take to convince him he is beaten?"

Carlysle sank down on the settle. "You don't remember Venya, do you?"

"No."

"If you did, you would understand why it is so hard to let it go. Venya was—"

Eredor waved a hand. "A paradise where *filidh* and *fheara* lived as one. I *know,* Sean. I've heard it all before. But what matters is the future, not the past. We cannot continue to drift along in some dream world, bestowing gifts only on the worthy while we wait for the prince to lead us home. We must make our own future here on Serilla, and that future lies with the trade routes. Don't you see? The world has changed, and we must change with it."

"Bastyon would say that some things never change."

"Bastyon is an old man. He's given good service, and don't think I don't admire him, but his day is done. The Prince of Venya is a thief and a pirate, and to continue to profit from his crimes is to share in his dishonor. It is time Serilla had a new leader, one who can help the *filidhi* out of this mire of superstition and false hopes."

"That new leader being you?" Carlysle asked dryly.

"Perhaps. But by all the gods, Sean, that is not what I am after. I am *not* the prince."

Carlysle smiled faintly. "No, you are not. Don't underestimate him, Earnán. That would be a grave mistake."

"I don't. He is what he is—Leander help him, how can he be otherwise? Born and bred for one purpose only, and that denied him. He is . . . a relic. An unnecessary relic chaining us to a dead past—and I'm not the only one who feels that way. Many of the younger *filidhi* agree with me already. You may not believe it, Sean, but I feel sorry for the prince. The time is coming when everyone will see he simply isn't needed anymore."

"Perhaps," Carlysle agreed. "But that time is not yet."

"Still, it is coming. No one can stop it now. And whatever I can do to hasten it, I will."

Chapter 31

SIGURD went swiftly up the stairway of the inn, keeping to the shadow of the wall. The meeting place was set, his orders clear, conveyed to him by Richard's sorcerer in the hour before dawn. They had argued in fierce whispers until the sorcerer's form was no more than a shimmer in the growing light, but all Sigurd's passion could not move King Richard's emissary.

"I thought Richard wanted to be rid of him and the princess both," Sigurd said, "and this is the perfect opportunity."

"I have told you, Sigurd, his plans changed. He wants the princess returned to him alive and the Venyan brought to Valinor for execution."

"Fool. My way is much better."

"I agree," the sorcerer said, surprising him. "King Richard has no appreciation for the finer points of pain. But he is the king and we do his will, so you must find your amusement elsewhere. Do not fail us, Sigurd, or it will be you who takes the prince's place beneath the axe. Do you understand me?"

He vanished without waiting for an answer.

Now Sigurd reached the doorway and tapped lightly on the wood. "My lady, it is Sigurd," he called softly. "May I come in?"

"It is open."

"The council meets below," he said, ducking beneath the lintel and closing the door quietly behind him, "there will be no better chance to slip away."

The princess sat before the window, looking out into the storm. "Sigurd, there is no need for such secrecy. The prince has assured me that I am free to leave."

"Then I suggest you take him at his word. You do want to go to Jexal, do you not? Or have you changed your mind?"

"I am not certain," she answered slowly.

Sigurd muttered a curse, dragging a hand through his bright curls. "I was afraid of this."

"Of what?" Her voice was cool, and her dark brows lifted, warning him of her incipient displeasure.

"That you would fall prey to his blandishments," Sigurd answered bluntly. "Come, lady, surely you know you're not the first he has beguiled into his bed! I thought he might have some respect for your rank, but I see I was mistaken."

She leapt to her feet, her body taut with outrage. "That is enough. Please leave me now."

She turned her back on him. *Oh, princess,* Sigurd thought, touching the poiniard in his sleeve as he eyed her slender neck, *do not tempt me beyond endurance.*

Once he had almost liked her; enough, at least, to be sorry for whatever fate Richard of Valinor had in store for her. He had thought she might be different. But she wasn't. She was just like all the rest of them, so cool and proper to a man they thought beneath them, but eager enough to spread their legs for the Prince of Venya's pleasure.

She had no idea who Sigurd really was or the power he wielded, which was far beyond anything the prince could command. She would not look at him so coldly if his blade was at her neck; then she would not speak to him so haughtily. She would beg. They all did in the end. They cringed and cried and pleaded for their lives, a gift that he alone could grant. It would be pure pleasure to leave this one lying in her blood, a parting gift to the prince.

A pretty problem that would be, when Richard cried to the world that his beloved niece was stolen and offered such a ransom as would make the common people gasp with wonder. Let the Prince of Venya talk his way out of that one! Once the murder of the princess was discovered, his noble dreams would fall in ruins all around him. But even that would not be the best of it.

What the prince would call his strength, Sigurd knew to be his greatest weakness. A true prince would take exactly what he wanted by whatever means he liked. He would never allow his actions to be questioned by his council or suffer any man to live who once opposed his will. But the Prince of Venya was both fool and weakling, his wits so bound and hampered by his so-called honor that he had not even a skilled assassin at his beck.

Honor? Sigurd was often hard put not to laugh when he heard that word applied to the Prince of Venya. It was vanity that made the prince imagine himself as one of the heroes in the old tales; hoping, in his secret heart, to win a place among their company. Sigurd could make that dream come true. One cut of the blade would ensure the Prince of Venya's immortality. His name would live forever as a byword for treacherous depravity. Death would be nothing in comparison to such a fate.

Almost it would be worth the loss of wealth and rank and vengeance to see the mighty Prince of Venya brought so low and know that he, Sigurd Einarsson, had done this.

But worth his life? A bit more time and he would far surpass King Richard's sorcerer in power. But as that time had not yet come, Sigurd dropped down upon one knee and bent his head contritely. "Forgive me. Be assured that only the deepest concern for you could make me so forget myself. Lady, I beg you to turn from a path that can only lead to ruin. Save yourself while there is still time."

She rounded on him, her face cold and still with anger. "You wrong him."

"He wrongs you!" Sigurd cried, moving forward on his knees to catch her hand. "While I—I ask nothing but to serve!" He pressed a fervent kiss upon her wrist. "You are so beautiful—so kind—do you not know that I would die for you?"

"A noble sentiment," a cool voice drawled behind him, "but I trust such desperate measures will not be called for."

The prince leaned in the doorway, arms folded across his chest. Damn him, what was he doing here? Surely the council meeting could not be finished yet! The princess snatched her hand away.

"M-my lord," Sigurd stammered, "I did not expect you."

"Obviously. Get up, I think your point is made. Tell me, Sigurd, exactly what service were you offering the lady?"

Sigurd scrambled awkwardly to his feet and ducked his head as though embarrassed. "I thought—that is, at one time the princess expressed a desire to go to Jexal—and as I know the desert—and her uncle, the *Melakh*—I thought she might need a guide."

The prince looked from Sigurd to the princess. "Is this so, lady? Do you wish to go to Jexal?"

"You and I have spoken of this, my lord," she answered cautiously.

"And other things besides. Or had you forgotten?"

"No." She held her chin high, though her face flamed crimson. "I have not forgotten."

The prince walked into the chamber and stood by the window, a shadow against the storm without. "A ship leaves for Padaea on the evening tide. 'Tis but a merchantman, I fear, and the journey will be long, for the ship is old and and the captain will not go directly. He has a fear of pirates, you see, having been attacked several times in the past along this route. I had hoped to find one that could take you a bit closer to Jexal, but this is the best that I can offer. If you wish to be on it, you must make haste."

"Padaea?" she repeated faintly.

"Yes, it is unfortunate," the prince answered, as though landing at the doorstep of Jexal's ancient enemy was a trifling inconvenience. "But I hear there is an active smuggling trade between the two countries. You should be able to arrange something along those lines. Unless, of course," he turned to Sigurd with an ironic half-bow, "your escort has found some better means of transportation. Was there another ship you had in mind?"

Sigurd had not even inquired at the docks. He shook his head and mumbled, "I was awaiting the princess's decision."

"As was I. As I am still," the prince said, though it was not to Sigurd that he spoke. "What is your will, lady? To begone with Sigurd on the evening tide? Or . . . ?"

Or what? Sigurd thought, looking from one to the other. There was another conversation going on here, made up of glances and half-spoken thoughts.

"I would think on it a while longer," the princess demurred.

"No time." The Venyan held out his hands and shrugged, his eyes locked with hers. "I doubt even Sigurd could find a ship bound southeastward once the autumn trade winds blow. I fear that it is now or—well, perhaps not *never,* but at least until the spring, at which time I will be far from Serilla and unable to assist you. If you would go, you must go now."

Sigurd knew an ultimatum when he heard one. So, apparently, did the princess, for the color fled from her cheeks. But there was more at stake here, some alternative to such an ill-planned flight known only to the two of them.

"You need not go alone, lady," Sigurd put in. "I can—"

"Leave us," the Venyan said simply, gesturing toward the door without so much as glancing Sigurd's way. Oh, what joy it would be to wipe that arrogant expression from his face. *Patience,* Sigurd told himself, managing a jerky bow, *'tis but a minor setback. He will fall in the end. And I will be there to see it.*

WHEN the door closed behind Sigurd, Rose sank into her seat. This was all happening too quickly. The prince had transformed yet again, this time into a stern stranger who would send her off to Padaea on the evening tide. She searched his face, hoping for some hint that he did not really mean this, but he was not even looking at her. She followed his gaze to the window, where the storm still raged outside and huge waves crashed against the cliffs.

"Well?" he said, not turning. "Which shall it be, lady? Padaea, or . . . have you reconsidered my proposal?"

"Why?" she asked. "Why would you wed me?"

He gave her a sideways glance. "There is a chance that you are carrying the heir to Venya."

"I am not. That much is certain."

"Still, I need to marry. Obviously I must marry a woman of noble birth. As you are without home or kin . . ."

She waited, but he did not go on. It was not that she expected or even wanted him to repeat his stilted words of love, but common courtesy demanded that he add some small profession of regard. Even Cristobal, in his one blotted missive, had signed himself, "your loving husband" and vowed to keep her letter next to his heart until the day they should meet. But apparently the Prince of Venya had no regard for custom. Or courtesy.

"Please, say no more," she said, when it was clear that he had no intention of doing so. "Your simple eloquence has already left me breathless. You are desperate. I am available. What woman would not swoon at such a thrilling declaration?"

He clasped his hands behind his back and gazed up at the ceiling. "I'm not doing this very well, am I?" he said to no one in particular.

"No, you are not."

He sat down on the edge of the bed and took her hand in his. "Let me start again. Lady Rosamund, do you believe I will return to Venya one day?"

"Yes," she said, so decisively that he smiled.

"So do I. But there are others who do not believe it, and still others who would stop me from attempting it."

"Is this your council you speak of?"

"Unfortunately, it is." He stroked her fingers one by one. "It is not merely a princess I seek, but an ally. One who believes in what I'm doing. One who understands that nothing in this world can come between me and Venya."

He continued to stroke her hand, his fingertips moving lightly up her wrists.

"I travel often, usually without warning or idea of when I might return. It would help enormously if I had someone I could trust—someone with your intelligence—to sit on the council in my absence."

He was saying one thing with his words, but quite another with his hands. Responsibility and duty were certainly one part of marriage, he was reminding her, but there was another part as well, the part that involved the two of them alone with the curtains drawn around the bed.

Her hand was almost lost in his, and his skin looked very dark against her own. The contrast was . . . exciting. She remembered his hands on other parts of her body and lost the thread of the conversation altogether. His voice went on, saying something about the council, and she dragged her gaze from their joined hands. But that was even worse, for now she found herself staring at his mouth.

There was something very pleasing about the shape of his lips. So neat. So precisely chiseled. The dip of the upper lip was sharply defined, the lower lip a bit fuller, a little softer. Very mobile lips, she thought, remembering their touch upon her own. One minute his kiss had been light and teasing, the next implacable. Like him, it had been confusing. Exhilarating. Impossible to predict from one moment to the next.

These were not the qualities she desired in a husband, or so she'd always thought. Now, though, as he continued to caress her, she knew she could never look at any man without comparing him to this one. She listened to his voice—not his words, they were beyond her, but just the music of his accent—a bit Sorlainian, a touch of Venyan, a hint of what she thought might be Ilindrian—a cadance that was uniquely his. Then it stopped and he looked at her, awaiting a response.

"Would you really force me to go to Padaea if I refuse?"

He composed his expression almost instantly, but she knew this was not the response he had expected. He waited a moment before replying, and when he did, it was without a trace of the annoyance she had glimpsed upon his face.

"You mistook my meaning," he said patiently. "I would not force you to do anything, though I fear you cannot remain upon Serilla unless we wed. Your uncle—both your royal uncles—would take it much amiss were we to form such an . . . irregular connection. No matter how innocent it was, the world judges such things harshly."

She forced herself to smile. "Is it my reputation you are worried for or yours?"

"'Tis a bit late to worry about mine, and yours is, of course, your own concern. But I cannot afford a scandal of this nature now, not when I need all the support I can muster. I am sorry, but I dare not risk it. I had hoped to avert it by a marriage that would seem to be of advantage to us both. But you are free to go where you list. I will aid you insofar as I am able without compromising Venya's interests."

Rose felt her throat tighten. They both knew she had nowhere to go but Jexal and no way of reaching there before the spring. He was offering her a place, a home, respectability—she would be a fool not to jump at such a chance. One day he would break her heart, but at least she would be alive to bear the pain.

"Surely the council would never allow a woman to sit among them," she said, a feeble protest that made him smile.

"Surely they would! I know it isn't done in Valinor, but you must remember that my mother was Queen of Venya in her own right. I don't just need any wife; I need a lady of good sense and sound judgment who will one day rule Venya at my side. I need *you*. I want you. Will you have me?"

Despite the hours Rose had spent considering this very prospect, she had a mad desire to burst out laughing. *Me? The*

Princess of Venya? One day Queen of Venya? He cannot possibly be serious.

But he did not look like he was jesting. He looked . . . weary, she thought, noting the shadows beneath his eyes. Worried. If she did not know better, she would say frightened. His hand was cold in hers, and she could practically feel the tension vibrating through his muscles. There was more here than she understood; he had not told her everything. But she thought at least part of what he *had* said was the truth. He did indeed look like a man in desperate need of an ally.

"Yes." She sighed. "I will."

"Thank you." He raised their joined hands to his lips, then released her and stood. "The wedding will be at sunset, then. If that is agreeable to you."

He didn't even kiss me, she thought, and now he looks so . . . grim. A chill spread through her, pooling in her stomach as his last words reached her.

"Sunset? Yes, that is fine. Perfect."

She winced at the sound of her own voice, too loud and very much too eager. To cover her confusion, she leapt to her feet. "I'll just get ready, then, shall I?"

She smiled brightly and looked about for something to occupy her hands. There was nothing. She had no finery to change into, for her lovely pink gown had been ruined by the storm. No silver circlet to polish. No *carna* blossoms to tuck into her bodice. No ribbons with which to weave a bridal sash.

"I'll send one of the women," he offered. "Tell her what you need."

I need my mother, Rose thought, staring at the floor through a shimmer of tears. *Or at least a friend. Oh, how I wish my cousin Jeannie was here! She would make me laugh, though I can't imagine how.*

"Thank you," she managed.

"Rosamund, I—" He started forward, one hand extended, then stopped, his arms falling stiffly to his sides. "I know this isn't—I'm sorry."

"So am I," she said, and meant it with her whole heart. "But we'll manage."

Chapter 32

THE woman who arrived an hour later was a young Venyan lady, obviously well born and just as clearly simmering with resentment. A sly smirk on her lips, she draped a gown over the narrow, lumpy mattress.

It was red. Not crimson or burgundy, but the raw color of fresh blood. The bodice was cut very low and bright with cheap embroidery. Rose looked from it to the woman.

"I cannot wear this."

The woman shrugged. "It's the best that I could do."

"Then I shall wear what I have."

The woman scowled. No doubt she had her orders from the prince, and though she might try to get around them, open defiance was another thing entirely.

"Very well," she muttered, snatching up the red gown. "Perhaps there is another somewhere."

"Send to the *filidhi* hall. I am sure Magea Avenic would be pleased to send me something suitable to wear."

She shot Rose a darkling glare. "I'll see what I can manage."

"You do that. In the meantime, have them send up a bath."

Alone, Rose sank down on the bed and stared blankly out the window. Princess of Venya. Me! Oh, Jeannie will be so surprised when she finds out!

"Jehan's garters! Not Rose? I never thought she had it in her! Oh, why couldn't it be me?"

Jeannie was the best of her cousins, Rose thought, though they'd never known each other well, and she suspected that Jeannie had always thought her something of a bore. Now her little cousin would be entirely flummoxed, wild with envy and very proud. Oh, if only she were here tonight!

It was easier to think of Jeannie than the one person she wanted with a longing too deep for tears. She wondered suddeny what her mother would have said about this marriage. Would the dutiful Najet, daughter of a desert kingdom, have been shocked by her daughter's willful behavior? Would the Queen of Valinor have been proud?

She would have had *something* to say, for Najet had been a woman of strong opinions. But whether she approved or disapproved of her daughter's choice, she would have defended it as fiercely as she had always defended Rose herself.

Even to the death. Rose knew that it was so, though she had no proof that her mother had been poisoned. The physician had denied it absolutely. But of course he would. He was Richard's physician, after all.

On reflection, Rose thought Najet would have been pleased with this marriage. For at heart, she was a desert woman, and did they not say that an enemy's enemy was a friend?

Chapter 33

THE sun was sinking over churning water in a sullen red cloud when Rose emerged from her chamber. She tugged at her robe, trying one more time to arrange it in flattering lines, then abandoned the attempt.

Magea Avenic had sent an entirely suitable gown—that is, if Rose had been headed for a life of silent meditation. The wool was fine, the color a dull burgundy, and the cut was very like that of a *filidhi* robe: absolutely shapeless. Rose thought of the young *filidh* Caelan, who had looked so neat and trim in her robes. But Caelan was tall—at least for a Venyan—and slender. Rose was built on very different lines, and the robe made no allowances for such superfluities as breasts and hips.

She wished it was at least an inch or two longer, so it might hide the truly hideous shoes she wore, adorned with garish paste buckles so horribly at odds with the gown that she shuddered every time she looked at them, passionately regretting her decision not to wear her old slippers. A size too large, they flapped with every step, which made them not only an embarrassment, but a dangerous one, as they were so high at the heel.

The one bright spot in her attire was the gift that the prince—*Florian,* she thought, *I must get used to that*—had sent. They glistened in her hair now, two gold-washed combs studded with tiny pearls. More precious to her was the note that had accompanied them, in which he lamented the lack of a proper silver circlet and hoped she would find them an acceptable substitute.

She looked like a hideous pudding. She wouldn't blame the prince—*Florian*—if he turned and bolted from the chapel.

The taproom, she amended as she flapped down the last step and hesitated in the doorway. She stepped into the room, and silence fell. No one greeted her. Not a single face turned in her direction showed any sign of welcome. They simply stared as though she were some exotic insect they had found crawling through their supper. She raised her chin and looked past them, her eyes narrowing when she spotted the Venyan lady who had attended her standing by the hearth, a cup of wine in hand and a simple, flowing gown of palest green draped about her slender form.

Her dark eyes met Rose's, and she smiled slowly, lifting her cup in a silent salute. Rose forced herself to smile back.

She flapped a few steps into the taproom and hesitated, her resolve wavering beneath the weight of silent disapproval. The ladies, in particular, were looking at her with murder in their eyes. Magea Avenic nodded from her place at the hearth, but the young *filidh*, Caelan, who sat beside her, did not even give Rose that much of a greeting.

"Diddle them all," Jeannie's voice said clearly in her mind. "*You're* the Princess of Venya, not any of those drabs!"

She watched the sun vanish into the angry sea until only a few last streaks of red lingered in the sky. At last someone—Lord Bastyon, she thought—pressed a cup into her hand. He turned away before she could thank him, leaving her alone again.

The landlord lit the candles. They hissed and smoked on the scratched trestles, the fat adding its own distinctive aroma to the crowded room. Rain pattered against the roof, first lightly and then in a steady roar. A few men from the ship came in, their loud voices and laughter soon dwindling to uneasy murmurs beneath the weight of Venyan disapproval.

Ashkii, in particular, looked as if he wished he could vanish, for the Venyans studied him with a horrified fascination that Rose resented hotly. She cast him a reassuring smile, but he did not see it, for his green eyes were fixed on the floor between his feet. The air grew so thick she could scarcely draw a breath, and sweat gathered at her temples.

She had just turned to set her empty mug upon the trestle when she was aware of a ripple of movement, a collective indrawn breath. She turned to see Florian in the doorway.

For once he had abandoned his accustomed black. He was

clad all in tawny silk and amber, his tunic embroidered with the Venyan arms and belted low on his hips with links of gold and topaz. His hair was loose, caught back at the temples in small braids to fall in a golden ripple over his shoulders. A circlet sat upon his brow, and a topaz glistened in his ear.

There was a long silence, during which Rose forced her jaw shut with a snap. Then he was stepping forward, holding out his hand. Moving in a dream, she went to meet him, stumbling as her shoe flapped against the rough wooden floor.

He glanced down and his lips twitched. "Kick them off," he suggested in a low voice as his hand closed over hers. "Before you break your neck."

She obeyed, sinking several inches lower as she took his hand. "Ready?" he asked and she nodded.

"Quite."

"Lord Bastyon, if you would . . . ?"

Bastyon turned to face them. His gaze was cold, his face so stern that Rose was certain he would refuse. She glanced quickly at Florian. He was taut, wary, intensely alert, his head held high and a terrible stillness in his face.

All conversation halted. It seemed no one dared to move or even draw a breath. The rain stopped, not trailing off into a drizzle as it did at home, but instantly and completely. The hush that followed was deafening. Rose found herself counting the slow drip of moisture from the eaves, measuring each moment as it passed.

Drip. Drip. Each one ratcheted her nerves a little tighter until she felt she would scream.

"Can we begin?"

It was her own voice shattering the silence, she realized with mingled terror and astonishment. Bastyon and Florian both glanced at her with identical expressions of shock; as though, she thought, some inanimate object—a stool, or perhaps a table— had burst into speech. Then they turned away, resuming their silent battle.

"The hour grows late," she hurried on, hardly aware of what she said, "and while I have no wish to rush you, I think—that is . . ."

She trailed to a stop. Still no one spoke. No one moved. It was time for desperate measures. She drew a deep breath and plastered a smile on her face. "I don't know about you, my lord," she added in a high, clear voice, "but *I* would like to get to bed."

Widening her eyes, she gasped, one hand flying to her mouth as though she had just realized the implications of her words. The blush she did not have to feign.

A muffled giggle came from behind her, followed by a flurry of throat-clearing and quickly stifled coughs. Then the guests exploded into laughter that held an edge of tension suddenly released.

"Well said, my lady," the prince drawled, "indeed, 'tis the very place I long to be."

The words were lazily amused, as was his grin, but his eyes were warm with sympathy for her gaffe. She dropped him a tiny wink, and his eyes widened in a flash of startled comprehesion.

"My lord." He turned to Bastyon with a graceful inclination of his head. "Shall we begin?"

Bastyon had not laughed with the others, but it seemed to Rose that the faintest hint of a smile touched his lips.

"Forgive me, my lady," he said with perfect courtesy. "The words escaped me for a moment. But I am ready now."

LATER, sitting in the skiff with moonlight spangling the water, Rose could not remember much about the ceremony. Embarrassment. A bit of fear. The warm glow of approval in Florian's eyes when he looked down at her, his steady voice as he repeated the vows that bound them as one forever.

She could not remember her own responses, though she supposed she must have made them properly, for three rings now shone on her fingers. She held out her hand and looked at them again, just to be certain.

"They do fit, don't they?" Florian asked, resting the oars in their locks.

"Yes. Perfectly. They are lovely."

He smiled and bent to the oars.

Once the ceremony was over, Rose had sipped another mug of sour ale as a confusion of people appeared before them, knelt, and murmured their good wishes. They all fell back as Sir Ewan strode forward and knelt. "Congratulations, my lord, my lady," he said in his deep rich voice. "Princess Rosamund, welcome among us."

She glanced quickly at Florian, smiling, but he was staring into the crowd. Following his gaze, she saw a young man with dark hair and a high-bridged nose returning Florian's stare. Who could he be? she wondered, even as she thanked Sir Ewan.

Next came Lord Bastyon, going slowly down upon his knees. "My lady," he said, "my lord, please accept my congratulations, as well."

"Thank you, Lord Bastyon," Rose said, impulsively reaching out to help him to his feet. He pulled away, his face tightening with some emotion she could not identify. Annoyance? Disgust?

Florian nodded, his expression tense, as Bastyon rose stiffly. He let out a soft breath when a dark-haired man with a scarred face knelt as well and presented his good wishes.

"Thank you, Lysagh," he said quietly, grasping the man's arm. "I won't forget this."

Lysagh nodded, unsmiling, and walked away. Florian stood very straight, then, his eyes fixed on two men who stood a bit apart with Lord Bastyon and Sir Ewan.

"What is it?" Rose whispered. "What is wrong?"

Florian shook his head slightly. "Perhaps nothing. We shall see in a moment."

The two men came forward at the same time to kneel before their prince. They barely touched one knee to the earthen floor before they were rising again. One was the young Venyan man Rose had marked earlier. He spared her one glance from beneath raised brows, then turned and walked away. The second man, older and much smaller, hurried after him.

Florian let out a long breath. "It could have been worse, I suppose," he murmured. Raising his voice, he called, "Master Innkeeper, bring out the wine!"

The crowd sent up a cheer. Ewan, standing at Florian's elbow, grinned. "That's right, lad. It could have been much worse. You're a lucky devil, are ye no?"

Florian raised Rose's hand, and she shivered as his lips brushed across her skin. "Indeed, Ewan," he said, "I am just beginning to realize how very fortunate I am."

Chapter 34

THE deck of the *Quest* was strangely quiet. "Where is the crew?" Rose asked, instinctively lowering her voice as Florian led her to the quarterdeck, lit by half a dozen lanterns. A small table had been placed beneath a canopy of sailcloth.

"Drinking our health at the tavern," he said, pulling out her chair. "I gave most of them leave for the night."

The table held a curious assortment of dishes. One goblet was of chased gold, the other of slightly dented pewter. None of the plates matched, and most were chipped, but the lantern light washed everything in glowing tones.

"You look very . . . lovely," Florian said politely, pouring a very pale yellow wine into her golden goblet. "That gown is . . ."

Rose laughed and raised the goblet. "Yes, isn't it? And you look . . . different. I didn't know you owned anything that wasn't black."

"Just this. Tomorrow it will go back into the chest."

"Because you always wear black?"

"Yes."

"Why?"

He frowned. "In fulfillment of a vow."

"I see," she murmured.

"A rather stupid vow," he added after a moment. "I was sixteen at the time, impulsive . . ." He smiled wryly. "It does have its advantages."

"Why, because it's frightening? Or because you never have to bother about what to wear?"

He laughed. "A bit of both. And now it's expected of me, isn't it?"

"And of course you always do what's expected of you!"

She meant it as a jest, for of course the Prince of Venya was a law unto himself, but his laughter died abruptly. "I try. Have some of this lobster," he added quickly, lifting the lid of one dish in a cloud of fragrant steam. "There are mussels, as well . . ."

Rose nibbled at her food, though she had no appetite. The prince refilled her cup after every sip. The wine was his favorite Tiernaviel, very light and fragrant, and went down easily. After the second goblet, she put her elbow on the table and rested her chin in her palm.

"So," she said, "the tales about you—are they true?"

"That depends on which tales you are referring to."

"Oh, you know," she said, embarrassed. "All of them."

"No."

"Ah." She fiddled with her goblet. "I see. Well, then, let us start at the beginning. You told me of your first journey into Venya, when"—when his best friend had betrayed him. What had she been thinking to bring up such a subject now? Still, now that she had done so, she was determined to learn something about this man who was her husband—"when you visited the forest pool. But you never said how you escaped."

"Luck," he said shortly. "Leander's will. Call it what you like."

"What about the marshes?"

"What about them?"

"They say you killed a score of my uncle's soldiers single-handed and fled into the marshes."

"There were not above a dozen, and I only killed the one who held me. Won't you have some more wine? Or would you like—"

"Were you really all alone?" she interrupted.

He sighed. "Yes, I had been cut off from my party. You should really eat some—"

"Armed only with a dagger?"

"Venyans are not permitted to bear arms," he explained with a smile that looked forced. "As I was in Venya at the time, I only had a dagger to hand."

"And then you went into the marshes. What were they like?"

"Putrid." He set the flagon down and stared at it. "They set upon me outside an inn, and I was wounded in the fight. But I was quick—terror will do that," he added dryly. "They were right behind me when I reached the marshes, and they did not easily give up the hunt. I was there for some days. I'm not sure how many. Once the fever set in, I lost track of time. I really don't remember much about it, only . . ." He shrugged uncomfortably, "I believe it was Leander's will that I survived. Certes, 'twas was no great courage or cleverness on my part, no matter what the songs might say. And there was a price . . ."

"What was it?"

He was silent for a long moment, then he grinned. "An ugly scar. Likely when I'm old, I'll be able to tell the weather by my aches and pains. Are you sure you'll have nothing more to eat?"

She shook her head. "But I would like to know—"

"Another time, I will answer all your questions. But now it's late. I don't know about you, my lady," he added with a lift of his brow, "but *I* would like to get to bed."

"Mmm. Yes. Shocking, wasn't it?"

"Quite. And quite effective, too."

She shrugged slightly. "You said you needed an ally."

"I did. I do. But while you may have spoken from expedience, I was quite in earnest." He stood and held out his hand. "Come, Rosamund. Let us go to bed."

Chapter 35

FLORIAN stripped off his tunic and folded it neatly over the chair, aware that his pulse was racing. Rosamund was a desirable woman. He had done his best to forget just how desirable she was, but now the memory returned to him in a rush.

The details were clouded, and he would be the first to admit that once they kissed, his objectivity had vanished, along with his control. What followed had seemed very sweet to him, but he could not forget that immediately after, she had expressed the desire to jump ship and bolt for Jexal. Hardly the response of a woman who had been satisfied by her lover. It was the sort of thing that could make any man a little nervous on his wedding night.

She looked very sweet lying in the bed, with her bright brown hair spread around her. He slid under the coverlet and took her hand in his. Poor girl, her fingers were icy.

"This all seems a bit too formal, doesn't it?" he asked, chafing her hand between his.

"It does," she answered, turning her head upon the pillow. "I don't feel like myself at all."

"Well, you're not, are you?" He brought her hand to his mouth, running her fingers lightly across his lips. He had always admired her hands, so pretty and graceful. He touched his tongue to her finger. "Mmm. You taste like cloves."

"From the oil. For my bath. What did you mean, I'm not myself?"

"Well, now you are my lady. And I am your lord. So you see this is a new situation for both of us."

She smiled, a faint spark of humor lighting her eyes. "But I don't suppose *you're* terrified."

"Well, no," he said, placing her hand upon his heart. "I'm rather . . . excited, actually."

Her hand was cool against his skin. She did not move it, but she did not withdraw it, either. "I suppose I should be, too. I wish I was," she said with an honesty that made him smile.

"Perhaps you will be later."

Her hair fell in a sheaf over the clean line of her neck and shoulders. He stroked it for a time, not speaking, once again reminded of the tiny pool hidden deep within the Venyan forest. He waited patiently for her to relax, letting his mind drift as he breathed her scent and watched the candle's flame flicker over the hues of her hair and skin.

When he judged the moment was right, he tugged her gently forward and brushed his lips against hers. The second time he lingered longer, then broke off and kissed her eyes, her cheeks, slowly working his way down to lips that had grown softer, would have parted beneath his had he asked that of her. But he did not. Not yet. He pressed chaste kisses on her mouth until her arms encircled him, drawing him to her, pulling him down and down into her embrace . . .

Into that sweet oblivion he craved. He sank into the dream, let himself be carried on the dark tide that swept away all care and worry, and gave himself up to the sensations stealing through him like a drug.

No past. No future. Only the scrape of her teeth against his lip, the dance of tongue on tongue, the whisper of her skin against his own. No words—no words at all, he did not want them, for words were lies. The truth was in the texture of her skin; her breast, the peak so soft and yielding and then hard beneath his lips and tongue. The quick, indrawn breath as he touched her secret place, released upon a shaking sigh. The instinctive movement of her body against his, her fingers lightly stroking him until his own breath came as raggedly as hers. *This* was real, the pleasure they shared, as bright and beautiful as foam upon a wave and equally ephemeral. *But no, don't think of that, don't think how false this closeness is, don't think at all, just let it happen . . .*

She was ready, he could sense it in her scent, the pattern of her breathing, the subtle shift of her body beneath his. He raised himself, poised above her, and looked into her eyes. *Now,* he thought, *now* . . . She raised a hand to touch his cheek, and her lips moved, forming a word that shot through him like an arrow, shattering the dream into a thousand pieces that danced crazily inside his head as he tried desperately to re-form them to reality.

But this was no reality he knew.

He had been here many times before, clasped in a woman's arms in the instant before joining, looking deep into her eyes. It was the moment of pure magic, when all barriers had fallen and everything was possible.

In this moment he had heard many things; sweet endearments whispered in a dozen tongues, prayers, entreaties, blasphemy. But never once in all those nights, had he heard this.

It seemed that somewhere far away, a door had opened and light was streaming into the dark places in his heart. Part of him longed to walk into that light and bask in its warmth, but another part, the greater part, urged him to turn and run, to lose himself in the darkness—

"Florian," she said again, and he was caught, bound by the sound of his name upon the lips of the one woman who had the right to speak it. The light flared into a brilliance that drove the darkness out, leaving him no refuge from the truth.

She was no dream, no phantasm who would vanish in the sunlight. This was Rosamund. Clever Rosamund, always so quick to leap to his defense. His Rosamund, with skin as soft as swansdown and hair like forest leaves, who made him laugh as she bested him at tiles.

When dawn came she would be here. When night fell again she would lie beside him in their bed. And the next night. And the one after that, for as long as life should last.

Not just an ally, but a wife. His *wife.* His own bright sun to warm him, the sweet rose of his world. His for now and always, for so she had promised, and his Rosamund would never lie.

Moisture stung his eyes as he bent to kiss her lips. It was a kiss like no other he had ever known, so sweet it left him dizzy.

And when he joined with his lady, it was unlike any of the couplings he had experienced. No drugged oblivion, this, his mind was clear, clearer than it had ever been before. She moved against him, drawing him more deeply into herself, and stronger than the physical pleasure of the moment, he felt a piercing joy, very bright and clear, experienced as much through her flesh as through his.

He was burning in her flame, drowning in her sweetness; it was too much, he could not last ... and yet would, he must ... until she cried out again, this time in release. Only then did he surrender, his own cry mingling with hers until the last shuddering tremors had subsided and they were at rest, his cheek against her breast and her hand twining in his hair.

My lady, he thought, turning his head to press his lips against her damp skin. *My wife. My Rosamund.*

Mine.

HE dozed for a time, Rosamund curled in his embrace, her cheek pillowed on his shoulder. He drifted into awareness of her and him and the candle guttering on the table beside them. He reached over her, fumbled in the drawer, lit a new candle from the dying remnants of the old, and fitted it into the soft wax in the holder.

"Let me look at you," he whispered, holding her hands apart beside her head. "I want to see you."

He wondered that he had never seen before how beautiful she was. Her lips were touched with carnelian and her cheeks still slightly flushed, her long eyes heavy-lidded as she gazed up at him. He traced the arch of her brows, the lines of brow and cheek and jaw with eyes and then with lips, slid down and rested his head beside hers on the pillow. He brushed a strand of hair from her cheek, and she made a low sound, a little purr of pleasure. Smiling, he stroked her face and neck until her eyes fell shut. He closed his own eyes then and caressed her shoulders, his hands moving lazily down her back. She stiffened slightly when he touched the space between her shoulder blades.

"And what is this?" he murmured, not understanding what his fingertips were telling him.

"Nothing of importance."

He raised himself on one elbow to peer over her shoulder. "Where did you get these?"

He scarcely knew his own voice, suddenly so sharp and harsh. She flinched a little and rolled over on her back.

"A small souvenir from Malin Isle," she answered with a brittle smile. "I didn't realize they had left a mark. Are they very ugly?"

"Rosamund, you don't think—surely you don't think I am complaining. What did they do to you?"

"Purified me. Or at least they tried. I'm afraid I did not take it in the proper spirit."

"Leander's balls—what did you do to earn such drastic . . . purification?"

"Oh, many things. But I'm sure you don't want to hear about them now."

"And I am sure I do."

She sat up and wrapped her arms about her knees, her hair falling about her face. Between the rich brown strands her cheeks were flushed, her eyes brilliant. "Then do *you* mean to make your confession, my lord, once you have required mine of me?"

He touched her hand lightly. "Require? No, Rosamund, no, you do not understand me. I require nothing. I am not your judge. I only want to know what you would tell me freely. Forgive me. I will not ask again."

She rested her brow on her knees. "No, it is I who am sorry. It's just . . . I don't like to think about it. And there is not much I *can* tell you, save to say that I displeased my uncle, and in doing so, brought Lord Marva's wrath upon my head. *He* will not abide a disobedient woman, you know. Look what happened to poor Jehan."

"What did happen to her?" Florian asked, sitting up as well. "I know she quarreled with Lord Marva over Leander, and was sent into exile for a time. But then he forgave her—Lord Marva's mercy fell over her like a mantle, isn't that how it goes? He took her back and made her his queen."

"And crowned her with a garland of carna blossoms," Rosamund said with a shudder. "Yes. But there is more to it than that. She—no, I cannot tell you that part, I'm sorry, but it is forbidden. But I—well, now I know where Jehan went during her exile and why she was willing to kneel at Marva's feet when she returned. And it had nothing to do with mercy."

"You displeased your uncle in Riall," Florian said slowly. "And he sent you to that place where they—I'm so sorry—"

"It wasn't your fault."

"Wasn't it?" he said bitterly. "If I hadn't gone to—" He broke off, cursing himself. He had not meant to speak of Kendrick's

Mine tonight. He tensed, braced against the inevitable question. He didn't want to lie to her, not now. And yet he knew he would.

She gazed back at him, green-flecked eyes filled with depth upon depth of understanding. Almost as if . . . but no, she couldn't know, it was impossible.

"It seems," he said harshly, "that every time I set foot in Venya, disaster follows."

"No, *Richard* follows. It is he who causes the suffering in Venya, not you."

He turned to her, pushing aside the curtain of her hair to frame her face with his hands. "I will kill him one day," he promised, "not only for Venya, but for what he did to you." He kissed the small scar on her brow. "Was this from Malin Isle, as well?"

"No." She sighed. "That was the result of my own stupidity."

"You are many things, Rosamund, but never stupid."

She laughed and drew him down to the pillows, resting her head against his shoulder and drawing lazy circles on his chest, winding her fingers through the fine light hair. "Oh, but I am, sometimes. I've only told you about my successes in Riall. I had my failures, too. This was one of them. I heard the captain of the guard talking about some trouble he was expecting at the gate, people trying to break through. I tried to stop it, but . . ." She sighed. "It was no good."

"You tried to stop it? How?"

"I thought if I could get there first, I could convince the soldiers to draw back. I hoped that if I held my place, they would see reason."

Florian drew back and stared at her. "You put yourself between Richard's soldiers and a starving mob?"

She frowned. "An ill-judged plan. It did no good at all. They wouldn't listen, wouldn't stop . . ."

"And this . . . ?" He touched the mark on her brow.

"It wasn't bad. Nothing compared to others. The Venyan people were very kind to me, though, they carried me straight to an inn and stanched the wound in no time." She raised a hand to her head and smiled. "Why, within a week, I barely noticed it at all."

Florian tightened his grasp on her. "You could have been killed," he said, his voice strangely hoarse.

"Others were," she said solemnly. "People died that day. Too many people. I should have found a way to stop it."

She should have found a way. A woman alone in a strange land among people who were no responsibility of hers. Yet she had made them her responsibility. And having no better plan, she had used her own body as a shield. The same body he held now, so terrifyingly fragile in his arms. He wanted to rage at her, to hold her close and never let her go, to fall on his knees in gratitude for such a foolish, gallant act.

Which must be, he realized, how every Venyan at the gates that day had felt when Richard's soldiers struck her down. Rosamund was not a legend, not a memory, but a woman of flesh and blood who had appeared in Venya's darkest hour when their prince was nowhere to be found. Was it any wonder that her name, not his, was held in reverence? Unfair, he had once thought it. Unjust. What a blind fool he had been!

He wound his body around hers, his fingers lightly stroking the scars between her shoulder blades. She shivered suddenly, and he tightened his arms around her. "You can tell me about Malin Isle," he said gently. "I'm not afraid of some silly curse."

"That's because you don't know—you haven't seen—" She wound her arms around his neck and buried her face against his shoulder. "I wish I *could* speak of it, but I can't. Don't ask me to."

"Shh . . . it's all right, *shasra*. You needn't tell me anything you don't want to. But if you do, I will listen."

"It's all right now," she said with a smile that lanced him to the heart. "It's only sometimes—when I think of it—but I won't anymore. But after a time there, I was—I couldn't—I wasn't thinking very clearly. And when Richard ordered me home again, I'm afraid I lost my head."

"What else could have sent you to me?" he said, dropping a kiss on the top of her head as he remembered their first meeting.

He had thought her mad. Perhaps she had been, a little, and not without good reason. After all she had suffered, it was a wonder she could think at all, let alone remember the words that had brought her to him. The words she had learned in Riall while risking her own life doing what Florian should have done himself.

"And I tried to leave you in that tavern," he said bitterly. "Rosamund, I am so—"

She laid her hand against his lips. "You did not know me. You had no reason to trust me. Believe me, Florian, I do not blame you in the least."

She smiled, looking for all the world as if she meant it. But how *could* she? She was not stupid; surely she *must* blame him, if not for attempting to abandon her, then at least for the nightmare months in Riall and everything that followed.

"Rosamund, I have so many things to thank you for I hardly know where to begin."

"I only did—"

"What anyone would have done. I know. If they had thought of it, that is, and they had the wit and courage to see it through. But no one did. Only you." He bent and kissed her brow. "I am blessed. Far, far beyond what I deserve."

She blushed crimson and ducked her head. "Then that is well, my lord," she said, so softly that he barely caught the words, "for so am I."

Chapter 36

IT was afternoon before they left the *Quest*. Florian would just as soon not have left at all, for he had never so enjoyed a morning. It began with him waking to find Rosamund beside him, her breathing deep and regular. There was no hurry to get up, no awkwardness as they both remembered the intimacies of the past night while fumbling for the words to say farewell. No farewell at all, but just a sigh and a smile when he woke her with a kiss.

The whole thing was so enoyable that he wanted to go back to sleep just so he could wake again. But not before he had enjoyed a drowsy, languid exploration of the pleasures of the marriage bed. He loved the shape of it, Rosamund turned on her side, still sleeping, hip and shouder jutting toward the ceiling and the sweet dip of her waist between. He loved the scent of it, rich and musky, the warmth of her body beneath the coverlet and the brush of her hair against his skin.

He laughed at the sound she made when he kissed her awake, beginning with an irritated murmur and ending in a sigh. She made other noises, too, as they charted this new territory together, an enchanted landscape of desire and fulfillment. He was surprised and gratified to find that Rosamund never left him guessing as to whether he was pleasing her or not. When she enjoyed something, she let him know, at one point with such enthusiasm that she clapped a hand over her own mouth, blushing to the roots of her hair. He pulled it away, laughing, and assured her that the sailors were quite deaf, or at least they would pretend they were, which amounted to the same thing.

"I suppose this is nothing new to them," she said, frowning

a little. "They must have heard plenty of this sort of thing."

"This sort of thing? Oh, no, Rosamund, never. Never anything like it."

"No?" Her laughter was strained, and she turned her face away, hiding her expression. "Then they must be deaf indeed."

He grasped her wrists lightly and pinned them beside her head, insisting that she meet his eyes. "Whatever the sailors might have heard, it was not my lady, the Princess of Venya, my own wedded wife, telling me how I might please her in our bed. It is a sound unlike any other." He lightly traced the tip of his tongue around her ear. "I hope to hear it often."

She shivered delicately. "I daresay if you apply yourself . . ."

"Like so?" He took her earlobe between his teeth. "Or . . ." He drew his hands slowly down her arms.

"Mmm . . . yes, like that."

"And this?" He dug his fingers into her ribs, and she let out a startled whoop of laughter.

"No! No, not like that—" She shrieked as he tickled her belly, fending him off with her hands while he continued to attack. He finally allowed her to push him off, though he caught her as he fell and rolled her atop him.

"Quiet," he whispered sternly. "The sailors might hear."

"Churl." She nipped him sharply on the shoulder. "Lout."

"Already the abuse begins!" He heaved a great sigh. "Will the princess become a fishwife?"

"Only when the prince deserves it."

All at once his chest constricted and he tightened his arms, as though if he held on very hard, he could somehow keep her exactly as she was right now, soft and tousled and glowing in the aftermath of love.

This marriage had been necessary, a duty he had assumed for Venya's sake. He had not looked for joy. Yet he had found it nonetheless, so piercing sweet it frightened him. He knew such happiness must have a price, and it tore his heart that he would not be the only one to pay it.

"Florian?" He heard the hesitation in her voice and his fear sharpened. Already they were so attuned that she could sense his change of mood.

"It is nothing." He kissed the tip of her nose, striving to recapture the easy playfulness between them. "Only—"

"Only what?"

Only that I have fallen in love, he thought. He caught himself before he spoke the words, knowing he had no right to them, just as he'd had no right to claim her as his own, even in his own thoughts. *I was better off alone,* he thought, *everything was so much simpler then.*

But then she smiled and he found that he was smiling as well. It was too late now to stop and count the cost. Perhaps he didn't deserve to be this happy, but he was, and there was nothing to be done for it today. "Only that I am famished," he said. "There is a tavern in the village where they make the finest stew in all Sorlain."

"Aren't we meant to go to the *filidhi* hall?"

"Oh, I doubt they'll be expecting us today. Come, my lady, and let us retire to our wedding feast."

Chapter 37

THE sun was westering in a cloudless sky when they left the tavern. What started as a private meal had had turned into a sort of wedding feast after all. Once Florian was recognized, every fisherman and farmer in the place had felt the need to toast their marriage. Then someone—Rose could not remember who it was—had called for music, and a group of men had roared out from the tavern to seize a passing piper.

Rose had danced with every one of them. To refuse would have been impossible, to even try, an insult. Florian grinned and shrugged helplessly as she was whirled around the floor. He stepped in when an argument began and whisked Rose from between her overeager partners. By the time the fight had broken out in earnest, he had neatly danced her out the door.

Now he took her hand and swung it as they passed the livery stable and the old inn, humming the last song under his breath. Everything seemed a bit unreal, as though she had wandered into some enchanted land. Rich sunlight washed the little village in golden tones that softened the tiled roofs to pink and lit the bougainvillea trailing down the whitewashed walls in brilliant hues of orange and crimson. The scents of orange and lemon blossoms wound through the salty air, a perfume more intoxicating than the wine she'd drunk.

She stopped for a moment to gaze about and draw a deep breath. She knew that the village was only a village, no different from a hundred others. Logic told her that the stew had just been stew, the wine merely wine, the piper barely competent. Yet her heart said differently. There had never been a wedding feast of such surpassing fineness, or a village so beautiful as this, or a day so warm and sweetly scented. And surely, since the dawn of time itself, there had never been a woman as happy as she was right now.

"Perfect."

She did not realize she had said the word aloud until Florian laughed. "Just what I was thinking."

And right there in the street, he put his arms around her and kissed her, to the great amusement of a group of boys outside the livery stable. He broke the kiss and looked over her shoulder, grinning, and lifted one hand in a gesture that Rose had never seen before. The boys returned it, along with several others, hooting with laughter. Rose had studied Sorlainian for years, but the words they called out had not been included in her lessons. Florian shook a fist at them, still smiling, then flung an arm around her shoulder and walked on.

"What was that?" She began to make the gesture he had first made, but he covered her hand with his.

"Nothing that a lady needs to know."

"And the things they said—they should not speak to you like that!"

"They haven't any idea who I am. And I did ask for it. 'Tis most improper to kiss where anyone might see. I'm afraid your reputation is quite ruined. No respectable man would have you now."

She elbowed him in ribs. "Then I'll have to make do with you."

They wandered through the village, and he plucked a handful of flowers from a hedgerow lining the path. He paused beside a stone set in the center of the square beneath the lemon tree and squatted to set the flowers on the weathered surface. Rose leaned close, pushing the blossoms aside to look at the inscription.

"Gracia and Sophia," she read aloud. "Grace and Wisdom. What does it mean?"

The prince glanced up at her. "Surely you have heard of Gracia and Sophia of Serilla!"

Rose shook her head. "No."

"Oh, your education has been sadly neglected." He sat down, his back against the stone, and offered her his hand. "No one can be allowed to visit Serilla without hearing their tale. Come, sit down, and I will tell you."

She joined him on the grass, sitting cross-legged beneath the lemon tree and inhaling its scent with pleasure. Across the square she could glimpse a bit of turquoise water between the shops, framed by scarlet blossoms trailing from the tiled roofs. Florian did not release her hand, but kept it in his, running one finger idly across her palm.

"Once upon a time," he began, and she smiled at the classic storyteller's beginning. "There was a great storm on Serilla. Great bolts of lightning split the sky, the thunder crashed and the wind shrieked, the sea rose to the tops of the cliffs, and great hailstones smashed the fishing boats to splinters. In the midst of this magnificent tempest, a village woman bore twin daughters, whom she named Gracia and Sophia. An old wise woman present at the birth predicted a great future for the babies. She said each of them would bear sons who would be kings. Well, it hardly seemed likely, but the villagers had a good deal of respect for the wise woman, so they watched the girls with interest as they grew."

"I'll wager," Rose said, "that they were lovely."

He squeezed her hand. "Of course! Hair of spun gold, eyes like sapphires—all the usual attributes. And as like to each other as two oysters in a pot. Yet no one in Serilla would ever mistake one for the other. Gracia was a wonderfully accomplished maiden. She could bake bread so light it almost floated from the pan, sew invisible seams, and sing as sweetly as a lark. But she was never too busy to perform countless acts of charity."

"She sounds"—Rose laughed—"rather horrid, actually."

"Doesn't she? Let us say, then, that she was a pretty girl who worked hard about the house and was kind to the poor. But Sophia . . ." He shook his head, sighing. "Ah, Sophia might have been her sister's twin, but she was not her equal. Sophia's bread was merely bread, she skimped her chores, and her songs were those she learned on the docks. Her days were spent at the water's edge, skirts tucked up, helping bring in the nets and begging to be taken out on the boats."

"Shocking. And unless I miss my guess, I know which one ended up with the prince. There is a prince in this story, isn't there?"

Florian laughed and twined his fingers with hers. "He arrived in springtime, driven ashore by another one of those convenient storms. One look at the beauteous Gracia, and he was lost. Of course the usual muddle ensued. He asked her to be his mistress, she refused—sweetly, but very firmly—and he went away an angry and disappointed prince, vowing to forget her. But all the ladies of the court could not banish her memory from his heart, and so he returned to Serilla, only to be refused again. So on and on it went until, in the end, her virtue was rewarded with a crown."

"What sort of story would it be if it was not?" Rose smiled wryly. "No doubt she bore a son."

"Indeed. They called him Esteban. In due time he became King of Sorlain."

Rose started, coming back to reality with a jerk. "You're making this up!"

"Truly, I am not. I grant that Queen Gracia's origins are not widely remarked upon—King Juan hushed it up as far as he was able—but you have my solemn oath it is the truth."

"What happened to the other sister? Sophia?"

"Once Gracia was established, Sophia went to court. All the village tongues were wagging, and they expected news of a royal betrothal any moment. But court life did not agree with Sophia. In the end, she kicked over the prophecy, came back to Serilla, and married her childhood sweetheart."

"Did she really?" Rose asked, pleased by this unexpected twist. "Well, the wise woman was half right, at least."

"That's exactly what the villagers said," Florian agreed. "Poor Sophia did not seem to care that she had disappointed the entire population of Serilla. She and her fisherman husband were very happy, and quite prosperous in a modest way. They bought land—this land we're sitting on, in fact, and the acres where the *filidhi* hall now sits. They opened the inn and the livery stable, planted grapes and oranges and lemons, and they, too, had a son."

"I wonder if the other boys used to tease him," Rose mused.

"Dreadfully. They called him the Prince of Serilla and would have made his life quite miserable, but luckily for him, he was a big, strong lad who had the rare gift of laughing at himself. His parents expected that one day he would manage their holdings, but all he ever wanted was to go to sea. So he sailed the world, living as he pleased, taking berth on this ship or that as the fancy struck him. One day he put into Venya and went with his captain to deliver letters to the castle. He walked into the Queen's presence chamber, the two of them took one look at each other, and"—he slanted Rose a glance—"two weeks later my parents were married and the prophecy fulfilled."

Rose's jaw dropped. "Your *father*—?"

"King Rafael of Venya. I'm sure you have heard he was a sailor," Florian said, smiling at her surprise.

"Well, yes. Yes, I have heard that. But I thought—"

"That Richard lied? No, indeed, he was a witness to their meeting because he was your father's envoy to Venya at the time. The part he always leaves out is that a few days earlier, he himself had offered for my mother's hand."

"She refused him . . . and wed a common sailor?" Rose said, then blushed, realized how rude that sounded.

"The nephew of the King of Sorlain," Florian corrected her, then grinned. "And yes, a common sailor. Of course, one could say the two of them were helpless in the hand of prophecy."

"One could, I suppose, but I don't suppose my uncle took much comfort in that notion."

"No, I don't suppose he did. Especially considering . . ."

"Considering what?" Rose asked curiously as he hesitated.

"My mother was a lady of high spirit," Florian said slowly. "She was a strong ruler, very bold and innovative, and much loved in Venya. She was also a woman who always said precisely what she thought. I've wondered sometimes in what terms she refused your uncle's offer."

"I don't know if there is any good way to say no to an offer of marriage."

"Perhaps not." He sighed, rolling over on his back and looking up at the sky through the branches of the tree. "My mother bequeathed me a kingdom; my father, half a fishing village. And now the High Magea calls herself Serillan and concerns herself with trade routes, Leander help us all."

Rose leaned against the trunk of the tree and stretched out her legs. The prince shifted, pillowing his head on her thighs. Today he was clad in a light wool tunic—black, of course—his arms bare and a plain leather belt slung low on his hips. Save for the fineness of the wool and the gold clasp of the belt, he could have been a farmer come to market for the day.

Was that his father in him? she wondered. Or perhaps Sophia, who had given up a life at court to wed a fisherman? Golden-haired Sophia, she thought, smoothing the shining strands from Florian's brow, who lived on in her grandson. Lying here, with his eyes closed and the dark gold of his lashes lying against his cheeks, he could almost have passed for a Sorlainian, bronzed deeply by the sun. She wondered idly if the mighty King Esteban had inherited his mother's looks as well, and if he had ever visited his mother's birthplace and met his wayward aunt. A sudden thought struck her, and she sat up a little straighter.

"You are kin to Cristobal, then," she said. "Do you know him?"

"I met him once, years ago. After Venya fell, we went to Esteban—Bastyon, Ewan, and I—hoping he would lend me an army. Needless to say, he refused, though he did offer to foster me at his court. Cristobal was eight then, a year older than I was. He was quite keen on the idea. Said he'd always wanted a little brother."

Rose drew her hand across his forehead, smoothing away a faint crease between his dark gold brows. "What did *you* want? Or did anyone bother asking?"

"Esteban did. He insisted on it. He sent everyone away and spoke to me himself, kinsman to kinsman. I was tempted—I would have been mad not to be tempted. Paloman Castle is magnificent, and Esteban was very kind, but . . . by that time, Bastyon had made dead certain I knew just what was expected of me, and I couldn't bring myself to let him down. Poor Cristobal was distraught—he kept trying to give me a puppy, I remember, and Bastyon kept giving it back, saying I couldn't keep a hound on shipboard. In the end, Cristobal burst into tears." Florian smiled wryly. "Bastyon was appalled. And so we went off to . . . Moravia, I think it was. Or maybe Jexal."

"Do you regret it?" Rose asked. "Do you ever wish you had stayed?"

The golden lashes lifted, and he looked up at her. She knew then that he would never be mistaken for a Sorlainian. Even for a Venyan, his eyes were extraordinary; not merely brown, but amber, deep-set and sharply slanted at the corners. The whites were very bright, standing out in sharp relief against his skin. *He has the best of both his parents,* she thought, and felt a stab of sorrow that they had never had the chance to see their child grow to manhood.

"No," he said. "Though I have sometimes wondered what it would have been like . . ."

"You would have been a pampered little princeling," Rose teased, "with a hundred servants and a wardrobe the size of the *Quest*. A different jewel for every hour—"

"—and scores of court ladies to . . . dance with in the rose gardens."

"You would have been insufferably proud," Rose said.

"Probably," he agreed. "But I never really thought about those things. The only thing I regretted was—well—" He shrugged, looking a bit embarrassed. "I would have liked to have Cristobal for a brother."

Chapter 38

THE next day, when they reached the *fildhi* hall, it was Rose who lifted the knocker. "The Princess of Venya seeks entrance to the hall," it sang.

She laughed, delighted. "Go on, do it again," Florian whispered. "You know you want to."

The door opened before she had the chance. This time it was an older man who answered, clad in a gray robe belted with scarlet. "Your Highness." He bowed formally. "We had thought to greet you yesterday."

"I was unavoidably delayed," Florian answered gravely.

The *filidh* glanced at Rose and smiled. "I see. Please, come in. I will find Magea Avenic for you."

"Thank you. In the meantime, I'll just look in on the apprentices. They are at supper now?"

"Yes, in the hall." The man gestured toward a doorway across the entrance. "Allow me to announce you."

"Oh, no. That won't be necessary. I'll announce myself. Then I'll just look in on Magea Avenic in her study."

The *filidh* looked a bit shocked, but he only bowed his head. "As my lord wishes."

"Announce me." Florian grimaced as they passed through the door and down a wooden corridor. "We've grown very formal here on Serilla lately."

The dining hall was a long room of wood, the bare walls reaching high above to shadowy rafters. Rose judged there were about fifty young men and women gathered at a dozen long tables. They were roughly divided by the color of their robes, though this did not seem to be any strict rule, for they moved about quite freely, dropping into empty seats to visit with their friends. Apart from their sober robes, there was no formality in this gathering. The rafters rang with their voices, and bits of bread flew across the tables as they pelted each other amid gales of laughter.

Florian stood in the doorway, watching them for a time. He smiled, but Rose fancied there was something a little wistful in his expression. "Were you one of them once?" she asked.

"Me? Oh, no, I never studied here. I didn't have the time." His eyes moved across the hall, and he took her hand. "Look, there is our friend Daigh from the stable. Let's go greet him."

They kept to the wall, arriving unnoticed at the table where young Daigh sat with half a dozen companions. He was leaning forward in his seat, his face intent upon the point that he was making. Florian put a finger to his lips and leaned against the wall, eavesdropping shamelessly on their converstation.

"—a complete waste of time," the young woman across from Daigh was saying. "All those kings and queens—what difference does it make now?"

"If you cannot see that for yourself, you do not belong here at all," Daigh answered loftily. "The deeper mysteries are tied to Venya."

"Deeper mysteries!" a green-robed boy sneered. "A bunch of moldy superstition. Come on, Daigh, surely you don't believe all that?"

"Unlike you, Ren, I am a *filidh* of Venya, not just a clever craftsman."

Ren rolled his eyes, and the others laughed. "Right, you are a *filidh*, and the rest of us are rubbish. But you were born here on Serilla, weren't you?"

Daigh's shoulders were very stiff. "No. I was born on Venyan soil."

"And lived there for what, a month?" a young woman put in. "What difference does it make, anyway? You were born in Venya, and I on Serilla, and I'm just as much a *filidh* as you are. If we have to learn history, it should be Sorlainian. But history is useless anyway. We all know that most of it is lies."

"Look at the Prince of Venya—" Daigh began.

"Well, I can't, can I?" The girl laughed. "He never shows

himself. Not that I would mind if he did," she added, nudging the girl beside her. "They say he's worth a look."

Rose frowned at Florian. He gave her his most innocent look, holding out his hands in a gesture of helplessness.

"The Prince of Venya," the apprentice Ren sneered. "He's a fine example of royalty. They're all the same, you know—or you would, Alara, if you would stay awake in history. They don't care about anyone besides themselves. All this nonsense about deeper mysteries and the union of the *fildhi* and *fheara* is just their way of keeping us under their thumb. This war the prince wants—it has nothing to do with the *filidhi*, really, or the *fheara*, either. It's all just vengeance, plain and simple, and no concern of ours. *Fildhi* can look after themselves. We don't need any kings and queens to tell us what to do."

Florian pushed himself from the wall and dropped down in the seat beside Daigh. "The blessings of the day, good *fildhi*," he said pleasantly. "May I join you?

"This table is for apprentices," Ren said. "Tradesman eat at the far end of the hall."

"Hello, Daigh," Florian said, turning to the apprentice on his right.

Ren looked at Daigh, brows raised. "Oh. Is this—this fellow a friend of yours?"

"I'd like to think so," Florian said quietly. "Why don't you introduce me, Daigh?"

"You don't have to," Ren put in. "Say the word, and I'll toss him out."

Florian smiled at the apprentice. "Alone? Somehow I doubt that, lad."

"Oh, really?"

Daigh laid a hand on Ren's arm. "My lord," he said to Florian, "this loud-mouthed lout is Renault, this farily presentable one is Phelan, and the silly chit across the table is Alara. Get up, you fools," he hissed to them, "and greet the Prince of Venya."

Florian nodded amiably and gestured Rose to join him. "You may have heard that you have a princess now, as well. This is my lady, Rosamund."

They studied her intently as they bowed, stammering out congratulations while Florian helped himself to bread and honey. "Sit down," he said, waving a piece of bread. "Don't let us interrupt your conversation. You have some . . . original theories about royalty, Master Renault. But any scholar can tell you that there is no substitute for source material. So why don't you ask me whatever you want to know?"

They looked at one another, obviously trying to remember exactly what they had been saying, and panic showed on every face.

"Don't worry," Florian said easily, "I'm not planning any executions. So you think of yourselves as Sorlainian, do you?"

Again, the apprentices exchanged nervous glances. At last the girl, Alara, said, "We were born here."

"True enough. But you wouldn't be here if your parents didn't have Leander's gift. And I'm very much afraid, Alara, that if you were to travel beyond Serilla, you would find that even if you consider yourself Sorlainian, the Sorlainians most definitely do not. Do you know Andra?"

"Yes, he is our teacher."

"Ask him. He'll tell you just how welcome Venyans are throughout Sorlain. They don't much like us, really. In time—oh, in a hundred years or so—they might come to accept us as their own. But long before that time, I intend for us to all be back in Venya. There are many reasons for this, most of which I'm sure you already know. Reasons of state, and responsibility to my people, and yes, Renault, to exact the blood-price for the murder of my parents. That is my duty as a prince . . . and as a son."

Ren flushed and bent his head over his trencher.

"But there is another reason, one that touches you directly. Each of you is bound to the fate of Venya, just as I am. Deny that, and you deny the very wellspring from which your magic flows. The bond already strains; should it be broken, your magic will begin to fade."

"But Master Roland says—" Ren began, then broke off as Daigh elbowed him.

"No, go on," Florian said. "What does he say?"

"He says our talent is inborn. He says it has nothing to do with Venya at all, but is a gift."

"A gift from whom?" Florian asked softly.

"Well, from"—Alara waved a hand—"from the gods."

"Oh, the *gods*." Florian waved his hand, as well, with a gently mocking smile. "Do these gods have names?"

The apprentices from other tables had gathered round, as the news of Florian's arrival went through the hall. Now a new voice spoke, that of a slight young man with burning coal-black eyes.

"No," he said decisively. "The masters use that word, but it doesn't mean anything, not really. We were born with abilities that no one can explain, so they call it god-given. But it usually runs in families, doesn't it? Like black hair or blue eyes."

"But this ability is a Venyan thing," Daigh said.

"Well, obviously," the slight young man said. "Venyan *filidhi* generally married each other, didn't they? They kept it in the family, so to speak."

"Not always," Daigh argued. "The gift is not confined to *filidhi* families. It can appear in any child. Any Venyan child, that is."

"There is many a seed sown outside the manor field. Some of these will come to flower—even in a dung heap," the young man added, drawing laughter from the crowd.

Florian had been sitting back, watching, but now he leaned forward. "And what of these wild seeds, young master? Are they not *filidhi*, just as you are?"

"No, my lord, they are not. My father's bastards may have black eyes, but that does not make them Gilverans."

"The first Gilveran was a groom, you know," Florian remarked casually, "and earned his title by his courage on the field. Nobility is a monarch's gift to a subject, just as the *filidhi* talent is Leander's gift to his people. And Leander, like the monarch, bestows his gift according to his purpose."

"But," Ren put in, "a gift once given belongs to the recipient. Surely we are free to use it however we see fit?"

"This gift is lent to you for a purpose. It is Leander's hand that has touched you, and his blessing that you bear. And Leander was no tradesman. He did not set up shop and sell his goods. True magic cannot be bought or sold. The blessing must flow from Leander through his children and out into the world. Freely."

"Would you have us starve in the service of Leander?" young Gilveran demanded.

"Are you starving?" Florian raised his brows, looking pointedly around the hall. "Do you lack for a place to learn your arts?"

"No," Alara said, "and we all know you're responsible for that. But we cannot go on like this forever. We want to do something useful."

There was a general murmur of agreement from the apprentices.

"We aren't children," a voice cried, "we want to earn our keep!"

"But that is not the *filidhi* task," Florian said patiently. "It is for the *fheara* to till the earth and herd the cattle and fish the seas. This does not," he added sternly, "mean they are your servants. Every Venyan is Leander's child, each serving according to his gifts. *Filidhi* are not complete without *fheara*, and Venya is our home. I am pleased that you wish to be useful, but to sell what should be given freely will only diminish you. Not in your lifetime, and perhaps not in your children's, but your children's children will know nothing of Leander's gift. So Magea Gwythian of Venya has said, and you discount her wisdom at your peril."

He slid from the bench and rested a hand on Rose's shoulder, urging her to remain. "Now I had better go see Magea Avenic and tell her I am here. Those of you who have kin in Venya may like to know how matters stand there now. It has been long since I have seen my home, but as you may have heard, my lady spent some time in Riall last year."

Silence fell as he named the city, for the news of Richard's occupation had reached even this sheltered haven. Florian squeezed her shoulder in a silent question, and she nodded, her hand moving to grasp his.

"Daigh, would you be so kind as to bring Lady Rosamund to me when she has finished her meal?"

"Yes, my lord," Daigh said. "I would be honored."

Florian bent and kissed Rose's brow. "Thank you," he murmured, then walked off. The apprentices stared after him, some thoughtful, a few hostile, though most just looked a little dazed.

Then as one they turned to Rose. She sat a little straighter, fighting back a wave of nerves as she looked at the earnest young faces all around her.

"Lady," the young lord of Gilveran said, sitting down beside her, "will you tell us of Riall?"

"Yes," she said, drawing a deep breath, "I will."

Chapter 39

ROSE wasn't sure what woke her. She sat upright, staring about the unfamiliar chamber in confusion. Then she remembered. She and Florian had dined with his council earlier and decided to stay in his chamber at the inn rather than go back to the *Quest*. But now the bed beside her was empty. She touched the pillow and found it was cold.

She stood and went to the window, staring out into the darkness. Quickly donning her shift, she pulled Florian's cloak around her shoulders. She slipped out the door and down the stairs, thinking Florian might have woken hungry, though after the enormous meal they had consumed, it seemed hardly likely. But the taproom was deserted, the candles doused, and the fire was merely a red-gold glow in the grate. She had just turned to go back up the stairs when someone spoke behind her.

"Looking for the prince?"

"Who is there?" she demanded, peering into the shadows. A figure rose from the settle, silhouetted against the dying fire.

"Eredor. At your service." He began to bow, then caught the edge of the settle and laughed. "Do you mind if I sit down? Wouldn't want to fall on my face."

"I do not mind in the least. Good night." Rose started up the stairway, but Eredor's voice halted her.

"Your lord husband is down at the docks, provisioning his ship so he might go off and chase his Ilindrian alliance. Pressing matters, don't you know. It's always pressing matters with him." His hand rose against the firelight, holding a goblet. "Here's to

THE PRINCE 257

our prince and his pressing matters. Not a moment to be lost, you know, there never is."

"I believe you are in your cups, my lord," Rose remarked mildly.

"Quite right. Not as much as you might think, and surely not as much as I would like, but I am taking steps to rectify the situation. I have planned the whole thing out, and anyone will tell you that I am a very careful planner. No imagination, of course, they'll tell you that as well, but I come in handy for all those the dreary little tasks that no one with imagination can be bothered with. But we were talking of the prince, not me, and why he left his bride to a cold bed. Shall I tell you why, my lady?"

Eredor had been at dinner earlier, though Rose did not remember him speaking a single word during the meal. Florian had warned her that of all the council members, Eredor would be the most difficult to work with, but she had not been prepared for the hostility in Eredor's tone. Still, he was a council member, and she had promised to do her best to win him over, so she bit back a sharp retort and said simply, "Not tonight. Perhaps tomorrow, we can—"

"Oh, but you really ought to know. *Someone* should tell you what is going on."

Rose sighed. "Go on, then, I'm listening. Say what you want to say."

"Want? Oh, no, lady, it is not what I *want* to say. For even a man of no imagination can see that you have been most cruelly duped, and it would take a far more callous man than I to take pleasure in the telling. For the Prince of Venya is a man obsessed, and he does nothing that will not further his ambition. I pointed out this very thing to him not long ago. Of course he did not listen. Though I will admit—being as you have noticed, somewhat in my cups—that I did not do it very well. Your lord . . . irks me. And that makes me incautious in my speech."

"It does indeed," Rose said. "And I think it would be best to end this conversation here and now."

"I ramble, don't I? How very strange. My words are usually aimed precisely to the point. Before you flee, let me just tell you how matters stand between the prince and his council. Two days past he stood before us, expecting us to go on supporting his obsession. And I'm afraid I gave him a rather bad time."

Eredor paused, and Rose heard the gurgle of the flagon as he refilled his cup.

"Are you sure you will not join me, lady?" Eredor said. "The wine is foul, but after the first cup or two you scarcely notice."

"No, thank you, my lord. You were speaking of the council meeting . . . ?"

"Ah, yes. Well, first I pointed out that your lord's reckless ambition was endangering the colony, though he cared naught for that. Or for the fact that the majority of his council no longer sees Venya as an option. So I was forced to remind him that not only has he failed to win a single monarch to his cause, but he has no support left in Venya, either. And when I had his back to the wall—speaking metaphorically, of course—he countered with his wedding plans. But I would wager anything that you had not agreed to such a marriage at that time. Tell me, lady, do I win or lose?"

When she made no answer, he laughed softly. "Just so. Another bluff. I should have called him on it."

"I fail to see what difference it makes when we agreed—"

"Do you really? And here I thought you were so clever! Your performance at the vows was masterful—oh, I marked it, and you have my deepest admiration, all the more because your shot was fired in the dark. You have no idea what's been going on in Venya, do you? I'll wager the prince has not told you how very much the people of Riall admire and respect you. Or how bitterly they blame him for what happened there. They hate him now, but you . . . ah, you are their Rose; Rose of Riall, the Shield of Venya, the very flower of virtue and honor and high courage."

"You exaggerate—"

"I do nothing of the sort. It is the simple truth. They make songs to you in Venya and spit upon the prince's name. I thought this time he must admit that he is finished, but once again, he pulled a miracle from up his sleeve. Venya's people have turned against him? Not a problem, he will wed the one woman who can possibly command their loyalty. So for the time, he has managed to keep his delusion alive, and it matters not to him who pays the price or how much they are hurt. I could almost admire him, did I not despise him so completely."

Rose fumbled for the banister. "You are finished, I trust?"

"Not I," Eredor replied, heaving himself to his feet. "Though

I'm sure your lord would like to think so. But I am for bed. Good night, my lady."

WHEN Florian returned to the inn, he found Rose seated before the fire, his cloak thrown around her shoulders and a cup in her hand.

"What are you doing up?" he asked, sitting down beside her.

"Drinking wine," she answered, leaning forward to pour him a cup. "Why don't you have some? It is rather foul—Eredor got that much right—but as he pointed out, you hardly notice after the first few cups."

Florian stared at her. Her eyes were overbright, her color high, and beneath the cloak, she was clad only in her shift. "You were drinking with Eredor? Here? Like *that*?"

She waved a hand. "No, no. Talking. Or rather, he was talking and I was listening. I didn't start drinking until after he was gone."

"What did he say to you?"

"Many things." She peered at him over the rim of her cup. "But let us start with the council meeting and your announcement of our marriage. Strange," she took a sip and licked a drop of wine from her lip. "I thought I had a choice in the matter."

"You did. I did not force you."

"Nor did you tell me everything, did you? Rose of Riall, the Shield of Venya." She stared into the fire, her expression pensive. "It has a nice sound to it, doesn't it? Is it true that they spit on your name, or did Eredor just add that detail for color?"

Three days. That was all that Florian had asked, just three days that belonged to him and Rosamund before the world crashed in upon them. Damn Eredor!

"I've never actually seen anyone do it," he replied carefully, "but I have no trouble believing it."

Rose nodded. "Yes. That's what I thought. It takes imagination to think up something like that, and my lord Eredor assures me he has none. He's a very bitter man," she added, "I would not turn my back on him if I were you."

"Which is why I asked you to sit on the council in my absence. Rosamund, I can explain."

"Oh, good." She gave him a bright, false smile. "Another story."

"The situation in Venya is—problematic."

She snorted delicately. "Indeed. So you decided to bolster your support by marrying me. A prudent move. Even Eredor grants you that. But I wonder why you did not tell me? Or no—" She held up a hand. "I know why. You handled the whole thing very cleverly, now that I reflect on it." She took his hand and let her fingertips drift across his palm. "Why, I hardly heard a word you said. How could I think, while you were doing this?" She trailed her fingers through his. "So much more effective than the truth."

"I did not lie to you," he said evenly.

"Really?" Her dark brows rose in courteous disbelief. "Then there really was a ship leaving for Padaea? The last ship of the season, I believe you said. Perhaps you did not hear Sir Ewan at supper when he mentioned that the autumn trade winds will not begin for another six weeks. I thought he must be mistaken, but now I do believe he had the right of it."

"Yes, well, it is true that—"

"I can be content with very little, Florian. I do not care if I never see the inside of a castle again, or if I wear the same gown for a year. I don't expect you to be faithful—"

"You should," he said fiercely. "Have I not sworn—"

She cut him off with an angry gesture. "I don't need pretty words, and I don't want empty promises. The one thing I do ask—that I demand—is honesty between us. I have spent too many years among people who lie as easily as breathing. I cannot bear to go back to all that, weighing every word you speak, never quite believing anything you say." She dragged a wrist across her eyes. "I can stand a great deal—anything but lies."

She made it sound so simple, but she had no idea how terrible the truth could be. Or how dangerous. Oh, she would not betray him willingly, he trusted her for that, but one slip, one misplaced word or hesitation would be the end of all.

"If I had told you about Venya, would you have stayed with me? Or would you have allowed my besotted surgeon to save you from my wicked wiles and sweep you off to the Jexlan court?"

"Not fair." She laughed unsteadily. "It is too late—you don't deserve an answer. But now the deed is done. I know that—that what we've had these past days won't last. I don't expect it to. But I think—I hope we can be friends. Only"—her voice broke and she looked away—"you mustn't lie to me again."

He could not promise that, but he gave her all the truth he could.

"I told you earlier that all I do—every word, every action—is done for Venya, and that was not a lie. For Venya's sake, I needed to wed Rose of Riall. I had to, and I meant to, by whatever means would serve. If I had disliked her—if I despised her—it would have made no difference. If I found her repulsive, I would have bedded her to get an heir."

He grasped her jaw and turned her face to his. "What has happened between us was not something I expected. Had I known how it would be, I would have gone about this very differently. But I did not know."

She jerked away from his hand. "What? What did you not know?"

"That it would be like this." He pulled her into his arms and brought his mouth down on hers, until her lips parted and she clung to him, shaking. "That, Rosamund," he whispered raggedly against her cheek. "That is what I did not expect. There is no other for me now, nor ever will be. Believe me now or not, it makes no matter; my deeds will prove my words. Had I a thousand years to live, there would never be a single day when you would have the slightest cause to doubt me."

He buried his face in her hair, breathing in the faint scents of lavender and chamomile. "I will not deny that our marriage was made for Venya's good. But had I been free to follow my own heart"—he drew a shaking finger across her lips, swollen from his kisses—"oh, Rosamund, it would have led me straight to you."

Chapter 40

BEYLIK leaned against the rail and stared up at the quarter moon, hanging low above the shadowed rooftops of Serilla. It was a pretty place, though he wished they were away. The simple village and olive groves were too like Jexal for his peace of mind.

He turned at the sound of footsteps behind him, exchanging a nod with Jarrett as he passed by. All quiet. Another hour and he would be in his cot. He yawned, resting his elbows on the rail again and watching starlight ripple in the black water of the harbor. He stiffened as a hand was clamped across his mouth.

"Quietly, now, *beylik*. Just step this way."

He jerked against the restraining hand, then froze as cold steel touched his throat. "I said quietly." Sigurd removed his hand but not the blade. "Step into the surgery. I'd like to have a word with you."

Sigurd closed the door behind them, then pushed Beylik up against it, one large hand fastening around his throat.

"Take your hand off me, *debsh*," Beylik spat.

"*Tsk, tsk,* such language! And you were so eloquent the other day, rallying the men to the prince! I saw you up there, and I wondered where you had learned those words, those thoughts. Surely not among the flocks of Jexal! No, you are something more than a shepherd. Or you were, before you became one of the nameless."

"Let go of—"

"Quiet. It is your turn to listen. I have here a letter for the prince, one that you shall bring to him with a story of the Ilindrian messenger who brought it. I care not what you say, so long as the prince believes it."

"I will not—"

"You will." Sigurd loomed over him, the knife flashing in his hand.

"Do you think I care for that?" Beylik flicked his eyes toward the knife. "You filthy traitor, I would die before I—"

Sigurd laughed softly. "But you are already dead, are you not, *beylik*? No, it is not death I offer you. Quite the contrary, in fact."

"I do not care what you offer. I will never—"

"Listen, *beylik*, and you shall hear what I can give you."

He leaned close, his breath warm against Beylik's ear as he whispered two words. Beylik jerked away with a hoarse cry and stared at the surgeon, incapable of speech.

"Ah, now he listens. Now he hears. *Now* the *beylik* knows who I am."

Beylik turned his face away, his eyes squeezed shut. "You are a deev," he whispered.

"Perhaps." Sigurd brushed a tear from the boy's cheek. "But I am your deev now, and you will do exactly as I say."

Chapter 41

ROSE pulled her chamber robe more closely round her throat and bent to the sheaf of parchments on the table. The wind rattled the shutter in its frame and gusted down the chimney, making the fire leap and dance against the blackened brick. In Valinor, this weather would be typical of late summer, but a month of long, hot Serillan days had thinned her blood. She wore a woolen gown and hose beneath her robe, and still she shivered as cool currents drifted through the thin plank walls and across the floor.

A proposal for a trade agreement was before her, page after page of writing. The plan, as she understood it, was to refit the *Endeavor* and the *Golden Net* as merchant vessels. The estimate of the refitting was buried within a tally, in Eredor's careful hand, of the lost income from the two pirate ships compared to the profit they would bring.

As Eredor reckoned it, the difference was negligible. It was all rendered to the last copper, and yet . . . Rose turned back to the proposal, one ink-stained finger tracing the closely written text. No, she did not see it. She seized her quill and scribbled a note into the margin.

"Overland travel? What does that include? Portage fees—tithes—bandits—bribes? How much? Who to pay?"

But even as she penned her questions, she was impressed. Eredor might be a churlish boor, but now that she began to understand his vision, she could not help but admire it. There was no question that Florian's coffers needed filling. The colony was expensive, and what had been saved was not enough to launch a full-scale attack on Venya. Now Eredor had found a way that rendered piracy unnecessary. Not only was it morally sound, it made good sense.

Her mind played with the image of Florian as a respectable trader of Venyan goods. Not forever, of course, just long enough to ensure that when he went to Venya, he had an army at his back and a solid network of support awaiting his arrival. Three years . . . five . . . With luck, she might have seven years before he risked everything on war.

Her heart leaped as the door opened and Florian himself walked in. He was drenched to the bone, his rain-darkened hair plastered to his cheeks and a grim set to his lips that did not bode well for the Ilindrian alliance. Was it wrong, Rose thought, to feel so glad of that?

"How did your meeting go?" she asked, leaping up to take his cloak and spread it before the fire.

"It did not go at all," he answered, sweeping the dripping hair impatiently from his face. "The Ilindrians were forced off course, so the meeting place has been changed. I must leave tomorrow."

"So soon?" She sighed, then added cheerfully, "Well, at least you are here tonight."

He glanced down at the document she had been reading. "What is this?"

"A draft of the Avrilan trade agreement. Florian, I know how you feel about this, but now that I begin to understand Eredor's plans—"

Florian flicked over the documents. "You should not waste your time on this. Once I have met with the Ilindrians, I will prepare for war at once. You and I will go to Venya and rally the *fheara*, and in three months I will attack."

Rose's mouth was suddenly dry. "That is very sudden—"

"I would not call eighteen years of preparation sudden."

"The council will not agree to this."

"Then I must live without their agreement," Florian snapped, setting his dagger on the table and drawing the poniard from its sheath.

Rose tried to smile. "A bit difficult, as they hold all your wealth. And Eredor has some very interesting ideas to increase it. If you would give him five years, you will be much better placed—"

"So they've gotten to you, have they?" he asked irritably, throwing down the poniard. "Well, it will do them no good. I will not wait another moment."

"But Florian," she said carefully, "I have some stake in this, too; you know how I feel about Richard's occupation of Venya. But now is not the time to act. If you would only work with Eredor—"

She was not reaching him. He was frowning, shaking his head, but before he could speak, she hurried on. "I know the two of you don't get along, but you really cannot afford to go on ignoring him. His plan is sound, Florian. I have looked at it from every angle, and it's very well thought out. It would be folly to let him go ahead without you! For he will, he's quite determined and he has the support of the *filidhi*. But he needs you. He would never say so, but he does."

"Rosamund—" Florian began, but she cut him off.

"Eredor is a wretched negotiator—he lacks authority, and he knows it and tries to make up for it with bluster. He's not familiar with charts or ships, and he doesn't have the first idea how to talk to sailors. He needs you, but his pride won't let him ask again. And honestly, Florian, he shouldn't have to. He is your subject, working for the good of your people. The least you could do is acknowledge him!"

Florian's eyes sparked with anger. "So you think I am unfair to Eredor?"

"Well, yes," she answered cautiously, "I do think you've been a bit unjust. Not that I blame you altogether," she added hastily. "He can be terribly rude. Yet he is no worse than Ashkii, and you have patience enough with *him!*"

"Ashkii never challenged my authority," Florian said tightly. "When I give him an order, he obeys."

"Eredor is not a common sailor—"

"Nor is Ashkii."

"Yes, I know his mother is a princess of Ilindria, but Eredor is one of your own barons. Can you not see the difference?"

Apparently Florian could not. He waved a hand, as though her words were a cloud of buzzing insects to be brushed aside.

"Just listen to him, Florian," Rose implored, "work with him, and he will work with you. Earnán is clever; his help would be worth having."

"Oh, *Earnán* now, is it? Strange, he never asked *me* to call him by his given name. It seems the two of you have grown quite friendly in my absence. Just how much time have you spent with Earnán on this?" He flicked the document and a few pages drifted to the floor. "What else have you two been getting up to while I was away?"

"Are you—surely you are not suggesting—" Her temper flared. "Do you believe, my lord, that I have betrayed you with Lord Eredor?"

"If I believed that," Florian ground between clenched teeth, "Eredor would no longer be an issue. He would be dead."

He paced to the hearth and laid a hand upon the mantel, golden head bent. "Eredor's ideas do have merit," he said after a moment. "I have never denied that. In time they will be useful, but that time is not now. *Venya must come first*. That is my final answer. I have given it to him not once, but many times, and his continued refusal to accept my decision—his plotting and planning behind my back, even with my own princess!—is treading perilously close to treason."

"But if your decision is wrong—"

Florian whirled to face her. "Then it is wrong! And once I have seen that it was wrong, I will do what I must do to make it right. But in any dispute, *someone* must have the final word! By right of birth, that duty—that privilege—that *responsibility* is mine. Think you it is something I take lightly? I assure you, it is not. Nor do I believe myself infallible. But by Leander's beard, once I have thought a matter through, once I have consulted and considered and come to my decision, I will not continue to defend it to anyone who disagrees!"

Had Florian been King of Venya, sitting on his throne in Diarmuiden Castle, his word would indeed be the final answer to all questions touching on his kingdom. But he was not a king. He was a prince without a throne, weighted with the responsibility for all his people yet continually denied the authority to direct the future of his realm.

As a child, Florian might have accepted that position, but no more. For the first time she saw the royal pride unleashed; head thrown back, eyes flashing, he stood before her, prepared to lash out at anyone, be it Richard or his council or even his own wife, who denied his right to rule. Rose understood, and sympathized, but the truth still remained that in choosing this matter as his battleground, he had chosen badly.

"What you are saying," she began carefully, "is that your right to command Eredor as his liege lord has been called to question, and you are right. But I beg you to consider carefully, my lord, how this challenge is best answered. As you yourself once told me, loyalty isn't worth much if it doesn't run both ways. Your council has concerns, serious concerns, about this Venyan expedition that remain unanswered. It is all well and good to order obedience, but a wise ruler—a just ruler—will work with his barons, not against them. Sometimes it is necessary to give a little—"

"I have given all that I intend to give," Florian snapped. "Now the time has come for them to give something in return." He turned away, his shoulders very stiff. "I thought you, at least, would take my side."

"But I do! It's only—no, Florian, wait, I understand, but—"

He hesitated at the door and looked back at her, his expression chill and shut. "You understand nothing."

She viewed him suddenly across a chasm, as though he had drawn the battle lines and placed her on the other side. Fear sharpened her voice as she tried to reach across the gulf between them. "Then explain it to me! Don't just walk away. Make me understand!"

He considered her coldly for a moment, then shook his head and twisted the latch.

"Are you afraid?" she said, "is that it?"

His jaw tightened. "Oh, so now I am coward as well as tyrant?"

"No." Her heart was pounding in her ears, her legs trembling with fear. "No, of course not. But you are acting like what they say you are, a man so obsessed that he is deaf to reason."

"If that is what you choose to believe," he said, his voice clipped, "then so be it."

"I don't want to believe it." Rose took a tentative step toward him, her hand outstretched. "But—"

"Pray excuse me," he said coldly, "I have much to do before I sail tomorrow."

Rose stared at the door, her hand falling slowly to her side. Tears gathered in her eyes, but she blinked them back. This was no time to weep; she had to think of what she would say to him when he returned. She sat down before the fire and marshaled her arguments, choosing each word carefully, honing every point until it glistened with unanswerable logic.

The fire died to embers. She threw on the last logs in the basket and drew Florian's cloak, now dry, around her shoulders. The flames rose, then fell again into twisting, writhing patterns of red and orange and black. The thread of her argument unraveled in her mind, then wove itself into a dream in which the door opened and Florian walked into a different chamber, bright with sunlight and scented with lavender, where a long window looked out upon a sea of flowers and a tabby cat stretched lazily on the hearthrug. Rose jumped up from her seat beside the window, the shirt she had been mending tumbling to the floor in a drift of snowy linen as she ran, laughing, into his arms, feeling the strength of them enfold her as he lifted her . . .

Hovering between sleep and waking, she felt wool against her cheek and turned her head against Florian's shoulder with a sigh, breathing in his own distinctive scent, salt air and tar and a trace of Jexlan spice. His tunic was wet against her skin—he'd gone out without his cloak, she thought with swift compunction, he must be frozen through. She remembered why he had left without his cloak, but their argument seemed far off and unimportant now.

The mattress was deliciously soft and welcoming, and she waited for him to join her. After a moment she felt the brush of cool lips against her brow and heard his footsteps going from the bed. She opened her eyes and watched him bend to the table where his weapons had been laid, the last vestiges of sleep clearing from her mind.

He was *leaving?* Oh, but he couldn't, not yet, not before he heard what she had to say. She struggled to one elbow, still tangled in the folds of his cloak, trying to remember the perfect argument she'd spent half the night constructing.

"Florian," she said, a bit more sharply than she'd meant to. He stilled, and it seemed to her he sighed before he turned his head. The predawn light lay starkly on his stubbled jaw and deepened the shadowed hollows beneath his eyes.

"Yes?" He straightened and slipped his poiniard into its sheath at the small of his back. "What is it now?"

His tone was perfectly polite; only the slight emphasis on the last word betrayed his annoyance. Stung, she cast off the cloak and sat bolt upright. Dismiss *her*, would he? A few well-chosen words—and oh, she had them ready—would wipe that infuriatingly stubborn, all-knowing look right off his face.

Armed with the absolute belief in her position, she nearly missed the significance of his expression until a small warning chord sounded in her mind. That look . . . had she not seen it in the past? Had she not met the man who stood before her—bored, impatient, with far greater matters on his mind than whatever *she* might have to say? Yes, they had met before, in a sweltering little chamber behind a dockside tavern. And now she knew her true opponent: the Prince of Venya.

Florian was gone, buried deep behind the mask he wore when confronted with potential danger. He wore it often, she thought, though she had not recognized the difference until today. Just so did he look when he faced his council and the *filidhi* in their hall. It was the face he turned to anyone who might transform from friend to enemy and strike him unawares.

Which was, she realized with a dull shock, everyone. The councilors who had created the Prince of Venya to their own design were now ready to abandon him. The *filidhi* he had sheltered declared him obsolete; the *fheara* believed Richard's lies over the honor of their prince—even the one friend of his childhood had turned informer. Somewhere among his people—perhaps on his very ship, among the men he had fought beside, drank with, laughed with—a traitor lurked. Everyone he had ever dared to trust could betray him in a moment.

Everyone but her.

This was not about trade routes or strategy or politics. It never had been. The Prince of Venya was fighting for his life and realm, and that he could no longer distinguish between an enemy and the woman who loved him should come as no surprise. It hurt more than Rose would have imagined possible, but she could not dwell upon that now. She must fight, too, and cannily, for the Prince of Venya was above all a survivor.

He would walk away from an enemy without looking back, and if that meant severing the fragile bond she and Florian had forged, so be it. He had lived alone for a long time now. Rose could argue herself hoarse, but no matter how clever or reasonable her arguments might be, once she had been ranked as an obstacle on the path to Venya, he would not hear them.

It might be wrong. It was certainly unjust. But it was the truth that must be faced before she lost him for all time. So be damned to Eredor and the council and the *filidhi* of Serilla. They could look after themselves. It was Florian who mattered now, and somehow she must find the words to reach him.

In the time she had spent on these reflections, he had continued to arm himself—a small knife to his boot, his sword into his belt, the thin stilleto to the sheath he buckled to his forearm. Now he shook his full black sleeve over the taut sinew of his wrist and shot his jeweled dagger into the scabbard. He scooped a few loose coins from the table and glanced toward the window.

"I fear we must talk another time," he said. "The tide is turning and—"

"I'm sorry," she said simply, holding out her arms. "Florian, I am so sorry."

He went completely still, his face expressionless. Rose sat, empty arms outstretched, her heart drumming a frantic rhythm in her ears. And then, between one beat and the next, the mask dropped and it was Florian who stood before her, proud and beaten, angry and repentant, his eyes filled with such naked longing that her own stung with sudden tears.

And it was Florian who came to her, swiftly as an arrow, sliding into her arms and bearing her back upon the mattress, his beard rough against her cheeks. "So am I. Poor Rosamund, did you sit up all night?"

"It doesn't matter. Only . . . don't go, don't leave me yet."

"No." He kissed her cheeks, her eyes. "Not yet."

"I never meant to doubt you," she said unsteadily, "and I don't. You were right—"

He lifted himself on his elbow. "That wasn't what you said last night. Don't tell me you have changed your mind!"

"Not my mind. Call it a change of heart, my lord, and you will have the truth. We may not always agree—and when we do not, you will hear about it—but Jehan forbid that I should ever give you cause to doubt my loyalty. Or my love," she added in a whisper.

"I do not doubt either," he said, bending to set his lips upon her brow. "Not now."

She wound her arms around his neck and pulled him down, then winced and drew away as the hilt of his sword poked her in the ribs. "Let me disarm you."

He fell upon his back, arms outstretched. "I think, my lady, that you already have."

"Perhaps," she said demurely, "but all the same, I'd like to have your sword."

"Would you?" He caught her wrist and drew her hand downward. "Then by all means, take it."

She collapsed against his chest. "I didn't mean *that*."

"It seems to me," he remarked to the ceiling, "that no *loyal* subject would laugh at such a moment. One might call it treason to . . . giggle when presented with the royal sword."

"Treason, is it? Well—" Her words ended in a yelp as his fingers found the sensitive spot beneath her arms. She countered with an attack upon his ribs and belly, delighted to discover that he was nearly as ticklish as she. At last he fell back, holding his hands up in surrender.

"It seems to *me*," she choked, resting her hands on his shoulders as her hair waved about his face, "that a—a truly *loyal* subject would risk a charge of treason to prevent her liege lord staining his fresh sheets with her blood. Or gelding himself."

He winced. "Since you put it that way, you have my leave to disarm me. Or at least," he amended, his eyes gleaming between half-closed lids, "you have my leave to try."

The sword he gave up easily, allowing her to unbuckle the belt and set it carefully upon the floor. The dagger was a bit more difficult. Once she had both hands upon the hilt, though, he surrendered. The poiniard proved a problem, for he had only to roll upon his back to defend it. After several fruitless attempts, he grinned, folding his arms beneath his head. "You could try distracting me."

His shirt had come untucked during their battle. She slid her hand beneath it, feeling the hard muscle of his belly contract beneath her fingertips. "Like that?"

"It is a beginning."

Her hand drifted upward to his chest, pushing the folds of his shirt before it. He obligingly held up his arms so she could remove it and fling it over her shoulder, and she took the opportunity to divest him of his stiletto. Then she dipped her head and trailed a line of kisses from breastbone to navel, feeling the sharp intake of his breath when she slid a finger into the waistband of his trousers, then withdrew it and eased first one button, then a second, from its buttonhole, only to halt at the third. "You must allow me to order you new breeches," she murmured against his skin. "These are far too tight."

"They weren't when I put them on."

"Do lie still, my lord. I cannot seem to quite . . . manage this button."

"Keep doing that," he said hoarsely, "and it will burst."

"Perhaps this one . . . or this . . . If you would turn a little . . . ha!" Her hand fastened on the poniard. "No sudden moves, now. I would hate to have an accident." She drew the blade slowly from its sheath, nudged Florian to his back, and sat astride him. "Too easy," she said, a triumphant smile on her lips as she dangled the weapon before him, then slowly extended her arm and dropped it point-down toward the floor.

Florian's gaze never left hers. He hardly seemed to move. Yet before the poniard hit the wooden plank, he had caught it by the hilt. The next moment Rose found herself beneath him, wrists pinned above her head by one of his hands as the other raised the weapon to her throat.

"When a thing seems too easy, it often is." He drew the blade slowly down her neck until it reached her bodice, then slid the tip beneath the first lace. "Quietly now, no sudden moves. We wouldn't want an accident." The lace parted with a little pop. "You were doing very well," he said, severing the next lace. "Had me at your mercy, didn't you? And now"—his voice dropped to a purr—"it is my turn."

"Be careful," Rose said nervously, flinching a little as cold metal touched her skin. She hardly dared breathe until the last lace snapped and with a flick of his wrist Florian tossed the poniard aside. It hit the wall beside the window and stuck there, quivering.

"Oh, I will be." He parted her bodice and looked down at her. The first rays of the sun gilded his shoulders to bronze, yet his face was shadowed. A tiny shiver, half fear and half excitement, moved through her and she tried to pull her hands free.

He tightened his grip. "Not yet. I like you where you are." His lips were soft and cool against her skin, his mouth hot as it closed around her breast. She gasped at the sensation, and he raised his head slightly, his breath fanning her moist skin. His free hand slid beneath her skirt to stroke her calf, her knee, her inner thigh, moving slowly upward, then drifting down again, a slow, tantalizing journey that he repeated with endless patience until she drifted into a world of pure sensation.

Bright pleasure melted into need, sharpening with every

moment. She arched upward, only to have him move away and to
find herself powerless to follow, still caught fast at the wrists.

"Enough," she gasped, "Let me go—"

"Soon." His mouth hovered over hers. "Remember, you began
this game, not I."

She raised her head, blindly seeking, but he eluded her, his
lips skimming down her neck, across her breasts, then up again
until he reached her mouth. This time he lingered there, teasing
her lips apart before pulling away to look into her eyes.

"What do you want, Rosamund?" he whispered. His fingers
relaxed their grip upon her wrist. "Show me."

She clasped his neck and dragged his mouth to hers, her body
melting like quicksilver in his arms.

CONTENT. That was the word she wanted . . . or was it? No,
content was too calm, too passive for this feeling. She was . . .
happy. Completely and utterly at peace. If only everyone could
feel like this, there would be no war or strife, no discord at all in
a world so perfect. Slowly she became aware of Florian's hand,
stroking the hair back from her cheeks, his body warm and heavy
upon hers, his lips against her neck.

"Am I dead?" she asked. "Is that what this is?"

He laughed low in his throat. "If you are, then I am, too."

"Oh. That's all right, then."

Turning, he pulled her into his embrace, his body wrapped
around her, and her head resting on his chest.

"Next time," he murmured, "you will think twice before deciding I am helpless."

She suspected he meant more than the game they had just
played, though she wasn't sure he was aware of it.

"Next time," she answered, running a languid hand down his
belly, "I will tie you to the bedposts to be sure."

He considered this in silence for a moment. "I'd like to see
you try," he said at last.

"Is that a challenge . . . or an invitation?"

His chest shook with silent laughter. "An interesting question.
As soon as I've found the answer, I'll let you know."

She smiled and nestled closer, searching for a rejoinder, but
before she found it, she was asleep.

Chapter 42

AT midday Florian stood at the window. Sunlight danced on the harbor below, and a warm breeze carried the scents of sea and lemon and the sounds of shrieking gulls into the chamber. A fair day. A wasted day. It was shameful to linger here when there was so much to be done. Looking back into the shadowy chamber, he could just make out Rosamund's form. She lay on her side, one knee bent, a hand tucked beneath her cheek, and her hair tumbled on the pillow. She looked, he thought, quite ridiculously young and innocent.

He smiled, remembering the beguiling touch of her hands, her mouth, her delighted grin as she waved his poiniard in his face. He felt his body stir at the memory of her beneath him, writhing at his touch.

But Rosamund was more than the most delightful bed partner he had ever known. She was a woman with her own mind. It was a good mind, he thought, turning back to the window, and once convinced she had the right of an argument, she would not easily abandon it. He did not deceive himself that he had won this round; he had merely gained a reprieve. If he had any sense, he would leave before she woke and began the whole tiresome business over again.

But he did not have *that* much sense. Try as he might, he could not regret it.

Perhaps, he mused, sitting down at the table, the day was not really wasted. They might have conceived a child. Leander knew that Venya must have an heir, and the sooner the better. For a moment, though, he did not see the heir of Venya, but the child he and Rosamund might make together, a little girl with leaf-brown hair and her mother's smile, or perhaps a golden boy with long, dark eyes.

Smiling, Florian wrote a quick note to inform his men that their departure was delayed until the morrow. It wasn't until he was finished that a sudden tremor shook his hand, spraying sand across the table. He stared at the fine grains sparkling against the wood, his skin pricking hot and cold together as a fine sweat broke out over his body.

This wasn't happening. Not now. Not yet. It had only been a few weeks since the last time; he should have months before the fever returned.

Unless time was even shorter than he had thought. Unless he himself had somehow hastened things by resorting to the Ilindrian elixir.

He stood and walked carefully to the bed.

"Rosamund." He touched her arm. "Rosamund, wake up."

"No," she groaned, pulling the pillow over her head. "Come back to bed."

"I need you to do something for me."

It was happening too fast. His temples pounded fiercely, and the sunlight seemed unnaturally bright. Rosamund sat up, looking at him curiously.

"What is it? Is something wrong?"

"I am a little . . . unwell."

"Is it the marsh fever again?"

"Yes."

"Poor Florian, how tiresome. Shall I send for Sigurd?" she asked reluctantly.

"No!" Florian blinked hard to keep her face in focus. "Please go to the *filidhi* hall. To Magea Gwythian."

"Yes, all right."

She threw back the coverlet and pulled her shift over her head, then picked up her kirtle. "Oh, dear," she said, pulling the gaping bodice together. Florian tried to return her smile, but from the look on her face, the effort was a failure. She stooped and put her knuckles to his brow.

"You're burning! Lie down," she ordered.

"Not yet. Rosamund, listen, you must tell only Magea Gwythian. No one else." He caught her wrist. "Do you hear me?"

"I hear you," she said soothingly, "but what if she is not receiving visitors? They must have other healers who can—"

"No!" He tried to hold onto her, but his fingers slid from her arm. "Only Gwythian."

"What does it matter who I bring so long as they know what to do?" she said reasonably. "Just rest and I'll be back—"

He stood unsteadily, grasping the bedpost for support. "Never mind. I'll go."

"You—? Don't be absurd." She put a hand on his shoulder and urged him down again. "You are not going anywhere. All right, Magea Gwythian it is."

"Speak to no one else."

"I won't. Only do lie back now, that's the way, and let me cover you. I'll be back as quickly as I can."

She cast him a doubtful glance over her shoulder, threw his cloak around her, and went quickly out the door.

Chapter 43

"HE insisted that I only speak to you," Rose said to Magea Gwythian of Venya. The old woman showed no surprise at this; she merely nodded, not looking at Rose but staring pensively out the long window of her chamber.

"Sigurd said it is a marsh fever," Rose added.

Gwythian turned. "Who is Sigurd?"

"The surgeon on the *Quest*. He said it is a recurring ailment that lasts a day or two. He said it is not serious," she added uncertainly. "And the next day my lord was well again."

"When was this?"

"Some weeks ago . . . eight, perhaps, or ten."

Gwythian seemed to relax slightly. "I see. You did well to come to me." She looked fully at Rose for the first time, and smiled slightly. "Please sit down, my lady. I will be with you in a moment." She stood, leaning heavily on her staff. "Would you take a cup of wine while I make ready?"

Rose sat down. "Yes, thank you." She smiled wryly, tucking her loose hair back into her cloak. "I came out in a hurry." She accepted the cup with a nod and sipped, then, as the Magea began to pour for herself, she said, "I misspoke before. My lord has been ill since, though I am not certain it was the same ailment."

Gwythian stopped. "When was that?"

"The day the *Quest* was nearly overtaken. He was fevered, I remember, when he came back to the deck, but he said it was a reaction to the . . . the . . ." She waved a hand. "To whatever it was he did to the ship."

Gwythian sat down slowly. "What exactly did he do, my lady?"

The Magea did not interrupt her, though it seemed the color faded from her face as Rose recounted what had happened on the *Quest* that day, when Florian climbed to the topmast and turned the ship against the wind, guiding it through the Valinorian vessels.

Gwythian leaned her brow against her hands, folded on her staff. "My lady, would you be so kind as to ring the bell for me?"

"Of course. Is something wrong?"

"Yes," she answered simply, then held up a hand, forestalling Rose's next question. "Please wait a moment."

The door opened and the young *filidh* Caelan came into the chamber. She looked as though she'd been outdoors; her cloak was thrown back and her cheeks were ruddy.

"Yes, Grandmother? Oh—my lady." The *filidh's* voice cooled. "Good day to you."

"Caelan, the prince is ill." Quickly she recounted all that Rose had told her. "You must go to him at once. You know what to bring."

"What is wrong?" Rose asked.

"I will tell you when I've seen him," Caelan snapped, her robe swirling as she ran for the door. "Come, my lady, hurry."

FLORIAN tossed restlessly upon the bed, sweat-soaked strands of hair clinging to his cheeks. His eyes glittered between half-closed lids, yet he did not seem aware of them, nor did he answer when Caelan questioned him. At last the young *filidh* drew the coverlet up.

"Sigurd said," Rose began, her voice shaking, "that the fever will not last beyond a day. He said it was inconvenient, but no more."

"This is not marsh fever."

"Then—"

"Lady, come sit down," Caelan said, so gently that Rose felt every muscle in her body tense. "Please," she added, gesturing toward a chair. Rose lowered herself carefully, as though a sudden movement might shatter her.

"Sigurd is a very good surgeon," Rose said, her voice strangely high-pitched. "My lord has every confidence in him."

"I am sure he is an excellent surgeon, but if he believes this is a marsh fever, he has been deceived." Caelan took the seat across from her. "The prince is a royal Venyan, and like all his line, he has inherited Leander's gift. Unlike the others, it never fully manifested. My grandmother first thought the events in Venya—the terrible death of the king and queen, which apparently the prince witnessed—had simply delayed the process, and at fifteen, he did begin to show the first signs. But then he went to Venya and became quite ill—"

"From the marshes?" Rose asked.

"Yes. After he recovered, the little progress he had made toward realizing his gift was lost. By the time he passed his nineteenth year, he and my grandmother both came to accept that for whatever reason, it would never manifest."

"But—" Rose began. Caelan halted her with a gesture.

"Please let me finish. Then I will answer all your questions—or those I can. Soon after, the prince began to experience a recurrence of his illness. His surgeon at the time attributed this to marsh fever and treated it accordingly, and for a time, his remedies served. But what was happening was more serious, for the prince's gift, denied its natural outlet, was burning him away from within. My grandmother had never seen such a thing before, but she had read deeply and knew that such a condition, though rare, was invariably fatal."

"*Fatal?*"

"Not immediately," Caelan said quickly. "Grandmother judged the prince had years before him still."

"How many years?"

"Perhaps twelve. Ten, at the least, assuming we could find no remedy. Grandmother and I devoted years to the search, and we did find a way, a ritual that could only be performed in Venya, for it required the taking of a living opaline crystal from the earth. Last spring the three of us went to Venya together, but the ritual was never completed. Richard was there before us."

Rose looked up. "At Kendrick's Mine," she said, the words not quite a question.

"Yes. We did not expect to be met by soldiers, but we were, and barely escaped with our lives."

"So that is why he was in Venya," Rose said softly. "That is why he went to Kendrick's Mine."

"And left with his errand unfinished. We have tried to find another way, but so far it has eluded us. Now . . ." She shook her head. "What precisely did you see that day on the *Quest*? Tell me everything you can remember."

Once again, Rose recounted what had happened on the *Quest* the day of their escape from the *Lord Marva*.

"But that is impossible," Caelan said.

"I saw it—everyone saw it. It happened right before our eyes. He turned the ship against the wind and guided it through the channel."

"But how? Unless . . . Tell me, had he by any chance lately visited Ilindria?"

"Yes, but—"

"Fool." Caelan rose and stalked over to the bed, frowning down at the prince. "How could he have taken such a risk? Or no, not even a risk, you couldn't call it that, for he knew the price full well."

"What price?"

"Tell me what happened next," Caelan ordered sharply. "Everything."

"He fell—lost consciousness. Sigurd gave him something and—and he was better."

"Porga." Caelan shook her head, a reluctant smile touching her lips. "They say he has Leander's luck, and I'm starting to believe it. The prince took Ilindrian elixir, and it woke his gift, as he knew it would—not a true awakening, but a—a flash of power. It would have killed him, had the surgeon not contained it. *Porga* is made to block Venyan magic, and so it did. For a time." Caelan glanced over at the bed. "But now . . . I fear time is running out."

"What do you mean?"

"It is obvious that the Ilindrian elixir weakened his defenses, though I suspect that even before that, he was worsening. He should have come to us. He should have told us."

"Why?" Rose demanded. "What could you have done? You have admitted already that your cures have failed him."

Caelan's dark eyes flashed. "When I said I had given several years of my life to the search, it was no idle boast. From the time I was twelve and showed some glimmer of a seer's talent, I was kept cloistered. Five years I spent in a cell, lady, five years without seeing sunlight or speaking to another living being save for my grandmother, and all to clear my sight so I might see the means to cure our prince. In the end, it was granted to me, but to no avail. I would have tried again, had Grandmother not forbidden it. But if my death would have released the prince, it would have been required of me. And given freely."

"Caelan." They both started at the sound of Florian's voice, coming weakly from the bed. He struggled to one elbow, throwing off the coverlet. "Mistress, no one told me—I would never have allowed you to be shut away like that—"

"It was not yours to decide." Caelan drew herself up, dark eyes flashing. "I serve Venya."

Five years, Rose thought, Caelan spent in silent solitude. Upon her release, with the world all new before her, she had sailed off to Venya with her prince to rescue him from certain death.

Who knew what part a priestess of Venya would have played in that ill-fated ritual? Or what dreams the girl had cherished during those long and lonely years, when her every thought had been devoted to her prince's welfare? The outcome, Rose thought, had been inevitable. She could see it clearly now; the longing beneath the priestess's haughty gaze, the anguish barely concealed by the proud tilt of her head.

"I, too, serve Venya," Florian said hoarsely.

"Then submit yourself to the Magea," Caelan said coldly, "as has every ruler before you, and allow her to seek some means of undoing the damage you have done."

Florian's eyes were fever-bright, his bare chest gleaming with sweat. "How much damage?" he demanded. "How long do I have left?"

Caelan shook her head impatiently. "You would know the hour of your death? What do you take me for, some dockside gypsy? The future is not one certainty, but an endless stream of possibilities that appear and disappear with every action taken or not taken, every word spoken or unspoken. One wish, my lord, one prayer—a single thought has the power to alter it forever. You could be dead by sunrise. So could I, for that matter, or your lady here, or any mortal who walks beneath the sky. What you ask is impossible. I bid you good night and leave you to your lady's care."

Caelan turned, her robes swirling, and started for the door. She paused briefly by Rose and pressed a twist of parchment into her hand.

"Give him wine, well watered, as much as he will take," the younger woman ordered coolly, "and add a pinch of this to each cup. The fever should be gone by midday. My grandmother will send to you."

"Lady, you have chosen an ill time to bandy words with me." Florian's arms were trembling with the effort of holding himself upright, but his voice, though hoarse, was very firm. "Since you insist, I will rephrase the question. Given that I do not succumb to injury or accident, speaking solely of the malady with which you have been so concerned and which touches so closely upon the future of Venya, tell me what you have seen."

Caelan halted, hand outstretched toward the door, the color draining from her face. "My lord," the young priestess said, her voice shaking, "Do not ask this. I-I cannot—"

"In Leander's name, I order you to speak."

Caelan closed her eyes. "One year for a certainty," she whispered. "Perhaps as much as two. No more than that."

Rose's hand clenched on the twist of parchment, the slight rustle seeming very loud in the dead silence that had fallen on the chamber. Two years. Or less. The words repeated in her mind, over and over, their meaning undeniable. Yet try as she might, Rose could not fit them into any reality she understood.

"Thank you," Florian said politely. "That is what I need to know."

WHEN Caelan had gone, Rose poured a bit of wine into a cup, filled it with water, and added a pinch of the grayish powder. She carried it to the bed and handed it to Florian.

"Drink it all," she ordered shortly.

She turned away without waiting for an answer and began to gather discarded bits of clothing from the floor and fold them into tidy piles. Next came the weapons; dagger, poiniard, and stiletto were set carefully on the table, ordered by size and arranged in a meticulous line. She swept the ashes from the hearth and built up the fire, then gathered the fragments of her lace from the floor and tossed them into the flames.

Rummaging in a drawer, she found a ribbon and took it to a seat by the window, then slipped her kirtle over her head. Sitting in her shift, she began to thread the ribbon through the bodice. The ribbon was crimson; it sat oddly against the dull green of the kirtle, but she did not search for another.

She dared not pause. If she did, if she stopped what she was doing for a single moment, she might begin to think, and then anything might happen. Better not to think at all; better to keep busy. One side was finished sooner than the other, and she saw the ribbon straggled like a drunken thing, winding a crooked path between the holes. She picked it out and began again, only to end up no better than she had started.

Cursing beneath her breath, she tried a third time, concentrating fiercely. When she reached the end, she stared at the ribbon in disbelief. It couldn't be . . . and yet it was. She turned the kirtle in her hands, trying to puzzle out where she had first gone wrong, but she could no longer remember what the pattern was supposed to look like. It was too complicated, too tangled to ever be made right again . . .

Jumping to her feet, she threw the kirtle to the floor. Then she seized the flagon from the table and flung it into the fireplace, followed by her cup, the candle, and the inkwell. Breathing hard, she rounded on Florian. He lay against the pillow, watching her.

"I'm sorry, Rosamund," he said. "I did not know how to tell you."

"Didn't know? You didn't *know* how to *tell* me? Well, that is very strange, Florian. You had no trouble telling me many other things. Oh, but of course! I see the problem now! It is only the *truth* you are incapable of speaking!"

"Rosamund, you are upset. Sit down—"

"For once, Florian, just for once I want the truth from you!"

"What truth is it you're looking for?" he asked wearily.

"You knew of this—this illness—"

"I did. But you heard Caelan, they thought it could be ten years, and they were searching for a rememdy—"

"But you did not believe you had ten years or even five. You've known you were getting worse. That is why you have been in such a rush to get to Venya, isn't it?"

"I did not know. I suspected. And yes, that is part of the reason I do not dare delay. The tide is ebbing," he added very low, "Should I miss it, all is lost. Rosamund, I have seen it—'tis Leander's will—"

"Don't speak to me of Leander's will," she cried.

"But I must." He turned his head restlessly on the pillow. "You don't understand. We were bound, the land and I, when I was in the marshes. My life was spared, but chained to Venya. The drought, the fires—my illness—are all one."

"That is nonsense. Fever talk—"

"Truth. You said you wanted it."

"Very well," she said, her voice straining with the effort to speak calmly. "If your healing will bring about Venya's, then you must do as Caelan said and submit yourself to the care of the Magea."

"She is wrong. 'Tis not the way. She's twisted the prophecy. The land reborn, it said, hope springs in the land reborn. But that is after—"

"What prophecy is this?"

"Caelan made it," he said, his voice a hoarse whisper. "On the night we fled Kendrick's Mine, she prophesied Venya's freedom, the land reborn."

"After what?" Rose demanded. "You said it would be after. What must come first?"

His eyes were closed, his breath rasping in his throat. She slipped an arm beneath his neck, lifting him so he might drink.

"Tell me," she said when he had drained the goblet. "What must happen before the land is reborn?"

"A sacrifice."

"What sacrifice?" she asked, setting the goblet very carefully upon the table.

"Not—Rosamund, not you! You don't think I would—"

"I think," she said evenly, "that you would do anything for Venya. But very well, if the sacrifice is not me, what is it?"

He closed his eyes and turned his head away. "The uncrowned king."

"Of course. I should have known." She poured the goblet full again and left the pitcher of watered wine on the bedside table beside the twist of powder. "I will be back tomorrow."

"Rosamund, wait—"

"Tomorrow," she repeated. "I will speak to you then. Not of gods and bargains and prophecies, but of the truth. By Jehan's garter, either I will have that from you or I will leave on the next ship."

Chapter 44

FLORIAN watched the *filidhi* hall take shape against the eastern sky. In the hour before dawn, the village was wrapped in slumber. The harbor was dark, save for tiny glow of the pinnacle light shining on the *Quest*. He wasn't aware that he was waiting for a sound until the bell rang out, soft but very clear, measuring the passing of a watch that would never come again. The last note lingered sadly for a moment, then faded into the rhythmic crash of breakers against the cliffs.

The truth. That was what Rosamund demanded. As if there was one truth to be told, not the dozen that were tearing him apart. But he could not afford to fall to pieces now. There *was* a truth, and she deserved to have it.

He heard the door open behind him. The fire had subsided to embers, not enough to show the details of her face, but he could see her weariness in the line of her shoulders and hear it in her voice when she asked him how he did this morning.

"Much better," he said. "Caelan's draught worked wonders."

He blew up the fire and lit a candle, which he placed on the table between them. The warm light revealed the windswept tangle of her hair and the sand on the damp hem of her gown. "Did you spend the whole night walking?" he asked, but she only shook her head, rejecting this attempt at conversation. He saw her eyes move over him, watched the comprehension spring into her face.

"You are leaving."

"Yes," he said. "On the first tide."

"I see."

Moving stiffly, she began to rise from her seat. He caught her wrist and pulled her back. "No, I don't think you do. Rosamund, you asked for the truth. Do you want to hear it or not?"

"All right," she said indifferently. "Go ahead."

"When I was seven," he began, "I woke one night to the smell of smoke. Before an hour passed, I saw my parents murdered and watched my home go up in flames. Nothing made sense to me. It was all a jumble of faces and words I couldn't understand. But then Bastyon explained that Leander had spared me for a purpose. And he knew—he knew without a doubt—what that purpose was. One day I would go home, drive Richard out of Venya, and avenge my parents' death. It was so simple that even I could understand it."

"You were a child—" Rosamund began.

"*Then* I was a child. But later—later I was not. There was a time, after that first journey into Venya, when I could have turned my course. It was not only I who had been betrayed, but the entire network of support it had taken nine years to assemble. We had no outside allies, no hope of raising an army. Even Bastyon was ready to admit defeat. But I was not. No one asked me to prey on Richard's ships, no one suggested I turn privateer. That was my decision.

"I have killed, Rosamund; I have stolen, and I have sent good people to their deaths. The only comfort I could offer their families—and myself—was that their lives had been given for Venya. Take that away, and I am nothing—worse than nothing, a common pirate, a thief, a murderer who deceived my followers and betrayed the honor of my people. And that I cannot be. I will not."

"Yes," Rosamund began slowly, "I understand. But I cannot see how allowing the *filidhi* to save your life will be a betrayal of anyone's honor. In fact, I would think your first responsibility is to stay alive."

"My first responsibility is to complete the task for which Leander spared me. One year is all I can count upon. I will need every moment of that time to prepare for war."

"Do you mean to tell the council?"

"No. I did not mean for you to know—I am sorry, I know you think I should have told you, but I could not risk it. The council has little enough faith in me as it is; what would they say if they knew I had so little time? It would be the end. I cannot force you to silence, but I hope that you agree it is the only thing to do—or at least that you respect my decision."

She put a hand to her head as though it ached. "I will say nothing."

"Thank you."

She lifted her head. "But do not mistake that for agreement. Or respect."

Florian kept his face carefully expressionless. "Then I must settle for your silence."

"Really? I don't think so. The Ilindrians are not to be relied upon. It will be only Venyans who face Richard's army on the field. Say we can rally the Venyans—and I say we, because you'll need more from me than silence. You'll need my full support."

"Yes," Florian admitted.

"Suppose I give you that. We go to Venya and if we are lucky—and I mean very, very lucky—we manage to escape Richard's notice long enough to put together something resembling an army. But it won't really be an army, will it? Not like the one Richard has, with knights and archers and pikemen who have years of training and experience. How long do you expect a ragtag collection of farmers and fishermen—armed with Jehan knows what and totally untrained—will stand against Richard's forces? It will be a slaughter."

"Do you imagine I have given this no thought? I have studied every battle ever fought, the tactics that worked and why they worked, the strategies that failed and how they could have succeeded. You are right; we don't dare meet them in open battle, but there are other methods of warfare that have been successful against larger forces, even ones better armed and more experienced. And you mustn't forget that our men will be fighting for their homes and freedom against soldiers who have no real stake in the outcome. It makes a difference, Rosamund."

"Yes, I'll give you that. But I have read of battles, too. I don't claim to be an expert, but it seems to me that such a war as you describe is not won quickly. It can take months—sometimes years—for those sorts of tactics to succeed."

Trust Rosamund to put her finger on the most glaring flaw in what was, at best, a desperate proposition. "Even if I were perfectly well, there is no guarantee I would live to see a victory. That is in Leander's hands. But *I* must begin it. And if I should fall—"

"If?" Rosamund interrupted. "No, not if. *When.* Let us confine ourselves to truth here, Florian. You don't expect to be King of Venya. What exactly did Caelan prophesy?"

He looked toward the window, where the *Quest* lay at anchor, the first sunlight gilding the mast.

> *"The sword to conquer Venya's foes,*
> *The shield protects us from our woes,*
> *The sacrifice of uncrowned king,*
> *Offered in the sacred ring,*
> *Then two are one by oath forsworn,*
> *And hope unites the land reborn."*

Rosamund rested her chin in her palm and stared at the table, a small crease between the dark wings of her brows.

"Let us have the coronation, then," she said.

"One does not clap on a crown and call oneself King of Venya. There are rituals involved, all of which must take place on Venyan soil."

"Then we'll go to Venya and do it."

"The last time I went to Venya for a ritual, it was a disaster. And I can hardly steal into my own kingdom, declare myself king, and slink out again before I'm caught. No respectable *filidh* would take part in such a travesty, and nor would I."

"Very well. Say the prophecy again."

When he had done so, she said, "What does it mean, the sacred ring?"

"Originally it was a part of an old custom, the Game of Kings. At one time—centuries ago—it was held every seven years and the winner was named High King until the next game. All the kingdoms on the Western Sea took part, and each one hosted it in turn. It was abandoned ages ago—too many deaths. But even before that, back in the days when Venya and Valinor were divided into a hundred petty kingdoms and there was little outside trade, it was used to settle disputes between the tribes. Two would enter the sacred ring, but only one would leave it."

"Somehow I cannot imagine Richard accepting such a challenge."

"More's the pity. I've issued him several, just on the off chance he might be insulted into it, but he does not deign to answer. Of course the reference is symbolic. War is inevitable and through it, *fheara* and *filidhi* will be reunited and Venya reborn."

"And the sacrifice of uncrowned king is part of this . . . rebirth? But that is rubbish! What good can you do Venya if you are dead?"

"Shasra." He took her hand. "You know the answer to that as well as I. If that is what the land requires . . ."

"Superstition," she snapped. "We are not savages. We do not sacrifice our kings every time there is a drought and water the land with their blood."

"Nothing is certain," he said. "Believe me, I do not intend to walk up to Richard unarmed and let him cut me down. I intend to fight him. I intend to *win*."

"You say that," she began in a low, shaking voice, "but you don't mean it. You—you've given up, haven't you? You gave up years ago. All your talk of winning is just talk. You don't believe it can really happen, no more than the council does. But you will do it anyway, all because some girl had hysterics and babbled a bunch of nonsense that could be twisted to mean anything!"

"Caelan is not 'some girl.' She is a *filidh* who has dedicated her life to Venya's welfare. You do her a disservice to mock her."

Rosamund put her head in her hands. "Yes. You're right. I'm sure it did mean *something,* but there is no possible way that you or anyone can be certain what that is."

"Nothing is certain," he said again, reaching out to pull a leaf from her tangled hair. She caught his hand and held it tightly in both of hers, scowling down at their linked fingers and blinking hard.

"But I know my duty," he went on. "I've known it all my life. I should have told you before, I see now that it was wrong of me to keep this from you, but I was hoping you would never need to know. I'm sorry. But I must fulfill my destiny."

She lifted her head and looked at him directly. The green flecks in her eyes shimmered in the sunlight streaming through the window. "You are afraid," she said, sounding faintly surprised.

For a moment he could only stare at her, too shocked—too hurt—to answer. Then he forced himself to laugh. "This is the second time you've named me coward. Once more and I shall have to call you out."

"No. No, you're not a coward. It isn't physical danger you fear or even death. But you *are* afraid. It is . . ." She made a subtle gesture he did not recognize. "What is the word? Dishonor? Obscurity? What in Jexal they would call the nameless death."

"Every man wants his life to have had meaning."

"But your life is not yet finished. If there is one thing I know about prophecies, it is that they are seldom what they seem. And Caelan—all praise to her name—said herself that no one can foretell the future. To make decisions on the basis of a—a riddle makes no sense."

Her voice was calm, but she gripped his hand so tightly that her nails dug into the skin. "Caelan found one ritual to heal you, but who is to say there are not others? We can send for healers from Jexal and Moravia and Ilindria—"

"Do you think we have not tried that?" he said gently.

"Then we must try again."

"You shall do whatever you think best. But still, I go to Venya."

"To fling your life away? It is folly—worse than folly. The Prince of Venya?" She threw his hand from her. "The *martyr* of Venya is more like it! You would choose a hero's death over the chance of life!"

Florian was shaking with anger. "What I do—all I do—is done in the service of my people."

"In the service of your pride! They were right, all of them, you *are* obsessed—"

Florian stood abruptly. "You are talking nonsense. This war can be won. That is not pride, it is a simple fact, and I intend to make it happen by any means that serve. If my death can serve as an inspiration to the Venyan people, it is the least that I can offer them."

Rosamund leapt to her feet and leaned across the table, her palms flat upon its surface. "It *is* the least! You would do better to offer them your life by giving the *filidhi* time to heal you."

"I *have* given them time."

"Then you must give them more."

"No," he said flatly, starting for the door. "And that is my final word."

"Is it?" she asked softly from behind him. "Then hear mine. If you persist in this—this madness, do not look to me for support. I will not go to Venya. I will not speak for you there."

As soon as the ultimatum had been spoken, Rose realized her mistake. He would never give in to a threat or retreat from such an open challenge. When he turned back, his face was perfectly expressionless. Faultlessly polite, he inclined his head and said, "You must do as you see fit."

"But—but you said yourself that you cannot possibly rally the *fheara* without me."

"Then it seems I will be fighting Richard alone. But as you have made abundantly clear, that it is no longer your concern."

She slipped past him and put her back against the door. "I spoke in anger. Of course I want to help you. And I can, I know I can if you would only listen." But she wasn't reaching him. He wasn't hearing her at all. "This is my life as well as yours," she cried, "my future you are deciding."

He regarded her coldly. "*Your* life. *Your* future. Pressing matters, to be sure, but not quite so pressing as the lives of my people and the future of the Venyan throne. These are my concerns, and if you will be so kind as to excuse me, I will go deal with them."

"But—"

"Move," he said in a voice of deadly calm.

"Not until we have talked this through."

All at once, his calm shattered. "Talk? What else have we been doing? Talk changes nothing. Get out of my way, Rosamund, or by all the gods, I'll—I'll—"

"You'll what?" She folded her arms across her chest, daring him to finish.

"I will carry you to yonder chair and tie you down."

She was momentarily speechless, suspended halfway between tears and laughter. For of course he couldn't mean it. Florian would never do such a thing.

But the Prince of Venya might.

"Be reasonable," she pleaded. "I am well aware of *our* responsibilities to *our* subjects. You know that. You've just forgotten, not that I blame you. This whole thing is like some ghastly nightmare, and of course you're overwrought. Jehan knows I'm a bit overwrought myself, and that's exactly why we must calm down and discuss this rationally."

"I have made my position clear. So have you. If that leaves us in opposition, I am sorry for it but it simply can't be helped. So if you will kindly let me pass—"

"I will *not*. Don't be an ass, Florian, you can't possibly do this all alone. You know you need me—"

He leaned forward, resting both hands on the door beside her head, trapping her within his arms. "I need no one," he said in a low, fierce voice, his eyes blazing into hers. "*No one*. This is mine to do, and I will do it in whatever way seems best to me. I trust I make myself clear, even to a woman overwrought."

"Quite clear."

He stepped back, his arms falling to his sides.

"Go, then," she said, opening the door. "I won't stop you. But if you do, Florian, if you shut me out and insist on doing this alone, you are making a very serious mistake. One that I will not soon forgive. If ever."

He walked past her into the corridor. "I will be back as soon as possible. I can only hope you are more reasonable when I return."

"Who is to say I'll be here at all?" she shouted after him, and when he continued on without any sign of having heard her, she slammed the door with a crash that splintered the frame.

Chapter 45

FLORIAN stood on the deck of the Ilindrian ship, slapping his gloves impatiently against his thigh. Half a dozen of his men leaned against the rail, eyeing him apprehensively. Well, that was no wonder, his mood had been foul since he left Serilla.

Though it was still three hours until sunset, the lanterns had been lit against an early dusk. The sea was choppy, the heavy stillness of the air punctuated by sudden gusts of wind that snapped the furled sails against the mast and rattled the hanging lantern. Florian frowned, staring up at the sails. A very sloppy job they'd made of them. Someone would catch extra watches when the captain saw this mess; Ilindrian captains were the tautest he had ever known.

"Your Highness, a thousand pardons for keeping you waiting!"

The Ilindrian hurrying across the deck was a stranger to Florian. His pale skin was flushed, his thinning reddish hair hanging in limp strands about his narrow, pointed face. The House of Sungila, Florian thought, wondering whether he should be insulted. He'd never met a Sungila who held a higher rank than cup-bearer at the *Qaletaqa*'s court.

"Please," he said, gesturing toward the hatch, "if you would step this way, Dichali Keme awaits below."

Florian hesitated before passing down the hatch. "After you," he said to the Ilindrian. "Dichali . . . ?"

"Akando, my lord. At your service," he added hastily, putting hand to heart and bowing deeply.

Sloppy, Florian thought again. He'd never met an Ilindrian who needed prompting for an introduction, and this one had been one step from rude. Hand to heart was used to an immediate superior; two fingers to the brow was the proper salutation for a prince.

The man was obviously no courtier. His tunic was of silk, cut very finely, but there was not a thread of Sorlainian purple anywhere about him. Even the lowest of the *Qaletaqa*'s servants usually had a strip about the hem or sleeves, the width increasing with the importance of the wearer. The *Qaletaqa,* old Heammawihio himself, covered his vastness in acres of the stuff, an extravagance that never failed to astound visitors to his court.

If the *Qaletaqa*'s chosen servant was a measure of his regard, this whole charade was a waste of precious time.

"Beylik, you are with me," Florian said. "The rest of you, wait here."

"Perhaps it would be best if they returned to shore before the storm comes, my lord," Beylik suggested quietly. "We would not want any . . . unfortunate incidents to mar your meeting."

Florian doubted that anything could hurt—or help—this meeting, but the men were looking ill at ease and there was no need for them to suffer a drenching. He gave the order over his shoulder as he followed Akando down the steps and into the captain's cabin. A quick glance showed nothing out of place. Two men were seated at the table, heads bent over a large piece of vellum. They both fairly leapt to their feet, hands flying to their brows as they bent nearly to the floor.

"Dichali Dohosan at your service, Your Highness," the younger of them said, "and may I present Dichali Keme. Please, sit down, rest yourself. Such a close day—this poor wine is nothing, but it is chilled. Will you do me the honor of tasting it?"

"Thank you, yes." Florian lifted the goblet. "To the *Qaletaqa*."

"Long may he reign," the two answered in unison.

Beylik slid silently into place at Florian's left shoulder, his back against the wall and one hand resting casually on the dagger in his belt. Dichali Akando, having delivered Florian safely, stood with his back to the door, twisting the tassels on his sash.

"You leave the princess in good health, I trust," Dichali Dohosan said. At least, Florian thought, their network of informers was performing with Ilindrian efficiency.

"Quite good, thank you. And the *Qaletaqa*? He is also well, I hope?"

"Oh, yes, in health and spirits."

The formalities completed, they sat in silence for a moment while the ship rocked on the choppy sea and the sweat dripped down Dichali Dohoson's pale face.

"The *Qaletaqa* requested this meeting, Dichali," Florian said. "Perhaps the time has come to tell me why."

"Yes, of course," Keme said, drawing the vellum forward. "The *Qaletaqa* has long considered you a friend, Your Highness, and remains, as he has ever been, sympathetic to your cause. An alliance between Venya and Ilindria would fill his heart with joy. Indeed, it is his dearest wish that such an alliance will be joined . . ."

"Does that mean he intends to form one?"

The two Ilindrians stared at him, identical expressions of shock upon their faces. Florian knew he was being unpardonably rude by Ilindrian standards, but his head was aching and he wanted nothing so much as to be out of this cabin and back aboard the *Quest*.

"Well," Keme said slowly, "that is a delicate matter."

"Yes, indeed," Dohosan chimed in with a disapproving frown. Florian half expected him to cluck his tongue as Bastyon always did when Florian had committed some glaring breach of etiquette. "Very delicate indeed."

"Then perhaps you would be so courteous as to explain it to an ignorant Venyan," Florian said, giving in as graciously as he could.

"With the greatest delight," Keme answered, smiling. "Over a meal. It is nothing much, a poor collection of scraps, no more. But you would honor us by tasting it."

Florian turned sharply at a sound and saw two servants busy at a far table. He repressed a sigh. "Thank you. But it must be a short meal. I am expected back on my ship. As we wait, let us carry on, Dichali. Shall we begin with this?"

He pulled the vellum forward. Dichali Keme rose and leaned over it. "Yes. You will see here the terms you have suggested to the *Qaletaqa*."

Florian scanned the document quickly. It had been written by a poor hand, the writing so cramped and curled that the words were all but indecipherable.

"I can't quite make this out," he said, pulling the candle closer. "Can you read it for me, Dichali?"

"Where?" Keme leaned closer, pointing. "This?"

The band about his wrist glinted violet in the candlelight. It was very close, Florian thought, but it was not the deep rich purple of Sorlain, a shade impossible to duplicate.

"Yes," he said. "That clause."

The *Qaletaqa* would never send an emissary so meanly clad. It would be an affront to his royal dignity, just as those sloppy sails would be an insult to any honest Ilindrian captain. Florian bent over the vellum, ostensibly following Keme's finger, his mind measuring the odds. Two servants, the two Dichali at the table, Akando by the door. Who knew how many up above. At that moment, the ship lurched, and Florian realized they were moving. Dichali Keme froze, his glance sliding toward the servant.

Florian caught the glint of steel from the corner of his eye. One flick of his wrist and the stiletto was in his hand. Another flick and it was quivering in the chest of the servant who stood a moment, dagger raised and an expression of incredulous surprise on his face.

Before the body hit the floor, Florian was on his feet, his own dagger in one hand and his poiniard in the other. While Keme and Dohosan gaped, the foxlike Akando reached into his flowing tunic and drew out a knife, which he threw with cool and deadly accuracy. Before it left his hand, Florian had dived over the table, carrying Keme with him to the floor, Akando's knife buried itself in the Ilindrian's back.

Two down. That left Dohosan, Akando, and the second servant.

"Beylik." Florian glanced quickly over his shoulder to find Beylik still leaning against the wall, his gaze fixed on the ceiling, one hand resting on the dagger that had not left his belt.

"Beylik!" Again, Florian called, his voice sharp with disbelief. Again, there was no answer.

Florian pulled the knife from Keme's back and threw it toward the door. A shimmer of silk, a thud, and Akando bent to twist the blade from the wood where it had lodged, inches from his heart.

Dichali Dohosan was shouting—not in Ilindrian but in some form of Jexlan—looking past Florian to Beylik, who stood unmoving, as deaf to Dohosan as he had been to Florian.

Florian could not think of Beylik now. His attention was focused on Dohosan's hand, moving toward his sash as he continued to shout a furious stream of Jexlan. Before the Ilindrian could draw,

Florian was on him. A moment later, he leapt back from Dohosan's body and hit the wall hard as Akando's knife whipped past him.

In the instant it took for Akando to arm himself again, Florian launched himself forward, sensing rather than seeing the servant's curved blade slice the air where he had been. But Akando was his prey, and gods, the man was quick, twisting at the last moment so Florian's poiniard sliced through silk, and then turning fiercely to the attack. They went down together, Akando's hands locked around his throat.

The Ilindrian was strong as well as quick, wiry, and lithe, and his grip was unbreakable. Florian let himself go limp until black spots danced before his eyes, then brought his knee up sharply. It was not enough to break the Ilindrian's grip, but for a moment it slackened just enough for Florian to twist and slice upward with his poiniard.

From the corner of his eye, he saw the last man hovering over them, blade in hand, waiting for the chance to use it. In the next moment, Florian forgot him. Akando was only wounded, and he grappled to regain his grip on Florian's throat, nails digging gouges in his neck. But his grip was weakening. Another twist and Florian was free. One quick thrust and Akando's heart had ceased to beat.

Florian expected to feel sharp steel in his back even as he drew the poiniard from its gory sheath and whirled to engage his last opponent. He found himself facing Beylik, who was wiping his dagger upon the sleeve of the dead man at his feet.

"You left it a bit late," Florian rasped.

Beylik straightened and sheathed his dagger. He gazed down at Florian, his young face hard and unsmiling.

"You knew."

Beylik's expression did not change. "I knew." He prodded Akando with his toe, turning him onto his back, and stared into his face. "He was a paid assassin, this one, the lowest of the low. And now he has been called to the halls of learning." His eyes turned to Florian. "No man is summoned there except by name."

"Gods"—Florian swiped a wrist across his brow—"is that what you were promised? Your *name?*"

He watched numbly as his cabin boy went to the door and pressed his ear to the wood. "Nothing yet," he said, "but they will come soon. The crew. To see what has happened."

Beylik turned, his back against the door. The cabin was a charnel-house, dead men sprawled everywhere, blood pooling on the floor beneath them. So much blood. His legs felt oddly weak and shaky. He slid down the door and closed his eyes so he wouldn't have to look at all the blood and think about what it meant.

"Lock it," the prince said. "Lock the door. *Now*."

It was easier to obey than to argue. Beylik fumbled for the latch and twisted the heavy key. "That will not hold them long."

"Long enough."

For what? Beylik wondered, but he didn't bother asking. It made no difference now. He heard the prince moving around the cabin and wondered dimly what he was doing, though not enough to open his eyes and look. *Why does he bother?* Beylik thought. There is no way out.

"Beylik, get over here. Help me with these crates."

A great crash followed his words. So much wasted energy, Beylik thought, and all for nothing. It was over. It was useless to fight; far better to accept whatever was to happen and try not care too much when it did.

There was a time when he would have argued passionately against such weakness, and for years he had clung to the memory of the young man he had been with all his ideals. But that young man had known nothing of the real world.

Beylik could see him now, setting out from home, a book tucked beneath his arm and his mind on fire with the passage he had read. He strode down the hillside, passed into the olive grove—had there been a rustle? A footfall? If there was, the young man did not hear it. He never saw them, either, for they struck him from behind.

He woke to find himself chained and collared, just another *beylik* among many, his future a gray path leading to the nameless death. He only wished they had taken his memories, as well. Then he would not understand how completely he had betrayed not only the prince, but the name he had once valued. But no more. It was worthless to him now. Better, far better that it be lost forever than stained beyond redemption.

Florian looked up sharply as the latch rattled inches above Beylik's dark head. "This is no time to swoon, Beylik," he called sharply. "Get over here and help me."

When Beylik made no answer, Florian seized his wrists and pulled him roughly to his feet. "Lash those crates together." The lad stared at him, his eyes blank, and Florian struck him a stinging blow across the face. "Look alive, man."

Beylik obeyed without a word as Florian gathered every flagon he could find and filled them with water. They, and all the food on the table, went into a bundle that he tied securely to his back. Then he picked up a heavy chair and smashed the stern window. "Come on," he said over his shoulder, pulling himself through the frame. "Stay close."

"But you—I—" Beylik made a helpless gesture encompassing the dead men and the door, now quivering beneath repeated blows from without.

"Bring the crates."

Beylik held them out. "Take them."

"No, I told *you* to take them."

With a muttered curse, Florian seized the boy by the collar and dragged him through the window as the door burst open behind them.

Chapter 46

ROSE sat at the window of her chamber, watching sunlight glitter on the empty sea. The latest draft of the trade agreement was spread before her, but she could not bring herself to read it. When a knock sounded at the door, she pulled a chamber robe over her shift. "Come," she called.

It was Ewan, but her welcoming smile faded when she saw that he was not alone. The entire council filed into the chamber. None of them looked at her directly. They studied walls or ceiling or stared down at their feet. Only Bastyon met her gaze.

"Lord Bastyon," she said. "Is it my lord?"

"Yes."

"What has happened?"

"We had word from the Ilindrians two days ago. They were concerned that the prince had missed their rendezvous. Then, today, this lad arrived—"

It was then Rose noticed Ashkii hanging back by the door. His skin looked almost transparent, and his green eyes were rimmed with red.

"My lady." He knelt before her, his silvery head bowed. "When the prince did not return from his meeting, Gordon went to look for him, but the ship was gone. The *Quest* is in pursuit."

"A trap," Rose said.

"The prince took Beylik," Ashkii said. "I wanted to go—I was meant to, but then I fell sick. I thought it was something I had eaten, but now—now I think Beylik gave me something. He stopped before they went and left me his things and a letter. I didn't think anything of it, we all do the same before a battle, but when he didn't come back, I opened it, and—and it said—" He covered his face with his hands.

"It was a full confession," Bastyon said. "He claims the surgeon was involved as well."

"Sigurd?" Rose sank down to her seat. "And Beylik?"

Ashkii made a choked sound of agreement.

"How long ago did my lord leave the *Quest*?" Rose asked.

"Two days, my lady," Carlysle said.

Rose stood and reached for her gown. "I assume the *Endeavor* is ready to sail. I will be with you in a moment."

Eredor cleared his throat and shifted from one foot to the other.

"My lady." It was Bastyon who spoke. "Is there any chance you are with child?"

"With . . . ? I-I suppose there is a chance—"

"Then there is no question of you joining any search party," Carlysle said.

"I fail to see what difference that makes," Rose said. "I am not ill or helpless, and my lord—"

"Is dead," Carlysle said with brutal frankness. "And you, my lady, shall remain exactly where you are."

"Do not presume to give me orders," Rose said coldly. "Get out of my way."

Ashkii was staring up at them, his eyes moving quickly between Rose and her councilors.

"If there is the slightest hope," Bastyon said, "you must allow us to indulge it—and you—with the best care we can offer."

"If there is a child," she said evenly, "the best thing you can do for it is to let me find its father."

"My lady," Eredor said, his voice surprisingly gentle, "you can leave that to us."

"I will do no such thing. I will not stay here—"

"Indeed you shall," Carlysle said. "We would be remiss to allow you to do otherwise."

"*Allow* me? Have you forgotten who I am? Get out of my way at once."

It was no great matter to push Carlysle aside, but then she found herself face-to-face with Ewan. He put his hands on her shoulders and looked into her face. "Ye bide here, lady. I'll see to it." He gave her a little shake. "Let me be about it, lass."

She nodded. "Very well, Ewan. I trust you."

"Come," Eredor said, "sit down. You have had a shock, you must rest. Can I send for someone—a woman—from the hall, perhaps?"

"Yes," Rose said. "Please send for Caelan."

Chapter 47

THEY finished the food on the third day. That was not the problem, though; a man could survive a long stretch without food.

As long as he had water.

Two days more, Florian judged as the sun rose for the fourth time since they had gone into the sea. One sip at dawn, another at noon, one more at sunset, today and tomorrow. Beylik would not rouse; Florian had to pour his ration into his mouth and hold it shut when he choked and sputtered.

That had been at dawn, when Florian was still capable of movement. Now the sun stood straight overhead, glaring from a cloudless sky. Its weight was a solid pressure on his back, pinning him to the crate.

His mind was as empty as the sea stretching to every side. No hope, no fear disturbed him. He had always been here, rough wood pressed against his cheek, Beylik's wrist beneath his hand, legs floating slackly behind him, lifting and falling with the gentle rocking of the swells.

His unfocused gaze moved over the crate to the water lapping at its edges. He watched without interest as a hand fastened on the wood. The fingers were long, webbed at the base, the skin tinged with blue. A sleek head appeared, and eyes as dark and fathomless as death stared straight into his.

"So, Venya, it has come to this."

There seemed no answer, or none worth making, so Florian remained silent. He blinked, and when his eyes opened, the merrow was gone—if it had ever been there at all. It did not seem to matter either way.

Beylik's wrist jerked beneath his hand, and instinctively he tightened his grip. Slowly he turned his head to see the merrow across the crate, one long arm about Beylik's shoulders. The boy was insensible—perhaps dead. The merrow hissed and tugged again. Florian lifted his head.

"He is mine," the merrow said. "Mine by right and custom."

"No."

"He will be dead soon. Give him to me now." A flicker of hunger passed over her face as she looked at the dying cabin boy.

"Sod. Off."

Florian forced his legs to move. One kick, then another, and the crate inched forward. The merrow dove and came up beside him. She rested a pointed chin on folded arms, her face inches from his own.

"A swift death, Venya, for both of you. Take what I can offer."

"Help us," he said, forcing the words past his swollen tongue and cracked lips. "You have some interest in Venya—you said so once—"

"It is too late. We would have seen the mine closed, for it has befouled the waters of our spawning grounds. A small chance, we judged, but the only one we had. And now no chance at all, for you have failed us."

"Not failed. Not yet. Not while I live. Help me and—"

Her fingertip was cool against his lips. "It is over. You have tried, we give you that much. But it is finished."

"No."

"Yes," she said gently. "It is the truth, and what is more, you know it. Is it not better to die here and now, before the legend tarnishes beyond redemption?"

A legend. Is that all he was, a legend? A story told to children, a song sung by drunken sailors in a tavern?

"You would choose a hero's death over the chance of life!"

Someone had said that to him. He could not remember who it was, only the bitterness of the accusation. But that wasn't what he wanted . . . was it?

Cool fingers brushed his brow, trailed over his cheeks, and stroked his cracked and swollen lips. "Why do you suffer when you could be at peace? Die with youth and honor intact—is it not better thus? Would you live to see your name become a jest remembered only by a few?"

The merrow's hand cupped his head, and her mouth was cool and sweet against his own. With a burst of strength that left him dizzy he jerked away, squinting hard against the sun.

"Hush. Quietly, my love. Do not be afraid."

Sleek arms slipped around him. Dark eyes blotted out the sea and sky, drawing him into their depths.

"No."

"Shh. It will be well. Let me help you."

Her voice was kind, her hand gentle as she stroked the precious, wasted moisture from his cheeks. She bent to him, her mouth fastening on his. He struggled only briefly, then his lips sought hers, drinking in her sweetness as they slipped beneath the waves without a splash.

Chapter 48

❧

ROSE stood at the cliff's edge, staring blankly at the endless sea, spellbound by its constant motion. For two days she had burned with a pain that consumed her from within, searing flesh from bone. She had paced the chamber, only succumbing to sleep when exhaustion claimed her, starting up at the least sound to begin her restless round again. She allowed Caelan to stay; the *filidh* did not trouble her with talk or bother her with food, though today she had brought Rose fresh clothing, combed her hair, and led her to this place.

Now Caelan sat beside her, hands folded in her lap, her dark eyes fixed patiently on the sea.

"Lady?"

Rose glanced down to find a small boy beside her. He looked familiar, though she couldn't quite remember . . .

"They say—I heard that—" His face crumpled. "He said he would take me back to Venya. He said we'd go together. Now—I want to go home, lady—"

"Don't worry, Corin, Leander will send him back," a high voice said decidedly. A girl strode up the hill, the wind tugging at her skirt. Her hair was cropped short, and she held bunch of wild-flowers in her hand. She was followed by more children, the bigger ones helping the smaller up the rocky slope.

"Isn't that right, lady?" the girl asked, looking up at Rose. "I know who you are. My mother's sister had a lover in Riall, and he was at the gates the day you faced down the soldiers. He said that even when they charged you didn't run. He said you could lead an army—like Queen Niahm in the old songs—and he'd fight in it.

So would all his friends. And when you and the prince go back to Venya, I'll be one of your shieldmaidens."

She marched to the cliff's edge and addressed the sea. "My father was wrong about the prince," she declared, holding out a flower. "He really did care about all of us. He sent Sir Ewan to bring us here, so I reckon we all owe him our lives. I won't forget it, or the way he came to the *Endeavor* that day. We need him back, so please see to it, Leander."

She let the blossom fall and turned back. "Shana is my name," she said to Rose, bobbing her a curtsey. "You can find me in the kitchens at the *filidhi* hall. Send for me when you need me."

A young man in a patched tunic accepted a flower from Shana, then limped up to the cliffs. "The prince sent his own surgeon when I was sick. Keep him safe, Leander."

He tossed the flower over and stepped back. "Lady, I am Tam, apprentice saddlemaker. I can read and write and look after your soldiers' gear."

He bowed and turned away as the next child took his place, and then another and another.

"The prince found my brother—"

"—gave us the *filidh* hall—"

"—remembered my da when he was hurt—"

"He gave me a chance to prove myself when no one else would. Lord Leander, watch over him and bring him home."

Rab, the ostler, turned to her. "Lady Rose, I offer you my skill with horses," he said, then stepped back and rested a hand on Corin's shoulder. The *filidh* Daigh stood beside him, with Ren and Alara and the young lord of Gilveran and a score of other apprentices from the hall, amid a crowd of village folk. The Magea had not come, Rose noted, nor any of the council. Or no, she realized, there was one council member. Eredor stood behind her.

"What do you here, my lord?" she asked, her voice rusty from disuse.

"I-I am not certain. Only that I had to come."

He stood quietly at her shoulder as one by one, *filidhi* and *fheara* and Serillans walked up to the cliff. When the last of them had spoken, the crop-haired girl, Shana, offered a wildflower to Rose.

"I do not know you, Leander, but for Jehan's sake, she who

freed you from Lord Marva's dungeon, I beg you to hear your children's prayers."

Holding out her hand, Rose let the blossom fall. It caught the wind and spiraled slowly down into the foaming waves, flecked with gold and blue and scarlet. A movement on the horizon caught her eye as a sail appeared around the headland. Hope flared—perhaps there was something to this Venyan ritual—then died again when she realized it was not the *Quest*.

"That ship," Caelan whispered from behind her. "I know not what it is, but—lady, you should come away."

"Not yet."

The people left as quietly as they'd arrived until the cliff was empty once again and the last petal had vanished into the churning sea.

"Come now, you must rest," Caelan said firmly, and Rose allowed herself to be led back to her chamber. Moving as if in a dream, she took off her gown and let down her hair, then picked up her comb and went to the window.

"Let me," Caelan offered, reaching for the comb. She froze, her hand arrested in midair, as the sound of voices drifted up from the courtyard below.

The comb dropped to the floor between them. Rose could not move. She could not speak. It seemed her heart had stopped as she strained to listen. She could not make out the words, but that voice . . . it couldn't be, and yet it sounded like . . .

She leaned as far out as she dared, but could not see the men who stood below. Throwing her chamber robe over her shift, she started for the door. Caelan caught her wrist. "No. Wait."

The sound of laughter came from below, and Rose's heart began to thunder in her breast. She wrenched free of Caelan, ran lightly down the steps and out the door, blinking in the sunlight as she burst among the group of men standing in the courtyard. Bastyon was there, and Ewan and Carlysle, talking with a man clad in glittering silver and purple, whose back was turned to her. She did not see Florian, which was strange, for she could still hear his laughter plainly.

"Where is my lord?" she cried. "Is he—"

She stopped, the words frozen on her lips, as the stranger turned, still laughing. Florian's laugh. Upon a stranger's lips. Or no, surely this was Florian . . . and yet it wasn't. He was heavier across the chest and shoulders, perhaps an inch or two above Florian's height. His skin was a shade paler, his hair a shade darker. He could have been Florian's brother—or Florian himself, had he come to manhood in a peaceful Venya.

But of course he was neither of these things. He was Florian's kinsman, the second grandson of the twins Gracia and Sophia.

He was Cristobal of Sorlain.

He smiled, his eyes lighting with pleasure and admiration. His eyes were blue, the same clear hue of the sea behind him. Rose was suddenly aware that she was clad only in her shift, a thin chamber robe hanging from her shoulders, with her hair unbound and streaming in the wind.

"Tell me you are Rosamund," he said. His voice, the very pitch and timbre of Florian's, was marked by the rolling Rs of Sorlain. "Say only that, and my joy will be complete."

She clasped the robe about her throat with a shaking hand, incapable of speech.

"Indeed, Your Majesty," Lord Bastyon said. "Please allow me to present you to Lady Rosamund. My lady, His Majesty of Sorlain."

Cristobal bowed. Rose did not move. He took her unresisting hand in his and raised it to his mouth. His lips were warm against her icy skin.

"Forgive me for not warning you of my arrival," he murmured. "Yet this morning, I found I could not wait another moment to meet you for myself. And I am glad I did not wait," he added with a dazzling smile, "for to see you as you are right now is a memory I will forever cherish."

His words washed over her in a tide of sound, though the sense of them eluded her. But she dimly realized that he must have said something flattering, for the men all laughed indulgently.

All save Ewan. He did not even smile.

"Come inside, Your Majesty," he said, "and let us offer ye refreshment."

Crisobal ignored him. "My father was a wise man," he said to Rose. "He ruled Sorlain justly and with honor. While he lived, I gave him my obedience, not only for the sake of duty but for the love I bore him. And we agreed well together . . . in most things."

Rose wished she could sit down. Her knees had begun to shake so badly that she feared that she might fall.

"One thing on which we did not agree was you, my lady."

Cristobal slipped a hand beneath her elbow and led her across the courtyard, where a few sawed-off casks had been filled with earth and planted with brilliant blossoms, set beneath spiky gray-green leaves that rustled in the breeze, giving off a spicy scent. Cristobal sat on a rough wooden bench and drew her down beside him.

His hand moved to the jewel-encrusted breast of his tunic, slipped inside, and drew forth a tattered bit of parchment. Rose stared in disbelief as he unfolded it and she saw her own childish handwriting, faded now, upon its surface. "I kept it, Rosamund, just as I promised, though I lost the one your brave squire carried. We were seen that day, he and I, and it was taken from me. Oh, love, I wanted so desperately to come to you then, but I was forbidden."

His warm fingers closed around her icy hand. "I am sorry it took me so long to answer, but I am here now. And I swear to you, Rosamund, I swear upon my mother's soul that I came to you the moment I was free."

"Cristobal. I-I—" Rose wasn't sure whether she wanted more to laugh or cry. For years, this had been her fondest dream. Now here he was, everything and more than she had hoped for, saying just the words she had imagined he would say.

She blinked hard against the sudden stinging in her eyes. "Thank you," she said softly. "I thank you with all my heart. I understand completely why you could not come before. But now—oh, Cristobal, I am so sorry, but now it is too late."

"No, Rosamund," he said just as softly, "you are wrong. It is not too late at all."

"Perhaps you do not understand," she said. "I am already married."

"I understand that you went through a ceremony with the Prince of Venya, but it was meaningless. You are wed to me. You have been since we were children. Now I have come to take you home."

Chapter 49

FLORIAN floated helpless beneath the water, supported only by strong arms wound about his waist. For a single blinding instant he was one with the merrow. He knew her every thought, her every need, shared the flooding of her senses as his life force was drawn inexorably into her own.

Inky hair billowed about them, a blue-black cloud that brushed softly against his skin. Bare feet slipped off cold scales as his body moved instinctively in a parody of lovemaking.

The merrow's silent laughter filled his mind. *More,* she urged him, *give me more,* and for a moment he was filled with shame and horror. Then it was all gone, all forgotten as he roused to her with shattering intensity. She drank in his desire with greedy hunger, urging him toward the ecstasy of death.

The taut peaks of her breasts crushed against his chest. An image flitted through his fading consciousness, a distant memory of a woman who had held him just like this. Rosamund. Her name rang out like a warning bell through heavy fog. Rosamund. He could see her, then, her back against the door, pleading with him not to leave her. "I want to help you," she had said, but he hadn't listened. He'd turned away from her and walked out . . . He couldn't die, not now. He had promised to return . . .

With an effort that seemed to wrench every muscle in his body, he lifted slack arms and caught the merrow round the neck, deliberately pulling her against him as he sought to reclaim what she had taken, using the bond that she had forged between them. Her shock and anger whipped through him like an icy lash when she realized what he was about.

They hung suspended for a moment, and then, at last, just as Florian was sure his lungs would burst, a surge of energy lent him strength as the merrow struggled in his arms. She twisted and he sought to hold her, but she was stronger than he had expected. With a flick of her powerful tail, she surged upward, tearing herself from his embrace. Florian broke the surface just behind her, bursting into sunlight with a gasp. His reaching fingers brushed wood and fastened on the crate, where Beylik lay just as he had left him.

The merrow regarded him from across the crate. "No man has ever attempted that," she said.

Florian coughed out seawater. "I know."

Her teeth flashed in a smile. "Yesss. You know me now—a little. I know you somewhat better. There is more to you than I imagined."

"Thank you," Florian said with an ironic nod.

"You have earned another chance, Venya. Use it wisely. But perhaps, something more is needed . . ." She rested an elbow on the crate and leaned her pointed chin in her palm. "Yes. Leander had his gift from my mother's mother. Now I shall give one to his heir."

"A gift?" Florian eyed her with suspicion. The little he had shared of the merrow's consciousness did not inspire trust. "What sort of gift?"

She tipped her head back, laughter bubbling from her blue-tinged lips. "Not a prophecy, I think. The one you have has confused you quite enough. Tell me, are you good at riddles?"

"No."

She laughed again. "Then I will make it easy for you.

> "*To gain what you desire most,*
> *Surrender what you would not lose,*
> *Consider well, lest both be lost,*
> *The game begins when once you choose.*"

As Florian's heartbeat slowed to normal, his energy was fading fast. He tightened shaking fingers on slick wood. "Water would have been more helpful."

"No imagination." The merrow shook her head, her hair billowing around her slender shoulders. "That is the trouble with

Chapter 50

"I make it four years," Rose said, passing a document across the table. "What do you think?"

Lord Eredor studied it with the same meticulous attention he gave to everything, tipping it so Caelan could read over his shoulder.

"We could do it in three without this," Caelan said, pointing. "Why allow the *filidhi* hall so much when it will soon be abandoned?"

"We will not close the hall," Rose said firmly. "The *filidhi* who wish to remain may do so. If they do not come to Venya freely, we have no use for them."

"I suppose this might be possible," Eredor said slowly, "though it is ambitious."

"It is based upon your own estimates, my lord; 'tis only the scope that has changed. Make any corrections you feel are necessary. You must keep in mind, though," she added quickly, "that this is all subject to my lord's approval."

Eredor looked away.

What am I doing? Rose thought in sudden panic. Florian would never agree to this—he had told her as much before he walked out.

"Of course." Caelan smiled. "That is understood."

During the past days, Rose had come to rely upon the young *filidh*, not only for her companionship, but also for her unflagging composure and good sense. "Did not the prince ask you to see to his affairs in his absence?" Caelan had scolded two days ago, with a cunning that was not lost on Rose. "What will he say when he sees how idle you have been?"

There was no answer to that, so Rose sat down at the table and listlessly flipped through the pile of documents before her. One was a new proposal from Eredor. Her wandering attention was caught when she saw that he had set aside a portion of the profits to arm and train soldiers for the prince and another portion to be sent directly into Venya.

A concession, though a grudging one, for the amounts were minuscule, and he allowed a full ten years to prepare for a war. "Oh, come, my lord," Rose had murmured, reaching for a quill, "surely we can do better than that." What had started as a way to pass the heavy hours had soon absorbed her completely.

Now it had gone too far. To continue without Florian's leave seemed as though she thought—as though she did not believe—

She snatched the document from Eredor's hands and tore it in two. "This was a mistake. Forgive me for wasting your time."

"But lady, it is brilliant—" Eredor began, but Caelan cut him off.

"No harm done," the *filidh* said lightly, "our time is yours to command. Shall we—"

She broke off at a knock upon the door. "If it is His Majesty of Sorlain," Rose said, "please tell him I am resting."

"You cannot avoid him forever," Caelan said.

"I can try," Rose muttered, leaning her head on her hand. Cristobal was annoyingly persistent. He simply would not go away, no matter how many messages she sent him asking him to do just that. She could not bear the sound of his voice, so close in timbre to Florian's, or to look at his familiar-unfamiliar face.

But it was not Cristobal at the door. It was Sir Ewan's voice she heard, and Rose stood, trying to summon a smile for the knight.

He strode past Caelan into the chamber. "Rosamund," he said abruptly. "Sit down."

Rose felt the blood rush from her face. She swayed, but Eredor was at her side in an instant.

"Sir Ewan," the *filidh* snapped, "what mean you by bursting in like this?"

"I am sorry," Ewan said, "but ye must sit down and listen, Rosamund. There are two things I must say to ye, and ye must hear them both before ye speak."

Rose sat. Caelan stood protectively behind her, hands resting lightly on her shoulders. "The *Quest* has been sighted," Ewan said. "We've had two reports—it will be here at any time. The prince is aboard. He is alive."

Rose started to rise, but Caelan pressed her back into the seat. "Wait," she said. "That is only one thing. What is the other, Sir Ewan?"

"This." Ewan held out a piece of parchment addressed to the Prince of Venya. A heavy purple seal dangled from its edges. "Aye, I opened it. Read it," Ewan said. "Quickly."

"My dear brother of Venya," it began. "Some time ago word reached me that my lady wife had taken refuge on your ship."

Rose paled, and the parchment trembled briefly in her hand.

"King Richard is full wroth with his niece, but I have reminded him that it is my place to correct her, should correction be needed. But fear not, cousin. I admire her spirit and am grateful that you brought her unharmed to Sorlain, where we have been at last united.

"We both rejoice that you are once again at liberty to pursue your throne. As you know, Sorlain has long been sympathetic to your cause, and I think the time has come when I am able to give you more tangible proof of my support. I am certain that my bride would have it so, and it is the sole desire of my heart to please her in all things.

"I regret that I cannot stay to greet you, but my people are right eager to meet their queen and so we must away. As both an ally and a kinsman, I look forward to the day when I shall come to Venya and share in the joy of your victory."

"What a horrid letter," Rose said in an unnaturally bright voice, handing it to Lord Eredor. "But Cristobal cannot simply whisk me off. Not if I refuse. And I do refuse."

"Aye," Ewan agreed, though he wouldn't meet her eyes. "Ye can do that."

Caelan's fingers dug painfully into Rose's shoulders. "His Majesty has offered to support the prince's cause," the *filidh* said. "My lady, he is offering us *Venya*. We could go *home!*"

Rose turned to look out at the harbor, where any moment now the *Quest* would appear. Florian would be standing on the quarterdeck in his old black shirt, perhaps with a mug of kava in his hand. Florian, who had told her so many times that nothing in this world could stand between him and Venya.

"But why?" Rose cried. "Cristobal knows that I am wed. Why would he insist on this? It makes no sense! Does it, Caelan?" She turned to Caelan, who was also staring toward the harbor, her eyes bright and hot color in her cheeks.

"I cannot say, my lady," Caelan answered. Her hands fell from Rose's shoulders, and she stepped back. All at once she was a *fil-idh* of Venya again, remote and unreadable.

Rose turned to the knight. "There must be a reason, Ewan. He cannot be doing this simply to honor some childish promise."

"I canna say what his reasons are," Ewan said heavily.

"The prince will never agree to this," Eredor said, tossing the letter on the table. "Lady Rosamund, you mustn't fear—"

The door opened again, and Cristobal walked into the chamber. He took in the situation at a glance.

"You have read it, then."

"In my lord's absence, his correspondence comes to me," Rose said coldly. "Please explain the meaning of this."

"Leave us," Cristobal said, "I would speak with Lady Rosamund alone."

"Stay," Rose said. "His Majesty does not give orders here."

"I think I do. We are in Sorlain," Cristobal reminded her gently. He gestured toward the door, and Caelan went at once. Ewan and Eredor followed more slowly.

"We'll be just outside, lady," Eredor said. He shut the door and she and Cristobal were alone.

He was clad in black today, heightening his resemblance to Florian. But his tunic was soft velvet, trimmed with gold and peppered with small diamonds that flashed as he moved toward the window, blocking her view of the harbor.

"You do not seem to understand that I am already married," Rose said, "to the Prince of Venya."

"No, Rosamund, you are married to me," he said patiently. "We have been wed these many years."

"Well, for the past months I have been living as the Prince of Venya's wife. In all respects," she added pointedly.

Cristobal merely smiled. "As I have not been entirely faithful myself, I am in no position to complain."

"But—but I could be carrying the heir to Venya!"

"Rosamund, we both know you are not."

She stared at him in horror. Had Caelan told him that? Or had he bribed the laundress?

"I am not accusing you of any wrongdoing," Cristobal continued in that same patient voice, which was beginning to grate on Rose's nerves, "nor do I accuse the Prince of Venya. At the time, you both believed yourselves free to marry, a misunderstanding for which I accept full responsibility."

"But it wasn't a misunderstanding," Rose argued, her voice rising. "It was the truth. Your father did not believe the marriage was valid—"

"Of course he did. He knew full well that it was valid. He decided for his own reasons to ignore it and made me promise to do the same, but he never denied that it was legal."

"But if you promised him—"

"A promise that I made unwillingly. Before his death, he released me from it."

"Then let me make haste to do the same. I release you from our vows, Cristobal, freely and with no reservations. I make no claim on you at all."

"And yet," he said, "the claim exists. We are married, Rosamund. Nothing you can say will alter that."

"But what I have *done* has done so. I wed the Prince of Venya before witnesses. It was a proper marriage—"

"As was ours," Cristobal interrupted.

"But this one was consummated. Legally, that means—"

"Do not speak to me of legalities. What court do you imagine would hear your case? Valinor? Venya? I hope you do not think to plead it in Sorlain."

"But why?" she cried. "There are plenty of princesses who would be thrilled to wed you! Why would you want me? Forgive me if I speak plainly, but I do not want *you.*"

"Want!" He waved a hand contemptuously. "You want, I want—you are talking like a child. This hasn't anything to do with *want.* I do what I *must.* I do my duty."

"What duty?" she shot back. "Not your duty to Sorlain, for I bring nothing to this marriage. Surely not your duty to me! So what duty is it that you perform here? What are you not telling me?"

"Enough," he said curtly. "We have wasted enough time as it is."

"Cristobal, the only thing I ask of you is to leave me as I am.

Why in Jehan's name would you of all men choose to saddle your-self with a wife who despises you? For that is all you will get."

He turned to gaze out the window. "I am sorry to hear that," he said, and the terrible thing was that he did sound genuinely sorry. "But it changes nothing. Rosamund, you are the daughter of a royal house. You understand how these things are done."

"But—"

Cristobal whirled to face her. "This is a wretched situation, do you think I do not see that? What *you* do not seem to see—or do not *want* to see—is that you are not the only victim here. None of us wanted this to happen, but it did. I accept full responsibility for this fiasco. I am prepared to make what amends are in my power both to you and to the Prince of Venya. In return, I only ask that *you* accept your place as Queen of Sorlain."

He had heard nothing. Or, hearing, he had chosen to ignore every word she said. There must be something more to say, some argument that she had not yet tried—

"Gather your belongings," he ordered. "It is time we were away."

"You would have me leave without so much as a farewell?" Rose demanded incredulously.

"I would. For such a parting would undoubtedly be painful, and things might be said and done that we would all regret, though none so bitterly as the Prince of Venya. Rosamund, I do not want to fight my kinsman. I *will* not fight him unless directly challenged, but should he challenge me, I would have no choice but to accept. And that is a fight that he can never win."

She folded her arms across her chest and looked him up and down. "Are you so sure of that?"

"Yes," Cristobal said tightly. "For no matter what the outcome of our encounter—which is by no means certain, whatever you might think—he will still lose. And if he is the man I think he is, he would welcome a clean death before living with the knowl-edge that he has thrown away that which he has proven so many times means more to him than life itself."

He drew a deep breath, then went on more calmly, "Given time, I am certain he will reach the same conclusion. To deny him that time would be the height of selfishness on your part and irresponsibility on mine."

Rose turned away abruptly, leaning her elbows on the table and pressing her palms hard against her eyes.

Think, she ordered herself desperately. Forget the legal position, it doesn't matter now. Forget the moral superiority of her argument; if Cristobal would not hear it, she might as well save her breath. It was time to focus on essentials.

Her options had narrowed down to two: either go with Cristobal or refuse. If she refused outright, Cristobal might relent and wait for Florian's return. If he did not relent, if he tried to carry her off by force, she could put up a fight. Ewan would come to her aid, and Eredor and Ashkii, and perhaps the people of Serilla would rise up in rebellion against their king. But even if she were prepared to see men die for this, their lives would only purchase time until Florian returned.

What would happen then, she was almost too frightened to imagine. He had told her plainly that Venya was his goal, and he would use any means to get there. Sorlain's support was a gift undreamed of—he would never turn down such an alliance, and it was folly to think of it. Even if he did, his only recourse would be to issue Cristobal a challenge. Florian might be bested. She didn't think it likely, but what was the alternative? If Cristobal should fall, Sorlain would unleash its wrath upon the man who was responsible for the death of their young king, no matter why or how it had been done. And it would not be only Florian who suffered, but all belonging to him.

Cristobal was right. Florian *would* rather die than live to see such devastation wrought by his own hand.

She raised her head and looked at Cristobal directly. "I beg you not to do this."

All at once his mask of lordly confidence dropped away. He looked very young and terribly uncertain, almost frightened for a moment. Then the mask dropped back in place.

"I must," he answered simply.

"Why?" she whispered. "Just tell me why. Surely there is some other way, and I would help you find it. Only don't—don't—"

He held out his hand. "Come with me, Rosamund. If not for my sake or yours," he added bitterly, "then for his. If you care for him at all, you must see you have no choice."

Chapter 51

FLORIAN walked swiftly up the path from the docks, a bunch of violets in his hand. He was halfway to the inn when Ewan hurried to meet him.

"We have been expecting ye this hour past," he said. "Where have ye been?"

"Good day to you, as well." Florian laughed, continuing up the path. "There was a squall—the damnedest thing I've ever seen. It came right out of nowhere, lasted an hour to the minute, then vanished."

They topped the rise to the village square. There was the old inn at last, the bleached sign creaking in the light breeze. Florian quickened his steps.

"Your Highness," Ewan began, putting a hand on his arm.

"Later, Ewan."

Florian shrugged him off and burst into the inn. He found his council gathered at the bottom of the stairway.

"Welcome back, Your Highness," Bastyon said. "You look none the worse for your adventure."

"I'm fine, Bas, never better. You're all well, I hope?" Without waiting for an answer, he made to push by them, but they pressed together, barring his path. "Bad news?" he said, looking at their grim faces, "well, it will have to wait. I'd like to see my lady."

Bastyon held out a piece of parchment. "King Cristobal was here," he said. "This is from him."

"I said later," Florian began, but something in Bastyon's expression halted him. He put the violets on a table and took the letter. "It's been opened."

"Aye," Ewan said. "I opened it."

Florian read the first lines and looked up sharply. "His *wife?* What the devil—"

"Apparently there was a proxy marriage," Bastyon said, "performed when they were both small children. When King Osric died, King Esteban thought it prudent to conceal it from the world and seek a more advantageous alliance for his son. Now that Esteban is gone, Cristobal has decided—"

"Decided?" Florian interrupted. "He can't—"

"Aye, he can," Ewan said heavily. "And he has."

"Where—?"

"Perhaps you should sit down," Bastyon suggested quietly, gesturing toward the empty taproom, "and finish your letter. Then we can discuss it."

Florian ignored the offer of a seat. He scanned the message quickly, then realized that he had not absorbed a word of it. He was aware of them all watching him. Waiting for an answer. He tried reading it again, but only disconnected phrases reached him.

". . . my lady wife . . . Sorlain has long been sympathetic to your cause . . . tangible proof of my support . . . my people are right eager to meet their queen . . ."

"Where is the princess?" he asked evenly.

"Gone," Carlysle said.

"You let him take her?"

"Your Highness, no!" Eredor protested. "She insisted."

"You lie."

Eredor did not flare at this insult. He merely sighed and shook his head. "You tell him, Ewan."

" 'Tis the truth, Your Highness."

"She realized it was the only possible solution," Bastyon said. "And accepted it with dignity."

"But this—this is laughable," Florian said, though he had never felt less like laughing. "We were married—you all witnessed it—"

"His Majesty had the prior claim," Bastyon said. "And he has offered you compensation."

"Compensation?"

"Venya," Carlysle said impatiently. "Did you not understand?"

The letter fell from Florian's nerveless fingers. "To gain what you desire most, surrender what you would not lose," he whispered.

"What?" Carlysle demanded.

Ewan silenced Carlysle with a sharp gesture. "My lord," the knight said gently, "I know how difficult this must be for ye. But we want to be careful here. We don't want to go making an enemy of Cristobal, who has said himself that he's disposed to help—"

"I am not in the business of selling women," Florian said coldly. "No matter how high the price. Particularly when the woman is my wife."

Eredor stood back from the group surrounding Florian, nor had he joined his voice to their arguments. He met Florian's eye and nodded slightly.

"You are not thinking clearly," Bastyon admonished Florian. "Had Sorlain not remained neutral, all would have been lost years ago. Now Cristobal is on the throne, and you must—my lord, you *must* keep his goodwill. Think of your people here on Serilla, under Sorlain's dominion. Think of your people in Venya and what this alliance could mean to them. Once you have reflected, I am certain you will see that Lady Rosamund showed great courage."

Courage? Is that what they called it? Florian walked past them and up the stairs to the chamber he and Rosamund had shared. There were no gowns tossed on the neatly made bed, no shift laughingly abandoned on the floor. The hooks were bare and the table empty of Rosamund's belongings. Or no, not entirely empty. A pair of combs and three rings shone on the polished wood beside a folded scrap of parchment. He stepped into the room and picked up the rings, remembering the moment when he had put them on her hand. He slipped them onto his smallest finger, then stripped off his damp clothes and dressed again.

When he could find no further excuse to delay, he sat down on the bed and opened the parchment.

"Florian," it began abruptly, "Do not think I have been carried off. Now that I understand the position in which I've placed you, I know what I must do. As you once told me, your marriage is a matter of state, and Venya will not be served by our continued alliance. I do this of my own will, and I trust you will accept my decision, reached after due reflection and made for the good of all concerned."

The parchment dropped from his hand. Well, that was that. Cristobal had his wife; Rosamund was safe and would be queen of a country into which both Valinor and Venya could be easily absorbed, leaving twice as much again. In return, Florian would have what he desired most. Bastyon must be relieved at how neatly everything had fallen into place. Florian knew he should be relieved as well.

He didn't feel relieved. In fact, he didn't feel anything at all. But he knew from bitter experience that this numbness was a temporary state. Already he could feel the pain crouched, waiting for the proper moment to spring and rip him into shreds.

He bent and retrieved Rosamund's letter, intending to burn it. Instead he lay down on the bed and closed his eyes. His path to Venya was clear now. He had exactly what he'd always wanted.

Venya would be free. His people would be safe. He tried to summon the image of the forest pool, but all he could see was Rosamund's hair rippling over his arm and hear himself saying that their marriage had been undertaken for the good of Venya. But had he not said, too, that his heart had led him to her?

No. That wasn't right. He'd said that if he were *free* to follow his heart, it would have led him to her. But he was not free, and she was Queen of Sorlain. Now that Venya's interests were no longer served by their union, it must be abandoned. Everyone was very clear about that, from Bastyon to Cristobal to Rosamund herself.

Abandon. The word echoed through his mind. She had said that she would leave him, but he had not believed her. Certainly he had not expected her to walk away without so much as a farewell, leaving him no more than a note announcing her departure. And such a cold note, so ruthlessly to the point. She had not bothered with endearments or regrets, let alone apologies for the lies she had told when she swore that nothing in this world would ever part them.

But if he was going to start tallying up lies, he must in fairness count the ones he'd told to her. Could he really have expected her to refuse Cristobal of Sorlain for him? He should be grateful that she hadn't left him sooner.

"My lord? I knocked, but you did not answer." Caelan looked in through the half-open door. "Can I do anything for you?"

Florian hiked himself up on his elbows. "No. Or—yes. Come in. Tell me, did you meet His Majesty of Sorlain?"

Caelan walked to the table and sat down, folding her hands before her. "Yes. Several times."

"What manner of man is he?" Florian asked.

"Young," she said. "Very elegant, but not haughty at all. He has a very pleasing manner."

"And his person? Is that pleasing, too?"

"He is very like *you*, my lord."

Florian wasn't sure why that should bother him, and yet it did. "Well, our grandmothers were twins."

"Yes," Caelan said serenely, "he visited that little stone in the square and walked all about the village. Apparently Queen Gracia had told him stories of her childhood. He was very curious about the *filidhi* hall, as well, and spent an entire day observing their lessons. He was quite knowlegeable," she added thoughtfully, "and particularly interested in weather-working. He asked if we had any masters of the art."

"Do we?" Florian asked.

"No, it is not a Veynan gift. 'Tis not unknown in Sorlain, though very rare. It seems that Gracia and Sophia were the only ones Serilla has ever produced."

Florian sat up. "Weather-working tends to run in families, doesn't it?"

"Generally, yes, though they say it skips a generation."

"Damn him." Florian swung his legs over the side of the bed. Caelan raised her brows. "My lord?"

"Cristobal. He is one. He sent a storm, earlier—it must have been him. Coward," he spat, pacing to the window and back again. "He wouldn't face me. He didn't dare. He summoned that storm and held me off until he was away."

"Your Highness," Caelan said, "sit down. Let me pour you some wine."

"I don't want wine," Florian snapped.

"But you should have it just the same," Caelan said imperturbably. "His Majesty of Sorlain seems genuinely sorry for this situation. I believe he wanted to do the right thing."

"Well, if that was what he wanted, he had a damned odd way of showing it. An honorable man would have stayed to talk the matter through, not snuck in here like some thief and walked off with my lady."

And she walked off with him, he thought, all the anger draining out of him. He sat down and took the wine, though he did not drink it. What did it matter if Cristobal had summoned the storm or not? Rosamund had gone with him willingly. She had told him so herself.

"As I understand it, His Majesty was trying to avoid a confrontation that would only bring you pain."

Florian laughed harshly. "Was that Lady Rosamund's excuse, as well?"

"She—she did what she thought was right."

"Of course." Florian tossed back the wine. "Well, I can hardly blame her for wanting to avoid a scene. But if she thought I would have tried to keep her here by force, she was mistaken."

"But—" Caelan caught herself before another word escaped her. She poured Florian's cup full again, and added a drop to her own, though she'd scarcely touched it. Her composure restored, she said, "My lord, this has come as something of a shock to you, but in time you will see it is for the best."

"Best for who, Lady Caelan?" a cool voice asked from the doorway. "Our princess has been taken from us, and we have nothing in return. I can hardly see how that is best for anyone."

"Eredor," Florian said, "King Cristobal would not offer what he is not prepared to give."

"But what has he offered? Vague promises of some future aid to be decided at his pleasure. Hardly a shrewd bargain on our part. That is, if we were in the business of selling women. In that case, we could have set a far higher price on the princess, for His Majesty was quite desperate to have her." Eredor advanced into the chamber. "Did they tell you, my lord, that when you were believed to be dead, she refused him many times, and in such terms as left no doubt of her sincerity?"

Florian looked at Caelan. "Is this so, lady?"

Caelan turned her cup between her slender fingers, staring into its depths. "Yes, it is true. It was only when the news came that you lived—when she knew what was at stake—that she agreed. It was what was right for you—for *Venya*."

Florian set his cup down very gently. "She did not want to go? You *know* this?"

"Everyone knows it," Eredor said. "She made no secret of the fact that she found His Majesty's suit unwelcome. She never gave up hoping that you would return, even when it seemed all hope was gone. Your lady is nothing if not loyal. To you *and* Venya—though in truth, she made no distinction between the two.

Her faith in you was quite . . . persuasive." He dropped a torn and crumpled parchment on the table.

"What is this?" Florian asked.

"I had sent you a new plan, one that gave ten years to the building of an army. This was her reply. Should you ever bother to read it, you would find it a bold vision grounded in reality, one that had every hope of success. But I don't suppose you will. Instead, you have traded your lady—forgive me, *gifted* her—to Cristobal of Sorlain. And we all must wait to see what *gift* he chooses to grant you in return. Well, to my mind, there is nothing he could give us that could ever compensate for such a loss."

Eredor spoke more truly than he could know. Nothing could ever take Rosamund's place. *My Rosamund,* Florian thought, *how can I let her go like this? But no, she is not mine, I have no right to think it. I never had that right.* Black rage rose in him, but he forced it back. "What would you have me do, Eredor," he demanded roughly, "declare war on Sorlain? Venya needs—"

"*She* is what Venya needs," Eredor said. "If you doubt me, ask your subjects. Do you really not know how they love her? She is their Rose of Riall, their Shield of Venya, and they—"

"Their *what?*" Florian seized Eredor's wrist. "What did you just say? Their *shield?*"

"It is their name for her in Venya," Eredor said. "You must have heard it before now."

"No. No, I never did." Florian looked at Caelan. "Did you?"

"Yes," the *filidh* said. "But I don't see—"

"The shield. The *prophecy,* Caelan."

"What prophecy is this?" Eredor asked.

> *"The sword to conquer Venya's foes,*
> *The shield protects us from our woes,*
> *The sacrifice of an uncrowned king,*
> *Offered in the sacred ring,*
> *Then two are one by oath forsworn,*
> *And hope unites the land reborn."*

Florian looked at Caelan. "The shield. It is Lady Rosamund."

The color drained from Caelan's face. "But—no, my lord, it is a coincidence, it means nothing."

To gain what you desire most, surrender what you would not lose . . . the game begins when once you choose.

Florian stared out the window, where the sun had reached its zenith. "The sacrifice—the sacred ring. We thought it meant war, but the merrow said a *game*, and that once I made the choice, it would begin. What if the game isn't war?"

"The *merrow?*" Eredor raised his brows.

Florian waved him to silence. "You said that the future was always shifting," he said to Caelan. "You said a word could alter it—a thought. Surely a vow could do so. My lord." Florian turned to Eredor. "Thank you. You spoke truly when you said that Venya needs its princess. Lady Rosamund is my wife, oath-bound for as long as life should last, and not even the King of Sorlain can alter such a vow."

"What do you mean to do?" Eredor asked uneasily.

"Restore her to her people. But there are things that we must do before I go, and they must be done at once. Fetch that quill, if you would, and write down exactly what I say."

When Eredor had finished writing. Florian read it over, then signed it and impressed it with his seal.

"My lord," Eredor said, "I am not sure I understand this."

"I think you do," Florian answered quietly. "My lady has accused me of treating you unfairly and I have come to see that she is right. Should you need to use this, I trust that you will use it wisely."

"I—thank you, my lord. Of course Lady Rosamund will have my full support. But you—"

"Don't worry about me. I can look after myself."

Eredor glanced down at the parchment and sighed. "I would feel much easier if I understood your plan."

"I haven't got one. Yet. Come, Eredor, don't look so glum. Everyone knows that the Prince of Venya can always think of something!"

Eredor looked up sharply, but after a moment a reluctant smile touched his lips. "Is that so?"

Florian touched his shoulder briefly. "I heard it in a song," he said, "so of course it must be true."

Chapter 52

TWO guards were posted outside the door. Not that they were needed, Beylik thought, pacing the length of the surgery and back. He had no desire to leave this place, and Sigurd was not going anywhere. Thanks to the letter Beylik had left, the crew had made dead certain that Sigurd would remain just where he was until the prince could bring him to trial. In the meantime, the Moravians had reached their own verdict and carried out their sentence on the surgeon, stopping short of death so the prince might have that pleasure for himself.

Sigurd lay facedown on his cot, his back a mass of scabs and bruises. The only thing he seemed capable of moving was his eyes, and they turned now to Beylik, a tiny gleam between swollen, purpled lids.

"Planning our escape?"

Beylik ignored him and lay down on his own cot. He had no words for Sigurd, nor for anyone. Whatever was to happen would happen, and he no longer cared what it was, save for a vague wish that it would just be over.

His wish was granted immediately. The door opened, and Gordon, the first mate, strode into the surgery.

"The prince has summoned you," he said to Sigurd.

The surgeon rose slowly to his feet. Though he swayed dangerously, there was a difference in the way he held himself. The stoop was gone, and his bearded chin jutted proudly. "Forgive me if I don't dress for the occasion."

"He doesn't give a damn if you come naked as a babe. Just get your worthless hide moving."

And me? Beylik thought. *Am I to be judged as well?* No one stopped him as he followed Sigurd out the door and to the prince's cabin. The prince stood at his table, hands braced on either side of a chart, Ashkii at his shoulder. *In my place,* Beylik thought, a small dart of pain breaking through his numbness. Gordon took a seat at the table beside the second mate, Nohraimen.

"Sigurd Einarsson," the prince said without looking up. "You stand accused of treason. What say you?"

"That it is a lie," Sigurd answered, his voice ringing with sincerity. "Where is the evidence of this charge? There is none—there can be none, for I am innocent."

"Beylik?" The prince glanced at him. "What say you to this?"

Beylik shook his head, trying desperately to clear his thoughts. "Sigurd gave me the false letter," he said. "It was he who arranged the meeting and said what I must do. He is in league with Valinor."

Sigurd laughed. "My lord, this is utter nonsense, a tale concocted by this *beylik* to bring me to disgrace." He turned to Beylik. "Where are your witnesses?"

"There were no witnesses," Beylik cried, his voice trembling, "you know there were none—"

"I do know it," Sigurd declared, "for I never said such things to you or gave you any letter. My lord, you know me—have I not served you faithfully since I came aboard the *Quest*? This *beylik* does the will of Valinor, he has admitted as much. Surely you will not take the word of a confessed traitor over *mine!* I do not ask for mercy—that is for the guilty—but I demand justice."

"That is your right," the prince said, "and you shall have it. Without any witness to this conversation, I cannot accept one account over the other. Venyan law makes no exceptions on that point, as no doubt you are aware. You may go, Sigurd. Here are your wages"—he held out a small sack—"and we shall set you ashore."

"You are sending me away?" Sigurd cried. "My lord, I have done nothing to deserve—"

"Whatever you have done or not done," the prince said evenly, "I am sure that after the recent unpleasantness you have no wish to remain aboard the *Quest*. Gordon, please escort Sigurd to his cabin and allow him to gather his belongings. Have the skiff lowered, and ask Timmon, Jarett, and Monk to take him to Mirana. Nohraimen, you are with Mr. Gordon." He turned back to the chart spread before him. "Ashkii, please bring that candle over here."

Sigurd made a sudden motion toward the prince, then froze, his face twisting as though he had been struck. "You release me from your service?" he demanded hoarsely.

The prince made no answer, nor did he lift his head.

"This way," Gordon said, taking one of Sigurd's arms while Nohraimen seized the other. "Come along now, let's do this quietly."

"Wait—" Sigurd twisted in their grasp. "My lord—"

"Enough." Nohraimen pulled Sigurd sharply toward the door. "You have been dismissed."

"Then let him say so! My lord, please! It—it is the custom of my people—I need to hear you say the words—"

The prince glanced up. "Sigurd Einarsson, I release you from my service. Now go."

"There, now, are you satisfied?" Gordon said as he kicked the door shut behind them.

The prince marked the chart, then turned to his writing table and pulled a pile of parchments forward, scrawling his signature on one after the other. Ashkii dripped wax onto each one as it was signed and the prince impressed it with his seal. Beylik hovered near the doorway, uncertain whether he should stay or go.

"Thank you, Ashkii, that will be all for now," the prince said at last. Ashkii gave Beylik a sad look as he passed by, the last remnant of their friendship shimmering between them before he, too, was gone.

A heavy silence filled the cabin as the prince gathered up the documents he had signed and tied them with a ribbon. Just as Beylik decided that there was no point in staying, the prince spoke. "Are you sure you should be up already? You're very pale."

"I am recovered."

"Well, you would know best." The prince raised his head. "So, Beylik, what now? Will you leave us, too? Not with Sigurd, of course," he added with a slight smile. "We'll set you down somewhere else."

It was the kindness in his voice that undid Beylik, bringing back the memory of a thousand other kindnesses the prince had shown him. *I'm sorry,* he wanted to say, *forgive me, don't send me away.* He opened his mouth, but no words came out. He could only shake his head from side to side. *No. No. No.*

"Then would you bring me some kava?"

It took Beylik a moment to understand the question, but then he fairly flew out the door and down the passageway. But by the time he reached the galley, he knew that he, like Sigurd, had been tried and sentenced by the crew. No one spoke to him. They spoke *of* him, but only to each other, muttering behind his back just loud enough to be sure that he would hear the threats. No one looked at him, either, yet he felt their eyes upon him, and he was tripped twice on the journey, the second time sprawling headfirst against a table's edge.

He picked himself up and touched the back of his wrist to his split lip, saying nothing. Laughter followed him as he went grimly to the galley, where stony silence greeted his arrival.

"Thank you." The prince accepted the mug without looking up. Ashkii was back, once again standing in Beylik's place, and Gordon stood on the prince's other side. They leaned over the table as the prince spoke rapidly, his finger moving over the chart.

"Just here," he said. "The *Endeavor* will be waiting. If neither the princess nor I appear at the rendezvous, you are to join them *here* and pursue the *Corazón*. You will board her, but you will keep keep bloodshed to a minimum. On no account is the King of Sorlain to be injured or mishandled. Take the princess and return to Serilla, where Lord Eredor will give you further instructions. I have written this all out and expect my orders to be followed to the letter. Questions?"

"What men will you take with you?" Ashkii asked.

"None. I go alone."

"If you miss the rendezvous—" Gordon began.

"Do not wait for me; there can be no delay. If that is all . . . ?" He emptied the mug and handed the bundle of documents to Ashkii. "See that Lord Bastyon gets these."

Ashkii, Beylik thought, his chest constricting painfully. *Ashkii, not me. It will never be me again.*

For the second time in his life, Beylik felt as though he had stumbled into a dark dream from which he could not wake. But this was worse, far worse than the slave market. That, at least, was something that had been done to him. This time he had no one but himself to blame. Only now did he see how his bitterness had blinded him to the gifts he had been given: a home aboard the *Quest,* duties he enjoyed, the companionship of the crew.

Gone. All gone. Home, friends . . . and honor. He had betrayed the man who had taken him from the galleys, struck off his collar, shown him nothing but kindness and respect. No matter how he might regret it now, the deed was done, and he had done it of his own will and the crew would carry out their own brand of justice. It would be an accident, of course. That's what they always said. *Just an accident, m'lord, a damned shame, but some folk are just unlucky.*

Knowing he deserved it did not stop the terror. The prince was leaving—Beylik would be alone with the crew, and no one would lift a hand to help him. Frozen, he watched the prince rise from his seat and take a long look around the cabin.

"Right," he said briskly, "we should be close now."

Beylik had to bite his torn lip hard against the plea struggling to escape. He would not beg. He *would* not. The prince paused in the doorway and looked back. Beylik managed to hold himself upright, but he could not stop the tears rising to his eyes. Ashamed, he bowed his head and watched the floor blur between his feet.

"Beylik," the prince said, but Beylik could not answer. He did not even try. There was nothing left to say.

"Beylik," the prince repeated gently. "Come. You are with me. Step out, lad, that's the way, I've things to do tonight."

The others fell back so Beylik could take his place. One pace to the left, one to the back, a position only granted to one whose loyalty could not be questioned.

Despite his need for haste, the prince did not go directly to the quarterdeck. He walked through the mess room, full at this hour, stopping to greet many of the men by name. Now they looked at Beylik directly, though none acknowledged him.

The prince took the long route across the foredeck, and Gordon hurried to meet him in the waist, saying that the *Corazón* was just where the Serillan harbormaster had promised it would be, at anchor on the far side of the island.

"Very good, Gordon. Thank you. Beylik"—the prince took the dagger from his belt and handed it to him—"I hope you will not need it, but . . ."

Beylik dropped to one knee and took the prince's hand. "My

lord, I—there are no words to thank you—or none I can find. But I must know—why? You know what I have done—"

"And why you did it. When we were on the sea you told me many things I had not known. Do you not remember?"

"No, nothing after that first day."

"My lady told me once that I should watch over you more carefully. As always, she was wise. Any thanks belong to her."

Beylik stood and touched his brow. "May Lord Leander keep you safe from harm until we meet again."

"And you. But if we do not, you are to look after the princess for me. Understood?"

"Aye, my lord. With my life."

The prince left him then and walked toward the larboard rail. Beylik stood a moment, regretting that he had not paid more attention earlier. Why was he going all alone to the *Corazón*? The princess was aboard, or so it seemed, and there had been something about a rendezvous that might be missed and orders to pursue and board the King of Sorlain's ship to bring the princess back.

I should go with him, Beylik thought. He actually took a few steps forward before he stopped himself. His orders were clear. He was to remain aboard the *Quest* and stand ready to give the princess any aid she might require. In the meantime, he would put the prince's cabin in order. He was halfway to the hatch when the first sailor bumped against him, pushing him into a second.

"Watch your step, lad."

The man shoved him hard, and the first sailor put out a foot and tripped him. "Clumsy sod," he said, bending down and dragging Beylik upright by his collar. "I don't know what lies you told the prince," he hissed into his ear, "but *we* know what you are."

Beylik jerked away, instinctively looking toward the prince. What he saw made his heart leap to his throat. Everything went very slowly then, as sometimes happens in a dream. Beylik cried a warning, but the prince did not hear. Then he pushed between the sailors and ran as he had never run before, certain he would be too late.

Sigurd stood behind the prince, his hand rising, rising— Beylik cried out again as the blade reached its height and began its swift descent. The prince whirled, one hand moving to his empty scabbard, then leapt back, narrowly avoiding Sigurd's blade. Beylik stumbled into him, knocking him off balance, flinging up his own arm to block the blow as he raised the prince's dagger.

There was no pain—not then—just the satisfaction of knowing his blade had found its mark and a dizziness that drove him to his knees.

"Beylik?"

"I'm fine," he said, and he did feel well enough, save for the dizziness and a sharp stinging in his eyes. He lifted a hand to wipe them and felt his wrist seized.

"No, don't touch it." That was Gordon's voice, though Beylik couldn't see him. "Lift him gently—get him to the surgery. He'll be all right, my lord." He lowered his voice, but Beylik heard him say, "We'll try to save the eye."

"Do all you can," the prince ordered. "I would not lose him."

"Aye, m'lord, we will. Handsomely lads, that's the way, don't jar him—just lie still, Beylik, we've got you—pity about Sigurd, he'd have patched you up in no time." There was laughter then and a deep voice said grimly, "He's sharks' meat now, and good riddance to the bastard. I'll sew the lad myself."

Beylik managed a grin. "Not you, Jarrett, I've seen your work. Let Ashkii have a go at it."

"What, the demon? You'd let one of them—"

"Shut your mouth, Timms, the Ilindrian's all right—"

"Aye, t'lad's right, Mr. Ashkii sews a fine seam. Someone fetch him—"

"Here, lad, drink this down, you won't feel a thing," they said with rough kindness, and Beylik choked, too dazed to protest as they poured a river of *usqa* down his throat.

Chapter 53

CRISTOBAL stood as Rose entered his cabin. His outfit was the match of her own, plain white satin with only a single ornament; a brooch that matched the one on her breast, a diamond C and R entwined.

She took the seat across from him and spread the heavy napkin, her fingers smoothing and smoothing it across her lap. She did not want to look at Cristobal. A single glance had been bad enough, sending such sharp pain lancing through her heart that she was struck dumb.

"My lady?" he prompted, and she realized he had asked her something, though she had no idea what it was. She steeled herself and raised her head to see Florian looking back at her.

There were differences, of course, and she concentrated on finding them, hoping that by doing so she could minimize their likeness. Cristobal's hair was not the color of moonbeams, but ripe wheat beneath a summer sun. His eyes were blue, not amber, and though they had an upward slant, the effect was merely attractive, not exotic. Perhaps the chief difference lay in the fact that his face was still young, full-fleshed, instead of lean and hard beyond his years.

". . . to your liking?" he said in his beautiful low voice with its musical Sorlainian accent.

"Yes," she answered, with no idea what she had just agreed to. But what did it matter? Whatever he asked, she would agree to. It would be easier that way.

"I am so glad," he said, lifting the cover of a dish. A spicy aroma filled the air. "Not everyone cares for them. Here, let me help you.

Thank you, Galeno," he added to the servant hovering over them, "we will not be needing you tonight. Take the others and go."

Rose had not been aware of the servants until they moved, half a dozen of them gliding on silent feet toward the door.

"Do you speak our tongue at all?" Cristobal asked as he filled her dish.

"A little," she answered in Sorlainian, "and I fear not well. I had lessons when I was a child, but that was long ago."

"Oh, no, you speak it beautifully! Your accent is hardly noticeable. Your teacher must have been a good one."

"She was the widow of one of my father's men and had been born in Savrelo."

"It is a beautiful place," Cristobal said eagerly. "The people there are herders, for the most part, and their flocks are sold at Neroja market. That is a sight to see, for it lies in a sheltered valley where the gypsies keep a settlement. Market days bring them all down from the mountains, and the air is filled with music. There are no finer dancers than the gypsies of Neroja, not in all the world. I will take you there—that is, if you like."

And there it was again, that tiny flash of uncertainty that would have been disarming had only things been different. If he had arrived at Larken Castle as she'd once hoped, she would be dizzy with her good fortune. But it was too late for that. Her heart had been given already, and not all the magic of Venya could will it back again.

"Yes," she said tonelessly. "I'm sure I would enjoy that."

No matter how much she wanted to dislike him, he made it difficult to do so. He chatted on lightly through the meal, telling her of his childhood in Paloman Castle. It sounded very grand, she thought, with so many servants and tutors they could not be counted, let alone named. But for all the people constantly surrounding him, she sensed that he had been a lonely child.

"Do you still have fourteen hounds?" she asked, curiosity overcoming her apathy for a moment.

"No." He smiled suddenly. "I have thirty now."

He told her a little of his hounds, and of his mews, and of his stables filled with the finest horses in the world. He told her of the famous rose gardens of Paloman Castle and its breathtaking view of the mountains on one side and the sea upon the other.

His determined cheer faltered only once, when he spoke of his father. "Do not hate him, Rosamund. He did what he thought best for Sorlain. It was his chief care . . . his only care. My mother died when I was born, you know, and he never married again. Sorlain was everything to him. He was a great king," he added reverently, "the greatest ruler our land has ever known. Even when he was ill—when he was dying—he never faltered in his duty. He was loved and respected by all his subjects."

"And by his son?" Rose asked.

"More than any," Cristobal answered solemnly. "If he seemed . . . stern, at times, it was only that his burden was so heavy. He was determined that I should be fit to bear it as he did, with dignity and wisdom."

Rose studied him across the candles. "Admirable," she murmured. "And yet . . . it seems an awfully heavy burden for a child. Did you never rebel?"

"Oh, no." He smiled a little and bent his head, the candlelight gleaming on the deep gold of his hair. "Which is not to say I did not think of it. I had my dreams . . ."

"What were they?"

"Oh, daring adventures, thrilling deeds, true love—" He laughed. "What boy does not see himself as a hero? But I could dream them only so long as I was prince. Now I am king." He set his knife neatly on the table, adding in a lower voice, "And kings are not permitted dreams."

He looked up, his smile back in place. "Are you finished? Would you like to sit on deck?" he asked politely as they both rose from the table.

Rose shook her head. "I'm weary. I shall retire now."

"Really?"

From the light in his eyes, Rose knew she had said the wrong thing. Surely he didn't expect to bed with her tonight! But of course he did. He was her husband, after all.

He smiled, and her heart twisted savagely in her breast. It was Florian's smile, but Florian was gone, vanished back into the mists of legend, and she was Queen of Sorlain.

"Not yet," she began, taking a step back. "Please, can we not wait?"

"Yes, of course," he said, taking a step forward. "We will wait.

But there are other ways in which we can become . . . acquainted. Other ways in which we might find pleasure," he said softly, stroking a finger gently down her cheek.

"But—"

He laid his finger on her lips. "Shh. Do not say no. Do not say anything, not now. Let us begin—not too quickly, for we have all the time we need. Slowly," he said, his hand brushing her neck. "Softly. Like so . . ."

He bent to kiss her. She stiffened, overcome with the desire to push him away and flee. But he was true to his word. He made no demands but kissed her lightly, and, she thought, with a very practiced skill. But then, he had said he'd not been faithful . . .

Faithful? To her? Dear Jehan, could this man really be her *husband?* No, this was a dream, a nightmare—and yet it wasn't. It was all true. Florian was gone—she would never see him again. Never again in all her days would she wake up beside him or hear his laughter or feel his arms around her. It was as though he had died.

Or she had. Surely she could not feel more alone if she were in her grave.

Cristobal pulled back and looked into her eyes. "It is him, isn't it? The Prince of Venya. When I kiss you, you think of him."

"He was my husband until this morning. Did you imagine I would forget him by tonight?"

"No." Cristobal frowned. "But in time, you will. It is as though you were a widow," he added, speaking more to himself than her. "And widows recover. They forget and learn to love again."

"Some do. Not all."

"I am sorry," he said, and once again, he sounded as though he meant it. "It gives me no pleasure to see you suffer. I will do anything to ease your grief, give you all I have to give, and one day you will learn to love me."

"That is beyond what we have bargained for. You should not hope for it. I will be your wife, for so I have promised, and will fulfill my duties. And with that, Cristobal, you must be content. Or if you will not be content, you must release me."

"I cannot," he said sharply.

"Why?" Rose demanded. "Why *can* you not? Do you mean you *will* not, or is there something you have not told me?"

He made an impatient gesture. "Cannot, will not, what

difference does it make? Do not ask it again. Ask anything else, but not that."

He turned from her and lifted his goblet. His hand trembled slightly as he raised it to his lips and drained it, then set it down and spoke without looking at her. "All my life I have heard about my cousin Florian, so bold and brave and clever. In truth," he added with a bitter laugh, "I grew quite weary of his name upon my father's lips. Tell me, lady, is he really such a man as they say?"

"Yes. He is all that and more."

Cristobal refilled his goblet. "More? What more is possible?"

"He is . . ." Rose's throat closed, and she shook her head mutely.

"Beyond words?" Cristobal drank again. "Indescribable? It has been said that there is a resemblance between us. Is it the truth?"

Before Rose could reply, a voice spoke from across the room. "Why don't you see for yourself?"

Rose whirled, her heart stopping with a jerk when she saw a familiar black-clad figure leaning casually against the doorpost.

Cristobal's eyes narrowed, but a moment later he smiled. "It must—surely it must be the Prince of Venya!"

"Indeed. My lady," Florian made her a sweeping bow, the effect only slightly marred by the water dripping from his hair and clothes. "You're looking very lovely tonight. And Your Majesty, I was so sorry to have missed you earlier."

"A pity, yes." Cristobal waved a casual hand, his rings flashing in the candlelight.

"But I couldn't let you sail away without paying you a visit." Florian laughed and added, "I must say you don't make it easy to drop in unannounced."

"The guards—" Cristobal began.

"Are still enjoying their game of tiles. You should have a word with your captain about that."

Florian smiled as he advanced into the cabin, leaving wet footprints on the carpet. "Perhaps I should have sent word, but all that ceremony is so tiresome. It's so much simpler this way, just the two grandsons of the Serillan twins. I've always been sorry that I never met them, but Gracia must have been very proud of your abilities. That storm you sent earlier—" He reached the table and

•

pulled out a chair. "Do you mind if I sit down? And if it's not too much trouble, could I have some of that wine?"

Rose held her breath during the small tense silence that followed.

"Of course," Cristobal said at last. "Allow me to pour."

Florian drained the goblet in a single draught. "Much better, thank you," he said, waving a hand toward the empty seat across from him. "Won't you join me?"

Again there was a silence as Cristobal frowned down at the flagon in his hands. Florian glanced at Rose and raised a finger to his lips.

"Please," he mouthed.

What was he doing here? What game was he playing now? Foolish, reckless—she bit her lip hard to keep from bursting into tears. He was here. He had come after her.

"Yes," Cristobal said, "very well." He sat down in Rose's empty place, staring with wary fascination as Florian hooked one leg casually over the arm of his seat and lifted the cover of a serving dish to peer inside.

"You were saying . . . the storm . . . ?" Cristobal prompted.

"Now that was an excellent piece of work," Florian said approvingly. "I must admit that it defeated me completely. Of course," he added with a grin. "I didn't know then who had sent it. Next time you won't catch me off my guard."

Cristobal laughed. "There won't be a next time. We are allies now, remember?"

"Ah, yes." Florian refilled his goblet. "And that's precisely what I want to talk about tonight."

"I suppose I wasn't entirely clear about the help that I could give you—"

"Oh, please don't think I doubt your word. If you say you'll help Venya, then you will. We're both men of honor, aren't we?"

"Yes, of course. Men of honor," Cristobal repeated softly, as though savoring the words.

"That's just as I thought. But Your Majesty—"

"Cristobal."

"Cristobal, then. I do hate to say this since we're getting on so well, but men of honor really don't go about stealing other men's wives. It simply isn't done."

Cristobal laughed, but Rose saw the wary tightening of the

skin around his eyes. "So I have been told. But fear not, cousin, I'm fully prepared to put the whole thing in the past."

"Are you?" With a lightning change of manner, Florian slammed the goblet on the table and sat up very straight. "Well, I'm not."

Cristobal's throat worked as he swallowed hard. "Lady Rosamund was my wife before ever she was yours. Be reasonable—"

Florian laughed. "Reasonable? Me? I think you have mistaken me for someone else."

"Then you must be mad." Cristobal's eyes narrowed. "No, not mad, not you! Not the Prince of Venya! You're up to something—but what?" He leaned back in his seat, bringing his steepled fingers to his chin. "Obviously she has value to you. Why else would you have stolen her?"

"Stolen?" Rose interrupted, and both men turned to her. Florian frowned, shaking his head almost imperceptibly.

"Your uncle has told me the true tale of your abduction. But now I think he may have overstated the case. Obviously you were not forced. But I believe you were . . . persuaded."

"Ah," Florian said. "I see. You think I used magic to enchant the lady."

"I will not speculate on *what* you used," Cristobal said dryly, "but I will venture to guess that you did whatever was necessary to secure the lady's agreement to this marriage. And your motives are crystal clear. After the disaster in Riall, you needed Lady Rosamund to bolster your support in Venya. Do you deny that?"

"No. I do not deny it."

"It was a clever move. Richard is livid," Cristobal added with a slight smile. "Did you know that? When he speaks your name, his face turns red and his eyes bulge in a most amusing fashion."

Florian grinned and lifted his goblet. "Then let us hope he speaks it often. I confess that vexing Richard is a pleasure."

"You have vexed him mightily this time! Venya has become troublesome, he tells me. So much toil on his part, and now all will be undone. Add my support to your Venyan allies, and you will see that you have no further need of Lady Rosamund."

Florian nodded. "That seems a logical conclusion."

"Then I ask again: What are you doing here tonight?"

"It is a very simple thing," Florian said apologetically. "Nothing to do with Richard at all. Has it not occurred to you that I might miss my lady and want her to come home?"

"You?" Cristobal laughed. "Oh, no, cousin, that did not occur to me. Why, 'tis common knowledge that you have already betrayed her half a dozen times! Forgive me, my lady," he added, turning to Rose. "But I think you know this already. And if you do not, you should."

"I suppose Richard told you that as well?" Florian's voice was casual, but his knuckles whitened on the goblet.

"He did. But he did not have to. It stands to reason, does it not? They say you've had a hundred women—"

"A hundred?" Florian murmured. "Really? Where *do* I find the time?"

"—so what's one more or less? Lady Rosamund has served her purpose; you are now free to seek another bride, one with all the wealth you need so badly. Your choice will be almost unlimited."

"I could say the same to you. Surely you are the most eligible groom in all the world! Why do you insist on the woman who has plighted her troth to your kinsman, however unworthy you might think him to receive it? Why do you seek to take my lady, when you have shown me such generosity in all other things? I could ask these questions, but I do not, for I do not want to quarrel. Apart from all the practical considerations, I have so little family that it grieves me to think of us at odds."

"I think," Cristobal said a little pompously, "you must concede that I have done all in my power to avoid a quarrel."

"You made me a very handsome offer," Florian admitted. "Please don't think I am ungrateful. And I would be a poor excuse for a prince if I were to do anything to endanger our new friendship."

"Then we are agreed!" Cristobal half rose from his seat.

"Well, no, actually we are not," Florian said with a disarming smile. "Say rather that we have reached an impasse. But I'm sure we can find some way to resolve it."

Cristobal sat down. "How?"

"We could . . ." Florian gave his kinsman a long, measuring look. "No," he murmured as though to himself, quickly suppressing a smile. "That wouldn't do. Let me see . . ."

"*What* wouldn't do?"

"Oh, it was just an idea . . ." His smile widened to a grin. "I thought we might have a wager."

"You would have me wager Lady Rosamund? My *queen?*"

Rose's jaw dropped. *This* was Florian's plan? Oh, it was beyond reckless, it was madness.

"Do you take me for a fool?" the Sorlainian asked coldly. "Such a wager is unthinkable!"

"Well, yes," Florian said, with the air of one explaining the sum of one plus one. "That's the whole idea, isn't it, to do the thing that no one else has thought to do? Of course, it could be no ordinary wager, won or lost on the fall of the tiles or even at sword point. It would have to be something very special. Perhaps . . . the Game of Kings?"

Rose had heard those words before. Where, she did not know, nor could she remember. Her mind seemed frozen, yet her body reacted with a thrill of fear that rippled through her belly and down the insides of her thighs. Florian gave her a quick glance, and in the second their eyes met, she knew exactly what he planned.

"The Game of Kings?" Cristobal laughed. "That is but a child's tale, a legend."

"Oh, no, it has been done, though not for two hundred years or more. It seems the later monarchs lacked the talent to attempt it." Florian leaned forward and lowered his voice. "Or perhaps it was the courage."

"Perhaps it was no lack at all," Cristobal said coolly. "Perhaps they grew too wise to indulge in a such a perilous amusement. It could be that they were more concerned with duty than with—"

"Honor?" Florian interrupted smoothly. "Yes, of course, that must be it! I'm afraid wisdom has never been my strong suit. I'm sure my lady—forgive me, I should say Lady Rosamund—"

"Her Majesty," Cristobal snapped.

"—would be the first to tell you that I can be irrational when it comes to any matter touching on my honor. I make no doubt she is right. Perhaps it *is* a sort of vanity that will not permit me to withdraw once a challenge has been issued."

Cristobal's face flamed. He straightened slightly and folded his hands before him on the table. "And if I was to agree to this Game of Kings?" he asked in his most judicious voice. "What would I gain if the victory was mine?"

Florian shrugged. "The satisfaction of knowing you'd defeated me. But never mind, I quite understand your position. With nothing to gain and everything to lose, why take the risk?"

Cristobal bit his lip, frowning. "That's right. Why should I?"

"Really, Cristobal, if you can't see it for yourself—oh, very well. The only possible reason to accept such a challenge would be"—the Prince of Venya smiled wickedly—"for the adventure."

Chapter 54

AN hour later, the small boat scraped sand. Florian was out in an instant, tugging Rose after him as Cristobal ordered the sailors to a small cove, where they were to remain in the boat until he returned. He wanted no witnesses to this game, and once Rose understood how it was played, she understood completely.

"You said the prophecy was symbolic," Rose said to Florian under her breath as they walked up the shore.

"It may have been."

She seized his arm, halting him. "What is going to happen when you walk into the ring?"

"Leander only knows." He touched her cheek and smiled. "Perhaps nothing at all."

"And then—?"

"That depends on you. If you would like to live in Paloman Castle—which is magnificent, Rosamund, as I am sure Cristobal has told you—I will congratulate Cristobal on his victory and take my leave of both of you. If not—well, then I will think of something else."

She caught his hand and held it between her own. "But you believe this is the game the prophecy foretold?"

"We'll soon find out." He turned as Cristobal joined them. "Shall we begin?"

Florian had explained the ritual on the way to the island. He and Cristobal stood back to back, then each walked in the opposite direction, pacing the beach from the waterfall to the sea, muttering under their breath until they met again and the circle was complete.

Florian held up his hands and sketched a pattern in the air.
"Thus it begins," he intoned, "the Game of Kings. The rules shall
be three. One: The stone must touch the water while in the grasp
of the contestant. Two: No life shall be taken here tonight. Three:
No blood shall be spilled save by necessity. My heart and hand
upon this pledge, my blood to answer should I fail."

Cristobal repeated the last words solemnly.

"Now we need a stone." Florian glanced about, then bent to
pick up a pebble. "Is this acceptable?"

"No," Cristobal said, "use this." He reached into his pouch
and held out his hand. An emerald the size of a walnut glittered in
his palm.

"Very nice," Florian said approvingly. "Much more fitting."
He swept the sand flat with his palm and set the emerald down.
"Withdraw to your side, Your Majesty," he said with a slight bow,
"and I to mine."

Florian approached Rose noiselessly through the moon-cast
shadows, the breeze ruffling his full black sleeves and catching
the edges of his silver-gilt hair. He held himself straight, every
muscle tensed, and when at last he stood beside Rose, she could
see that his eyes were clear and sharply focused.

"Listen to me," he said in an undertone. "If I fall—"

"Florian—"

He put a finger against her lips. "The *Quest* is anchored just
over that rise. Gordon will be here tomorrow morning. If you
choose to go with Cristobal, you need only meet Gordon and tell
him to depart in peace. Should he find neither of us here tomorrow, he will pursue the *Corazón* and take you first to Serilla, then
if need be, to Ilindria. It is in your hands, Rosamund. I give Venya
into your keeping."

"Me? Alone? You must be—"

"You will not be alone. Eredor will be with you, and Ewan, and
the rest of the council, in time. Caelan will speak to the *filidhi*. If
this is what was meant to be, then I believe—I must believe that the
way will be made clear for you. Rosamund, *you* are the ruler Venya
needs—wise and kind and brave, and I—" He broke off and
looked away, then turned back and smiled. "I will do my part."

"Don't walk in there," she whispered. "There must be some
other way! I'm frightened—"

He squeezed her hand. "I know. Not that I am anything of the sort." He brought her hand to his lips, then glanced up at her, one brow raised. "Frightened is far too mild a word to express what I am feeling."

"What are you two saying over there?" Cristobal called suspiciously.

"Lady Rosamund was just telling me I haven't a chance, and I was confessing that I'm trembling with fear," Florian called back, laughing. "But I am ready now. Are you?"

"Yes. Let's get on with it."

Florian released Rose's hand and turned to face Cristobal across the sand. "Then I wish you good luck, Your Majesty. My lady, would you count to three?"

"One," Rose said, her hands twisting in her skirts. "Two. Three."

The word had barely left her lips when Cristobal stepped into the circle. A moment later, his outline shimmered, and in his place was a falcon that beat huge wings against the warm, sea-scented air. Florian hesitated but a moment, then walked into the center. He stopped, his expression deeply wary, then advanced another step. His body jerked as though he had been struck and he fell to his knees, his face turned to the sky.

He knew, Rose thought, he knew this would happen. She started forward, then cried out as a wall of blue flame rose before her, barring her entrance to the circle. She leapt back, and by the time it had subsided, Florian was gone.

She stared in disbelief at the sand where he had knelt, then up at the falcon that had been Cristobal, silhouetted against the moon. Up and up it rose, and then, folding its wings, it dove. Halfway to the emerald it was knocked into a flurry of feathers by a white osprey hurtling through the night.

Rose caught her breath, hardly daring to believe what she was seeing as the falcon dropped almost to the ground. At the last moment, it spread its wings and caught the current once again. But now it began to change; its wings spread to an enormous breadth. Green scales replaced brown feathers, and the neck lengthened against the moon-bright sky.

The dragon bent its head and spat red flame. And there was Florian, himself again, standing just before the emerald. He lifted his hand and a shield appeared, emblazoned with Venyan arms. The flame turned against its surface, though his arm trembled

visibly with the effort as he bent awkwardly, his free hand groping in the sand.

The dragon dropped to the earth. It shrank and dwindled, became a panther that paced upon the sand, then threw back its head
and roared a challenge to the night. It crouched and sprang at Florian but was met midair by a lion with claws outstretched and
teeth bared. They collided just over the emerald and were both
knocked backward to sprawl upon the sand. Before the lion could
gain its feet, the panther was upon it. Once, twice, the huge claw
struck and the golden pelt was running with fresh blood.

Neither of them seemed to hear Rose's sharp cry of protest.
No blood spilt, that had been the agreement. But then, it always
had been. Yet men had died before.

The lion twisted and was gone. The panther paced restlessly
from side to side, searching for the emerald. Rose held her breath
as she caught a flicker of movement. A serpent glided through the
shadows, the green stone held between its jaws. The panther
leaped and transformed in midair into the falcon that dove, curved
beak striking the sand where only a moment ago the serpent had
been—and now only the emerald remained.

The falcon seized the stone in its talons and rose swiftly, turning toward the water, but its cry of triumph changed to one of
rage when an arrow whistled through the air and the stone fell
into Florian's waiting hand.

Florian sprinted toward the sea, swiftly but with none of his
usual grace. Between the tattered remnants of his shirt, Rose saw
the blood flowing freely down his back. Even through her own cry
of terror she could hear his gasping breath when he stumbled, then
went down upon his knees, straining against the tentacle wrapped
about his ankle. He turned back, and his face went deathly white.

This was no creature of their world that faced him, but something from a child's nightmare, all knobby legs and claws and
jagged teeth. Another tentacle lashed from jaw to temple, then
Florian shimmered and was gone.

A huge claw reached out, grasped the stone, and the monster
lumbered awkwardly across the soft sand. Rose choked back a
despairing cry as it reached the hard-packed shoreline and began
to move more swiftly, but she breathed again when the creature
reared back and fell, blinded by the torch Florian thrust before its
hundred eyes.

In a lightning movement, Florian plucked the stone from the creature's claw and raced toward the water. The beast struck out again, this time lashing his torn back, but Florian did not change his form. Rose feared that he no longer had the strength, but he was so close, just a few steps from the waterline—

He jerked back at the last moment, a whiplike tentacle wrapped about his throat. Florian grasped it one-handed, vainly trying to tear it from his flesh. He was forced back one step, then another, then he turned swiftly and moved toward the monster, wrapping the slackened tentacle around his hand and bracing himself, the heels of his boots sinking deep into the hard-packed sand.

What is he doing? Rose wondered, *does he really think he can shift it?* It seemed he did; his face was wrenched with effort, every muscle straining as he sought to drag the chittering monster forward.

For a moment it seemed to move . . . but it was no use. The thing was enormous, and it crouched back on its many legs. Now it was Florian who was dragged inexorably forward, his heels digging deep furrows in the sand.

Rose clamped her hands across her mouth as Florian moved closer, ever closer to the monster's gaping jaws. It was not Cristobal, not now. Cristobal was gone, vanished into the shell of the thing he had created. *This is how men die,* Rose thought dizzily, *this is how it happens* . . .

Florian released the tentacle. The thing that had been Cristobal teetered, thrown off balance for a moment. But only for a moment. Even as Florian twisted and dove for the water, it rose again, gathered its many legs beneath it, and leapt.

Rose lifted her skirts and ran, stumbling in the soft sand as she skirted the circle. She cried out to Cristobal, trying to reach the man, then halted, tears choking off her words. Florian had vanished beneath the hideous shell. All she could see of him was his hand, outstretched upon the sand. Even as she stood speechless, a wave rolled slowly to shore, its very edge foaming lightly over the emerald glittering in his palm.

Instantly the monster vanished. Cristobal stood beside his kinsman, laughing. "Oh, that was close! A moment more and I would have—Florian?" he said, bending over the black-clad form lying facedown on the shore. "Are you all right?"

"Of course he's not all right," Rose cried, running forward. "You have slain him!"

"Oh, no," Cristobal said. "I didn't hurt him . . . much."

"You shouldn't have hurt him at all! Were you not listening to the three rules?"

"Of course I was. But . . . well . . ." He knelt beside his kinsman and turned him over. "He will be fine . . . won't he?"

"That depends," Florian replied, opening one eye, "on how it ended." He sat up and touched a hand to his cheek, then examined the blood on his fingers, looking slightly stunned.

"You won," Cristobal said grudgingly, and Florian laughed.

"Did I? How splendid!"

Cristobal turned on his heel and walked away.

Florian hurried after him. "Cristobal," he said, laying a hand on his kinsman's shoulder, "wait, sit down a moment. Do you realize what we've done tonight? This the first time anyone has attempted this in centuries!"

Cristobal jerked away. "Do not patronize me."

"But I'm not! I can see now why the game was stopped, can't you? That sort of power is almost impossible to control—and yet we did. We both did. Your father would be very proud if he had lived to see this."

"Proud? He would be furious."

"I would hate to think so," Florian said, "King Esteban was very good to me. I was sorry I never had the chance to thank him for his help."

"He liked you, too. He always made it a point to keep informed of where you were and all that you were doing. The time off Parvia, do you remember when you took three of Richard's ships? He went on and on about it; I'd never heard him laugh like that before. Gods, for the first time, I am glad he is dead. At least he cannot see how I have failed him."

"No, of course he wouldn't feel that—"

"He would." Cristobal sank down on the sand and rested his brow on his bent knees. "You understand nothing."

Rose lowered herself to the ground beside him. "Cristobal," she began gently. Florian frowned and shook his head, but she ignored him. "You're right. We don't understand. Because you haven't told us what is happening, have you? But I think that now you must."

He shook his head without raising it. "I don't know what you mean."

"You do. Some of it you've told me for yourself," Rose went on gently. "You said your father was a good, wise king who never took a single step that would not benefit Sorlain. Right up to the end."

Cristobal groaned. "Do not remind me—"

"But you also said that he released you from your promise not to seek me out. Why did the King of Sorlain make that decision, Cristobal? He had a reason, didn't he? And it must have been a very good reason to convince him to change a mind that had been so firmly set against our marriage for so many years."

Cristobal shrugged slightly. "On his deathbed, he took pity on me."

"But he wasn't on his deathbed when he made this decision. You were in Valinor weeks before his end. That was why Richard ordered me home from Malin Isle, wasn't it? Why did King Esteban change his mind? What sent you to Valinor in the first place? As far as I can see, I have nothing that Sorlain could want. Richard has given me no dowry—"

"And yet," Florain said, speaking for the first time, "your father must have done so when he promised you to Cristobal. It would all be in the marriage settlement."

"Which was sent to Sorlain for safekeeping," Rose finished thoughtfully. "Yes. But I do not know what was in it that could be of such importance."

"Not gold," Florian said. "Sorlain has no need of that. Lands? What would Sorlain want with some bits of Valinor?" He turned to Cristobal. "If you have anything to add, please do."

"No," Cristobal said. "I have nothing to say. In fact, it is growing late, and I think I should—"

"You're not leaving," Florian said. "Not until we settle this."

"Bits of Valinor," Rose repeated slowly. "No, but not all Valinor's possessions are in Valinor. Not since Lord Varnet made his voyage. He brought us new alliances—small fiefdoms that were glad to swear allegiance to Lord Varnet's king. Richard lost most of them, the fool, but a few remain. Korin, Parva—but they are poor places. Agripe—"

"Agripe?" Florian repeated sharply. "Yes, that's right, Agripe belongs to Valinor. But they also trade with Sorlain. And they have . . ."

Cristobal made as if to rise, but sat down again with a sigh. "Yes," he said, "they do."

"I'd heard about the sickness in the *abulón* beds," Florian said. "But I think it was worse than rumor made it."

"Much worse," Cristobal agreed glumly. "It was devastation. Without Agripe—"

"Gods," Florian said softly. "You are in trouble, aren't you?"

"Wait," Rose interrupted. "What sickness? What is worse? And what trouble do you speak of?"

"The *abulón*," Florian said. "Used to make Sorlainian purple dye."

"It is made from their shells," Cristobal said. "It requires many shells and much labor to yield even a small amount. But the *abulón* were already harvested for food, and the fisherfolk prepared the dye in winter to supplement their living. In my father's father's time, this was a small trade, but once Varnet opened the Andrien pass, the Ilindrian demand far surpassed what we could readily supply. I fear in our attempts to satisfy that demand, we were too greedy. We took more and more, and what was left was weakened. In these past years, there has sometimes been a sickness in the *abulón* beds. But now the sickness can no longer be controlled. The beds are nearly empty. And we have no healthy stock to start again."

"And so you need to trade for them," Rose said.

"There is one island where they can be found," Cristobal agreed. "Only one. Agripe belongs to Valinor and formed part of your original dowry. It is yours, lady, gifted to you by King Osric. Richard is not aware of this—the deed rests in Sorlain—"

"If Richard thinks it is his, he would surely trade with you," Rose said. "If you but told him—"

"Do you know your uncle so little? Now, believing that my sole wish is to fulfill my vow to you, he plays his advantage for all it is worth. First he tries to foist one of his own daughters on me, then he dangles the promise of our marriage before my eyes, setting one condition after another, his pride swelling every time that I comply. If this is how he wields such a small amount of power, imagine what he would do if he were to learn the true value of what he has! He would set such a price as would beggar even Sorlain."

"Well, then, why don't you just take it?" Rose asked. "Valinor could never stand against Sorlain."

"Would that I could. But that would wreak nearly as much havoc as losing the *abulón*. We are bound to Valinor through a thousand agreements. Given five years, I could extract us from the web our fathers wove, but to slash it into ribbons would ruin thousands of my subjects. Either way, it means disaster. I was a fool to have agreed to this!" he cried. "How could I have been so irresponsible!"

"It happens to the best of us," Florian said. "If there is anything I can do to help you—"

"You could give Lady Rosamund back. That would make things right."

"Give—?" Rose choked. "Oh, I do not think so."

"You are right," Cristobal said quickly, "what we have done tonight is inexcusable. But all I said to you was true. I never did accept my father's will in this, and I have carried your letter. I never married because I hoped—I truly believed we were wed. You have seen me at my worst, but I swear to you that I am a better man than this. All I ask is the chance to prove it."

"I am sorry," Rose said, "but I must refuse. Cristobal, somewhere there is a woman who is worthy of your love. Be patient, and you will find her."

"I will never find her," Cristobal said, his voice breaking. "Not now. I have lost everything—gods, what I am to do?"

Florian could not help but pity him. Cristobal had no queen, no Agripe Isle, no option but to crawl to Richard and beg, a galling prospect on every level. The best he could hope for was an agreement that would bring hardship to his people. He had lost, if not everything, then far more than he could easily afford. Being only human, Cristobal would soon begin to look around for someone to blame for this disaster.

Florian groped for the words to comfort him, the magic phrases that would restore Sorlain's neutrality, but before he could find them, Rosamund forestalled him.

"Nonsense," she said briskly. "You have lost nothing. You made a mistake, that's all, in not confiding in me from the start. As for Agripe, you say you cannot take the island by force—"

"It is impossible."

"Then let the Prince of Venya do it for you."

Cristobal raised his head to look at Florian. After a moment, the two men turned to Rosamund.

"How?" Cristobal asked.

"He can invade it. Plunder its riches and occupy it. I see it as a peaceful occupation lasting . . . well, how long would it take to get sufficient *abulón* to Sorlain? A matter of a few months, I would think." She frowned, tapping a finger against her chin. "Yes, that should be manageable. But he cannot do it without your help. He will need ships."

"I suppose I could manage . . . two."

"Ten."

"Four. Really, Rosamund, that is the best that I can do."

"Florian, can you manage with that?"

Florian nodded, not trusting himself to speak.

"Four, then—though six would be better."

"Five," Cristobal said. "And it is no use asking more."

"Very well, five. He'll keep them after, of course—oh, and he will need gold, as well. And men—trained men, Cristobal, well armed and experienced in battle—who will remain with him as long as he has need of them."

"Florian?" Cristobal said. "Are you going to speak up?"

"Oh, no, I am enjoying this too much. I can hardly wait to hear how these ships are going to get to me without the world knowing Sorlain and I have joined forces."

"You are supposed to be a pirate, aren't you?" Rosamund asked impatiently. "So take them. After all that has happened to-night, I doubt anyone will wonder at a sudden animosity between Venya and Sorlain."

"Now, Cristobal," she continued briskly, "we do not want your sailors sacrificing themselves out of loyalty, so I think Florian should send you men to take command of the ships you mean for him to have. You will, of course, ensure that those ships are fitted out with valuable cargo. And Florian will, in turn, supply you with what you need."

She paused, frowning a little, then nodded once. "That is the meat of it. The two of you can work the details out yourselves. I'm going for a walk."

Straight-backed, she vanished into the trees, leaving Florian and Cristobal to stare after her in silent shock.

Chapter 55

FLORIAN found her sitting by a small pool beside the water-fall, weaving flowers into a garland and singing beneath her breath. The moonlight fell upon her white gown and glittered coldly on the diamonds she wore. He stood a moment in the shadows, his gaze traveling slowly over the hair dressed high on her brow, the long, slender neck that bent more gracefully than any flower. The low gown revealed the curve of her breasts, and as she reached to pluck a blossom, the movement had such beauty that the breath caught in his throat.

"My lady," he said with a bow.

"Oh, it's you," she answered carelessly. "Have you and Cristobal settled things?"

"We did."

He sank down to the ground beside her, drawing a sharp breath when his back touched the rough bark of a tree.

"You should have that tended to," she said.

"What, these scratches? They're nothing."

Her lips tightened, but she made no answer, all her attention fixed on the garland she was weaving. After a time Florian cleared his throat. "That's very pretty. Do you mean to stay all night to finish it?"

"Perhaps. It helps me think, and I have much to think about tonight. Life's very strange sometimes, isn't it?" she mused. "Yesterday I had two husbands, today I have none at all."

Florian tried to smile. "And tomorrow?"

"We shall see." She put the garland in her lap. "Why did you come to Cristobal's ship?"

"I realized that the prophecy applied to you—"

"Always the prophecy. Well, Florian, you might live your life according to some silly rhyme, but I refuse to do so."

Florian took the half-finished garland from her lap, his fingers nimbly twisting stems and blossoms. "You don't have to. The prophecy has served its purpose. We can forget all about it if you like; never speak of it again. And I won't even mention the merrow's riddle. Not once."

"Merrow? What—no, you won't distract me as easily as that. What about the sacrifice?"

"It's over. We had it all wrong, just as you said. Then I thought I understood, but I still didn't have it right. I'm afraid I'm sometimes rather stupid about these things."

"I have noticed. But I didn't think you did."

He slanted her a smile. "It's much easier when you are there to point it out to me."

They sat in silence for a time while the water rushed over the stones above and bubbled into the pool. The breakers rolling into shore were growing louder as the tide came in.

"Oh, and we were wrong about something else as well," Florian said. "The royal gift doesn't *have* to awaken before the eighteenth year. It usually does, but not always."

He held out the garland. The blossoms had lost their vivid colors and frozen into a shimmering crown of silver. Rose drew a sharp breath and reached for it, but the moment Florian released it, she held only blossoms in her hand.

"Yes, well," Florian said, "it was only an illusion. Not a bad one, really, for a first attempt. Don't worry, though, I'll get you a real one. If you will have it, that is. Venya needs a queen. Or I should say Venya's future king needs a queen. No," he said, "what I really mean is that *I* need *you*."

He took her hand and ran a finger over the slight indentation left by the rings she had worn. "I am sorry. I should have listened to you all along. But I was too . . ." His throat closed.

"Stubborn?"

Frightened.

"Can you forgive me?"

"For this?" Rose asked. "For Cristobal?"

"Yes. And for—well, for everything."

"Everything? Oh, you mean our marriage?"

"No. Or yes, but—"

"Or do you mean the lies you told me before we wed? Or that you forgot to mention that you believed yourself on the brink of death by prophecy?" Her voice rose and she tried to wrest her hand from his. "Are you apologizing for the fact that you played me for a fool?"

He held fast to her hand. "Yes. All of that."

"Oh!" Her laughter held a hard edge. "At least you admit it!"

"It would be pointless to deny it."

She sighed, then laughed, this time more naturally. "I know what you're doing. You think you can talk your way out of anything. The damnable thing is, you usually can."

"Rosamund, I have treated you very shabbily. And you deserve far more than I can offer you. Oh, you never complained, but I know what your life has been these past months. Comfortless. Lonely."

"'Tis true enough. The meanest herdsman lives more grandly than the Prince of Venya!"

The birds were waking, setting up a clamor in the branches overhead. In the growing light, he could see her hand clearly, pale against his own.

"Would it help," he said carefully, "if I were to beg?"

"Why don't you try it and find out?"

He smiled, though he did not raise his eyes to her. "I am not much of a bargain."

"You're not," she agreed. "Secretive, stubborn—"

"Don't forget unreasonable."

"—obsessed. I am not blind to your faults."

"I never thought you were. You see . . . much."

"But not everything." She tightened her grip on his fingers. "You are still capable of surprising me. You did tonight."

"I couldn't let you go."

"Because I can help you get to Venya?"

"Venya be damned," he said roughly. "I'm talking about you. About *us*."

"I know. But you would not have come tonight if you thought your people would suffer for it. I would not have wanted you if you did. I care for Venya, too, you know."

"I do know. Five ships, Rosamund? Five! You were magnificent."

She sniffed. "I was beginning to wonder if you'd noticed."

"It was rather hard to miss."

"Maybe there is hope for you. At least you aren't insisting on doing *everything* yourself, no matter how much you might suffer for it. It is a very tiresome habit of yours, and I won't abide it."

She glared at him, a slightly rumpled faery glowing in white satin and glittering with diamonds. He couldn't stop the laughter welling up in him. "I can change. I will put my whole heart into the task."

"Good. And you must never, ever lie to me again."

"Never. Not by word or by omission. But," he said, making one last effort, "are you sure this is what you want? I could not bear to make you unhappy," he added in a whisper. "Not you."

Her smile flashed out, brighter than the diamonds at her throat, warmer than the rising sun. "Don't be ridiculous. I am not unhappy in the least." Her fingers twined with his. "Now, let's send Cristobal on his way and get some rest."

The first pink and gold of dawn was streaking the sky as they joined the Sorlainian king by his boat. Rose took the diamonds from her breast, then pulled the jeweled combs from her hair. Freed, it rippled past her waist.

"Keep them," Cristobal said.

Rose shook her head and began to unfasten the gown.

"Really, lady, you can have the dress!"

"No, it's meant for your bride." She folded it carefully and ran one finger over the satin.

Cristobal grinned. "And the shift?"

"That I will keep"—she smiled back—"with thanks. Be well, Cristobal." She touched his cheek lightly and walked down the shore.

Cristobal watched her go, then turned to Florian. "I've been thinking about the risk you took, coming to my ship the way you did. She must mean a great deal to you."

"Oh, well . . ." Florian began lightly, then stopped and looked his kinsman in the eye. "More than my life."

"I envy you. They've always told me that love has no place in royal marriages."

"They told me that, too," Florian said, putting one hand on his shoulder. "But do you know something? They *lie*."

Cristobal laughed. "Farewell, Prince of Venya. I'll look for your men."

"You'll see them. Bright blessings on you, Cristobal."

Cristobal looked away, his jaw tightening. "Father used to say that. It was the last—the last thing he ever—"

"I'm sorry," Florian said quietly. "He was a noble king. I expect he was a good father, too."

"I knew he was dying," Cristobal said, staring down at the wet sand beneath his boots. "We both knew, though we never spoke of it. I thought I was ready. But now that he's gone—" He looked very young suddenly, his eyes filled with bewilderment. "I never knew my mother. My father—he was all I had, and now—"

Florian's grip tightened on his shoulder. "I know."

"You do, don't you?" Cristobal caught him in a hard embrace. "Bright blessings on you, too, cousin," he whispered fiercely, then stepped back, blinking hard, and turned away. "Look after your lady."

Florian followed his gaze. Rosamund stood a little distance off, staring out over the sea, the dawn breeze teasing the ends of her dark hair and fluttering the hem of her shift.

"I intend to."

Cristobal smiled crookedly. "Gods, I envy you the task."

He climbed into the boat and clapped his hands, rousing the sleeping oarsmen. In a moment, they were headed out to sea.

Rose joined Florian on the shore, lifting one hand in farewell and slipping the other about his waist.

"Those jewels were worth a small fortune," he remarked, his eyes on the departing boat. "Do you know they could have armed fifty men?"

She sighed. "It was a *gesture*."

"So I get you in your shift, is that it?" He turned and smiled into her eyes. "I'd rather have you out of it."

"And what would you do with me, I'd like to know? You can barely keep your feet."

"You have a point." He yawned. "Leander's ba—beard, but I am weary."

"Do you know, that's the first time I've ever heard you admit you're tired. And I saw how you were limping before. Here, take my arm."

"I don't need . . ." He stopped and drew a deep breath. "Thank you," he ground out between clenched teeth.

She grinned. "That's very good, my lord."

Laughing, he slung an arm about her shoulders, then winced. "I suppose you'll be thrilled to hear I've cracked a rib. And while I'm at it, why not make your joy complete and confess I've sprained my wrist, as well?"

"Does it hurt?" she asked sweetly. "Good. Maybe next time you'll think twice before rushing off into some mad adventure."

"Well, that's fine thanks! I swim miles to reach you—through shark-infested waters, I might add—and then . . ." He broke off, staring. "Oh, *shasra,* don't cry. I was only joking. It wasn't miles. And there was only one shark, very small, I hardly noticed it."

She gave a sobbing laugh. "I'm sorry . . . so silly . . . it's just that I thought . . . I was afraid . . . that I would never see you again. It doesn't matter now." She put her shoulder more firmly beneath his, wiping impatiently at her eyes.

He pulled her close against him, burying his face in the dark cloud of her hair. "Oh, but it does, my love," he whispered against her skin. "It matters very much to me."

Cristobal waved to the two shadowed forms upon the shore, the incoming tide foaming about their feet. Then he leaned back and stretched his legs before him with a sleepy smile. Had last night really happened? Or had it only been a dream? As the sun burst forth from the horizon, he looked back once more, but the small island was deserted, save for two sets of footprints vanishing among the trees.

The Fyne Curse

THE country of Columbyana, which stretches from the Cardean Ocean on the Eastern Shore to the border of Tryfyn to the west, and from the mountains of the Anwyn to the north to the fertile plains of the Southern Province, which extends to the Gulf of Beldene, survived a great twelve year war that ultimately left authority in the hands of the Beckyt House. The Beckyts made Arthes, a city in the Western Province, the seat of their government. There they built a great palace, a tower with tapering sides that rose ten levels high. They surrounded themselves with priests and warriors and with those blessed with sorcery.

In the fine palace emperors came and went, sons succeeding fathers. Some ruled with fairness and compassion, while others did not. Even those who abused their power were safe in their tower, because the House's strength had grown to a point where no one would dare to challenge them. Those few who dared to rebel did not live long. Either the priests or the sorcerers or the sentinels who served the emperor put a quick stop to any insurrection.

All the drama of Columbyana did not take place in Arthes.

In the third year of the reign of Emperor Larys, the fifty-seventh year of the reign of the Beckyts, a wizard who'd been spurned by a widowed Fyne witch responded to his heartbreak by inflicting this curse:

No witch cursed with the blood of the Fyne House shall know a true and lasting love.

For a hundred years, two hundred years, three hundred years . . . the Fyne women lived on the side of a mountain that came to bear their name. Some of them married, many did not. An unusual number of the men who dared to marry or consort with the Fyne women died before their thirtieth birthdays. Others simply disappeared.

Many of the Fyne witches tried to break the wizard's curse, over the years. All of them failed.

Prologue

The 365th Year of the Reign of the Beckyts

ALL night the narrow path had been dark, the moonlight and starlight dimmed by the thick foliage growing overhead. But for the occasional break in the intertwining limbs that offered a glimpse of the night sky, the men who marched silently along the trail might as well have been traveling through a long dark tunnel. They had to be careful to stick to the dirt footpath. To the left side the forest was thick with ancient trees that rustled with the wind. Animals growled and screeched in the darkness, but they did not bother the travelers. To the right the terrain dropped sharply. The deep ravine was so overgrown it was impossible to see until you were upon it.

The springtime chill penetrated their cloaks and trousers, even seeped through their boots. It was best to keep moving, to stay warm by marching ever onward. On occasion a rebel took a mis-step and a sword rattled, too loud in the stillness of night.

Sunrise was approaching, and Kane could begin to see a short way into the thick forest to the north. Fallen limbs were evidence of a storm that had passed a short while earlier. The animals that had made noise all night were now quiet, as if they had retired to sleep away the day. As it was no longer completely dark he could see the shapes of all the men who walked before him, not simply the back of Tresty's balding head. The battered rebels—one short of a dozen—moved silently along the trail that would take them to their leader Arik and the reinforcements. They had been defeated in battle and were weary, but they were not broken.

The emperor's soldiers had taken more than half their number in the last battle, four days gone. Kane Varden was one of eleven tired, hungry men. They had been beaten, and they had been wounded, but they were not ready to surrender. Not now, not ever. Not while the Emperor Sebestyen sat on the throne, hidden away high in his lavish palace while many of his people starved. It wasn't right for one man to have so much, while others had so little. It wasn't right for one man to take what he wanted at the expense of the common man of Columbyana, and like his father before him, that's exactly what Sebestyen had always done. Taken.

Kane's brother Duran, who had the best night vision of them all, led the way. Stopping only for short naps taken in shifts and what food they could catch or pick or steal, their journey would take another six days. Perhaps seven. They would join Arik in the northernmost reaches of the Eastern Province, heal, add to their numbers, and then be off to harass the imperial soldiers once again. Duran was young; barely twenty-two years. But like Kane, his heart belonged to this cause.

One day they would have the numbers to march into the palace itself, and Arik—the late Emperor Nechtyn's bastard son and Sebestyen's half-brother—would take the throne. Kane wanted to be there when that happened. He wanted that more than anything else in this life.

Duran stopped suddenly and raised a stilling hand. The rest of the crew halted as well. Kane laid his hand on the hilt of his sword, as did the men in front of and behind him.

When all was still, Kane heard what had alerted Duran. There was movement in the forest. Movement unlike the whisper of animals they'd heard throughout the night. The crisp rustle of leaves being displaced and the muted snick of metal on metal disturbed the quiet dawn.

Imperial infantrymen burst from the forest with a chilling cry, swords raised as they attacked from three sides. Clad in dark green uniforms that had allowed them to blend into the forest and as road-weary as the rebels, they broke from the shelter of the trees and surrounded Kane and what was left of his unit. The only direction that was clear of soldiers was the south, where the ravine dropped so sharply. In moments the rebels had their backs to that ravine as they faced superior numbers.

The strength of the imperial forces was daunting. How many soldiers poured from the forest? Thirty, at least, with more behind them. The odds weren't good, but it wasn't the first time they'd been outnumbered.

An imperial soldier raised his sword and swung out with a cry as chilling as that of any animal. Kane met the attack, stopping the arc of the sword with his own blade and then dipping down as he struck back with a skilled and fatal blow. When that soldier was down he engaged another. Then another. For a poor farmer's son, he was a damn good swordsman. As was Duran. As were they all. Arik had seen to their training, knowing that there would be moments like this. They did not brandish their swords in a manner that would impress; they practiced killing blows, simple and deadly.

But they were not sorcerers; they had no magic to protect them. They were men. Imperial soldiers fell, but so did the rebels. And the emperor's men kept coming. One fell, and two more took his place. It was as if an endless stream of soldiers poured from the trees.

One cry in the midst of many caught Kane's attention, even though it was no louder or more insistent than the others. It was simply more familiar. He turned his head to see Duran go down. A tall, thin soldier wearing a traditional emerald green uniform stood over Kane's little brother and struck once again. It was a death blow; Kane had seen enough to know.

"No!" He ran, frantically taking on one opponent and then another as he worked his way to Duran and the soldier who had already turned away to fight another rebel. It seemed that every imperial soldier was determined to stop Kane from reaching his brother. His skill with a sword was forgotten in favor of strength and brutality. He slashed and hacked his way through the fight, intent not only on surviving but on reaching his brother's killer. The clang of steel on steel faded, the faces of other soldiers blurred. The point of a clumsily wielded sword caught him across the back, and he spun to plunge his blade into the offending soldier's chest before continuing on.

As he drew closer to his goal Kane focused on the murderous soldier's face. It was gaunt and tanned, the eyes dark and slanted like those of a cat.

All the while, more imperial soldiers came. The rebels were going to lose this battle, and with enemy combatants on three sides and a sharp drop to the other, retreat was impossible. He could surrender and be taken prisoner, or he could die. It was no choice at all.

Kane swung his sword toward the soldier's neck, but the man who'd killed Duran saw the move coming and he jumped back. Not far enough or quickly enough. The tip of Kane's sword caught his cheek. Enraged to be cut, the man turned all his attention to Kane. He commanded his sword with skill, and they fought as the men around them fought. After a moment there was nothing else. No one but the two of them; no sound but their own harsh breathing and the clash of metal on metal. Everything else, the rest of the battle and the grief of Duran's death, faded from Kane's mind.

Kane held his own against the soldier. They fought like men who had been here before. Without conscious thought, without planning each and every move. Each blow was the result of instinct and innate skill and too many years of practice. They were well matched, until their swords met in midair and the blade of Kane's weapon snapped in two. He had a good weapon and such a thing should not have happened, but it did.

He dropped down and rolled to his right to reach for Duran's weapon. His hand shot out, he grasped the hilt and lifted the sword from the ground and stood, all in one smooth motion. But the delay, no matter how short, had given the green-clad soldier an edge. His furious blow caught Kane in the chest; the next one cut his arm. Deep.

Kane realized that he and the soldier who had killed Duran were the only ones who still fought. The once quiet road was littered with the wounded and the dead. A greater number of imperial soldiers than rebels lay dead, but that was little comfort. The battle, such as it was, was over. Kane Varden was to be the last man down.

"Fecking hick insurgent," the soldier said, his voice crisp with the accent of one who had spent his entire life in the capital city of Arthes. With a flick of his sword he ripped the weapon from Kane's hand. When Kane had been disarmed and the tip of the soldier's sword was pointed at his heart, the soldier paused to touch the blood on his cheek. "You marked me, you insolent malcontent. I should mark you ten times before I kill you."

"You killed my brother, you son of a bitch." Kane didn't back away from the tip of the sword. His family was gone; his home had been taken. He had nothing left.

The soldier glanced down at Duran, who lay perfectly still on the ground in a puddle of his own blood. His throat had been cut, and the soldier's slash had ripped his shirt and the flesh beneath.

"This one? He didn't even fight very well. Still, I'll happily put his pretty head on a stick and post it on the wall at Arthes until there's nothing left but a skull. Since you say you are his brother, I'll be sure to display your pathetic head close by."

He poked nonchalantly at Duran's body with the tip of his sword, and Kane lunged. He knocked the sword from the soldier's hand, and they grappled for control of the short knife the soldier drew from a sheath at his waist.

The other imperial soldiers found the hand-to-hand combat amusing. Winded and wounded, they gathered around to watch and cheer and close off any avenue of escape.

Kane fought hard, but he was losing blood and his strength faded fast. The soldier broke away, but the knife they'd fought for was in Kane's hand. If he could only kill the soldier before the others killed him, he could die in peace.

The soldier moved too quickly, spinning around and then lifting one leg and kicking. His imperial boot found Kane's wounded chest, and Kane flew backward. He tried to catch himself, knowing that if he ended up lying on the ground he was finished, knife or no knife. He'd almost managed to do just that, to catch himself . . . and then his foot found air where ground should have been. Momentum took him back another step, and then he was falling . . . tumbling. The air was forced from his lungs when he landed hard on the edge of a boulder. He rebounded, rolled back, and continued to fall. All he could see was a blur of brush and dirt, and then, when he landed on his back with a jarring thud, a brief glimpse of sunrise before everything went black.

ELIZABETH MINOGUE is a technical writer and editor. She has penned several short stories. She is also the author of *The Border Bride*, *Laird of the Mist*, and *The Linnet*, written as Elizabeth English. She lives in Pennsylvania. Write to her at P.O. Box 539, Kimberton, PA 19442.

NICOLE BYRD

Widow in Scarlet
0-425-19209-1

When Lucy Contrain discovers that
aristocrat Nicholas Ramsey believes her
dead husband stole a legendary jewel, she
insists on joining his search.
Little does she know they will be drawn
into deadly danger—and into a passion
that neither can resist.

Also Available:
Beauty in Black
0-425-19683-6

Praise for the romances of Nicole Byrd:

"Madcap fun with a touch of romantic
intrigue...satisfying to the last word."
—Cathy Maxwell

"Irresistible...deliciously witty,
delightfully clever." —*Booklist*

BERKLEY SENSATION
COMING IN DECEMBER 2004

Husband and Lover
by Lynn Erickson
When Deputy DA Julia Innes' husband is arrested for
the twelve-year-old murder of his ex-wife, she will
have to team up with detective Cameron Lazlo to
clear his name.

0-425-19938-8

The Sun Witch
by Linda Winstead Jones
The first novel in the Sisters of the Sun trilogy, which
tells the story of the Fyne women, who inherited
supernatural arts from their mothers—but a long-ago
curse makes true love unattainable for them.

0-425-19940-1

Echoes
by Erin Grady
Tess Carson's sister has disappeared after being
implicated in the murder of her boss. When Tess
begins to have visions, she suspects that she is the key
to finding her sister.

0-425-20073-6

Secret Shadows
by Judie Aitken
Tragedy on the Lakota reservation brings together an
FBI agent and a doctor, who share the same dreams—
and a passion for each other.

0-425-19941-X

He was the hero of a hundred songs and stories, the
sorcerer pirate whose name struck terror into every
captain on the nine seas. Bold and dashing, wily
and clever, the Prince of Venya was as deadly to his
foes as he was loyal to his followers. A single smile
from him had the power to melt a woman's bones
within her flesh. And he was her only hope...

Alone, desperate for her life and fleeing from her murderous
uncle, Rose of Valinor seeks help from the one person who
could outwit her uncle—the man he forced into exile, the
legendary Prince of Venya. But the man Rose finds is
nothing like the stories. Rather than a chivalric ideal, the real
prince is cynical, hardened, and cool—and refuses her plea.

Florian of Venya's one goal in life is to free his people
from the despotic rule of the usurper King Richard—
and he has no intention of letting Richard's niece
distract him from his goal. Especially since he
suspects her of being not only a madwoman,
but a spy as well. But when they're forced to
work together or risk being trapped by
Richard, they're able to see beyond to the
souls beneath—and find in each other a
love neither believed possible...

www.penguin.com

ISBN 0-425-19920

$6.99 U.S
$9.99 CA